# DISTURBING
## THE
# PEACE

# Pinnacle Westerns by Terrence McCauley

## *The Jeremiah Halstead Series*

BLOOD ON THE TRAIL

DISTURBING THE PEACE

## *The Sheriff Aaron Mackey Series*

WHERE THE BULLETS FLY

DARK TERRITORY

GET OUT OF TOWN

THE DARK SUNRISE

# DISTURBING THE PEACE

## A JEREMIAH HALSTEAD WESTERN

## TERRENCE McCAULEY

**PINNACLE BOOKS**
Kensington Publishing Corp.
www.kensingtonbooks.com

PINNACLE BOOKS are published by
Kensington Publishing Corp.
119 West 40th Street
New York, NY 10018

All Kensington titles, imprints, and distributed lines are available at special quantity discounts for bulk purchases for sales promotion, premiums, fund-raising, educational, or institutional use.

Special book excerpts or customized printings can also be created to fit specific needs. For details, write or phone the office of the Kensington Sales Manager: Attn.: Sales Department. Kensington Publishing Corp., 119 West 40th Street, New York, NY 10018. Phone: 1-800-221-2647.

PINNACLE BOOKS and the Pinnacle logo are Reg. U.S. Pat. and TM Off.

First Printing: August 2022
ISBN-13: 978-0-7860-4862-5
ISBN-13: 978-0-7860-4863-2 (eBook)

10 9 8 7 6 5 4 3 2 1

Printed in the United States of America

*To Aunt Rosie*
*Thank you for always being there.*

# Chapter 1

"Jeremiah Halstead!"

Halstead drew his Colt from his belly holster as he turned around on the crowded street to see who had called his name.

He spotted a fat man in the thoroughfare, beginning to raise a rifle in his direction.

Halstead fired and struck the man in the belly. The impact of the bullet caused the would-be assassin to stagger backward a few steps, but he managed to keep his feet.

He kept his rifle in hand, too.

Halstead's second shot struck him in the head, which sent him flat on his back.

As more rifle shots filled the air, Halstead dove for cover behind a horse trough. Bullets pelted the dry goods store where he had been standing and punched through the trough, sending a steady trickle of water onto the boardwalk.

The citizens of Helena, who had found themselves in the middle of a gun battle, screamed in panic as they scattered for the nearest cover they could find. All of the noise prevented Halstead from being able to tell where all of the shots were coming from.

"Keep firing, Luke!" a man yelled out above the gunfire and chaos. "We've got him now!"

Halstead pegged him. Left side, across the street. In front of the spectacles store.

When the gunmen stopped to reload, Halstead sat up and aimed his pistol at the gunman on the left. His target was in the process of levering in another round into his rifle when Halstead fired twice. One round missed. The second hit him in the chest.

Another rifleman on his right began to cut loose with a primordial yell before he began firing again. That yell had given Halstead time to lay flat behind the cover of the leaking trough. The screaming man's rifle went empty after three shots. When he heard the rifle hit the compact of the street, Halstead rolled over onto his stomach to see a man charging at him as he pulled his pistol from his holster.

Halstead squeezed off a round, and the bullet hit the charging man in the left hip, causing him to spin as he fell forward.

He landed face first on the ground but had not dropped his pistol.

Halstead quickly got to his feet as he kept the Colt Thunderer aimed down at the fallen man. "Push the gun away from you, mister. You don't have to die today."

But instead of pushing the gun away, he tried to raise it.

Halstead's shot hit him in the top of the head. His body went limp as Halstead watched life leave the stranger.

As he walked over to the man he had just killed, Halstead could hear the stifled whimpers of the citizens who had scrambled for shelter wherever they could find it. He stepped on the dead man's hand and picked up the gun. A rusty old Walker Colt. Halstead was surprised the gun had not blown up in his hand.

Halstead stood over the dead man, cracked his cylinder, and dumped the dead brass on the corpse. He was in the process of taking rounds from his gun belt and reloading his pistol when a boy from across the thoroughfare shouted, "This one's still alive, deputy!"

Halstead spun the cylinder and snapped it shut before he looked at a boy of about nine years old pointing down at the second man he had shot in front of the spectacles store.

He kept the Colt at his side as he walked toward the fallen man.

The boy backed away as Halstead drew closer, but he did not run off.

Halstead aimed his pistol at the fallen man as he approached. The gunman was barely still alive. His right shoulder was a ruined, bloody mess and getting worse by the second. The bullet must have hit an artery. He would bleed out in a matter of minutes. Not a lot of time for him, but more than enough time for Halstead to get the truth out of him.

The wounded man was still pawing for his rifle with his left arm when Halstead's shadow fell across him. He squinted up at the deputy marshal and laid his head flat on the boardwalk. "Go ahead, you bastard. Finish me. I'm done for anyway."

Halstead had no intention of letting him off that easy. He already knew the answer to his question, but he had to ask it anyway. "Who sent you?"

"Go to hell," the man spat as he struggled to raise his head. "You've already killed the others. Do the same to me."

Halstead placed his boot on the man's ruined right shoulder, causing him to scream.

"Last time I ask nicely," Halstead told him. "Tell me who sent you."

"Zimmerman, damn you!" the man cried out. "It was Ed Zimmerman."

Halstead removed his foot. He had been afraid of that. The ten-thousand-dollar bounty the outlaw had put on Halstead was double the bounty the territory had placed on Zimmerman. It had caused the lawman more trouble than he could have imagined.

He heard the citizenry mutter and scatter as they saw another man approaching with a rifle. But there was no reason to worry for the young man had a deputy marshal's star pinned to his shirt. It was his friend, young Joshua Sandborne.

"You hurt?" Sandborne called out as he aimed his Winchester down at the dying man.

"I'm fine," Halstead told him. "He'll be dead in a minute, so no need to go for the doc. Just keep an eye on him and let me know when he goes. Keep an eye on the street in case anyone decides to help him.

Halstead went to check the other two men he had shot. Both men were already facing whatever justice awaited a man in the hereafter. He just wanted to see if he knew them.

He heard some of the women on the boardwalk gasp at the sight of such death and carnage in broad daylight. They made a great show of clutching their pearls and turning their heads, but not their eyes. In his brief time in the territory, Halstead had learned that blood was a popular sport in Montana. Helena might have been the capital of the territory, but it was no different from Dover Station or Silver Cloud or any other frontier town in that regard.

Halstead looked down at the fat man he had shot first. His beard was long and sported a healthy amount of gray and white mixed in with brown. He looked to be about forty years old. What little hair he had left atop his head was also streaked with gray. His skin was weathered and had clearly seen more than its share of the sun. His overalls were faded and stained with sweat and grime that no amount of soap and water could ever wash out.

He looked less like a gunman and more like a farmer, which Halstead expected he was.

Halstead walked over to the last man he had killed. He looked to be younger than the fat man by about a decade or so, but decided he had been a farmer, too.

He had been forced to kill a lot of farmers and shop-keepers and drovers and cowboys and wanderers of every description over the past few weeks. Foolish, desperate men who had taken a gun in hand in the hopes of being able to claim what had been called The Outlaw's Bounty; the one Edward Zimmerman had placed on Halstead's head.

Halstead had to admit some admiration for Zimmerman. Not many men had the gall to openly put out a price on the head of a lawman, much less a federal lawman. Most people were appalled by the notion. Public officials and newspapers around the territory denounced it as a hindrance to the territory's efforts for statehood, which was assured to happen in less than a month or so.

But public condemnation of the bounty had only made word of it spread farther and wider than it otherwise might have. Which was why Jeremiah Halstead had spent every moment of the past several weeks on a knife's edge. His hand was never far from one of the two Colts he wore on

the fancy black leather gun rig he'd had made specifically
for himself. One on his right hip and the other in the
holster on his belly. The fancy two-gun rig normally
drew attention wherever he went. Now he drew attention
for a different reason. Men looked at him like they were
watching ten thousand dollars walking right by them.

He remained in the thoroughfare as he heard a horse
and rider approaching from around the corner. He did not
draw either of his guns for he could hear the chatter among
the crowd that Sheriff Aaron Mackey and his first deputy,
Billy Sunday, were approaching.

He watched Mackey round the corner first, atop the
black Arabian he called Adair. The marshal of the Montana
Territory was tall and lean and about thirty-five, which put
him ten years older than Halstead. The dark hat and clothes
he wore also served to make him look older.

As usual, Billy Sunday was right behind him, prodding
a man along at the end of a Winchester. The black man was
as tall and lean as Mackey and about the same age. The
two men had ridden together in the cavalry, and Billy had
been Mackey's deputy in Dover Station and now here in
Helena. Dover Station did not exist anymore, but their
friendship had endured.

Halstead noticed the prisoner was a sandy-haired man
who looked to be on the verge of tears. Halstead had seen
many a man cry when they found themselves at the wrong
end of a gun where Mackey or Sunday were concerned.

Halstead watched Mackey draw Adair to a halt in front
of the corpse at his feet. The black mare caught the scent
of blood in the air and tossed her head. Halstead knew the
smell of death did not spook her. If anything, it brought her
to life. Adair was a war horse in every sense of the word.

Halstead touched the brim of his hat to Mackey. "Good morning."

Mackey looked around at the two corpses in the thoroughfare. "Wasn't for them." He nodded over toward Sandborne. "Looks like you left one alive."

"Not for long," Halstead told him. "I hit an artery. He'll bleed out in a minute or two."

Billy stood up in the stirrups and cut loose with a low, long whistle as he kept the sandy-haired man covered with his Winchester. "Looks like it took two shots a piece to finish them off. You losing your touch already, nephew?"

Halstead expected some ribbing from the man he considered an uncle. "Just being thorough is all."

But Mackey had not been in a kidding kind of mood as of late. He was responsible for a territory larger than some European countries, which left little time for jokes. "They come at you because of Zimmerman's bounty?"

"That's what the dying one over there told me." Halstead looked at the sandy-haired prisoner whose eyes were already welling up. "Who's your new friend?"

"We came running as soon as we heard the shots," Billy said. "We found this one creeping up the street heading this way. Rifle in hand."

Halstead looked at the sandy-haired prisoner. He was trying really hard to look straight ahead instead of looking down at the corpse on the ground.

He grabbed the prisoner by the neck and bent it, so he had no choice but to look at the man at his feet. "You were with these boys, weren't you?"

"I was." The prisoner swallowed hard and shut his eyes. "But I don't want to see them like this, please. They were my brothers."

"Where'd you ride in from?" Mackey asked.

The man shut his eyes tight, forcing tears to stream down his cheeks. "We rode in here from Bisbee, Idaho, last night. We'd heard about that bounty the outlaw fella put on your head. Zimmerman I think his name is."

"Zimmerman." Billy frowned.

Halstead asked him, "You hear about the bounty from Zimmerman personally or from someone else?"

"We heard it from four men we met who rode through Bisbee about a few weeks ago. Said they were riding up here to put a bullet in a man named Halstead and collect the reward." The prisoner chanced a look at Halstead. "Seeing as how you're Halstead, I guess they didn't collect."

Halstead remembered them. Four loud-mouthed drunks who took him on after spending half a day in The Wicked Woman saloon drinking some courage. They had collected plenty of lead for their trouble, but no gold. "You boys farmers?"

The prisoner shut his eyes again and shrugged. "Tried to be. Ain't got much to show for it except aches and blisters and bills. When those boys rode into town on a Saturday night bragging about how much money they'd get for killing you, a bunch of us figured we ought to have a go at that reward money instead, so . . ."

Halstead waited for more but realized that was all the man decided to say. He was smarter than he looked. If he had kept talking, he would have talked himself into a noose. As it was, he was looking at ten years hard labor.

"Open your eyes," Mackey ordered him.

The man did as he was told and held a hand to his mouth as he saw Sandborne slowly lower his rifle. There was no need to cover a dead man.

"That's Reb," the prisoner said.

"Not anymore." Mackey beckoned Sandborne to come

over to them. When the young deputy got there, he said, "Take this man into custody and lock him up. Send word for the coroner to bring his wagon. I'll keep watch over everything until they get here."

The young deputy grabbed hold of the prisoner and shoved him in the direction of the jail.

As they watched Sandborne do his duty, Halstead looked up at Mackey and Billy. "The kid's really grown up this past year or so, hasn't he?"

"We all have," Billy said. "Guess we've had to."

Halstead could not disagree with them. In the span of about twelve months or more, they had gone from being the law in Dover Station, Montana, to being the law for the entire territory and with only a few more men than they'd had with them in Dover Station.

Mackey had gotten married and watched his hometown burn in the same fire that took his father. It was a lot of a change in a short amount of time. Most men would have buckled under the pressure or at least shown some signs of strain. But Aaron Mackey was not most men.

Mackey had always been older than his years, even when Halstead remembered him as a cavalry lieutenant in Arizona where Sim Halstead, his father, served as his sergeant. Mackey had been stern back then. The years since had only made him grow more so.

The marshal looked over the three bodies spread out before him. "Any sign of the constables?"

Halstead shook his head. "Guess they're too busy planning the big statehood celebration with the mayor."

Billy grinned. "Never let a shooting get in the way of a good party."

"This is bad business," Mackey said. "Zimmerman's bounty has turned out to be more trouble than I thought.

I figured the five-thousand-dollar reward would help people do our work for us. I didn't think he'd respond with a ten-thousand-dollar bounty on you."

"Neither did I," Halstead admitted. "And I never thought anyone would try to collect based on a rumor."

Mackey looked down at the dead man lying in the thoroughfare between them. "We've been lucky that no real hardcases have come for you, but luck doesn't last forever. Even people who look like you are getting killed."

Halstead winced at a memory that still ate at him. The week before, a man who bore a passing resemblance to him and wore all black was killed by a traveling fabric salesman looking to cash in on the bounty. The man he had killed had been an undertaker just arrived in town to look at opening a business in Helena. He could still hear the cries of the man's family as they gathered around his body. The salesman had shot himself in the head upon learning of his mistake.

"Seems like dead people follow me wherever I go."

"Knock it off," Mackey said. "You didn't do this. Zimmerman did. And it's going to keep on happening while you're in Helena. Good thing we caught a break this morning."

Halstead was suddenly interested. "What kind of break?"

Mackey deferred to Billy. "We got a letter from Jack McBride, the town marshal of Battle Brook and Hard Scrabble. Battle Brook is a boom town in the western part of the territory. Hard Scrabble used to be a jumped-up mining camp, but now it's a town on the decline."

Mackey added, "Our old friends Mr. Rice and Mr. Ryan are building up Battle Brook to serve the mines they have up in the hills."

Halstead held his tongue until they told him what all of this had to do with him.

Billy went on. "McBride wrote to tell us he's heard rumors from the miners that Rob Brunet is in the area. That name mean anything to you?"

"Sure does," Halstead said. The man was wanted throughout the West for a series of stagecoach robberies and homestead raids he and his gang had pulled. He was known for striking in Montana or other territories only to jump the border back into Canada. He'd also had more than a few run-ins with the Mounted Police north of the border. "I thought that bastard ran back to Canada last year."

"He's back now," Mackey told him, "but we don't know if it's just him or his gang is with him. McBride says he's heard rumors that he's fallen in with some bad company, possibly Ed Zimmerman."

"Zimmerman." Halstead said the name as if it was a curse. "Seems too far away from civilization for Zimmerman's tastes."

"Which makes it a perfect place for a man with five thousand dollars on his head to hide out," Mackey told him. "McBride thinks he's hiding out around Hard Scrabble. Makes sense since everything's relocating from there to Battle Brook."

Halstead felt a mixture of dread and excitement begin to spread through him. "Guess you'll be sending me out there to get him."

"I am," Mackey said, "but it's not my first choice."

Halstead frowned. "Thanks for the confidence, boss."

Mackey's jaw tightened. "It's got nothing to do with you and everything to do with the terrain. Those hills are dangerous for anyone, especially for someone like you who's still new to the territory. They're bad in summer and even worse now in late fall. Normally, me and Billy would go, but with all this statehood nonsense going on, we're needed here. That's why I'm sending Sandborne with you."

Halstead's dread overcame whatever excitement he had been feeling. He had nothing against Joshua. If anything, he was too fond of him to risk his life going against a man like Zimmerman. "Aaron, I don't think that's a good idea. He's a bit green and—"

Mackey looked down at him, and Halstead felt his throat go dry.

"Josh is young, but he's capable. He grew up here and knows how to handle himself in the snow and the mountains. You don't, so he's going with you."

Halstead knew all that, but there was more at stake here than just knowing how to handle the elements. "Zimmerman's not the kind of man you cut your teeth on, Aaron. He hits hard and he hits fast."

"So do you," Mackey reminded him, "and he's excellent at following orders. Unlike you."

The look Billy gave Halstead told him to stop arguing. And he had learned from experience that Billy was rarely wrong.

Halstead said what he knew Mackey wanted to hear. "Sounds like we'll be able to learn a good bit from each other."

Mackey nodded. The discussion was over. "McBride's a good man. Billy and I served with him a bit in Arizona. Tall man and tougher than he looks. And I'd appreciate it if you didn't give him the same kind of greeting you gave Sheriff Boddington in Silver Cloud."

Halstead closed his eyes. He wondered if Mackey would ever let him live that down. "That was different."

Billy said, "McBride's different, too. You two will get along just fine."

Mackey went back to looking over the bodies in the thoroughfare. "The train leaves in three hours. The journey lasts a couple of days, depending on the conditions of the tracks. You'll get off the train at a place called Wellspring. It's barely a town, and the sheriff is an old fool named Howard. No need to check in with him when you get there. If all goes well, you won't have to deal with him."

Halstead would remember that. "Anything else?"

"There's a stage that can run you up to Battle Brook," Billy told him, "but with the price on your head, I'd avoid it. That means you boys will have to travel off the road to get there. You'd best get busy outfitting yourself. Get a mule from the livery and put two tents and provisions for a three-day ride on our account at the general store."

Mackey added, "I'll give the warrants on Brunet and Zimmerman to Sandborne. He'll help get the animals loaded on the train for you. The governor would like to be able to announce we've captured Zimmerman and Brunet at the statehood celebration in a week or so, but don't let that rush you. Stopping them is more important than his announcement."

Halstead was glad Mackey saw it that way. "Sounds like I have a lot of work to do. Best get to it." He touched the brim of his hat as he began to head toward the general store when Mackey called out to him.

"One more thing. Best start getting in the habit of picking up your brass. I spend more on bullets for you than the rest of the marshals combined. It's cheaper to reload them than to buy new."

Halstead had no intention of reusing a bullet he had spent killing a man. But he saw no reason to argue with Mackey about it. "Guess it's a sign of how popular I am."

"Expensive, too." Mackey looked away as he stood watch over the carnage. "Bring back Zimmerman and Brunet, Deputy Halstead. Straight up or over the saddle. Makes no difference to me."

But it made all the difference in the world to Halstead. He had promised to kill the man once and that was exactly what he planned to do.

# Chapter 2

In the dense forest just outside of the dying town of Hard Scrabble, Edward Zimmerman led Rob Brunct through a snow-covered thicket and into a sparse clearing. The sky was slate gray, and the morning sun was blinding despite the thick clouds.

"Don't know how the hell you hope to find anything out here with all this snow," Brunct said. "If I didn't know better, I'd think you were setting me up to stop a bullet."

Zimmerman smiled at his fellow outlaw's angst. "Never fear, Robert. The only thing I'm setting you up for is success."

Zimmerman's mount, a skittish bay gelding, caught the scent of death lingering in the air and shied away from it. A spur to the belly and a sharp tug on the reins brought the animal back into submission. "Be mindful of your mount around here," Zimmerman cautioned. "I'm afraid I had to leave a couple of bodies behind when I was here last."

Brunet followed Zimmerman's lead. "As long as you don't aim to leave another one now, we'll be fine."

Realizing they were close enough to the spot; Zimmerman climbed down from the saddle and wrapped his horse's reins around a nearby bush. He reminded himself to get a better horse when he got back to town. The gelding was a bit too mild for his taste and purpose.

He stepped over the skeletal remains of a leg poking out of the snow and approached a heavy rock that stood out in the middle of the clearing. He bent at the knees and, with little effort, rolled the heavy rock aside so his guest could get a good look at what was beneath it. He took a couple of steps back and gestured down to the deep hole in the ground.

*"Voila, mon ami,"* he said to Brunet. It was all the French he knew, but enjoyed putting it to good use. "Behold the treasure I promised you."

Brunet produced a pistol from beneath his coat and aimed it squarely at Zimmerman's head as he looked over his horse's head and into the hole. "All I see is a sack in the ground, Zimmerman. Pull it out real nice and slow. And if you pull out anything more than money"—he thumbed back the hammer—"it'll be the last thing you do."

Zimmerman dramatically held up his hands and ducked his head. "Robert, my friend. Where's the trust? I already told you there's a pistol in the bag for emergencies, but I won't go near it."

The burly outlaw with the wild black beard grinned. "I didn't get this pretty by doing manual labor." He gestured with the pistol as he said, "You pull it out, leave it on the ground, and step over there where I can see you. And you'd better be as unarmed as you said or . . ."

"Yes, yes, I know. I'll be the next one left out here," Zimmerman said. "You've already threatened me enough for one day."

Zimmerman reached into the hole and hefted out a yellow bank satchel. The stenciling on the side of the bag had read "Wells Fargo" once, but the lettering had faded after repeated burials.

His treasure now out in the open, Zimmerman backed away and kept his hands visible as per his earlier agreement with Brunet. He was also unarmed, save for the rifle on his saddle more than twenty feet away. All of these precautions were taken at Brunet's insistence.

Zimmerman did not much like all of these measures. In fact, he found them quite insulting. True, the two men only knew each other by their respective reputations, but Zimmerman preferred to think they were somehow bonded together by their greed. Their mutual lawlessness. Their unending desire for more. Always more. More of what was a question he often asked himself. The answer was as unimportant as it was consistent. Just more.

Zimmerman was sure to stand particularly still as he watched Brunet climb down from the chestnut Canadian he rode. It was a fine-looking animal and better suited for this climate than the fretful beast he had.

Zimmerman tried to find the best word to describe Brunet as he watched him walk toward the last remaining testament to the Hudson Gang. Like Zimmerman, he was just shy of six feet, but not by much. And, like Zimmerman, he was a broad and powerfully built man. His physique came about naturally and was not the result of hard work. Both men were healthy and far from fat, but their size gave them a more menacing quality than a miner or farmer or other working man might possess.

That was where the similarities between them ended. Zimmerman preferred to shave every morning when he could. Brunet's thick black beard covered the upper part of his heavy buffalo coat. The floppy brim of his weathered brown hat served to keep the wind and the rain out of his face. The large brown eyes beneath it had a wild, almost feral quality to them.

Zimmerman regarded himself as a planner, while Brunet was a man who got things done. He often acted rashly and killed without purpose. Every man Zimmerman had either killed or allowed to live had been for a reason.

Zimmerman watched the outlaw descend on the bag of money like a wolf on a fallen elk. His greed had overtaken him, but like the wolf, not enough to make him careless. He opened the bag with his left hand while he kept Zimmerman covered with the pistol in his right.

Zimmerman took this to be an excellent sign. Wild men were not always careless men. And with the right influence, they could be tamed. Alexander Darabont had taught him that. He had taught him so many things by his example. He had learned as much from his former leader's mistakes as he had from his successes. Perhaps more.

And all he had planned for the past three months had led to this moment. To this grubby, monstrous man pawing all the money Zimmerman had in the world.

Brunet found the pistol Zimmerman had placed in the bag and tossed it aside as he dug his hand into the bag. His eyes grew wide as he lifted his hand full of coins and allowed them to slip from his fingers back into the bag as if they were grains of sand.

He looked at Zimmerman with toothless delight as he dug his hand deeper into the bag and came up with even more coins.

"Remember our agreement," Zimmerman cautioned him. "You can see the money. You can even count it. But all of it stays here. Neither of us takes a cent."

But Brunet seemed too consumed with the treasure to hear Zimmerman. "There's got to be a million dollars here."

Zimmerman prevented himself from laughing. If he had a million dollars at his disposal, even a quarter of that, he would have no use for Brunet's talents. "It's ten thousand to be precise. I joined my money with the loot of the Hudson Gang's after their unfortunate demise in Silver Cloud."

Brunet grabbed a single coin from the bag and bit it with one of his few remaining teeth. "It's genuine, by God." He allowed the coin to drop back into the bag and looked up at Zimmerman. "I'll admit I had my doubts about you, boy, but you're a man of your word. That much is certain."

Zimmerman thought it low praise coming from a mountain brute, but he feigned sincerity when he said, "Given the source, I take that as a compliment. Now, if you'd be so kind as to place the pistol back in the bag and put the bag back in the hole, I'll place the rock back on top of it so we can continue our discussion."

Brunet surprised him by not only doing as he asked but also pushed the heavy stone back on top of the hole as if it were a pebble. He was obviously much stronger than he appeared. Perhaps even stronger than Zimmerman. He took note of that.

Brunet stood upright and opened his buffalo coat just long enough to tuck his pistol away inside one of the hide's many pockets. He stood looking at Zimmerman. His short arms hanging from his sides like an ape. "You took a hell of a risk bringing me out here to see all this. I could shoot you now and take off with all the money."

Zimmerman shrugged. "If you did, you'd be riding away with ten thousand dollars and riding away from ten million.

You doubted my sincerity, which is understandable. At least now we know we can trust each other."

Brunet nodded his head down toward the skeletal foot sticking out of the snow. "That fella trust you, too?"

Zimmerman had wondered how long it would take Brunet to ask him about that. "There's another man about ten yards to your left. They were prospectors who had a donkey I could use to bring the gold up here. Once they had dug the hole and placed the rock over it, they had served their purpose. Like the Good Book says, "Three men can keep a secret if two of them are dead."

Brunet ran his thick tongue around the inside of his mouth. "T'ain't any scripture I've ever heard."

Come to think of it, Zimmerman doubted it was from the Bible, but it sounded good. "Well, if it isn't there, perhaps it should be." He gestured toward the horses. "Now, I don't know about you, but I think we've been out here in the cold long enough. What do you say we get back to the cabin where we can continue our discussion?"

Brunet showed his agreement by walking back toward his horse and climbing up into the saddle. Zimmerman made sure he was mounted and comfortable first before he did the same. He was aware that the outlaw was fully capable of killing him and taking the gold for himself but doubted he would do that. For if Brunet agreed to what he was proposing, the contents in the hole would be pocket change compared to the riches that lie ahead for each of them.

The two men descended the rocky hilltop in silence until they reached the flatland that led to the trapper's cabin they shared as their mutual hideout for the past day or so. The place had been a ruin when Zimmerman had stumbled upon it as he fled Halstead and Silver Cloud and had remained so until he had been well enough to fix it.

Zimmerman tried not to think of all he had endured in the days and weeks following his run-in with Halstead. How the gaping hole in his left side had almost crippled him in his mad scramble for the freight train as it stopped to take on water. How even breathing set his entire body on fire. How the saddle and saddlebags he carried with him only made it worse.

He remembered the feverish days he had been forced to spend in that wretched box car, surrounded by five forgotten men who looked at him as hungrily as Brunet had looked into the Wells Fargo satchel just now. He had counted himself fortunate that he'd had the good sense to shoot them all before the pain and the fever robbed him of consciousness. He had no doubt they would have done the same to him—and worse—as soon as he had passed out from the wound in his side.

He only regretted that the dead men were as poor as the lice and rats who dwelled in the box car. Their corpses had yielded little except to serve as a distraction for the vermin to feast on while he slowly recovered.

The only thing of value any of them possessed had been coffee and the fixings to make a small fire in a tar box they had found somewhere. The coffee grinds served as a poultice he used to fill his wound and the fire kept him warm on the cold, endless nights when fever dreams haunted him amidst the endless rocking of the westbound train.

He remembered how weak he had been when the train stopped and one of the crew decided to check the box cars for stowaways. He had not wanted to kill the man who opened the unlocked car, but he could not afford to allow himself to be taken prisoner, either.

He could not die or be arrested for he had unfinished business to tend to. Business that could not afford to be delayed by a lengthy stay in prison and the inevitable end he would meet on the gallows.

He could still hear the gunshots of the remaining members of the train crew echo in the distance as he struggled over hard ground, hauling his saddle and bags across the frozen land and through the unending forest that surrounded him. By the time the sun had dipped well below the horizon that wretched day, Edward Zimmerman knew he was done for. The cold Montana day had almost killed him. His fever was raging. The unforgiving night would surely finish the job.

He had thought his eyes had been playing tricks on him when he spotted the ragged darkness in a clearing just ahead of him. He did not know if it was real or if this was Death itself come to collect his soul before his body grew too cold. He stumbled toward it anyway. He'd had nothing left to lose.

He found it was an abandoned trapper's shack. It was little more than several dozen planks of wood nailed together and a slanted roof that kept the snow from piling too high atop it. The rusted steel traps that adorned its walls showed its past purpose.

He remembered a great plume of dust rose up as he collapsed on the crude mattress stuffed with crushed leaves and dried grass. The place had a door and a roof that did not leak much and a stove where he could make fire.

It was where he had spent weeks recovering. The same place to which he rode with Brunet now. The place that had saved him from death and allowed him to carry on the last bit of unfinished business he had left in the world.

That business being the slow death of Jeremiah Halstead.

The man who had wiped out his gang. The man who had put the gaping hole in his side. The man who had put him through a living Hell as he fought to survive.

Now, upon reaching the shack, the two outlaws stowed their mounts in the tangle of pine branches and wood Zimmerman had cobbled together to serve as a place to stow their horses. The animals were just as susceptible to the cold as humans and required some shelter from the elements. It was not much, but it was better than standing tethered to a porch post all night.

Brunet followed Zimmerman inside the shack. They had kept the fire in the stove burning before they left to see the gold, and Zimmerman quickly fed it more sticks and wood to make it even hotter.

Both men shucked their coats and warmed their hands by the growing warmth of the stove.

Brunet stomped his feet on the wooden floor Zimmerman had done his best to repair following his recovery. "Showing me that gold up there bought you a lot of stock with me, Ed, but I still need some answers."

Zimmerman had been expecting that. "And I'll be glad to give them to you."

"How'd you manage to find me?"

"By word of mouth," Zimmerman explained. "Once I was healthy enough to move around, I spent my time visiting the various mining camps in the area. I make a circuit of about ten of them or so. The big mines run by the mining companies and the smaller claims by Hard Scrabble. I told them I was just a simple trapper, so they paid me little mind. I'd play cards with them and drink with them. I'd listen to what they had to say. I even added a bit to that bag you just hauled out of the ground as a result of it. That's when Dippy pulled me aside one night and told me he thought I was Zimmerman. I was worried at first until he asked me if I wanted to meet you."

Brunet nodded at the memory. "Poor old Dippy. He never did know how to keep his mouth shut. Didn't like him letting on about me like that. Always looking to show the world how big a man he was." He looked at Zimmerman. "You did me a kindness by killing him for me like you did. He was the last one of my old bunch who stuck around."

"Killing him was the least I could do," Zimmerman said. "If he brought me to your hideout in the mine, he'd eventually lead someone else there, too. Maybe someone not as friendly as me. And, since he had figured out who I was, it was only prudent to kill him."

"True." Brunet rubbed his hands over the stove. "Though it'll put you in a bad way with the miners. When they notice Dippy is missing and you quit coming around, they might say something about it to the sheriff."

"My time with them served its purpose," Zimmerman explained. "I learned all about their operation. I know what shifts they work and, most importantly of all, when and how they get paid. They're particularly fascinated about all of the wanted men said to be hiding out up here in the hills. They love to talk about what they'd do with all the money they'd collect by bringing down a man with a big price on his head. Men like you and me." He laughed. "My scalp alone would bring five thousand dollars."

"That's nothing," Brunet sniffed. "I've got two countries hunting for me. Either one would bring twenty thousand easily. But I'd wager you already knew that."

Zimmerman did not bother hiding it. "As you already knew about the reward out for me. So I decided to play a game with them. I let them know that I'd heard Zimmerman was alive and well in California. Not only that, but he had placed a bounty on the head of the marshal who chased him out of Montana. Ten thousand to the man who killed him. All they had to do was make sure the killing got mentioned in the papers and Zimmerman would make good on his claim. Either to him or the man's family, if he had any."

Brunet laughed. "Heard that one myself. Mighty good thinking on your part. Putting out a bounty on the man who put one on you. What happens if someone comes to collect?"

"I'd gladly pay it," Zimmerman admitted, "though I doubt it'll ever come to that. No bounty hunter worth his sand would dare take on Halstead. He'd be finished for life. But I knew the amateurs who think ten thousand is a godly sum would gladly take a gamble, especially if they had nothing to lose. A few seconds' work with a gun beats a lifetime spent digging gold and copper out of the ground to men with few other prospects."

Zimmerman felt himself growing warmer and not just from the stove fire. "Word has spread far and wide and, last I heard, about ten men have tried to collect on my offer. They're all dead now, of course. Halstead isn't likely to be taken down by desperate farmers or miners or cow hands." He sighed deeply. "Still, I live in hope. And even if they miss, it keeps Halstead on his guard and distracted."

"Distracted," Brunet repeated. "You mean distracted from hunting you."

"Distracted until I am ready to hunt him," Zimmerman said.

Brunet ran that thick tongue of his along the inside of his mouth again as he thought that over. "I've got no more quarrel with him than I've got with any other man toting a badge, Ed. If we join up, I'm in it for the money, not the blood. I've never minded the killing part of it. You know that. But I'd just as soon let a man go if I can."

But Zimmerman had already surmised all of that. He knew Brunet killed whenever the occasion called for it. And he knew that, if they went up against Halstead, the occasion would certainly call for it. "I never thought different, Robert. I see men like you and I as shepherds in a way. We don't enjoy killing, but it's an unavoidable circumstance in our line of work."

Brunet thought about that for a while. "Could always get ourselves honest work."

The two men looked at each other across the stove before breaking out into laughter that filled the tiny shack. Brunet had a high-pitched cackle that did not fit such a deadly man.

As the Canadian pawed away tears of laughter from his eyes, he said, "Let's say you and me throw in with each other. We're going to need men."

"We most certainly will," Zimmerman agreed. "Good men and lots of them, too, if we're going to put my plan into place."

"About that." Brunet wagged a gloved finger at him. "You've been going on about this plan of yours for the past couple of days. You ever going to get around to telling me what it is or am I going to have to guess?"

"That depends." Zimmerman extended a hand to him across the stove. "Are we partners?"

Brunet regarded the hand for a moment and the man extending it to him. "I think we can do better than that."

Zimmerman watched him produce a knife from somewhere inside his buffalo hide. The large blade caught a glint of firelight before he pulled off his glove and drew the sharp edge across the palm of his right hand.

Zimmerman pulled the blade he kept tucked in the back of his pants and did the same. The two men clasped hands until their blood was intermingled. Some of it sizzled as drops hit the stove between them.

"A pact sealed with blood is the only pact I honor," Brunet told him as he gripped Zimmerman's hand tightly.

Zimmerman matched the strength of his grip. "All right, then. Now we can finally talk about how we're going to take over the territory."

# Chapter 3

Halstead had never understood why people enjoyed traveling by train. He had never liked the idea of putting his life in someone else's hands. It was a cramped, boring experience where people were constantly jostling him, elbowing for that extra inch that would give them more room. The cigarette smoke. The perfume. The snapping of the same newspapers read over and over again throughout an entire journey. The stops along the way that were either too long or not long enough depending on their purpose.

If he had not been ordered to take the train—and if it had not reduced a weeks-long trip into a matter of days—Jeremiah Halstead would have preferred to make the journey to Battle Brook on horseback. It would have required considerably more planning on his part, but riding along in a wooden box on wheels made him feel ridiculous.

And although Mackey had arranged for him to have a private car, having to share it with Joshua Sandborne only made it worse.

"Ain't this something, Jerry?" the younger man said as he looked out the window at the passing scenery. "We could never go this fast for this long on horseback."

He did not want to dampen Sandborne's enthusiasm, so he kept his mouth shut.

Sandborne looked around their private car. "And we've got this whole place to ourselves. Sure beats the bunkhouse at the JT, that's for certain. How'd the marshal manage to get us such good lodging?"

"The owner of the railroad is a friend of his," Halstead told him. "He always makes sure we have our own berth if he can."

Sandborne sank back into his cushioned seat and stretched out. "I could sure get used to this."

The constant rocking of the car and Sandborne's wonderment combined to make him nauseous. He preferred to remain focused on the business at hand. "I've decided we're going to sleep in shifts so one of us is always awake."

He was glad, but not surprised, that the young man grew serious. "Sure, Jerry. That on account of you having that price on your head?"

"That's part of it," Halstead admitted. "The other part is that Mr. Rice, the owner of the railroad, likes us to earn our keep while we're enjoying all this finery. He expects us to keep an eye on things while we're on board. Let the passengers know there are marshals on the train with them. Makes them feel safer knowing we're around. Also makes his railroad more popular with folks."

Halstead had no idea of whether or not any of that was true, just that Mackey had told him to do it.

"Sounds only fair," Sandborne said. "Trouble is, I ain't sleepy."

"You're *not* sleepy," Halstead corrected him. "Mind your grammar. The marshal doesn't want his boys sounding like a bunch of drovers, even if that's all we are."

"We're not drovers." The younger man sat up straighter. "We're lawmen, by God. Federal ones at that!"

Halstead did not think so. "Taking meat from one place to another makes us drovers when you get right down to it. This job's a lot easier to take if you look at it that way."

He watched Sandborne assume that look he always got when he was taking something to heart. It only served to make him look younger than he already did. Sometimes, it was hard for Halstead to remember that he was only four years older than Joshua.

When he had thought about it enough, Sandborne said, "Well, whether we're lawmen or just drovers, I'm still not sleepy."

Halstead almost admired the boy's consistency. He stood up and took his black hat from the hook by the door. "I think I'm going to take a walk around. Get the layout of the train now that we're underway. You stay here. Enjoy the view."

Sandborne gladly went back to looking out the window. "I surely will. Give a holler if you need anything."

He knew it was cruel, but he could not resist the urge to give Sandborne something to think about while he was gone. "There's just one more thing. We have to change your name."

The prospect of changing his name was about the only thing that could distract Sandborne from the window. "Change my name? Why?"

"I'm Jeremiah," Halstead explained. "You're Joshua. Both begin with 'J.' Even if you call yourself Josh and I go by Jerry, it's still 'J.' They sound too similar and people are liable to get us mixed up. Since we're working together, one of us ought to change their name. I'm older, so it ought to be you."

Sandborne's eyes went wide. "You're about ten minutes older than me. I'm twenty and you're twenty-four."

"Which still makes me older than you," Halstead reminded him. "So take some time and come up with a different name. Something simple. Like Sandy."

"Sandy?" The deputy frowned. "Sandy Sandborne? My pa had a horse named Sandy once."

Halstead smiled. "See? It's already broken in."

Sandborne folded his arms and frowned out the window. "I ain't gonna be called Sandy." Then winced when he caught himself and said, "I meant *not*. I'm *not* going to be called Sandy."

Halstead left the young man with that problem to keep him busy until he got back. Kidding that boy just might make this trip go faster.

The passengers who spotted Halstead coming toward them all looked the other way when he got closer. The pattern was always the same. First, they'd look at his face, then at the star on his lapel, then at the holster sticking out of his coat, then at anything else that was not him. A newspaper or a book or a window.

He knew they all mistook him for being half-Indian. A lousy half-breed with a badge.

He had almost grown used to it since coming to Montana. In El Paso, no one had ever taken him for being anything other than white with maybe a bit of Mexican blood in him. Down there, it had not really mattered.

But, as he constantly reminded himself, Montana was a

long way from Texas. Life was different up here. The people were different. And with statehood fast approaching, they wanted to distance themselves from the thought of anything that reminded them of their recent frontier past. From Indian raids and shoot-outs and train robberies.

In Texas, the past was never far away because the present hardly changed. Cities got bigger and the clothes got fancier, but Texas was still Texas. Life was still a precarious undertaking down there. If you got lost, either thirst would get you or the sun would bake you alive. Say the wrong thing to the wrong man at the wrong time, and you could find yourself in a fight for your life.

Trust the wrong men and a man could find himself in jail for three long years. He had learned that last part the hard way.

Yes, Montana certainly was a long way from Texas. Sometimes, that was bad. But when it came to his past, Jeremiah Halstead saw it as a benefit. And although he did his best to never look back, the treatment people gave him made it hard to remain in the present.

He reached the dining car and drew the same reaction from the customers there as he had from the passengers in the back. He paid them no mind and took in the setting instead. White tablecloths. Gleaming silverware and plates that had the railroad's initials engraved on them. Interlocking GNR in fancy letters for Great Northern Railroad. Only the black waiters in white coats bid him hello as he passed.

As he reached the end of the car, he saw a young lady sitting alone at a table. She was clearly doing her best not to cry but was doing a poor job of it. Her slender face was streaked with tears, and her blue eyes were already red.

Halstead did not know much about women's fashions

outside of the fine way Katherine Mackey, Aaron's wife, liked to dress. And by his estimation, she would have admired the light pink dress and hat this woman was wearing now.

He was old enough to know that pretty young women with tears in their eyes could only lead to trouble, but something about her made him want to know why she was crying.

"Something bothering you, miss?" he asked when he stopped at her table.

She looked up at him, hopefully at first, then her eyes dimmed. But he could tell it was not because of who he was or who she might think he was, but for a different reason. She was hoping he would be someone else.

She forced a smile anyway. "Is it that obvious, sheriff?"

"Only to someone who's paying attention," he said. "Everyone else in here is too busy with their food to notice. Your secret is safe with me."

She stifled a laugh and quickly covered her mouth with her handkerchief. There was something in the simple gesture that made his heart stop for a beat.

"I'm glad to hear it," she said. "I wouldn't want to make a complete fool of myself so soon after leaving Helena."

"The only fool on this train is the man who made you cry," he said without thinking. He immediately felt as foolish as he had made Sandborne feel earlier. "I'm sorry. I shouldn't have said that."

Yet her smile held. "I guess that was obvious, too. That I'm crying over a man, I mean."

"Only to me." *Why am I sounding like this?*

She gestured to the empty chair across from her. "Would you like to join me, sheriff? It appears that I have been abandoned at present. That is, unless you have official business."

The thought of saying no should have entered his mind, but it had not, so he sat down. "I was just taking a walk through the train to kill some time is all. And I'm not a sheriff, ma'am. I'm a Deputy U.S. Marshal. Jeremiah Halstead."

"And I'm far too young to be called 'ma'am.'" Her eyes told him she was far from insulted. "I take it you're *the* Jeremiah Halstead. The one everyone in Helena is talking about?"

He felt himself begin to blush. "The one everyone in Helena is gunning for is more like it."

"So I've heard." She thumbed away her tears with gloved hands that matched the color of her dress. "That can't be easy. Having to live in fear all the time of someone trying to gun you down."

"Fear will get a man in my line of work killed," he told her. "So will thinking too much, so I try not to think about it. Guess I'm lucky I was born stupid."

Her smile faded a little as she rested her chin on her gloved hand, looking him over with her reddened blue eyes. She had hair as black as his own only it was swept up somewhere under her hat. It made her skin look even more delicate than it already did. "You're far from stupid, Mr. Halstead. Quite far."

Halstead tried to make himself stop blushing. "Stupid enough to get shot at for a living."

"But smart enough to know I was hoping you were someone else. How did you know?"

He had not really thought about it. "Just the way you looked, I guess. Surprised and sad all at the same time."

"Perceptive *and* tough," she noted. "Admirable qualities in any man in any line of work."

"Qualities I'll bet the man you were waiting for just now doesn't have." This time, he did not regret what he had said.

Her smile returned a bit, and he was glad he had not upset her. "If he did, he would be sitting here right now instead of you."

He forced himself to look away out of fear he might be staring, which even he knew was impolite. "Guess I shouldn't have said that. I'm not very good when it comes to manners, but I'm working on it. My friend's wife said she'll make a gentleman out of me yet if it's the last thing she does."

"Men with manners aren't always gentlemen." She looked away, too. "You can take my word on that."

Halstead could not understand the rage that was suddenly building up inside him. Rage at a man he had never met. Rage at him for making her cry; a woman he had only met a moment before. A rage he did not fully understand but still consumed him. "He's a fool, whoever he is."

She cut loose with a sharp laugh that immediately embarrassed her and caused her to raise her handkerchief to her mouth.

He could sense she had drawn every eye in the dining car, but the sound of her laughter only made him laugh, too.

And now it was her turn to blush. "See what I said about manners? A proper lady would never allow herself to laugh like that, especially in such a public place. I have the worst laugh. My father said I yelp like a puppy."

"It's a good laugh," he said. "Honest. Nothing wrong with honesty. The world could use more of it if you ask me."

"Perceptive, tough, and a philosopher," she remarked. "You know, we've been chatting for more than five minutes now and you haven't once asked me my name."

She was right. He had not. "Maybe that's because I feel like I already know you and names aren't all that important to me."

"Unless they're on a wanted poster, of course."

He enjoyed her sense of humor. "You're not wanted for anything, are you?"

She looked away. "Not for what I'd hoped for. That much is plain now. Even to me."

He wanted to punch himself in the head. There he went, ruining it again. "I'm sorry. I didn't mean to say anything that upset you."

She folded her hands on the table and sat up straight as if she had just awoken from a long sleep. "You've done nothing of the kind. I've spent the last week feeling sorry for myself, and you're the first person to come along and make me feel appreciated. My name is Abigail Newman and if you shake my hand or any other kind of formality, I'll be bitterly disappointed."

Halstead had no intention of disappointing her ever again. "We wouldn't want that, now, would we? May I ask where you're headed?"

"Battle Brook," she said. "My work takes me there. You?"

"Battle Brook," he said. "My work takes me there, too."

She said, "I'm going there to teach school. It's a desolate little mining town but a growing one, and their children are in need of a teacher."

"And your friend?" Halstead asked. "What's he headed to Battle Brook for?"

"Adventure," she said, "which is supposed to be a more respectable way of saying he's a card sharp. Or at least thinks of himself as one. His bank account would beg to differ. He was a doctor when I met him. Quite a good one, in fact. But he grew tired of medicine and has decided to become a professional gambler. I'm sure he's somewhere on this train right now trying his hand at poker." She arched a thin eyebrow as she looked at him. "He has a new system, you see?"

Halstead winced. He had heard this story time and time again. A pretty lady following a gambler as he works his way around the card circuit, always just one game away from making his name and fortune. And when the luck runs out and the cash runs out, he runs out and leaves with just enough money for a single ticket on the next stage out of town. He leaves the pretty lady behind with the solemn promise that he'll send for her as soon as he can manage it.

But the longer she waits, the more she realizes he is not coming back, and she falls for the next smooth-talking man who comes along. She either leaves with him or obtains a reputation. And not much good happened to a woman who has the wrong kind of reputation, especially out in this part of the world. Or anywhere, for that matter.

"Why Mr. Halstead," Abigail said. "I'm touched."

For a moment, he feared he had been speaking out loud. "About what?"

"That look on your face," she said. "A look of pity and concern. Don't worry about me. After all, Thomas is using my money."

"Your money?" he repeated.

"Not all of it, of course," she told him. "But yes, my money. My mother died giving birth to me and my father made a fortune in shipping in San Francisco. And when he died last year, he left it all to me. The men who actually run the company pay me a handsome sum each month to simply sign what they tell me to sign and not ask too many questions. There's more than enough to allow Thomas to engage in his dreams of making a life for himself as a gambler, but I still control the purse strings in the partnership. He always sulks when I pull them tighter, but into every life a little rain must fall, even his."

Halstead was dumbfounded. He had never heard a woman talk this way before, especially about a man. Much less a man she supposedly loved.

Abigail looked at him and laughed again in a way that was far more subtle than before. "I hope you don't play poker, Mr. Halstead. You'd lose your shirt in about three hands. Even Thomas could beat you. Your thoughts are written all over your face as plain as day."

He said the first thing to come to mind. "If you've got all that money, why teach? And why let Thomas waste it all on cards?"

"Because I had a teaching position and Thomas before my father died," she told him. "I don't like change and I enjoy teaching."

"And Thomas?"

She looked down at her gloved hands. "I enjoy him less and less." She looked up at Halstead again. "I don't mean to give you the wrong impression, Mr. Halstead. I'm not all that wealthy. Not like Mr. Rice who owns the railroad, but I should be more than comfortable enough for the rest of my days if the business continues to prosper. If not, there's always teaching to fall back on, isn't there?"

The more he listened to Abigail talk, the more he was fascinated by her. He felt like he could sit and listen to her for hours without once growing bored. If he found his mind drifting from her words, he would have had those beautiful blue eyes to keep his attention.

They both looked up when one of the waiters appeared holding a silver coffee service on a silver tray.

"Sorry for the delay, Miss Newman," the black man said, "but we'd just run out of coffee and I put on a fresh pot just for you. I took the liberty of bringing a second cup for the deputy, here. You're in good hands with Deputy Halstead, miss. We all are."

"Thank you, Randall," she said. "That was quite thoughtful."

The waiter bowed to both of them and moved on to another table.

Halstead took this as his cue to leave. He still had the rest of the train to look over and besides, he did not want this Thomas fellow to come back, find him talking to Abigail, and make a scene. He sounded like the type who would. And Halstead was not the type to allow him to get away with it.

He hated to do it, but he pushed himself away from the table and got up before she had a chance to stop him. "I have to be moving along. Got to finish those rounds I mentioned."

She watched him get up and inclined her head in a most curious way. "I hope all this talk of money and Thomas hasn't scared you off."

"Not at all," he assured her. "It's just that if I don't leave now, I'm liable to sit with you until we get into Battle Brook."

That smile again. "Would that be so very bad, Jeremiah?"

"Not for me," he admitted, "but you'd get pretty bored and my partner would probably starve to death. He's a good kid, but this is his first time on a train. He's so taken with everything, he's liable to forget to eat. Not to mention your Thomas wouldn't be too happy that I occupied so much of your time."

"The only lady he's interested in these days is the queen on those damnable cards of his." She frowned. "But we still have a while before we reach Battle Brook. I'm sure we'll run into each other before then. At least I hope we do."

"So do I." He touched the brim of his hat. "Evening, Miss Abigail."

"Mr. Halstead."

He fumbled with the door between the cars, which made her laugh again, before he made it outside. It was not until he was already halfway into the next car before he could feel his legs again. Before he felt anywhere close to normal. Had he drunk anything while with her, he would have sworn she had spiked his drink. But as he had not drunk anything, that would be impossible.

But she had the same effect on him as too much whiskey. That much was certain. She had touched him in a way no woman had ever touched him before and without even coming near him.

It was strange and wonderful and startling all at the same time. He did not notice the odd looks he drew from the passengers until he was already through the rail car. Their opinion of him no longer mattered. Her good opinion of him was all that counted.

He decided some fresh air might help clear his head a bit, and he paused in between the next two cars. He tucked himself between the railing and out of the wind as the train sped along westward. He remembered the black Havana cigars he still had in his pocket that he had taken from Sheriff Boddington in Silver Cloud. He had smoked one with Billy Sunday upon returning safely to Helena. Billy usually preferred cigarettes but had never been one to turn down a good cigar if offered.

Halstead removed the cigars he had wrapped in brown paper from his inside coat pocket and took one out. He drew it under his nose and inhaled the rich earthy smell of the stick.

He tucked the rest of the cigars away, bit off the end of the stick, thumbed a lucifer alive, and shielded the flame from the wind as he lit his cigar. He puffed on it until he drew the flame deep enough into the cigar to know it was lit before tossing the match away.

He stood on the back platform of the train car, enjoying the smoke and all that had happened to him so far that day.

He was on his first long-range assignment for Aaron Mackey to a part of the country he did not know to go up against an evil man he knew all too well. He could accept those odds as they were if he did not have Sandborne to consider. His teasing of the younger man aside, Sandborne was a steady hand and would be less of a burden than Halstead had let on. He had proven himself time and time again in Dover Station and in Helena.

But he had never gone against the likes of Zimmerman before. He doubted anyone besides Mackey and Sunday had. Sandborne certainly had not. He only hoped his steadiness held out against Zimmerman if they found themselves facing him. For he knew that if Zimmerman managed to escape this time, he would only grow more dangerous in the months and years to come.

And with a villain like Brunet in the mix, Halstead knew his job would be that much more dangerous.

Halstead looked at the door of the opposite car when it opened and saw a prosperous looking man step out. He judged him to be about thirty or so, with a trimmed brown beard and a tailored pearl gray suit that matched his bowler hat. A silver watch chain went from a buttonhole on his brocade vest and disappeared somewhere beneath his suit coat. Following the path of the chain led Halstead to see a Colt on the man's right hip.

Halstead popped the cigar in his mouth and nodded to the man, subtly hooking his right thumb on his belt near his belly holster.

"Afternoon," the deputy greeted the stranger.

The man looked him over in the same manner everyone else on the train had. His complexion, then the star, then the silver handle of the Colt sticking out of his coat like a threat. But the stranger did not look away after that. He did not continue into the next coach, either. He spread his hands on both sides of the railing and grinned at him.

Halstead did not trust it when strangers grinned at him.

"I take it you must be the great Jeremiah Halstead."

"Great, no. But I'm Halstead. And just who might you be?"

"Thomas Ringham," the man said as if the name alone was supposed to mean something to him. "I understand you've been taking liberties with my woman. Miss Abigail Newman."

Now Halstead knew who he was. "I've never been good in polite society, Mr. Ringham, so how about you tell me what you consider to be a liberty."

"Sitting with her in public," Ringham explained. "Making eyes at her across the table. Trying to seduce her with that native charm of yours."

Halstead removed the Havana from his mouth. "That's funny. I've been called a lot of things in my day, but charming's a first."

Ringham glared at him. "It just might be the last if you keep going like you are."

Halstead allowed a stream of cigar smoke to escape from the corner of his mouth. "Careful. It's still against the law to threaten a peace officer, even in Montana."

"I'm not talking to a peace officer now," Ringham sneered. "I'm talking to the damned half-breed who's trying to seduce a decent white woman. I won't have it, Halstead. Star or no star, and neither will a lot of good men on this train."

Halstead eyed Ringham closely now. He had been in shape once, but too much time at card tables had made him softer than he thought he was. Too much whiskey had dulled his senses, too, and made him slower than he thought he was. "Don't see any of those men out here with us. Just see you and me. I'd say it's up to you to try to do something about it."

Thomas Ringham slowly stood up from the railing. He was about the same height as Halstead, though he had his feet spread too far apart on the rocking train to tell for certain. Standing that way also put his right hip lower than he thought it was. He would clank his pistol on the railing if he tried to draw, not that it would matter. If his hand moved anywhere near his hip, Halstead would shoot him dead.

"Want to know how I knew your name?" Ringham asked him.

"Someone probably saw me talking to Miss Abigail and ran back to tell you," Halstead guessed. "Gossip travels fast, even faster on trains."

"They did," Ringham admitted, "but I knew about you long before that in Helena. Heard there was a price on your head by some outlaw called Zimmerman. Ten thousand dollars to the man who kills you." Ringham's smile was meant to intimidate him. "A man like me could have himself quite a time with ten thousand in my pocket."

"He surely could," Halstead said. "Could pay back the money he owes his woman for starters. There's a word for a man who lives off a woman like that. Just can't think of it now."

Ringham's eyes narrowed. "Abigail told you a lot, didn't she?"

"She needed someone to talk to," Halstead told him. "And since you weren't there, I filled in. But this isn't about her anymore. This is about that ten thousand you mentioned. You're right about that price on my head. And here I am. Cornered. Stuck out here alone. Just the two of us. If you want that money, make your play for it." He flicked the ash on his cigar without taking his eyes off Ringham. "Make it right now."

He watched Ringham consider it. He watched him roll the idea around in his mind as he tried to get comfortable with it. He clearly liked it well enough, but not the odds.

Halstead decided he was not as dumb as he looked.

The gambler looked him up and down again before he went back to leaning on the railing with both hands.

Halstead kept his right hand tucked on his belt and went back to smoking his cigar with his left.

"Things being what they are," Ringham said, "I don't need the money just now. But my circumstances might change when we reach Battle Brook. I hear you're headed there, too. Might look you up then if I have the need."

"Circumstances might change," Halstead admitted, "but not the result. You'll end up just as dead then as you would've if you'd gone for that hogleg now."

Thomas Ringham laughed as he hung his head for a

moment before looking at Halstead one final time. "Well, I suppose we'll just have to see about that, Halstead. Won't we?"

"I hope not. For Miss Abigail's sake."

Ringham pushed himself off the railing and went back inside the train car, shutting the door behind him.

Halstead kept his right hand on his belt until he was reasonably sure Ringham would not be returning. Realizing whatever threat the gambler may have posed had passed, he went back to enjoying his cigar. He was glad the gambler had backed down. It was a good smoke and it would have been a shame to waste it.

# Chapter 4

Zimmerman saw no reason to fight the sense of pride he felt as he looked over the mangy group of twelve men he had managed to gather at the trading post. The place was run by Zed Sherman, who had proven to be no more scrupulous a man than most who ran trading posts. For a small fee, he allowed Zimmerman to hold his meeting and give them privacy with no questions asked. Traders rarely profited from curiosity.

Zimmerman watched the men as Brunet began to lay out the plan they had already agreed upon a few days earlier in his shack. Brunet had reluctantly agreed to allow Zimmerman to be the leader of the group as long as he did not make much of a show of it. Most of the men Brunet had brought here knew him, at least by reputation, and he did not want to look like he was playing second fiddle to anyone.

Zimmerman allowed him to have his way, at least for the time being. He intended on having each of these men eating out of his hand before the month was out.

"You boys know who I am," Brunet began. "Some of you have even ridden with me a piece before. This man here is Ed Zimmerman, late of the Hudson Gang. He's my partner in this here undertaking, and I want you to give him the same respect as you'd give me."

A swarthy, hunched man Zimmerman took for a Blackfoot Indian said, "Respect is earned, Brunet. And I don't know this Zimmer Man or whatever his name is from nothing. And what I do know of the Hudson Gang is that they're all dead and he's the only one still alive."

Some of the men around the crooked planked table grumbled in agreement while most just looked at Zimmerman as if they were deciding why they should not just kill him.

Brunet brought his heavy knife down and stuck the blade in the table. "I won't tolerate insolence, boys. Any man who won't do as I say best finish his beer and ride on now. And any man who signs on and changes his mind about that later will catch a bullet in the head for his betrayal." He looked at each man in turn before saying, "That bit's final."

The man Zimmerman had decided would be called Blackfoot looked down at his mug of beer and fell silent.

Brunet went on. "This is a simple, real sweet idea Zimmerman is hatching here. One that, if we do it right, will make us all rich and healthy before too long."

A stout man with welts on his face said, "Sounds almost too good to be true. I don't trust things that are too good to be true."

Zimmerman decided this man would be called Scar if he remained with the group. "Perhaps if you let Brunet speak, you'll feel better about things."

"Damned right," Brunet agreed. "The next one who speaks up before I'm done gets a whipping."

Two men got up from the table, drained their mugs,

and left. Zimmerman had not taken the time to take their measure but was glad to see them leave. Since they did not seem to like the rules, it was best they left now before they stayed too long and it became necessary to kill them later.

Brunet continued. "Figuring no one else wants to leave, here's the plan. We're going on a mining raid, boys. Not just one, mind you, but on the six biggest operations in the hills around here. It's not going to be as easy as you figure because we're not going to hit these boys and run away. We're going to hit all six over three days when their pay shows up. We're also going to have pack mules with us to handle all the money we'll be taking from them."

That detail set some of the men to grumbling, but Brunet spoke over them. "It'll mean some killing, but only as much as necessary. Just the guards and anyone else who tries to stand in our way. If we can cow the miners instead of killing them, all the better. Shooting them will only make people in town turn on us and make us hotter than we'll already be. A massacre will only get the army involved and none of us want that headache. But if we do it the way we tell you to do it, by this time next week we'll have more money in our hands than we've ever dreamed."

Some of the men looked at each other but only one raised his head higher than the others and looked like he had a question. The bald, skinny fool might have even raised his hand if he'd had any schooling, which Zimmerman imagined was minimal. He pointed at the man and said, "Go ahead."

"We taking any of the ore with us?" the man said. "We'll have the mules anyway, so why not load up while the getting is good?"

Zimmerman was glad the first question was an intelligent one. He would call this one Plato. "Ore will be heavier and more difficult to sell. I'll explain what we plan on doing with the money once all of you have formally joined our cause."

The men seemed to accept that for the moment.

Brunet continued with his talk. "Zimmerman here's got it all figured out. He's been in these parts for the past few months and he knows how the six biggest mines work. He knows when they get paid and when they ship out their ore further south of here to be ground up. Now these payroll wagons are apt to have a lot of armed guards, so if any of you leave here thinking you can hit them on your own, you're wrong. Zimmerman's got a way we can get rich and get away clean."

Another man who was just as bald as Plato, but without the benefit of a neck, looked like he had a question. Given his appearance, Zimmerman decided this man would be known as Bullet. "Six mines in three days sounds like a lot, don't it? It won't be just us ripping the strong box off a stagecoach. We'll have mules with us, sure, but they ain't exactly light on their feet and the going up around them mines is mighty dangerous even if you're taking your time. It's even worse when you're in a hurry."

Zimmerman knew Brunet understood that part of the plan and allowed him to speak.

"It has to be three days because they all get paid around the same time," Brunet explained. "Six mines, six wagons on account of the same wagons that bring the pay also haul the ore away. We hit them in the order that they're paid so we can get the money and move on. But we're going to have to be smart about this, fellas, not greedy. Taking the ore will slow us down, even if it's just a couple of nuggets we can fit in our pockets. I know it sounds funny, but we're raiding gold mines for cash, not gold. The ground won't allow for anything more than that, boys."

That fact killed off most of the grumbling and Brunet resumed his talk. "Three days is going to make for some tough riding and tough living, but you bunch are used to that. We're going to have to hit each wagon hard and fast and move on with the payroll even faster. We aim to hit two camps per day and clean out all six of them before it's all said and done. We're gonna have to be just as smart after we hit the last mine. That means hiding out for a while. Laying low. That means no heading into town. No whoring or getting drunk. At least for a little bit."

A man with a fleshy face scarred from frostbite said, "I didn't come here expecting to be turned into no god-damned monk for no amount of money."

Zimmerman decided he had earned the name Monk for his observation skills. "The money we steal won't do any of us much good if we're caught or dead. Going to town before we're ready is too risky. I assure you we'll have the rest of our lives to enjoy what we steal, but we need to be smart about it. All of us."

He looked at each man as he said, "I'll see to it that you all have your fill of whiskey or rum after we finish with the last mine, but the women will have to wait since we'll be hiding out with the money for a while. Anything else is just too dangerous. It's for your own good, I promise you."

"Sounds like my mother," Monk grumbled to the laughter of all.

A man with a sullen expression, thick black hair, and droopy eyes spoke next. "How come we have to hit the mines? Why don't we just wait until all them miners hit the towns on payday and take the money off them then? Or hit the ore wagons while they're full and on the road?"

He reminded Zimmerman of a tintype he had seen of Edgar Allan Poe once and he decided he would be called Poe. "Because any fool can roll a drunk in an alley. We want it before they get it. As for hitting the wagons hauling the ore, if you boys want to sift through a wagon full of rocks we can't carry or sell in its current form, be my guest."

Zimmerman could feel the mood of the men gathered around the table begin to shift from skepticism toward something like acceptance. They were not all the way there yet, but they were closer than they had been at the beginning. Dropping just a few more bread crumbs would bring them all the way into his lair.

He decided to add a little sugar to the pot. "We're not just talking about a single score here, boys. We're talking about something a lot more than that if you want it."

"More?" the heaviest man in the group said. His bearskin coat was even more matted than Brunet's. "How much more? And how much are you figurin' each of us will take as our cut? When all's said and done, I mean."

His question about money, combined with his prosperous belly, reminded Zimmerman of a picture of J. Pierpont Morgan he had once seen in a newspaper. This man would be called Morgan. "I'm afraid we've reached the point of our discussion where we're going to need a commitment from you gentlemen before I tell you that. A commitment not all of you may be prepared to make. This isn't like joining the army or signing on with a bunch who'll hit the odd stagecoach now and then, but something far greater than that. If you're in, you're in all the way until the finish. No getting your share and riding off after we hit the last mine. No backing out because you want to go back home. What we take will be split evenly among us and based on how many I see right now, that means a split twelve ways." He held up a finger. "And I did say evenly. Brunet and I get the same as each of you. The orders we give you must be obeyed, but only when it comes to hitting the payroll. The risk and the reward will be shared evenly. But Brunet and I will need more than your word on this. We'll need your blood."

The men all looked at each other as Zimmerman stood next to Brunet and both of them produced their knives and drew them along their right palms, reopening the cuts that had only just begun to heal.

Zimmerman said, "What we're proposing is that serious, men. Any man willing to do the same, step forward now and shake our hands, then shake each other's to seal the deal for now and for all time. We're bonded to you as you are to us in all future profits."

Some of the men hesitated, mostly those whom Zimmerman had not seen fit to name yet. But those he had already committed to memory got to their feet, pulled their knives, and cut their hands. Before the ceremony was over, all of them had swapped blood and forged the deal forever.

As he began to rebandage his hand, Zimmerman knew he was in uncharted territory now. Darabont had never demanded such a commitment from his followers. He had never bound his men to him in the way he and Brunet had just done. He had never sought such loyalty among cutthroats. Perhaps that was why he had found himself in a pit up to his neck with red ants devouring him slowly.

Zimmerman knew the nature of men such as these. He knew one of them would get greedy and seek to break the oath, the bond. And Zimmerman would kill him when he did. It would not matter who. Even if it was Brunet, the man's treachery would be a lesson for the others to learn to honor their commitments. And they would, for by then, they would see the riches that awaited them.

Zimmerman could feel his newfound power coursing through his veins as he finished rebandaging his hand. He looked at Brunet and asked, "Should I tell them now?"

"After all of that?" He smiled as he wrapped his hand. "I think you'd better."

Zimmerman decided to do the math for them. "There are about two thousand miners working the six mines we'll hit. Considering each of them gets paid about forty dollars a month, if we hit them right, I figure we're looking at a haul of about eighty thousand dollars. Split twelve ways, we'll be looking at a bit more than six thousand per man at least."

The men, including Brunet, whooped and hollered at the prospect of easy money. They slapped each other on the backs and slammed their mugs of beer together at the news.

But Zimmerman himself did not participate in their revelry. For he knew the true number that the amount came to. A number that would not mean much to this band of heathens, but one that pleased Zimmerman to no end.

The true take per man would be six thousand, six hundred and sixty-six dollars. The sign of the beast mentioned in the Book of Revelation.

A beast who, if Zimmerman had his way, would bow its head to him in admiration for all of the wrath he intended to unleash upon the Montana Territory.

"Six thousand," Monk shouted above the others. "I don't

think I've ever seen that much money in one place in my whole life."

Zimmerman drank in their greed and joy. "If you think that's a lot, just wait until I tell you what we plan on doing with it once we steal it."

And with that, he began to explain his true plan, which made their dead eyes come to life.

# Chapter 5

Halstead had never been so happy to be in the middle of nowhere in all of his life.

He stretched his legs as he walked around the platform at Wellspring Station. Sandborne was already fetching the horses and loading their supplies on the mule.

Before reaching Wellspring, the conductor had told him that the tiny railroad town offered all of the comforts of home. A couple of nice hotels, some decent places to eat, and a saloon where a man could slake his thirst for liquor and other things after a long train ride. The only law in town was a half-doddering old fool named Red Howard, who had been good with a gun once but not anymore.

Halstead was glad he and Sandborne had brought enough supplies for them to ride overland and straight for Battle Brook as soon as possible. It was not yet eight in the morning and he knew they could make good time in their journey. Every single day the rumors of Zimmerman's sighting went unconfirmed made it more difficult for Halstead to find him, much less arrest him. The man was like a weed. Easy to take root and difficult to pull out when the time came. And if he had managed to work out some kind of partnership with Rob Brunet, then taking him in would be twice as hard.

Halstead stood near the station building as he watched the other passengers disembark. He did not want to admit that he was looking for Abigail Newman, but he was. He had seen her several times since that first day on board, but never without Thomas Ringham at her side. The way she stole a glance at Halstead whenever they happened to see each other told him she felt the same way toward him. She never allowed her eyes to linger on him for too long, but long enough to let him know he had made an impression.

He hated not being able to talk to her, but if his presence had spurred the idiot to treat her better, then he was glad for her. It did not serve to make him like the gambler any better.

He watched one of the black porters struggle down the train stairs with luggage and place them on a hand cart before Thomas Ringham stepped down onto the platform. He was dressed in a different suit today, a dark blue number that was as well-tailored as any he had seen him wear on the ride out from Helena.

Halstead felt his chest tighten again as he saw Abigail take Ringham's hand and descend from the train. She was wearing a powder blue dress that he imagined Katherine Mackey would envy. She stopped on the last step to look around, and her eyes found Halstead leaning against the station building. He knew the brief smile she offered him from across the sea of bustling travelers would warm him on the many cold nights to come.

Ringham spotted him, too, though there was no such affection in his gaze. He continued to glare at Halstead as Abigail walked past him and attended the porter with their luggage.

Halstead did not look away. He was leaning against the building as he had seen Aaron Mackey stand so many times before. At an angle to his man, his left shoulder front, making himself as narrow a target as possible. His belly gun was easier to draw and shoot that way. If it came to that.

And judging by Ringham's glare, he thought it just might. He could tell the same thought was going through the man's mind. Halstead imagined he would have to kill this man one day. Might be best to get it over with right here and now.

But Abigail took Ringham by the arm and led him away before it came to that. Ringham reluctantly followed.

"This sure is something," Sandborne said as he came to Halstead's side.

It took Halstead a moment to snap out of the spell Abby had put on him. "What is?"

"This." He thrust a bottle at him. "Ginger ale. A whole bottle of it. A fella at the end of the platform is selling the stuff from a wagon. I had it a time or two back in Helena, but this stuff tastes better. Try it."

Halstead looked at the bottle for a moment before taking it. "You know, I *have* had pop before, Joshua."

"I know, but this stuff is local, meaning you can't find it everywhere." He took a healthy pull on the bottle. "And don't let the ale part of the name fool you. It won't make you drunk like regular ale will. The fella at the wagon promised me that. I imagine we'll want to keep a clear head on the trail."

Halstead could not help but enjoy Sandborne's enthusiasm. The kid would make a hell of a salesman if he wanted.

He took a good swallow of the stuff and immediately regretted it. The strong taste of ginger almost made his eyes water. He handed the bottle back to Sandborne.

Sandborne finished drinking his bottle and wiped his mouth with his sleeve. "Yes, sir. That'll wake you up."

"Hope it woke you up enough to see to the horses and the mule like I told you."

Sandborne was glad to report, "The mule is loaded. The canteens are full of fresh water from the station pump over there, and Col and Max are saddled. We are ready to hit the trail at your convenience, Deputy Halstead."

Halstead looked around the crowded platform for one last glimpse of Abby before they left. But the platform was a hive of activity and it was impossible. He hoped to see her again in Battle Brook. He began walking toward the horses, and Sandborne followed as he finished Halstead's ginger ale.

"Max," Halstead said. "That your horse's name?"

"My dun gelding." He sounded disappointed. "His name's always been Max."

"Guess it slipped my mind," Halstead admitted, then remembered an earlier conversation. "What about your name? Come up with a new one yet?"

"No," he said as he tossed the soda bottles into a garbage can on the platform. "Not going to, either. If you don't want me to use my first name around you, I won't. I'll just go by my last name. If people ask me, I'll tell them to call me Sandborne. Just Sandborne."

"A name that will strike terror in the hearts of every bad man who hears it," Halstead said. "Let's move. We've got a long road ahead of us."

* * *

After less than half a day on the trail, Halstead knew the maps he had seen were wrong. There was no way they could reach Battle Brook in a day or so. He was figuring more like three. The distance may have been short as the crow flies, but horses did not have wings and neither did mules. The terrain in this part of the venture was mostly up hill and rocky. He imagined the main road to Battle Brook would have been better. But with the price on his head, he didn't want to risk it.

The trail along the rocky hillside was wide and the drop off from the right side was a gradual one. The ground was slick with clear ice that had melted, only to freeze once again. Col's shod hooves broke the thin ice beneath her and Sandborne's horse did the same. At the rear, the mule had no trouble with its footing despite the heavy load it carried.

He had expected Sandborne to complain about the conditions, but he had not said a word since leaving Wellspring. He simply followed Halstead's lead up the gradual incline that would eventually lead them on the trail to Battle Brook. Every sign he had seen on the trail told him they were going in the right direction. He only hoped the ground leveled out a bit once they passed through a section marked Rocky Pass.

The road cut hard to the north through a wide jagged gap in the rockface wall. Halstead took a look at the left side of the road and saw several tons of rocks and rubble below. The deep cuts in the side of the rocks told him someone had used dynamite to create this passage long ago. Perhaps a surveyor for the railroad or some trappers looking for a shortcut to Wellspring where they could sell their pelts.

Halstead rode through the cragged opening of the pass

and was glad he had found himself on a plateau. The opening led into what he could only describe as a box canyon with jagged rocks jutting up all around him. A much wider split in the rocks was on the far side of the plateau and, from what Halstead could see, it went on straight as far as the eye could see. Maybe the road to Battle Brook would be quicker than he had imagined only a few minutes before. Maybe—

"Get down!" Sandborne yelled out from behind him as a bullet struck the ground in front of the horses. Halstead steered Col toward an outcropping of rocks on the right side of the pass as another shot rang out but did not hit anywhere near him.

He pulled his Winchester '86 from the scabbard under his leg as he spilled out of the saddle, then slapped Col on the rump and sent her back toward the pass entrance. Another bullet struck a rock on his left as he found cover behind a boulder.

Halstead looked to his left and saw no sign of Sandborne or the horses.

"Joshua," he called out in a whisper. "You all right?"

Joshua did not answer, and Halstead could not break cover to check on him. He scanned the tiny box canyon for any sight of a gunman or rifle. All he could see was the same kind of jagged rocks and boulders that could give a man cover for as long as he wanted it and his ammunition held out.

Halstead cursed himself for leading them right into a trap. And he eyed the rocks around his position carefully for a way to get them out of it.

He caught a glint of light off something halfway up the rock face on the left and ducked behind the boulder as another bullet bounced off a nearby rock and kicked up stone dust into his eyes. He knew there was more than one shooter in the canyon with them.

When he heard a rifle fire from the opening to the canyon, he knew Joshua had found a target.

"Got him," Sandborne called out.

Halstead was still trying to shake the dust from his eyes. He refused to use his sleeve knowing that would only do more harm than good.

When he cleared his eyes, he looked up to the left where he had seen the glint. All he saw now was a bloodstained rock. No one had ever questioned Sandborne's skill with a rifle, not even in fun.

"See anyone else?" Halstead asked him.

"I'm looking," Sandborne told him.

Halstead kept his Winchester ready as he looked over the rocks through a watery gaze. The sun was right above them now and was likely to catch any gunmetal raised in their direction. The center part of the outcropping looked clear and he began to look at his side of the box canyon.

A bullet struck the stone behind his head, gouging out a big enough piece to cut the skin on the back of his neck, causing him to cry out.

That brought several more shots raining down on his position. He had no choice but to scramble around to the side of the boulder for cover. Too many for just one gun. There had to be two shooters up there.

"You hit?" Sandborne called out from the canyon entrance.

"Just a scratch." He ignored the fire in the back of his neck. He knew it was a bad cut. He could already feel his blood beginning to run down his back.

The pain had at least cleared his eyes as he watched the rocks for any hint of movement. He looked for sounds of pebbles and dirt shifting as the gunman moved to get a better angle on him. He watched for any sign of a glint from anywhere.

He did not know who was up there, only that they were very good. They were as deadly as they were patient.

He caught movement off to his right and raised his Winchester to his shoulder. He saw a man moving among the rocks.

Halstead waited until the man was in the clear again before he fired. The big slug from the '86 struck the man in the back and bounced him off the rock behind him. His rifle clattered as it hit the dirt.

"That the last one?" Sandborne called out.

But Halstead did not answer. He remembered that last volley of shots that had been meant for him. He knew there was another man up there. His target was up in the rocks somewhere to his left, hunkered down while he waited for Halstead to move. He had just seen what happened to his friend when he had sought better cover. This man, if he was smart, would not make the same mistake.

Halstead would have to find another way to get the man to reveal himself.

Something Mackey had told him in Helena came back to him. *Mind your brass.*

Halstead ejected the dead cartridge from the Winchester and levered in a fresh round. He picked up the casing with his left hand and yelled in the direction of the shooter.

"I'm heading up top to make sure we got them, Joshua. Cover me. I'm almost there."

Sandborne came around the rocks and was shocked to see Halstead was still there. He signaled for the younger man to remain silent and fixed his attention on the general area where he figured the shooter was hiding.

He hurled the brass cartridge in as high an arc as he could and heard it ping off a rock somewhere above him.

A man behind a white rock jumped to his right and brought up his rifle. He did not reveal much of himself, but enough for Halstead to aim at and fire. His shot tore through the man's shoulder and struck him in the side of the head. He did not need to see the man fall to know he was dead.

Sandborne remained behind cover. "You think that's all of them?"

Halstead knew there was only one way to be sure. He slowly got to his feet and took a look around. No one fired. "Yeah. We got them all."

Sandborne stood up, too. His Winchester was at his side as he looked over the rest of the small canyon. "Why'd they hide up in the rocks? Why not just cut us off as we left through the other side? We'd have been sitting ducks then."

Halstead knew why. "If they missed, they'd have to chase us over open land. It would've been harder going for us if we backed out the way we came. That incline is dangerous even without the mule slowing us down. In here, they had cover and they thought that would be enough. Wished I'd been more careful before riding in here like that." He nudged his partner. "Might've worked, too, if you hadn't warned me. Thanks."

Sandborne shrugged. "I just called out when I saw a glint in the rocks that didn't look right is all."

Halstead ejected the spent cartridge and began feeding in new rounds into the rifle from his belt. "Maybe we ought to call you 'Hawkeye' Sandborne after this."

"No thanks. Sandborne suits me just fine." He gestured toward the rocks that surrounded them. "Why do you think those boys were shooting at us anyhow? Think they might be Brunet or Zimmerman?"

Halstead doubted it. "They'd probably heard we were on the train and riding this way. Figured they'd try for that bounty Zimmerman put on my head. Doubt it's Zimmerman or Brunet, though. They probably would've brought a lot more men with them. And they don't miss much."

"Neither do we," Sandborne said.

Halstead liked the way the younger man thought. "Best bring up the horses now. We've still got plenty of daylight left and I want to find a nice place to camp. Get those tents set up before the snow falls." And to make his friend feel even better than he already did, he said, "I'll be relying on you to pick the best place to camp tonight. You know more about that kind of thing than I do."

He would have sworn Sandborne had gotten choked up before he went back to gather the horses. Halstead had to admit that it made him feel good to give the deputy a compliment.

It felt even better to still be alive.

# Chapter 6

Back when he had finally felt well enough to ride a horse, the first thing Ed Zimmerman had done was ride into the sad little town of Hard Scrabble. The mining concerns decided they wanted a bigger, more proper town closer to their own mines, so they began to build Battle Brook. And despite the new town being less than a quarter finished, it had already managed to pull most of the businesses away from Hard Scrabble. Only The Miner's Bank and Trust, a saloon, and a few other places had remained to serve the several smaller mines in the hills around the town.

The general store was little more than a shack and, in addition to buying provisions for himself, Zimmerman had bought a pair of field glasses, just like those he had seen Halstead using to spy on them from that stand of pines outside Rock Creek when Zimmerman was part of the Hudson Gang.

He put those field glasses to work now as he looked down on the gold mine he and his men were about to rob. The company had called this particular hole in the ground "Mother and Country." He fought to keep his hands steady from the excitement coursing through his veins. He thumbed one of the scalps tied to his saddle horn to keep his emotions at bay.

"Well," Brunet prodded. "What do you see?"

What he saw was the future, though he did not dare say that to his partner. "Armor plated freighter to haul the ore. A team of eight horses. Clydesdales from what I can see. Six guards out front of the main office. No miners in sight."

He lowered the field glasses and set them in his saddle-bag. He could not have dreamed of a better setup for their first ride.

"Send in the men," he told Brunet. "The men in the buffalo hides first. Seeing those big furry bastards bearing down on them might throw off the guards enough for them to rush their shots. We'll hit the office at the same time. Leave no one alive."

Brunet grinned. "I thought you said you wanted to avoid killing if you could."

"I said miners, not guards or bosses. Now, best get to it before anyone else shows up. Hit 'em hard and fast. That's the way."

Brunet brought his horse around and trotted back to where the rest of the men were gathered, eager to make their fortunes.

As Zimmerman had expected, Brunet led them charging down the hill and out of the brush, where the men commenced to fill the air with savage screams that had even sent a chill through Zimmerman.

Pistol and rifle filled the air as the horde of outlaws rapidly closed in on the armed guards. The first two guards were killed before they even got off a shot. The remaining four were cut down before they could reach the cover of the iron wagon.

Zimmerman heeled his horse into motion and broke through the overgrowth just as Brunet kicked in the door of the office, where more gunfire erupted.

By the time Zimmerman drew rein in front of the office and climbed down from the saddle, it was all over.

Monk took a shot at the thick steel padlock on the wagon but flinched when his bullet bounced off it. Zimmerman called out, "You men form a line and keep an eye on that mine entrance. Anyone comes out, call out for me. You tell them to stay where they are. Don't let them bunch up out in the open or else they'll rush us."

Zimmerman walked into the office and found one guard dead on the floor with half of his face gone. The other man was behind the desk and bleeding badly from a hole in the left side of his chest. He was alive, but not for long.

Brunet laughed. "I've seen lambs put up a bigger fight than these two did."

Zimmerman took the man at the desk to be the mine boss. He pushed him upright with his boot and pinned him against the wall. "Where's the payroll box?"

"On the wagon," he said in a voice that was barely above a whisper.

Zimmerman looked at Brunet for confirmation. His pistol still smoked at his side.

"It ain't in here," Brunet said, "so he's probably telling the truth."

Zimmerman turned his attention back to the boss. "Where are the keys?"

"I don't have them," the dying man told them. "One of

the guards does. I don't know who. It changes every time they come. That's the truth, I swear it."

Zimmerman did not have to tell Brunet to begin searching the guards for the keys. He called out to Poe and Morgan to check the guards outside while he checked the dead guard in the office. After patting him down, he looked up at Zimmerman and shook his head.

Zimmerman took his foot off the dying man's chest and began pulling open desk drawers, dumping the contents on the floor. He found no shortage of keys, but none that looked big enough to fit the lock he had seen on the wagon.

"Found some," Morgan called to them from outside.

Brunet rushed outside while Zimmerman decided to ask the boss some more questions. But judging by the way the man's head hung slack on his chest, he could see he was already beyond answering them.

Zimmerman stepped outside and saw they had already managed to open the lock. One of the men he had not gotten around to naming yet was looking inside the wagon and, judging by the look on his face, the payroll box was empty.

"There ain't nothing there," the outlaw told him. "Damned thing's empty."

Zimmerman knew that could not be true. They had not loaded the ore yet, but the payroll must still be on board. "Climb up into the box and see if it's up there."

While the outlaw did as he had been told, he looked at Poe and Morgan. "You two get back on your horses with the others and keep an eye on that entrance. Those miners were bound to hear our shooting and they'll be sending someone out to take a look. Mind what I told you about letting them spread out."

The two men went around the other side of the wagon

and got on their horses while Zimmerman joined Brunet at the front of the wagon.

The unnamed outlaw had found a lock for a box built into the bottom of the driver's seat. He turned the key while standing on it and gave the lid a good pull, but it would not open.

"Damned thing won't budge. Probably got another lock on it somewhere."

Brunet looked like he wanted to shoot him.

Zimmerman held his temper. "That's because you're standing on it, stupid. Jump down from there."

The outlaw complied and Zimmerman climbed up on the wheel and pulled the lid open.

Inside were about a dozen canvas bank satchels neatly lined up for the taking.

His smile told Brunet all he needed to know.

"Poe," Brunet ordered. "Bring up the mule."

The outlaws cheered as Poe did as he was told. "Simmer down, men," Zimmerman warned them as he lifted the heavy bags out of the strong box and handed them down to Brunet. "We're not done yet."

Brunet and Poe helped secure them on the mule's sides to keep the beast balanced.

Zimmerman climbed down from the wheel as the last bag was slung on the mule. To Brunet, he said, "You and Poe take the money and ride on ahead to the hideout. The rest of us will be along in a bit."

But even the hard-bitten outlaw could not contain his excitement. "We did it, Ed. By God, it worked just like you said it would."

"And it'll keep on working if you do what I tell you. Now get going."

Poe and Brunet got to riding as Zimmerman climbed

into the saddle and joined the line of men facing the mine. He rode to Monk and asked, "Hear anything from them yet?"

Monk leaned over the side of his horse and spat a stream of tobacco juice before answering him. "Heard plenty, but ain't seen nothing yet."

Blackfoot said, "We've got plenty of time to ride on before they get out here, boss."

But Zimmerman was not going anywhere. Not yet. Not this first time. He had a point to make and he intended on making it loud and clear.

He raised his neckerchief to cover his face as he watched a miner emerge from the entrance. His face and clothes were caked with dirt and he was having trouble seeing in the harsh sunlight. He shielded his eyes with one hand and held a pickaxe in the other.

Several more miners soon filled the entrance behind him but did not venture out into the sunlight.

The man in front spoke with a brogue as he asked, "And just who the hell might you lot be?"

Zimmerman drew his .44 from his saddle holster and shot the squinting Irishman between the eyes.

The miners cried out as they saw their comrade fall to the dirt but did not dare move from the entrance.

Zimmerman called out, "Any other brave men want to join your friend here?"

No one moved, but one man shouted back, "You stealin' our money, mister?"

"It's not your money yet," Zimmerman told him. "It was the mining company's money. Now it's ours. They'll pay you what they owe you next month."

"What are we supposed to live on until then?" the same man called out. "We've got families. Credit to pay off."

"You don't have to live on anything," Zimmerman said. "All you've got to do is step right out here and I'll end all your troubles for you."

He waited at the head of his line of men to see if any of the miners came out. Still, not one of them did.

"I'm sure the good people of Battle Brook will see you through," Zimmerman told them. "And when the law shows up, make sure you tell them that this robbery was courtesy of The Spoilers. Tell them this is only the beginning." He pointed his gun down at the dead man on the ground. "Show them your friend here if they don't believe you and tell them anyone who stands in our way will get more of the same."

He aimed his pistol at the man who had spoken out. "Now, me and my boys have other business to attend to. Anyone who follows us won't like what he finds, and he won't die so easy."

Zimmerman looked back at Monk and nodded for him to lead the men out. They rode out of the mining camp in a single line the same way Poe and Brunet had gone. The same route they had planned to take from the beginning.

Zimmerman kept his gun on the single miner in the group until the last of his men rode out before he holstered his pistol, touched the brim of his hat, and rode after them.

He wondered if the miners could hear his laughter echoing along the hillside as he escaped with their hard-earned money.

The era of Zimmerman and his Spoilers had formally begun.


Brunet and Poe kept a steady pace as they sped through the narrow trail that led back to their hideout; a played-out mine that had been forgotten about for years. The entrance was deep enough for them to hide their horses while the men could bed down far enough away to keep from smelling them. Brunet knew the men did not like it, but it was ideally placed between the five other mines on their list and he doubted anyone would come looking for them there. Not before they had settled into their new home, anyway.

Branches and vines cut at Brunet's face and legs, but he felt too good about the robbery to concern himself with a few scrapes and cuts.

Despite its burden, the mule had allowed them to move at a good clip through the hillside, which made Brunet feel even better about Zimmerman's plan. He was hauling more money now than he had ever seen in all his life. All of it had gone exactly as Zimmerman had said it would and none of the men had gotten as much as a scratch, save for the greenery they encountered along the way.

For the first time in his life, Rob Brunet had a piece of something good. Something he could rely on. Between Zimmerman's brains and Brunet's brawn, there was no telling what they could do next.

He had not counted on Poe spoiling it for him.

When they were close enough to the hideout to slow down, Poe, trailing the mule behind him, rode up next to him. "How much you figure we took back there?"

"Won't know for certain until we count it," Brunet beamed. "And we will count it, together after we hit the second mine today. Every man will get his full share in due time. All of us. Equal, just like it should be. That's a fairer shake than any of those miners will get from their betters, I'll tell you that."

"I've never had so much money in one shot like this,"

Poe went on. "Not even after a year of robbing stagecoaches and wagon trains."

Brunet laughed for he knew it was true. "You just wait until three days from now. We'll be sitting on more money than we've ever dreamed."

"But we've already got that much right now," Poe continued. "You and me, I mean. Here. With us."

Brunet got quiet as they kept riding.

Poe kept talking. "I mean, if you and me were to just keep on riding instead of going to the hideout like we're supposed to, we could split this haul between us. Get away clean. No one shot at us this time, but who's to say it'll always be this easy? All I'm saying is that maybe we should quit while we're ahead."

Now that Brunet understood exactly what Poe was proposing, he drew his knife, edged closer to Poe, and pressed the blade against the outlaw's throat. Both men allowed their horses to slow to a halt.

Brunet had been told many times over the years about how his face changed when he was about to kill a man. How his eyes acquired a dark fire to them, and his face grew grim. He could tell by Poe's reaction that he looked that way now.

He pressed the blade hard enough against Poe's throat to draw a thin stream of blood. He removed the blade just enough to show it to the man.

"You made an oath, boy. Not just to me and to Zimmerman, but to the other men who ride with you. Men who'll die for you if it comes to it. And not just some words said over a Bible, but an oath in blood. Your blood and mine. Something like that can't be undone just because you're scared or greedy." He put the blade flat against Poe's throat and held it there, knowing how cold steel felt on a man's flesh.

"That oath can't be broken except by blood," Brunet explained. "So if you want to break it, tell me now so I can release you from your burden. I'll gut you where you sit and take the money on to the hiding place just like we're supposed to."

He scraped the blade up until it was just beneath Poe's jawline. "Choose now and choose final."

Poe's Adam's apple bobbed up and down as he shied away from the blade. "Jesus, Rob. I was just talking. I didn't mean nothing by it."

"Dangerous talk," Brunet said. "And if I ever hear anything like that from you again, I'll skin you alive."

Poe stammered something of an agreement and Brunet withdrew his blade and tucked it back into his buffalo hide.

The two men rode on to the hideout in silence. Brunet was beyond angry. He was disappointed.

There was nothing like a spate of greed to ruin an otherwise beautiful day.

# Chapter 7

"I've never been so glad to see a jail in my whole life," Sandborne said as they approached the outskirts of Battle Brook just before sunset.

Jeremiah Halstead could almost agree with him.

The mining town was different than Silver Cloud had been. Silver Cloud had one main thoroughfare lined with buildings of various sizes and uses on one street.

Battle Brook was so new, it was still being built. It had a collection of buildings of all different sizes along a series of streets that fed into a main thoroughfare they rode along now.

A steady rhythm of hammering and sawing drowned out the normal sounds he would expect to hear in such a bustling town. Wagons full of freight and building goods crisscrossed on their way to or from one construction site or another. He had seen at least three times where horses almost collided with wagons, but somehow managed to avoid disaster.

All of the activity reminded him of how Dover Station had been in the months before it fell. The memory of the sadness and death that rose from the ashes of that place then ruined Battle Brook for him now. He hoped this town had a better fate than Dover Station.

"This place sure is busy," Sandborne observed.

"It's a mining company town," Halstead told him. "Those boys don't let too much grass grow under their feet."

The main thoroughfare was much wider than he had seen in some other towns, but the hard dirt was just as rutted and pockmarked as he had seen anywhere else in Montana. He spotted The Bank of Battle Brook in the middle of the street. It was a long, dark building with a huge window with the bank's name hand-painted on it. He was glad it did not sport a tower. After all that had happened in Silver Cloud, he'd had his fill of clocktowers for the time being.

He saw the types of businesses one would expect to find in a town this size. A land office, a barbershop, a hotel whose sign told him it was The Standard Hotel, and a couple of dry-goods stores. There were plenty of saloons, of course, which he was glad to see appeared to be quiet now. That meant there were plenty of jobs around for any man willing to work. Battle Brook might be new, but it seemed to be an industrious place.

The alleys between the buildings were wider than he had seen in other towns, some wide enough to easily allow two wagons to pass at the same time. Heavy wooden planks were imbedded in the mud to allow people to go from one block to the next without getting themselves trapped in the sucking mud.

It would be a nice place for him and Sandborne to call home for the next few days while they searched the surrounding area for Brunet and Zimmerman.

Whatever lodgings The Standard Hotel provided them could only be a vast improvement of how they had spent the past two nights. The ride from Wellspring Station had been unexpectedly arduous. Even after their run-in with the men back at the boxed canyon, the rest of the trek had been all uphill, rocky terrain that had taken them the better part of two days to cover. Fortunately, Halstead believed in taking precautions and they had packed enough supplies to easily see them through despite the delay.

The tents Mackey had insisted upon had proven to save their lives. The snow fell fast during their journey, and the tents, if nothing else, served to keep them reasonably warm and dry while they slept. Sandborne had picked good places to camp where pine trees served to give their animals a measure of protection from the elements.

He decided to keep his younger partner on his toes. Complimenting him now would only make him cocky, and cocky could get them both killed under the circumstances. "Tell me what you see."

Sandborne looked around the town as they approached it. "Feed store. General store. A couple of saloons and a bank." He squinted as the sunlight off the snow made it difficult to see objects in the near distance. "Got a claims office, too. A dress shop and a hotel. That's all I can make out at present, besides the jail, of course. That sign is swinging in the breeze like it's welcoming us home."

Halstead knew Sandborne had been fixated on the jail for the last day or so, wondering if there'd be room for them to sleep in one of the cells. Before retiring from the service, Johnny Boggs had filled the young man's head with stories of having to sleep in cells with dangerous prisoners to keep an eye on them. Or in the hayloft of the local livery. Or, at the worst of times, in a house of ill repute.

The young man had soaked up the lies and stories of

the older marshals like a sponge and figured he would have to endure similar trials if he hoped to become as famous as them.

But Halstead preferred his comfort and would have a proper room if there was one to be had in town, even if he had to pay for it himself.

The jail was the last building at the far end of town, across from a couple of buildings that looked like houses. They even sported white picket fences around them.

Halstead and Sandborne brought their animals over to the hitching rail. The swinging sign on the boardwalk matched the sign on the door:

## JACK MCBRIDE
## MARSHAL, TOWN OF BATTLE BROOK

Halstead climbed down from the saddle but told Sandborne, "Find a livery that can take all our animals and store all of our gear. I want them tended to, especially that mule. That little guy was worth his weight in gold on this trip. Tell them I'll be along in a bit after I talk to McBride.

But Sandborne did not move. "Don't know if I can do that, Jerry."

Halstead had not been expecting that. "Why?"

"On account of the boss telling me to stick with you when you met McBride. Said he didn't want you roughing him up like you did Boddington down in Silver Cloud."

He should have expected that from Mackey. "I won't do anything. I promise. Now tend to the horses like I told you and come back here. If something goes wrong, I'll take full responsibility." He handed Col's reins up to him. "Go on, now."

Sandborne took the reins. "You promise?"

"You have my word."

Sandborne reluctantly took the reins and rode away along the hard packed mud of the thoroughfare.

Halstead rolled his shoulders and cracked his neck as he walked up the steps to the jail. It had been a few days since he had walked on level ground and it took some getting used to.

He knocked and waited for an answer.

*"Adelante!"* came a voice from the other side of the door. "That means come in."

Halstead stepped inside and found a man sitting behind a rolltop desk. It was a normal-sized desk, but given the man's height, looked like it was better suited for a child.

He had curly red hair and a long floppy moustache, but no beard. His pale skin and blue eyes gave him an almost wild look, but the star pinned to his chest read "Town Marshal."

The red-headed man looked him up and down, as most people often did, except he smiled at what he saw. "I guess you must be that deputy Ol' Mackey mentioned in his telegram." He stood up and came around the desk to greet him. Halstead was surprised the man towered over him. He must have been about six-feet-five inches tall and skinny as a sapling.

"Jack McBride. Town Marshal of Battle Brook and Hard Scrabble. Nice to meet you, Deputy Halstead."

The crick in his neck grew worse as he looked up at the man as he shook his hand. "Nice to meet you, marshal."

The gangly lawman clapped him on the shoulder. "You don't have to say it. Judging by the look on your face, I can tell you're disappointed. You thought I'd be taller."

Halstead shook his head. "I'd say you're plenty tall enough as it is."

"Well, don't worry. It's not contagious." He gestured for him to take a seat next to his desk while he went to the stove. "Sorry about the accommodations being what they are, but we're still getting set up in a way."

The first thing Halstead noticed, after McBride's height, was that there were no cells in the jail. Just an iron ring bolted to the wall at the back of the room. "Not much of a jail without a jail."

"Don't get me started," McBride said as he began to pour coffee. "See, I was figuring I'd have more time before we moved over here from Hard Scrabble on account of there being more law needing to be enforced over there. In fact, they just got started on building the actual jail yesterday. Ought to have the frame up by this evening, given the pace they're working at. This place is supposed to be a lawyer's office, believe it or not, so everything's temporary and nothing seems right."

He nodded over to where he had been sitting. "Take that desk for instance. As big as I am, I can't even see around the damned thing and I won't put it against the wall because I don't like sitting with my back to the door. I'm sure you can understand why."

"I can." Halstead frowned as he looked around the place. It was much smaller than the jail in Silver Cloud had been, though it had a water pump in the corner. The opposite corner had a line of white paint on the floor around it, but no bars. Just a heavy bed with a brass frame near the iron ring in the wall.

"Even the bed for prisoners doesn't fit. That monstrosity was being thrown out by The Standard Hotel, so they gave it to me for prisoners. The whole town's thrown together like that for now." McBride poured some coffee into a mug and handed it to Halstead. "And I imagine it will be for the foreseeable future. You ought to see the plans they've got for this place. Spreads out in six streets in either direction off Main Street. Gonna be a right beautiful place when it's done. I'm not complaining, mind you. The pay still comes regularly, which I guess is all that matters."

McBride moved his chair over so he could look at Halstead while he talked. "They tell me the jail will be ready in another month or so and I tend to believe them. It's getting colder by the day, so the men will be anxious to be working inside and out of the elements."

Halstead saw the gunrack behind McBride and noticed eight Winchesters that all looked to be in good condition. "At least you're well-armed."

"Always preferred the feel of a rifle to a pistol," McBride said. "Even got an old coach gun up there I keep for special occasions. Guess that goes back to my cavalry days. Never got close enough to the enemy for a pistol to be practical. I've never been much good with one anyway, so I prefer a Winchester. The sight of it calms the men down better when they see it. Racking in a round can be quite a sound at the right time."

He would get no argument from Halstead on that score. He sipped the coffee and found it was closer to mud than coffee. But it was plenty strong, just how he liked it, and he had no complaints. "How are you fixed for deputies?"

"Poorly," McBride admitted. "Mayor White and Mr. Ryan, in their infinite wisdom, said I can hire on some deputies when the jail's built."

Knowing Emmett Ryan a little, Halstead was not surprised to hear it. "What do you do if you need help?"

"Got a couple of volunteers who pitch in if I need them," McBride said, "but for now, there's not much cause for it. They're working these boys real hard. Both here in town and up in the mines. They seem to be finding more ore up there every day. We have a little trouble in the saloons come payday, but I've given the bouncers what my captain in the army used to call, 'a broad range of discretion' when dealing with them."

Halstead remembered something. "One of those captains Aaron Mackey?"

"For a bit," McBride said. "He was a couple of years ahead of me at The Point, but I knew him after that, too. Always a touch too serious. He never liked all that hero business they pinned on him after Adobe Flats. I only served with him a bit at the fort before they drummed him out of the army. At least they let him resign his commission. I suppose that counts for something. Not much, but something."

Halstead had often regretted not following in his father's footsteps and enlisting in the army. But when he heard stories like this, he was glad he hadn't. He was eager to change the subject. "I guess this is a pretty quiet town except for all the hammering and banging."

"Quieter still since payday was canceled this month, courtesy of The Spoilers."

"The Spoilers?" Halstead repeated. "Who are they?"

"I expect they have something to do with why you're here in the first place." He took a newspaper from inside his desk and handed it over to him. "I was saving this for you to read once you got here. It'll answer most of your questions."

It was a days-old edition of *The Battle Brook Bulldog,* the local newspaper. The headline said it all in large black print:

## THE SPOILERS STRIKE AGAIN
## HIT SIXTH MINE IN THREE DAYS

### Battle Brook Reels
### Scores Killed and Injured

Halstead skimmed through the article. McBride had been right. It answered some of his immediate questions but raised many more.

When he was done, he handed the paper back to McBride, who tossed it on his desk. "Makes for some tough reading, doesn't it?"

"Makes me think Zimmerman and Brunet have been busy."

"Robbing the payroll was bad enough," McBride said. "But the town can handle that. Mr. Ryan's already extended the men credit through next payday, which, as he reminded me in a letter, he was under no obligation to do. Like the old saying goes, 'A rich man and his money are not soon parted.' So while the money hurts, it's not what scares folks."

He pointed back at the newspaper. "They killed almost thirty men in those robberies without so much as a scratch on them. The last two sets of guards figured they'd be coming for them and they wound up just as dead as all the others. Killed the mine bosses, too. Folks are pretty riled up about that."

"Riled up enough to mount up and go looking for them?"

McBride shook his long head. "Nope. They say that's my

job. To ride up and get them. To do what a couple of dozen armed guards couldn't do. I'm crazy but I'm not stupid. That's wild country up there with plenty of places for them to hide. Old mines. Forgotten claims. Why I could ride around up there all spring and never find them. The snow up there only makes it worse."

Halstead would not have appreciated the terrain if they had still been in Helena, but he certainly appreciated it now that he had spent a few days in it. "I take it you've already been to all the mines that got robbed."

"Counted the dead, wrote up reports." He patted the desk at his side. "I'm happy to let you read them, but you won't find anything different than in that article you read. Whoever hit those mines knew when to hit them and how to get away without any trouble."

There was no place for Halstead to put his coffee, so he placed it on the floor next to his chair. "That sounds like Zimmerman to me. He's a planner."

"And Brunet is just about as soulless a man as you could hope to find walking the earth," McBride added. "They've managed to scrape together a pack of outlaws that's every bit as mean as they are. And if that wasn't bad enough, they've whipped them into shape. The miners tell me they move like soldiers and with all the discipline you'd expect from such."

"Any idea who they are?" Halstead asked.

He pointed up at the wanted posters on the wall next to the gunrack. "I heard there'd been some kind of secret meeting at the Sherman Trading Post last week. It took a lot of that 'broad range of discretion' I told you about earlier, but I got Zed Sherman to talk. A lot of the names and faces you see up there have signed on with them. Bank robbers, highway men, train robbers, murderers, rapists, and worse. One of them likes to set fire to a place after he kills everyone in it. Did it to a family over in Butte about a year ago."

McBride took a sip of coffee from his mug. "You'd think wild men of that sort wouldn't hold together under one man's rule, but Zimmerman seems to have proven me wrong."

The more McBride talked, the more Halstead realized getting Zimmerman and Brunet was going to be much harder than he had already known it would be. "The article didn't say how they do it. Did the miners tell you?"

"Every one of them told the same story. They ride in fast out of the bushes, kill the guards and the bosses, hit the pay wagon, and leave the miners alone. They only shot one and that was on their first raid. I think that was to make a point because, after that, I guess word spread to the other mines, and the workers didn't challenge them. And miners are a salty bunch. They don't take kindly to people stealing their money. Guess they figured it wasn't worth their lives."

Halstead could not blame them. If there was one thing Zimmerman did better than talking, it was intimidating people.

McBride asked him, "You've gone up against Zimmerman before, haven't you? Couple months ago over in Silver Cloud. Got shot up in the process of doing it from what I heard."

"Shot Zimmerman, too," Halstead said. "Thought I hurt him pretty bad. Guess it wasn't bad enough."

"Don't write that off as nothing," McBride told him. "You put a hole in the man. You hurt him not just in body but in pride. I've seen how that kind of thing can weigh heavy on a man's mind. I'd guess he'd give just about anything to get a shot at killing you."

Halstead did not have to guess. "He's already put a ten-thousand-dollar bounty on my head."

"So I've heard." McBride took another sip of coffee, only slower this time. Halstead could see he was thinking something over. "That's a hell of a lot of money to put on a man's head, especially a lawman. Could be that we just might be able to use his hatred of you against him."

Halstead was beginning to like the way McBride thought. "How so?"

"By getting the word out that you're here," he said. "I think maybe we ought to take a ride up to one of those mines he hit tomorrow after dawn. The Mother and Country was the first mine they hit. Same place where they killed a miner, too. Let the word spread that you're around. It just might make Zimmerman do something stupid."

Halstead did not doubt it, but the day was not over yet. He did not want to waste an entire day while Zimmerman and his Spoilers ran free.

And that's when he remembered something. "You're the one who let Mackey know about the rumors of Zimmerman being in the area just after you heard about Brunet, weren't you?"

McBride went to his desk and pulled out a pad. He flipped back a few pages and said, "That's right. I reported the Brunet sighting a month ago and the Zimmerman news last week. Why?"

"Who told you about Zimmerman?"

McBride pointed at his notes. "Says 'saloon gossip' right here in my notes." He pushed the pad back on his desk and rubbed his chin with his forefinger. "As I recall, I'd heard it second hand from the bartender over at The

Blue Belle. Al Goode's his name. And Goode only tells me what he believes to be true, which means he must've gotten it from Dippy."

Bartenders and drunks, Halstead thought. Same as Silver Cloud. Same as everywhere, he supposed. "Who's Dippy?"

"Last name's Dippy," McBride explained. "Not that it matters much. He's what I call a camp rat. He works odd jobs wherever they need him, but never down below. He's a chatty little bastard and he annoys most of the men. I'm surprised no one's buried an axe in him yet just to get him to shut up."

A picture began to form in Halstead's mind. "This Dippy character work any of the mines that got hit?"

McBride seemed to be catching on. "Since they're all owned by the same outfit, I'd guess he's worked at just about all of them at one time or another."

"Sounds like he might be a man we should talk to," Halstead said. "Got any ideas on where we can find him?"

McBride shook his head. "Come to think of it, I haven't seen him in a week or more. He's usually over at The Hot Pepper or the Belle when he comes to town, which is usually twice a week. Likes to try his hand at the poker tables. Does pretty well from what I've seen."

"It's what you haven't seen that bothers me." Halstead got to his feet. "He's our first link to Zimmerman and now he's missing. Finding him might help us find Zimmerman. Or at least get an idea of where he might be."

McBride said as he got to his feet, too, "Can't hurt to ask. I believe Al is working the bar at the Belle right now so we might as well go ask him."

The town marshal went to the rifle rack and took down a Winchester. "The Belle's a might prickly place, deputy. They're not welcoming of strangers. Might want me to go in first and do the talking. We'll get more out of them that way."

It went against Halstead's better judgment, but he remembered he had played it too rough in Silver Cloud. He decided to take it easier this time around. "If you see a wide-eyed kid join us along the way, don't get jumpy. His name's Sandborne, and he's with me. And while we're at it, you might as well call me Jeremiah or Halstead instead of deputy. I've never been much good at being formal."

McBride grinned as he racked a round into the Winchester. "Hell, Jeremiah. I'm just glad I've gone this long without having my nose busted. Heard you went through Boddington and his crew in no time flat."

Halstead was not surprised word had spread this far about him. "I'm glad I didn't have to." He opened the door for McBride. "Shall we?"

# Chapter 8

The Blue Belle Saloon was no different from any of the other dozens of saloons Halstead had seen in his life. Sawdust on the floor. A bunch of crooked tables with filthy green felt stained from cigar ash and spilled drink. Scuffed wooden chairs whose arms had been marred by hip holsters and legs that had been gashed by spurs. The place smelled of stale smoke and spilled beer with a healthy amount of desperation thrown in.

It was going on four o'clock, and the sun was already well on its way toward setting. Most of the oil lamps in the place were already lit. It was mostly deserted except for a few tables and a handful of men standing at the bar.

All of them eyeballed Halstead while McBride chatted up the bartender.

"How about it, Al?" the town marshal asked him. "See Dippy around lately?"

But the bartender was the one who was eyeing Halstead the closest. "Won't say if I have and I won't say that I haven't." He inclined his head toward Halstead. "Don't like his kind hanging around and we don't serve them, either.

You want to talk to me? Tell him to stay outside like a good Injun."

Halstead fought the urge to backhand the bartender. This was McBride's town. Better to let him handle it.

McBride slowly shook his head. "He doesn't matter here, Al. This is you and me talking, and we're talking about Dippy. You see him around lately?"

The bartender continued to glare at Halstead. "Not until he leaves."

McBride threw a long arm around Al Goode's head and slammed it down onto the bar and held it there after it bounced.

The men standing at the bar took their drinks and backed away. Some of the men at the tables pushed back in the chairs, but no one stood up. Halstead would have drawn if they had.

McBride spoke into Al's ear. "I just spent the better part of an hour telling the deputy here how friendly Battle Brook was and now you're making me look like a liar." He pressed the bartender's head down into the bar enough to make him yelp. "And we both know how I hate to look like a liar, don't we, Al?"

The bartender's arms flailed as he tried to pull himself free from McBride's grip on his head. "Let me up, Jack. Come on!"

"If the next words out of your mouth aren't about Dippy, I'll yank you across this fine bar and kick the hell out of you in front of everyone here."

He released Goode with a shove that sent him tumbling against the back of the bar. A few whiskey bottles rattled, but none of them fell, much less broke.

Halstead kept his eyes on the men at the tables.

Goode rubbed the right side of his head, trying to get the blood flowing into it again. "I ain't seen Dippy in about a week or more. The last time he was in here, he said he was sitting on something big. Bigger than any of us had ever seen before. I figured it was nothing but the whiskey talking, but he said it a few times. The last time he said he'd gotten himself a partner and they were going into business together."

"What kind of business?" McBride prodded.

"Any kind he wanted," Goode told him. "And that's the God's honest truth, Jack. He didn't say anything more. Just that. I got curious and asked him to spell it out more, but once he knew I was interested, he clammed up. He just spouted off about how he had this great big animal caged up in the mountains somewhere and when the time was right, he was going to let him loose on the whole territory. Crazy talk like that." He kept rubbing his head. "Nothing I deserved to have my head busted over."

Halstead eyed the gamblers while he listened to the bartender talk. "Where did he live?"

Goode hesitated until McBride went to grab him. "He had a shack at the Mother and Country, but he worked all the mines up there. They didn't pay him much and most of what he had was from playing cards with the miners."

Halstead had already gotten that much from McBride. He needed to know more. "He helped with the cooking at the mines, didn't he?"

"That's what he said. And what if he did?"

Halstead was not done asking questions. "He ever ride into town to buy things before he'd stop off in here?"

Goode surprised him by thinking about it. "Come to think of it, he had a mule with him tied up outside next to his horse the last time I saw him. I didn't think on it much at the time, but now that you mention it, I guess it was kind of strange. The cooks at the mine always had their goods brought up there. They never would've sent Dippy into town for that stuff. I don't think they would've trusted him to spend the money like he was supposed to."

Halstead saw one man seated in the middle of the room eyeballing him closer than any of the others around him. He had a clipped black moustache and nervous eyes. His breathing started to change, like he was working himself up to doing something. Halstead hoped he kept his mouth shut and his backside in the chair.

It was time to go. "Thank the man for his time, Jack. We've got some work ahead of us."

He let McBride step away from the bar and head to the door as he kept his eye on the man with the moustache before he began to back out of the saloon.

He had just turned to go when the man he had been watching called out. "You wouldn't happen to be Jeremiah Halstead, would you?"

Halstead turned slowly. Left shoulder at an angle. Right hand hooked on his belt buckle right next to his belly gun. "Just so happens I am."

"You the same Jeremiah Halstead with a price on his head? Ten thousand last I heard."

He heard Jack McBride shift his weight behind him. He hoped he had the sense to stay out of this.

"Funny. I heard that, too."

The gamblers around the man with the moustache slid their chairs away from him without getting up, leaving him alone in the middle of the floor.

The man with the moustache grinned. "A man could do an awful lot with ten thousand dollars."

"Only if he was alive to spend it."

The man cocked his head to the side. "I hear a lot of people have tried to get it."

"None still above ground. What does that tell you?"

The man smiled. "Tells me your luck is bound to run out sometime. Maybe even tonight."

Halstead remained as still as he had since the moment he had turned around. "Only one way to find out. Drop the ring and let's pull."

Even from more than thirty feet away, in the gloom of the saloon lamp light, he could see the man swallow hard. He was thinking about it. Thinking long and hard about whether or not he should go for the gun on his hip and make a play for that money.

But Halstead could practically see the man's mind working. He was sitting down and had a gun on his right hip. He would have to stand up to draw clean. By the time he even shifted his legs to get up, Halstead would have shot him three times or more. If only he had stood up earlier, he might have had a chance.

"If only" were the two harshest words in the English language.

The man folded his hands on the card table. "Got a good game going here. Don't want to ruin it by killing a man. Maybe some other time."

"Now or then won't change the result."

Halstead felt McBride's big hand on his back, which he took as a sign that it was time to leave. McBride covered him as he joined him outside.

As they began walking back to the jail, McBride said, "That happen a lot?"

"More often than I'd care to admit," Halstead said.

"You make friends wherever you go, don't you, Jeremiah?"

Halstead noticed Sandborne sitting on a bench in front of the jail and waved for him to come over to their side of the street. "All this excitement has made me hungry. Let's get something to eat, and tomorrow we'll take a trip up to Mother and Country to see about what happened to poor old Dippy."

"You don't think he's still alive, do you?"

"Probably not," Halstead admitted. "But sometimes, even dead men can tell you something if you know how to listen."

# Chapter 9

Early the next morning, Halstead, Sandborne, and McBride rode up to the Mother and Country mine to see what they could find out about Dippy and what had happened at each of the mines.

The trail up to the mines was steep and icy but well-worn, and the footing for the horses was good.

McBride led the way while Halstead and Sandborne followed close behind. The dinner the three had shared together the previous night at The Leather Apron had been a pleasant, if quiet, affair with none of the young lawmen deciding to talk much. McBride regaled his guests with stories about Battle Brook and how it had gotten its name way back when the town had first been settled about fifty years prior. It had been something about some kind of skirmish between the natives and the locals down by Tibbitt's Brook, though Halstead had been too tired to pay much attention to what McBride was saying. He had tried to appear interested enough, for McBride's sake, but thankfully, Sandborne had been sincerely interested in the town's history, thus saving Halstead from having to listen.

Sandborne's attention had allowed Halstead's mind to

roam over other subjects like Dippy and Zimmerman and Brunet. Where were the wild men now and what were they planning next? The paper had said they had stolen about sixty thousand dollars or more. A lot of money to split between men.

He could have understood if Zimmerman and Brunet joined up with a couple of men and raided a camp for the payroll, but they had not done that. They had hit six of the biggest mines in Western Montana and he had done it for a reason. Zimmerman, Halstead guessed, was too greedy to split the money twelve ways. He'd use the sixty thousand for something else. Something bigger.

The question was what. The question had been on his mind when he finally fell asleep in his bed at The Standard Hotel and had been waiting for him as soon as he woke up earlier that morning.

When his mind ran into the brick wall that was "what," his thoughts often drifted back to Abigail Newman and how a woman like her could wind up with a man like Thomas Ringham. He remembered keeping an eye on the window of The Leather Apron in the hopes of catching a glimpse of her passing by the dining hall, but his search had been in vain. He wondered if she was still on the stage-coach up from Wellspring or if she had already made it to town. He wondered what he would do when she did finally arrive and if she would stick with the gambler or seek love elsewhere. If she happened to look his way, he would con-sider himself most fortunate indeed.

But any thoughts of the pleasant Miss Newman were interrupted by McBride and the business at hand. The trail up to the mine had widened some and he held back his horse a bit to allow the two deputy marshals to catch up.

"I wanted to have a word with you boys before we get

up to the Mother and Country," the much taller man said. "Either of you boys work many mining camps?"

"Not really," Halstead admitted. There was no sense in lying about it. He did not want McBride to come up with a plan where Halstead turned out to be the weakest link. "But Sandborne here has been around them plenty. He lived in Dover Station most of his life."

McBride looked at the younger man, who had begun to blush. "That a fact?"

"Grew up on ranches, mostly," Sandborne said, "but I did law work for a time in Dover Station after Marshal Mackey and Deputy Sunday gave me a star. I learned how to handle myself around the miners whenever they came down from the hills to cut loose."

"Ever have to break up a fight between them?" McBride asked.

"People of every stripe knew better than to fight in town limits, marshal," Sandborne reported. "They knew Aaron didn't like fighting. And they'd like it even less if he had to break it up. But don't worry. I can handle myself when the time comes."

"He certainly can," Halstead agreed. Kidding him in private was one thing. Kidding him in front of others would sound like he was running him down. "Don't let that peach fuzz on his face fool you. He's seen his share of action in the past two years with Mackey. Saved my life on the trail as we came through the pass on the way into town."

"Thunder Pass," McBride said. "Great box canyon with a split on either side?"

"The very one." Halstead told him.

"No offense boys, but patrols have been wiped out riding through there," McBride said. "So, if you made it through there alive with people shooting at you, this deal with these miners will be a walk in the park for you."

Halstead decided they could talk about their experience at the box canyon another time. "Who's the man in charge at the mine?" No matter if it was miners, ranchers, outlaws, or Apaches, there was always one man above all others, no matter how they claimed different.

"Can't rightly say at the moment," McBride told them. "The main boss of the mine was killed with the guards. The Irish fella who kind of led the miners, a guy by the name of O'Hara, got himself shot in the head when he confronted Zimmerman and the others. Guess we'll find out soon enough after we get there. I'd like to visit all six mines today if we can. That way, we can put our heads together tomorrow to figure out what we learned from these folks. Maybe decide on the best place to start looking for them."

McBride looked at Halstead. "I think you two might want to sit back and let me do all of the talking at first. These boys don't take kindly to strangers, let alone federal boys like you. No sense in poking the bear if we don't have to."

Halstead knew what he actually meant. The men would think him a half-breed and refuse to cooperate. He did not like it, but he understood it. Getting Zimmerman and Brunet was all that mattered to him. If all he had to do was keep his mouth shut to find them, then he was more than happy to do it.

"We'll follow your lead, Jack," Halstead said, answering for Sandborne. "And we'll be there to back you up if you need it."

McBride glanced at Halstead. "Hell, Jeremiah. I already knew that. Just need your word you won't start swinging or worse if one of these boys shoots an odd comment your way. I'm not taking their part, you understand, but these are some pretty rough characters up here. You have to be in order to do the type of work they do. I'd feel a whole lot better if you didn't take what they might say to heart."

At least McBride was being honest. And he deserved the same amount of honesty from him. "As long as they don't get out of hand, Sandborne and I will be as quiet as church mice on Sunday morning, won't we, Sandborne?"

"We surely will," the deputy confirmed.

Halstead could not see McBride's face enough to see if the town marshal believed him, which was fine by Halstead. He was not sure he believed it himself.

The air at the top of the mining camp was thinner and much cooler than it had been down in Battle Brook, and Halstead was doing his best to not shiver from the cold.

He stomped his feet on the packed snow and stood as close to Col as possible to get all the heat he could from the mustang.

If the cold was bothering Sandborne, he was not showing it.

Halstead had stayed true to his word on the trail and had allowed Jack McBride to run the show. He spoke to one of the men in the office, who sent word down to the mine for all the men to come out for a special meeting. They did not bother telling them the reason for the meeting because half of them probably would have preferred to keep on working.

But the men groaned as they stepped out into the daylight and saw Jack McBride and the two men with him standing by the office shack.

They were all men of about five and a half feet tall and

bore the same disapproving scowls on their blackened faces.

Halstead imagined he was only part of the reason for their grumbling. He knew part of it had to do with him being a deputy marshal. They did not see many of them in this part of the territory. Most of them were looking at him because he had darker skin than them and therefore must be a half-breed. They saw even fewer of those out here.

Lucky for Halstead, he had not ridden out to the camp to be popular. He had come here for their own good.

The bald, grimy man Halstead took to be the acting mine boss began counting the men with the pencil he had tucked behind his ear. When he was finished counting, he turned back toward McBride. "They're all here, marshal."

"All except one," called out a man at the front of the miners. His brogue was thick enough to cut stone. "Seamus O'Hara isn't here. The best of us and the bravest of us." He pointed at the acting manager. "And as for you, Marsden, I'll repeat our demands that this mine be renamed in his honor and his memory."

Halstead glanced at the manager and saw the large, dark circles around his eyes. He would have been surprised if the man had slept more than two hours a night since the mine had been robbed. The man was in over his head and he knew it, but the job still needed to get done. "I've already told you that I've sent the request to the bosses back in Helena, Gorman," Marsden said, "but none of that has anything to do with why Marshal McBride and these other men are here today. I need you to listen to them and give them your full cooperation."

He made some kind of gesture toward McBride and came to stand by Sandborne and Halstead.

McBride placed his hands on his hips as he began to

speak to the hundred or so men who had gathered in front of him.

"Most of you men already know me," he began. "But since I see a few new faces here, allow me to introduce myself. I'm Jack McBride, the Town Marshal of Battle Brook."

Gorman interrupted him by saying, "Jack the Beanstalk, we call him for obvious reasons. And he's come to tell us a tale taller than himself about how he needs our help to track down and kill the men who stole from us. Ain't that right, Jack?"

McBride did not move as the miners laughed at him. But when they had quieted down some, he continued. "You'll get no tall tales from me, Gorman. Just the way things are. I know a group calling themselves The Spoilers hit your camp a couple of days ago. Took all of your pay with them when they left. This mine falls under my jurisdiction. You men and your families are under my protection."

"Your protection," Gorman spat. "A lot of good your protection did us when they rode out of here with a month's worth of our wages. What are we supposed to live on between now and then?"

The men cheered in support as McBride said, "On the credit the mine owners have arranged for you in town. That credit is good in Battle Brook or in Hard Scrabble. You know that because I told you that the last time I was here."

"Talk," Gorman said. "Just a lot of talk. Have you done anything to track the bunch who stole from us? No, you haven't. How do I know? Because you'd be dead if you had instead of standing there like the big gom you are, telling us all the grand things you're going to be doing to bring these killers to justice."

The men cheered him.

"I've been working on nothing else day or night, Gorman. And as a matter of fact, our friends in Helena have sent us some help in that regard. The man to my left is Deputy Jeremiah Halstead and to my right is Deputy Sandborne. They're both from the U.S. Marshals and they want Zimmerman and Brunet every bit as bad as you do, believe me."

Halstead heard the miners grumble to each other as they focused on the two lawmen McBride had just introduced. And as he had expected, most of them looked at Halstead. From head to toe and back again, just like in Helena and on the train. The face, the star, the silver pistol butt, then back up to his eyes. Same as everywhere.

Gorman did not appear to be impressed. "Well, isn't that grand? We've got a passel of murdering thieves on our hands and the wise heads in the capital send us a boy and a goddamned half-breed." He nodded at Halstead. "That dusky bastard over there is just as likely to cut a deal with Zimmerman and take half of the money with him."

Halstead fought to keep his hands from balling at his sides, lest his anger get the better of him. He had promised to allow McBride to handle this, but his temper was getting short.

"Even though they've been in Battle Brook for less than a full day, they've already managed to figure out someone who might've helped the men who robbed you. A camp rat by the name of Dippy. Likes to talk. Heard he used to work a couple of the mines up here, this one included. Anyone see him in the past couple of days?"

This time, Halstead noticed the men did not grumble. They looked at the ground instead, which told him all he needed to know. Miners were a notoriously loyal bunch, not given to talking about their own with strangers.

McBride placed his hands on his narrow hips. "Now's no time to play stupid, boys. I know you know him, or at least some of you do. He's not in any trouble. We just want to talk to him is all."

The men laughed.

Gorman spat in McBride's general direction. "Yeah. Just talk. Maybe have some tea with him. Talk about the weather. If you're looking for Dippy, then we'll be the ones to find him, not you. And if he's part of this robbery, we'll deal with him for that as well. We'll get more out of him with our fists than you will with your jail cell and your chains."

The men laughed again and jostled each other, encouraging the man to keep going. He chose to silently look at Halstead.

And Halstead looked right back at him.

"Unless, of course," Gorman added, "you plan on having the chief over there scalp him for you."

Halstead decided it was time for him to take over. He walked past McBride and stood in front of Gorman.

The miner stood up straighter, as did all of those around him. None of them was able to match Halstead's height, but every one of them was much broader than him.

"You like working the mines?" Halstead asked Gorman.

The Irishman's eyes narrowed. "What kind of question is that?"

"A simple one, so answer it."

"Sure, I like it well enough, I guess," the man admitted. "Pay's regular and the bosses are fair as far as bosses go."

"You like working in the mines enough to want to die in a mine?"

The men behind him moved forward as one but Gorman did not. "What was that you just said to me?"

"Guess all of that hammering and banging under the ground has dulled your ears some." Halstead leaned in closer and said, "Do you want to die in that mine?"

The man inched away from him. "Of course not."

One of the men in the back said, "That's a hell of a question for you to ask a mining man, mister. We can die any day. At any moment. We don't like talking about such things. It's bad luck."

But Halstead did not take his eyes off Gorman. He was talking to the group through him. "That's what I thought. It's funny the risks a man will take to put food in his belly and clothes on his back. The things he'll do to make sure his family has everything they need."

Gorman aimed his chin up at him. "What would you know about an honest day's work?"

"Plenty. You boys use axes and shovels to dig dirt out of the ground." He pulled his Colt from his belly holster and slid the barrel between their faces like a steel bar. "Just like I use this to sweep the dirt out of this territory." He tapped the star on his lapel with the tip of the barrel. "You boys face danger underground all day long. But when the whistle blows, your shift is over. You get to go on with your lives. Me? I'm a target every day and all the time. That doesn't bother me much. It's what I get paid for. But with a bunch of hardcases like Brunet and Zimmerman running around, you boys are targets just like me."

Gorman did his best to act like the gun in his face did not bother him. "How do you figure? He's already stolen from us once. What makes you think he'll do it again?"

"On account of Brunet is riding with him and he's not the type to let a soft target like you boys go. See, Brunet and his bunch hit a mine just like yours way up in Manitoba. That's in Canada for those of you who don't know.

Hit them on payday and took a fair amount of the gold they dug from the ground with him when he left, just like here. Normally, that would've been bad enough, but Brunet doesn't like leaving witnesses behind. So he not only killed the guards, he came back the next day, took some of that dynamite they had on hand, and blew the entrance to the mine just after the morning shift started. Turned the whole side of the mountain into nothing but rubble just by striking a match."

Halstead cocked and uncocked his pistol, making Gorman jump. "Just like that. Forty good men were lost that day all because Brunet took it into his head to make sure there were no witnesses left behind." Halstead inclined his head toward Gorman. "Hard working men, just like all of you."

Halstead stood up straight and began to look each of the other men in the eye. None of them raised their heads.

"You boys don't like me and Sandborne being here any more than we like being out here," Halstead told him. "We live mighty soft back in Helena. Nice bed and all the fixings. We're not out here because we want to be or because we want to give you a hard time. We're here because there's a group of outlaws on the loose who kill men like you and doesn't think twice about it. Now, you boys can josh and laugh and make fun of us all you want, but we're the best chance you've got to keep from winding up like those miners up in Manitoba."

Gorman swallowed first before saying, "You promise to kill him?"

"I'm promising that you helping us find Dippy will go a long way to keeping all of you alive," Halstead told him. "Men like Brunet and Zimmerman don't live on money alone. They live on fear. The kind of fear their names strike in a man when they hear it. All of you are witnesses. That means you're a threat to him because dead men can't testify even if we catch him. Telling us about Dippy will help us find him that much easier. You can help yourselves by helping us."

Halstead slid his Colt back into his belly holster and took a step back. "What's it going to be?"

The men did not grumble or complain or kid any longer. They simply looked at the back of Gorman to see what they should do next.

And Gorman, when he spoke, clearly spoke for them. "Let the rest of the boys go back to work and I'll tell you anything you want to know. No fooling."

McBride beckoned Halstead and the miner to follow him into the office shack while the rest of the miners went back to work.

# Chapter 10

It was just after nightfall by the time the three lawmen made it back to the jail.

McBride put on a new pot of coffee and relit the stove while Halstead and Sandborne looked at the map of the area on the wall across from the marshal's rolltop desk.

"Tell me something, Jeremiah," McBride asked as he waited for the pot to boil. "Was that business about Brunet and that Manitoba mine true or did you just make that up?"

Halstead shrugged. "What difference does it make? It got them all to talk, didn't it?"

McBride laughed. "Got me believing it, that's for sure, though I've never been the sharpest quill on the porcupine."

"I graduated from the Dominican Sisters Orphanage of El Paso," Halstead told him. "You graduated from West Point. I'd say that makes you pretty sharp, even though you try to hide it."

"What I am is sore." McBride lowered himself into the chair behind his rolltop desk and tossed his hat on it. "Six mines in one day. All we did was talk and ride all day long, and I'm wiped out. Guess that's why Zimmerman and Brunet's bunch only hit two a day."

"They did it that way because they're smart," Halstead told them as he watched Sandborne place a circle for each mine on the map in pencil. "They had a pack mule with them to carry the payroll every time. Probably have it stashed away somewhere right now as we speak. No one knew where or when or if they'd hit next. Being up in the hills like they were, Zimmerman wasn't worried about word spreading between the camps."

"The last two mines were aware of it by the third day," McBride noted, "but they were cowed by the news of O'Hara getting shot at the Mother and Country. Can't say as I blame them. If armed guards couldn't stop them, what could a bunch of men with pickaxes and shovels do? They'd be shot dead before they got within ten feet of them."

Halstead did not concern himself with the why of it. He already knew the answer to that question. Zimmerman and Brunet wanted the money, so they stole it. Built a fierce reputation for themselves while doing it, too. The only question was where the outlaws were hiding out now.

"Guess there's no point looking for Dippy anymore," Halstead admitted.

McBride agreed. "All he got was dead for his trouble. Your Mr. Zimmerman doesn't strike me as the type to tolerate a talkative man after he's milked him dry for information. Probably won't find the poor bastard until the thaw, if then."

But Halstead did not care much about Dippy's fate. That camp rat had already done enough damage by giving Zimmerman all the information he needed to steal the pay wagons. Whatever fate he had met, he deserved.

"This isn't your usual payroll robbery," Halstead said as he looked at the map. "The miners told us this bunch showed discipline. That's not like Brunet. That must have been Zimmerman's doing. I saw him act like that when I went up against him in Silver Cloud and those weren't even his men. Those were Hudson Gang boys. This bunch seems to be hand-picked by him. Dangerous and disciplined. A bad combination for us."

"If we don't catch them soon," Sandborne said as he continued to plot the mines on the map, "those miners will be in town telling everyone what happened. In a week, talk about The Spoilers will be down as far as Texas, maybe even Mexico. It'll certainly reach California. Kansas, too. They'll probably be legends by springtime."

Sandborne added, "There's nothing a cowboy likes better than a good drink, a good woman, and a good story to tell of his travels. And a story about The Spoilers certainly makes for good saloon talk. Only a matter of time the newspapers get hold of it."

Halstead had not considered that. With statehood coming in a couple of weeks, the governor had charged Mackey with the mission to keep things like this from spreading in the territory, much less beyond it. To hit the villains hard in their lairs or wherever they were to be found. Of course, men like the governor did not have to concern themselves with the details of finding them, much less facing them.

"Either way you cut it," McBride said as he eyed the coffeepot from his chair, "we're going to need more men. A lot more. Every account I heard today tells me we're looking at chasing down about a dozen outlaws. That's four-to-one odds as it stands now. What's more, they're familiar with the territory and know where to hide. I haven't gotten one single hint about where they might be holed up and believe me, I've already checked every saloon in town before you got here."

"Think they would've told you if they'd known anything?" Halstead asked.

McBride nodded. "They're worried The Spoilers will hit the town next. The memory of what happened in Dover Station is still mighty fresh in their minds. I know you boys lived through it, but they only know what they've heard, and it gets more gruesome with each re-telling."

Halstead had been at both towns when they fell. "The truth was worse than anything they could hear."

"Amen," Sandborne added.

McBride went on. "There's even some foolish talk that you're cursed, Jeremiah. That death follows you wherever you go."

Halstead was beginning to wonder the same thing. "As long as the right people die, that's fine by me."

McBride rubbed his hands roughly over his scalp as he got up to tend to the coffeepot. "No, sir. There's no other way around it. We're going to need more men."

Halstead agreed. "Yesterday you said you've got some men who help you from time to time."

"If a riot breaks out or a fight? Sure. The folks around here are good that way. But to ride into the timberlands after men like these? I'm sure some of them would be game, but they'd be more of a hindrance than a help. They've neither the sand nor the stomach for a hunt like this, especially now that the snow is already falling."

Halstead had been afraid of that. "What about the army?"

"It'd take the governor to ask them and that could take more than a week or so at the earliest," McBride said. "Besides, they wouldn't welcome fighting on terrain like that in weather like this. They might come around come the thaw, maybe."

Halstead realized there was only one place they could turn to for more men and fast. "What about Emmett Ryan? These are his mines they're stealing from. He ought to be able to send some men to help us."

"And I'm sure he will," McBride said, "but not until next month when the next payday and ore collection is due. We're not close enough for him to send any men before this time next week anyway. Even Pinkertons need time to gather supplies and travel."

The coffeepot started to shake as the water within it began to boil. McBride began pouring it into the mugs. "Not only are the odds against us, but the weather and terrain are, too. Any tracks this bunch leaves behind will be covered over as soon as the next snow falls, and it snows a lot each day up in those hills this time of year. I even tried to track them as soon as they left the Mother and Country and couldn't read a decent sign. Even the droppings of their animals get covered over."

Sandborne surprised Halstead by making some kind of sound. A cross between a gasp and a grunt as if he was choking on something. He had been looking at the map the entire time Halstead and McBride had been speaking.

"What is it?" Halstead asked him. "You going to be sick?"

Sandborne tapped the map. "I think I can see why they did it that way."

McBride took the boiling pot of coffee off the stove and brought over a couple of mugs with him to the map. "What did you find?"

"Depends on how good this map is," Sandborne replied. "This map any good, marshal, or is it just for show?"

McBride grabbed his own mug of coffee and rejoined them at the map. "It's always been as good as I've needed it to be. It's a bit out of date now that Hard Scrabble's drying up and Battle Brook is being built, but the terrain's the same. Why?"

Sandborne traced a thin line at the peak of the hill with a filthy fingernail. The line was in between all of the mines he had just dotted on the map. "Do you know what that is? Is it water or is that a trail?"

McBride was tall enough that he did not have to go on tiptoe to look at the area Sandborne was pointing to. "That's a trail. Trappers used it back in the old days. Some enterprising folks used to take wagons up there and sell the miners supplies so they didn't have to come to town. The mines use it every once in a while as a way to travel between each other."

Halstead watched as Sandborne traced the line down from where it started at the hilltop to where it ended.

"Good God," McBride said. "It goes all the way back to Hard Scrabble right along the spine of the mountain."

Halstead knew that was how Zimmerman had done it. He had used an old trail that ran between every mine The Spoilers had robbed.

He could not have been prouder of his friend for finding it. "Sounds like old Sandborne here is onto something, doesn't it, McBride?"

The town marshal patted Sandborne on the back. "It's an interesting proposition. Sure goes a long way to explaining a lot of things, but not everything."

Sandborne slowly lowered his finger from the map as he turned to face McBride. "What are you talking about?

We know the trail they probably used. We can trace it tomorrow and find out where they're hiding."

"Easier said than done." McBride took a sip of coffee. "That trail leads back to Hard Scrabble Township, which is plain as day to any man with two good eyes and a lick of common sense. That town's a shadow of its old self. Only a handful of stores and businesses still open to serve the smaller mining operations up in the hills. Everyone else packed up and headed over here to Battle Brook. People love new places."

Halstead could not see the point McBride was trying to make. "What's that got to do with us finding the trail and tracking Zimmerman and his men?"

"Plenty." McBride gestured toward the map with his cup. "First off is that those trails snake off in dozens of directions to dozens of claims. Some are still active. Some have been abandoned. Some are just great big holes in the ground and others go on for days underground. A man could get lost in any one of them and starve to death before he ever found light again. Plenty already have."

Halstead was beginning to understand McBride's meaning. "You think Zimmerman and his men might be hiding out in one of the abandoned mines."

"Could be," McBride allowed. "That's awfully unforgiving country. It's bad enough in warmer months when you can see where you're going. But with the snow cover, you could just as easily ride off the steep edge of a trail and not know it until you're dead. Could go in on foot, but then you'd have to ride out again. Either way, you're a sitting duck for any one of Zimmerman's men hiding behind a rock waiting to shoot you, which they most surely would."

McBride gave them more bad news. "They could also

be using Hard Scrabble as a place to hole up. They've got a general store in town that's still a going concern, so Zimmerman could get plenty of supplies with no questions asked."

"Good," Halstead said. "We'll ride out there tomorrow and see what we can see."

McBride held up a long hand. "Not so fast. Hard Scrabble's become a dangerous place, even for the three of us. A long time ago, a man named Aristotle said, 'Nature abhors a vacuum.' That's one of those fancy things they taught me at the Point. Hard Scrabble proves it's true. As the good people left Hard Scrabble for Battle Brook, a nasty element has moved in to take their place. The kind who break the law and kill a man because they like it. Hell, even the few good people who still live there feel like we've given up on the town for Battle Brook and they're right. We have."

McBride pointed up at the map. "If we ride up there tomorrow, we'd be going against about fifty or so citizens and I'm not talking about shopkeepers and barbers, either. I'm talking about hardened criminals. I'm not even counting The Spoilers. Going up there would probably mean killing civilians, even if they're wanted criminals. Hell, even if we did manage to get Zimmerman or Brunet, we'd be branded as murderers. Mayor White isn't known for his courage."

McBride shook his head. His decision final. "Yes, sir. Hard Scrabble has given itself over to wickedness, and there's not much the three of us can do about it. They'd likely welcome anyone who showed up with money to spend and wouldn't be too particular about asking where they got it. And Zimmerman wouldn't have to just stash his money in a mine somewhere, either."

The more McBride spoke, the worse Halstead felt. "Meaning?"

"Meaning they've still got a bank over there called The Miner's Bank and Trust. It's run by Cal Hubbard. Let's just say he's never been particular about who he does business with."

Halstead sat down in one of the chairs across from McBride's desk. Sandborne joined him.

Halstead shut his eyes. "A crooked man with a lot of money moves into town and takes it over. This is starting to sound like Dover Station all over again."

"You're not that lucky," McBride told him. "At Dover, you had a bunch of high ground around the town where you could peer down into it and see what was going on. Hard Scrabble's on a hilltop. A mighty steep one at that. There's no way anyone could sneak up on the place, not even at night, if they have someone watching. A man could see riders coming from a couple of miles out, which is more than enough time for someone to get word to Zimmerman and his boys to ride out or hide, assuming they're in town."

Sandborne sagged in his chair. Halstead would have felt sorry for him if they were not in the same predicament. And unfortunately, everything McBride had just told them was probably true.

"This is your town," Halstead said. "You know the area better than we do. What do you recommend?"

"I'd say you two should head back to Helena and don't come back until the thaw next year with more men," McBride said. "At least ten or more. Zimmerman and

Brunet are bound to settle into Hard Scrabble by then and they'll be dug in pretty good. Ten marshals in good weather would go a long way to keeping the citizens out of it."

Halstead felt his temper begin to rise. "That's months from now."

"It certainly is," McBride agreed. "But it's the best option I can come up with. If Mr. Ryan and his rich friends want to do something before then, let them hire Pinkertons to do it. I'd rather see them get shot up than us."

Halstead was still sore from his last run-in with Emmett Ryan back at Silver Cloud. And not just from the gunshot wound in his left shoulder, but in places where a man could not reach and no medicine could cure. He had seen how he could make a good man like Sheriff Barry Boddington into a bully, only to crawl when he bade him to do so.

He sensed an iron in McBride that would be tough to bend, but even iron bent if the flame was hot enough. And a man like Emmett Ryan could provide more than enough heat to do a job on McBride.

Halstead knew if he went back to Helena empty-handed, he would not only be disappointing Mackey. He would be giving up precious time to Zimmerman and Brunet to dig in and dig deep. Hard Scrabble would belong to them by then, just like Rock Creek had belonged to the Hudson Gang all of those months ago. And even if he came back in the spring with ten marshals, there was no guarantee McBride would still be on his side. Emmett Ryan was a businessman. Businessmen tended to cut their losses when the effort grew too expensive.

Halstead had no intention of ceding a town to Zimmerman and Brunet. He had been sent here to bring them in and that was exactly what they were going to do.

McBride added, "You boys are welcome to stay here the winter if Aaron will agree to pay for the room and board. God knows I could use the help. There's a nice rooming house that just opened that'll be a lot cheaper than The Standard Hotel you're sleeping in now. Can't judge the cleanliness of the place, but it's brand new. Just got finished last week, so it can't be too bad yet."

Halstead knew he had a lot of thinking to do and knew he could not do it sitting there.

"I think the best we can do is call it a night and sleep on it." Halstead stood up, and Sandborne stood with him. "Maybe a better plan will come to me in the morning."

McBride got up to shake their hands and nodded toward the cot where the cell would be built. "You know where to find me if something comes to you. This place will be hearth and home to me for a while."

McBride locked the jailhouse door behind them as Halstead and Sandborne unhitched their horses at the post. Sandborne went to climb into the saddle before Halstead stopped him. "Let's walk them to the livery. They've been carrying us through some tough terrain. They could use the walk. I know I could, too."

So the two deputies walked their horses along the rutted mud of the thoroughfare toward the livery at the far end of town. It was not as easy as walking on the boardwalks of the bustling town, but it was much less crowded. The workers who were building the town into what it would become had gone home for the night. A few establishments had horses tethered to hitching rails in front of them, but at least the chaos caused by the wagon traffic was over.

Halstead hoped the night air would do him some good and maybe clear his head a little. McBride had filled his mind with a lot of bad news. They were up against more than just Zimmerman or Brunet. They were up against the men who followed them. The dejected people who had accepted them. Even the weather and the terrain worked against them. He could use all the time he could get to think things through and come up with a plan. There had to be a way to simply find the gang without causing a massacre on either side. Arresting Zimmerman and Brunet would be a different story altogether.

Halstead was glad Sandborne had kept quiet as they led their horses to the livery. He imagined a bit of silence would do the younger man some good, too.

It was peaceful walking through town like they were. Not every business in Battle Brook had an oil lamp in front of it yet, but those that did had them lit. They cast a soft glow on the boardwalk, and the thin layer of snow on Main Street only made everything look warmer. He had not laid eyes on Hard Scrabble yet, but he could see why people were moving into Battle Brook.

It even smelled new and, like McBride had said, people liked new things, even when they brought their old ways with them.

"Jeremiah!" a woman's voice called out from above him.

Halstead looked up and saw Abigail standing on the balcony of a place called The Wild Cat Saloon. She had a heavy shawl wrapped around her shoulders to protect her from the cold night air.

He stopped walking his horse and so did Sandborne.

"Evening, Miss Abby." Halstead smiled up at her. "Looks like you made it here just fine."

"I didn't call out to you for compliments," she said. "Something's wrong."

His right hand moved to the buckle next to the holster on his belly. "What's wrong?"

"You need to watch out for Tom. He's got a couple of men with him. They've been drinking all day and are still at it. They're talking a lot about that bounty on your head."

Sandborne pulled the Winchester from his saddle scabbard as Halstead asked her, "Any idea of where they might be now?"

She pointed down. "In the gambling hall right here last I checked," she said. "Oh, they're awful drunk, Jeremiah, and I don't think they could hit the side of a barn even if they tried. Please don't shoot them if you don't have to."

Halstead said the rest for her. "Guess you don't want me to get hurt, do you?"

She shook her head slowly. Even in the dim light of the oil lamps, she looked beautiful to him. "No. I don't."

Halstead remained where he stood as he looked inside The Wild Cat Saloon. He could not see much with the door closed and the frosted glass, but he could hear the familiar sounds of a saloon. Men talking. Chips clinking. A piano somewhere deep inside the place playing "Old Dog Trey."

Sandborne asked him, "Want me to go get McBride?"

Halstead knew he probably should get the town marshal, but this was none of his business. Tom Ringham and his friends were threatening *his* life, not McBride's. Halstead had to take care of this himself, lest he look like he was hiding behind the tall man.

Halstead handed him Col's reins. "These horses need tending to. Take them down to the livery, then come in the back door of this saloon. If I'm still there, follow my lead. If I'm dead, shoot the bastards who killed me." He looked at the younger man. "Don't worry, Joshua. They won't kill me."

Sandborne looked like he might argue, but he did not. "I'll be back as soon as I can."

Halstead did not think it would take that long. It would probably be over by the time Sandborne reached the livery, which was not that far away.

As the deputy led the horses away, Halstead glanced up at Abby, who was still on the porch, and touched the brim of his hat. "Thank you, Miss Abby."

She surprised him by saying, "Try not to kill Tom if you can avoid it. Just because I don't love him anymore, doesn't mean I want to see him dead."

Halstead had finally heard some good news. She did not love Tom Ringham anymore. "That'll be up to him. Best if you get back inside and lock your door. It's going to get pretty noisy in a minute."

"Be careful, Jerry," she said, before heading back inside.

"I plan on it," he said to himself as he walked into the saloon.

# Chapter 11

From what he could see from the door, The Wild Cat Saloon was doing a fine bit of business with the mining crowd. There was not an inch of space to be had at the bar, and every table in the place was filled with gambling men. He supposed the credit Mr. Ryan had extended to the men was being honored here.

A Faro table and a roulette wheel were set up on the left side of the door. Both had customers three deep, shouting or groaning depending on where that marble ball landed or what card the dealer flipped over. Even the painted ladies who worked there had a difficult time moving from table to table to ply their trade.

Halstead was glad to see it so busy, for it meant no one had paid him much attention. It gave him the time he would need to spot Tom Ringham before the gambler and his friends saw him. Even a split second could mean the difference between life and death whenever gunplay might be involved.

He remained on the perimeter of the gambling tables, trying to spot Ringham. The gamblers did not like the idea of someone standing behind them and looking at their cards, but they held their tongues when they saw the silver star on the lapel of his coat.

Halstead peered through the cigar and cigarette smoke that had created a fine mist just above the tables. There were just too many men crammed together in the place for him to see anyone clearly. He saw at least ten men who could have been Tom Ringham, but none of them were exactly right.

He could push his way through to the back if he wanted to, but he did not like the idea of anyone being that close to him. Even before he'd had a price on his head, Halstead always liked to keep people at least two feet away from him. He was even more cautious now. No sense in giving someone a chance to slip a knife between his ribs and collect Zimmerman's bounty.

The longer he searched for Ringham, the more he was convinced the gambler was harmless. The boisterous crowd and the liquor and whatever card game he sat in on served to keep him busy. Murdering him was probably the furthest thing from his mind. And if he had been drinking as much as Abby had said, he would be no danger to him tomorrow, either. A hangover was always the best way to disarm a man.

But Halstead knew Ringham would not be hungover forever, and he had already mentioned Zimmerman's bounty at least twice. Once on the train and now here in town. Those who did not already know about it certainly knew about it now. And with enough liquor in them, someone else might try to collect it. Someone Abby did not know.

And the fact that Zimmerman had stolen the miners' payroll not only meant he was in the area, but that the man who killed Halstead would get his reward that much quicker.

He had to put a stop to Ringham's mouth soon before it got him killed. Maybe not tonight, but tomorrow after he had sobered up.

On his way out, Halstead stopped by the Faro and roulette tables to see if he might spot Ringham among the crowd gathered there.

No one at the Faro table resembled Tom Ringham.

He walked over to the roulette wheel where the crowd was much more animated. He had never seen the appeal of gambling. He had seen too many men die as a result of it, but roulette always struck him as being fair, if not exciting. Assuming the wheel was not rigged, of course, which was always a risky assumption.

And judging by the reaction of the crowd gathered around the wheel, some people were winning quite a bit of money. He saw the man cheering the loudest also had the most amount of chips in front of him. Two soiled doves flanked him and rubbed his back as he and the other players placed chips on numbers and colors on the green felt.

Halstead had found Tom Ringham. He remembered the man's tailored blue suit and thick black moustache. The blue derby hat looked new and was too small for his fleshy face. But Halstead was not there to judge his wardrobe. He was there to face him for threatening his life.

The dealer had already set the ball to spinning around the wheel when Halstead said, "I hear you've been looking for me."

All of the players grew quiet as they turned to face him. The ball clattered along the wheel before it stopped unnoticed on a particular number. None of the players cheered or groaned. They simply backed away from the table.

Only Ringham remained where he was, though his newfound lady friends had been quick to hide behind some of the male customers nearby.

Ringham clapped his hands at the result on the wheel and told the dealer, "I win again. Pay up before I lose my temper."

But the dealer had moved too far away from the table to do much of anything.

Halstead would not allow Ringham to ignore him now. "You deaf or just scared?"

Ringham kept his hands on the table railing as he slowly looked up at Halstead. "Neither deaf nor scared, especially not of a half-breed like you. Just playing a game is all. Winning, too. You're interrupting quite a run of luck on my part."

He did not seem drunk. His eyes were clear, and his words were straight. If he had been drunk before, he was sober now.

Halstead pushed the issue. "Heard you've been threatening my life. Been talking about how rich a man could be if he just had the nerve to collect Zimmerman's bounty." He rested his thumb on his belt buckle. "Here I am, Ringham. You got the nerve to collect?"

"I do," he said as he slowly stood erect and opened his suit coat. "But it just so happens that I happen to be unarmed at the moment."

Halstead saw Ringham's narrow eyes flick to somewhere behind Halstead before he looked again at Halstead. "But tomorrow will be time enough."

Halstead grinned. "Why wait? You don't think I can get the two behind me before I take you?"

Halstead heard gunmetal clearing leather. He turned in a crouch as he drew his Colt from the belly holster.

Two men with pistols in their hands, already raising their guns. He shot the one on his right first. A clean shot through the heart.

The one on his left rushed a shot that bit into the floor before Halstead cut him down with two shots to the chest. As the man fell, Halstead recognized him as the man who had called out to him the day before in The Blue Belle Saloon.

Both men were dead before they hit the saloon floor.

Halstead turned around and leveled the Colt at Ringham who had not budged an inch. He was still holding his coat open to show the world he was unarmed.

Normally, Halstead would have made a show of dumping his brass on the dead men and reloading. But he was in a crowded situation where most of the men in the place were armed. He did not want to be vulnerable, not even for a second. There was a time to be slick and a time to be cautious. This situation called for caution.

He motioned to Ringham with his pistol. "Get your sorry ass out here. Right now."

Ringham took his time as he made his way around the table, holding his jacket open so everyone could see he was not toting a gun.

The gambler looked at the dealer and said, "You'll keep my winnings on account for me, won't you, boy? I know how much I've got coming to me, and I'll be back tomorrow to collect."

The croupier nodded but said nothing. Neither did anyone else.

Halstead tracked Ringham's movements with his pistol until he reached the front door of the saloon, where he took the gambler by the back of the collar and pulled him off balance. He held him by the scruff of the neck like an alley cat for the entire saloon to see.

"I figure most of you know who I am by now, but in case there's any mistake, I'm Jeremiah Halstead, Deputy United States Marshal for the Montana Territory. I'm also riding with Deputy Sandborne out of Helena. We're here to track two murderous fugitives who have stolen pay from the hard-working men of the mines. We're going to find them and kill them, along with anyone riding with them. There's a five-thousand-dollar reward on the head of Edward Zimmerman. One of the men riding with him, Robert Brunet, will fetch a much higher price than that. You hear where they are, you let me or Marshal McBride know. When we kill them, and we will, you'll get your piece of the reward money. That's a certified fact. You can check with the marshal if you'd like."

He shoved Ringham forward without letting go of his collar. "There's also a rumor going around that Zimmerman's placed a ten-thousand-dollar bounty on my head." He took the time to look at all of the people staring at him. "That's all it is. A rumor. Anyone who tries to collect? Well, you can ask these gentlemen on the floor what happens next."

He pulled Ringham to the side and stood facing the crowd. His Colt still in his right hand. "Anyone else feel like trying their luck with me tonight?"

No one said a word. No one did much of anything except look at the man who had just gunned down two men in the blink of an eye.

"Very well, then." He touched the brim of his hat. "I wish you all a good night and luck."

He turned and pushed Ringham out the door.

The gambler stumbled onto the boardwalk and into Jack McBride and his Winchester. The town marshal took hold of him by the throat and pinned him to the wall of the saloon. He asked Halstead, "What happened? I heard shooting."

"This idiot got two other idiots to believe Zimmerman's bounty on me was real. They tried to collect."

McBride winced. "They are dead?"

Halstead looked at him until he realized how ridiculous the question was.

"Should've known better than to ask." He nodded to Ringham who was still squirming against the saloon wall. "What do you want to do with him?"

"Arrest him for conspiracy to commit murder of a peace officer," he said. "Disturbing the peace and just about anything else you can think of."

"I know what this is really about, Halstead." Ringham gagged as he tried to push himself off the wall, but the lanky McBride easily held him in place. "This is about you being sweet on Abigail. You want me out of the way so you can take a run at her yourself, don't you?"

"Miss Newman is a grown woman capable of making up her own mind," Halstead said. "What she does or doesn't do is her own business." He looked up at McBride. "You want me to lock him up while you stay here with the bodies?"

"They'll keep until the undertaker gets here," McBride said. "Someone's bound to have run to fetch him already. I think it's best if I run him in myself. You'd best get on to bed. Tomorrow's liable to be a lively one after tonight."

Halstead did not like the sound of that. "What does that mean?"

"Means Mayor White just stopped by to tell me the Town

Committee is going to want to have a meeting to discuss the robberies up at the mines, but after what you just did, they'll want some answers about that, too. That federal badge will buy you a lot of leeway with them, but they'll still expect you to say something about it."

Halstead shut his eyes. Everywhere he went in Montana, someone thought he owed them an explanation. "Do I have to go?"

"Probably not, but it's best if you do," McBride told him. "They can make a lot of noise with your boss if you don't. Maybe even the governor."

"Don't worry about the governor, half-breed," Ringham spat from the wall. "You'll have to answer to me first."

McBride pulled him off the wall and steered him toward the jail. "You'll be spending the night with a gag in your mouth if you don't learn to shut it. Now move."

Halstead watched the tall marshal force the gambler to keep walking toward the jail. He had no idea where Sandborne was. He had not seen him in the back of the saloon, so he figured he was still at the livery with the horses. It was probably best that way. He imagined there would be plenty of other times for him to learn about saloon fights in his young life.

He decided to take McBride's advice and began to walk toward his room at the Standard. He heard Abigail's voice from above. "That you, Jeremiah?"

He turned to look up at her. She still had her shawl around her shoulders but did not look as cold or as worried as she had earlier. "Yeah, it's me."

"I heard all the shooting," she said. "Glad you're not hurt."

"I'm fine. Just a disagreement is all."

"A pretty one-sided disagreement from what I could tell," she said. "You were the only one doing the shooting."

"This time," he said. "Next time's liable to be different."

He could not see her face from this angle. The moon was behind her and gave her a wonderful aura he could have spent the rest of the night looking at.

She said, "Sounds like Tom's earned himself a jail cell for the night."

"A lot longer than that," Halstead told her. "He threatened my life on the train, but I let it go because no one else was around. I can't have him do that in front of a saloon full of people."

"I'm just glad you didn't shoot him is all," she said. "Would've looked bad for you, considering what's going on between you and me."

Halstead could not believe the things this woman could say. "And just what's been going on between you and me?"

She wrapped her shawl around her and, although he could not see her face, he could tell she was smiling. "Well, if you haven't been able to figure it out yet, far be it for me to be the one who tells you." She turned to go back inside her room. "Good night, Jeremiah. I'm glad you're not dead."

Halstead heard her balcony door close and began walking back to The Standard Hotel. Abigail Newman was different from any other woman he had ever known. There was no arguing that.

# Chapter 12

"Drink up, boys, and be merry." Zimmerman loved the way his voice carried in the cavern. It made him sound and feel like a god. "We've nothing to fear from our enemies down in the mines, in town, or anywhere. Haven't you heard? The Spoilers are invincible!"

The outlaws cheered their leader again and took healthy pulls on their whiskey bottles. There was more than enough to go around. Zimmerman had seen to that. He had sent one of the outlaws he had not yet named into Hard Scrabble with the mule to pick up four cases of the stuff and bring it back here to the hideout. The man had even managed to shoot a deer on the ride back, whose meat was now being roasted on a spit.

Zimmerman did not care what his real name was. He had already chosen a name to befit the stocky outlaw with the pockmarked face and dead, brown eyes. He decided now was the time to announce it.

"And let us not forget to thank the man who not only risked life and limb to bring us our whiskey but our feast as well. The same man who, henceforth, shall be known to one and all as Hunter!"

The Spoilers cheered and raised their bottles to Hunter, who acknowledged them with a wave while he concentrated on roasting the venison over the fire.

Zimmerman had spent this past week watching each of the men closely. He wanted to know all about their strengths and weaknesses both on raids and at other times when it was quiet.

Out of all of them, the man Hunter seemed to be the steadiest. The quietest and the one man in the group who did not drink his fill. Brunet was his partner, as were all of the men in the hideout. But Zimmerman thought Hunter might be a good fit as his right hand.

Zimmerman clapped his hand on the man's back as he sat beside him at the fire. "You did well out there today."

The man shrugged. "Just did what you told me to do, Ed. Happened on the deer by accident. A happy accident as it turned out."

But Zimmerman had other reasons for talking to the man. "How did Hard Scrabble strike you?"

"Mean," Hunter said as he slowly turned the venison over the flame. "It always had an edge to it, but ever since they started building that new town a few miles away, things have gotten worse."

Zimmerman nodded. "Sounds like you know the place pretty well."

That drew another shrug from Hunter. "Used to winter down there from time to time. The rooms were always cheap, and the saloons served decent whiskey. They had a town marshal named McBride who used to keep the place buttoned up, but even he's in Battle Brook now."

Zimmerman was glad to hear it. "But the bank's still open, right?"

Hunter nodded. "General store, too. A couple of saloons. Barber. A rooming house."

Zimmerman did not care about that. He had something else on his mind. "What about lawyers? Did you ever have cause to use one when you were there? I'm looking for one lawyer in particular. A man by the name of Mannes."

"I know him," Hunter said. "He represented me once when McBride arrested me. Saved me from prison. I saw his shingle out over on Lawyers Row," Hunter said. "That's on the street behind the bank. As for whether or not he's still there, I can't rightly say."

Zimmerman imagined that was about all he was liable to get from the man. He clapped him on the back as he stood up. "Don't worry, my friend. This will be the last night we spend up here like mountain goats in a cave. To-morrow, we'll lay our heads down in Hard Scrabble."

"If you say so," Hunter said. "Might be safer to just stay up here. Saw a lot of hardcases when I was in town."

Zimmerman had expected that. "Harder than us?"

"Ain't hardly," Hunter told him.

"Damned right." Zimmerman laughed as he clapped him on the back again and retreated to his own dark corner of the mine. He still had some thinking to do.

The robberies of all six mines had gone better than he could have dreamed. All of the guards who had been hired to watch the payroll were dead, even when they surrendered their weapons. No witnesses had been left behind. He had imagined word of the robberies must have spread to the last two mines by the third day and expected more resistance from the guards. But the final dozen had proved as ineffective as the first dozen and they fell beneath the guns of The Spoilers just the same.

Hunter had brought more than whiskey and venison

back to the hideout with him. He brought back news. He had overheard the way the Irish and Scot miners in Hard Scrabble talked about them now. To see a Spoiler meant certain death.

He laughed to himself as he raised the whiskey bottle to his lips. God, how he loved the Irish. Still pagans at heart. Every gust of wind was a banshee. Every clap of thunder was God's anger. He could not have asked for a better reputation if he had written it himself.

As he drank the whiskey down, Zimmerman wondered if his old mentor Darabont would have approved of all that he had accomplished so far. He would probably not see being holed up in an abandoned mine for a week as a victory. He probably would have ordered the men to keep going until they had robbed every major mine in the area and then flee the territory to the west for better weather and fewer lawmen.

But Zimmerman knew greed had caused Darabont's downfall. Enough was never enough to a man like him. He always wanted more. He was always charging hard and fast toward the cliff to see if he had the nerve and skill to stop just before he fell off.

Zimmerman had a vision for his future. A plan to acquire more power than even Darabont could have dreamed of attaining. Zimmerman did not live for fear or blood. He saw them as tools to help him build an empire of his own. An empire that was already so close at hand, he could almost touch it.

After just three days of killing and stealing, The Spoilers had amassed a small fortune of about eighty thousand dollars. More than enough for him to put his plan into motion. He had chosen the perfect ground upon which to build his empire. He had the resources to make it so. He had the will to do it properly and, unlike Darabont, he had the gift of restraint.

And the next morning, he would ride into Hard Scrabble and strike the first blow that would help forge his future. His empire.

Not with a fist. Not with a gun. But with the mightiest instrument of all.

A pen.

His laugher filled the deepest reaches of the cavern and caused his men to join him. Even the sullen Brunet had joined in his delight, though none of the men knew what they were laughing at.

But Edward Zimmerman knew. And very soon, so would the rest of the world.


Just after dawn the next morning, Zimmerman rode into the town of Hard Scrabble. The place was as close to death as Zimmerman had ever seen.

The bones of a once-thriving mining town were still there. The elegant, hand-painted sign for The Iron Horse Dance Hall and Saloon still swung on rusted chain lengths in front of a large building. But the paint was peeling, and the shutters were cracked. The glass window on one of the closed front doors had been kicked out from the inside and no one had bothered to sweep up the glass shards from the boardwalk.

Most of the other buildings he saw in the soon-to-be-forgotten town were well on their way to similar states of disrepair. Windows that had once been boarded up were now broken, their insides open to the elements. He saw a few men sleeping inside abandoned stores. The residents of an old dry-goods store looked like they had a fire going for warmth. Some men were passed out in the doorways of long-abandoned businesses. Their thick buffalo hides being the only thing that kept them from freezing to death during the frigid Montana night.

The boardwalks all over town were beginning to warp and buckle with no one bothering to repair them. None of the many drunks he saw seemed industrious enough to bother repairing them.

All of that would change very soon.

Not every building in town was on its way to ruin. The Hard Scrabble Land Claims Office seemed to be in good condition. A quick check of the time piece he had taken from one of the dead payroll guards told him it would not be open for another couple of hours, which was fine by him. He had plenty to do in the meantime.

He turned his horse, a sturdy dappled gray he had taken from one of the dead guards at one of the mines, toward The Miner's Bank and Trust Building. He knew for certain it remained open to serve the few remaining miners in the hills. Its dark brown color and sturdy, thick-beamed construction gave the place a sense of permanence. And, with the amount of money Zimmerman planned on depositing in the place, he hoped to only add to that impression.

Zimmerman turned when he heard a door creak open and found a sturdy man in a duster stride out onto the crooked boardwalk and step down into the thoroughfare. The faded sign above the door said it had been the jail at one point, but the boarded-up window and busted door told him it no longer served that purpose.

Zimmerman turned his gray to face the man and crossed his arms on his saddle horn, taking hold of the handle of the .44 in his saddle holster.

"Morning," Zimmerman greeted the stranger.

"Certainly is." The man already had a Colt Peacemaker at his side and made no attempt to hide it. This must be one of the hardcases Hunter had warned him about. "And just who might you be, stranger?"

Zimmerman heard the challenge in his voice. "A prospector of sorts. And you?"

"I'm what you might call the tax collector around here," the man said.

Zimmerman grinned. "Is that so?"

"Damned right it is. You're in Hard Scrabble now and we've got ourselves a toll that strangers—"

Zimmerman drew his .44 and shot the man in the belly.

His victim kept his feet but dropped his pistol as he looked at the hole just above his belt buckle. He cried out as he used both hands in a futile attempt to keep the blood from leaking out.

Zimmerman left him screaming and dying in the street as he urged his horse forward toward the side street Hunter had told him was called Lawyers Row.

Many of the law offices along the side street had long since been abandoned by the attorneys who had once practiced there. He imagined they had been the first to give up on Hard Scrabble in favor of the new Battle Brook.

Only two offices appeared to still be in operation. The hand-painted letters on the windows of the Law Offices of David Parker, Esquire said Parker handled primarily wills and property transactions. Zimmerman had no need of his services.

The shingle above the door next to it was weather-beaten and hanging on by a single length of chain, though the lettering was still legible.

Mark Mannes, Attorney-at-Law.

The very man he had come to see.

Zimmerman thought he caught the smell of a stove fire going and stood up in his stirrups. Sure enough, a thin trail of white smoke was rising from the back of Mannes's law office. The lawyer was either living in the back of his office or was getting an early start on the day.

As Hard Scrabble's self-appointed tax collector continued to scream in the street behind him, Zimmerman climbed down from the saddle and wrapped the mare's reins around the porch post of Mannes's office. The hitching rail had fallen over long ago and had not been repaired. He would see to that after he accomplished what he had come to town to do.

He stepped up onto the creaky boardwalk and tried to look through the windows into the law office. It was dark inside, though he could see a bit of sunlight beneath a door that led to the back. He decided that knocking on the front door would be pointless, and he was too excited to wait.

He walked down the narrow alley between Mannes's office and a former bakery until he reached the back of the building. The whisp of white smoke was indeed coming from the back of the law office, where a back door stood half opened. He was about to knock when he heard a latch rattle from the privy about thirty yards away.

Zimmerman drew his Colt .44 from his hip and aimed it at the privy door as it opened.

He found himself aiming at a tall man as thin as a broom stick. His baggy long john underwear served to make him look even more timid than he already was. He had a thin crown of graying mouse brown hair around an otherwise bald head. Beady pale blue eyes looked at him from behind wire-rimmed spectacles. He was clean-shaven, which revealed he was bereft of a chin. And the look on his face was one of complete and utter blandness.

And as he looked down the barrel of Zimmerman's .44, it was obvious that the lawyer did not know whether he should run back into the privy, cry out for help, or simply surrender.

"What do you want?" the man asked him, unable to hide the quaver in his voice.

"That depends," Zimmerman said. "You Mannes, the attorney?"

He seemed to have to think about it for a moment. "Yes. I am."

"Good." Zimmerman holstered his pistol. "Then we have business to discuss. Best come inside so we can talk. I'll even let you fix me a cup of coffee if you behave yourself. You might not know it now, but your life is about to change for the better and so is mine."

Zimmerman even held the door open for him as he invited the attorney back into his own home.

He could not gauge the look the lawyer gave him as he trudged past him. "Fear not, my new friend. I'm not here to harm you. I'm here because of your skills with the law and your lineage."

Mannes squinted at him. "My lineage? What does that have to do with anything?"

Zimmerman gestured to the door. "Step inside and let's talk."

# Chapter 13

Two hours later, Mark Mannes and his new client, Edward Zimmerman, sat in the office of the president of The Miner's Bank and Trust.

The slant of light from the shaded windows still showed a thin layer of dust on the president's desk and even on the president himself.

The Honorable H. Calvin Hubbard looked exactly how Zimmerman thought a bank president should. He was a round-headed man with a slight double chin, thinning white hair, and an impressive set of thick white mutton chops and moustaches to match. He looked to be about sixty or so, but the light in his eyes and a lack of age spots showed him to be closer to forty despite appearances. His tan suit had been expensive when he had bought it some time ago, and it probably came from a respectable tailor in Helena.

The banker cleared his throat before saying, "My old friend Mr. Mannes here tells me you have quite an ambitious plan in mind for Hard Scrabble, Mr. Smith." He spoke the name as though he knew it was an alias. "Unfortunately, I fear it may be too late to put them into practice."

Mannes looked nervously from Hubbard to Zimmerman like a frightened rabbit looking for escape.

Zimmerman had never been a cultured man but had watched enough of them in saloons and gambling halls over the years to be able to ape some of their mannerisms and expressions. He crossed his legs and folded his hands on his lap. "What makes you say that?"

Hubbard frowned. "I'm not sure how much of the town you were able to see before you came to visit me this morning, but to put it mildly, Hard Scrabble is a town in decline. Once the Ryan and Rice mining concern increased their holdings in Battle Brook, most of our customers relocated there. This town is merely a shell of what it once was."

"Doesn't look so bad to me," Zimmerman said. "Some paint and a little hard work would fix this town up real nicely."

Hubbard blinked at him. "It's become a most dangerous place, too. Why, just this morning a man was gut-shot in the middle of the street."

"I know. I'm the one who shot him."

Mannes's stomach made a gurgling sound. Hubbard's mouth dropped open.

"It was for the town's benefit, I assure you," Zimmerman said. "Please, go on."

Hubbard forced a smile despite what he had just heard. "While we would be more than happy to take your money, Mr. Smith, there's not much hope for you to grow your investment. Why, just yesterday, one of our major depositors informed us that he may be closing down operations by the end of the year. If that happens, I'm afraid we'll have no choice but to shift the few remaining accounts we have to the bank in Battle Brook and close our doors."

Zimmerman noticed Mannes appeared to be on the verge of tears. Mannes had already explained all of this to him in his cramped kitchen over a weak pot of coffee. Zimmerman had insisted on seeing Hubbard anyway.

Zimmerman saw no benefit to allowing the lawyer to be afraid of him. "Mr. Mannes has already given me an honest assessment on the town's current situation. I can assure you I'm still intent on investing. In fact, I plan on investing heavily in Hard Scrabble, and I plan on starting today."

The banker furrowed his brow. "I don't know who you really are, Mr. Smith, and quite frankly, I'm not sure I want to know, but if you're looking for investment property, I must tell you in all good conscience that Hard Scrabble is hardly the place for you."

Zimmerman remembered why he was an outlaw. He despised polite banter and decided to cut to the chase. "This bank owns most of, if not all of the buildings in town, doesn't it?"

"All of them, I'm afraid," Hubbard sighed heavily.

Zimmerman did not give him a chance to speak. "And you're still part of Battle Brook?"

"Technically they're part of us," Hubbard told him, "but I expect that to change once we're granted statehood next month." The banker's eyes narrowed. "None of that seems to deter you, does it?"

Zimmerman smiled. "Why do you think I'm here?"

Hubbard began to stammer a response, but Zimmerman cut him off. "Battle Brook is owned by Ryan and Rice. You own Hard Scrabble, don't you?"

The banker's chins moved as he nodded his head.

"And you lent money to the mine owners in the hills?" Zimmerman pushed.

"All of them." Hubbard's eyes narrowed again. "How do you know all of this?"

"Good," Zimmerman said, "because after I make my deposit with you, I'll be your biggest investor."

Hubbard looked at Mannes, then back at Zimmerman. He ran a thick finger along the inside of his strained collar. "H-how much of an investment?"

"Eighty thousand." Zimmerman enjoyed the look on Hubbard's face. "All cash money, too."

He watched Hubbard's mouth move, but no sound came out. He reminded Zimmerman of a trout on the end of a hook.

When his voice returned to him, he said, "*Eighty* thousand, you said?"

"Cash," Zimmerman repeated. "I can have it here by noon. You have a reputation for discretion, Mr. Hubbard, and I'm counting on that discretion now. My name's obviously not Smith and I doubt you ever thought it was. My name is Ed Zimmerman, and I'm using my ill-gotten gains to buy your town from you. Today."

Zimmerman motioned for Mannes to explain what they had already discussed in his kitchen two hours before.

"My client will deliver eighty thousand dollars in cash by noon today," Mannes began. "At that time, you will transfer all of the bank's foreclosed properties to him, including the town hall. For legal purposes, I will be named the temporary mayor of the town until formal elections can be held. You will also provide him with a list of all the mines you currently have interests in. You will agree to allow my client to consolidate those independent mines into a single entity. Your shares of the mines will remain the same and you will continue to share in existing profits and future profits should my client invest in improving operations at particular mines."

Zimmerman thought Hubbard might throw up. It was a lot to take in all at once. "Consolidation? I don't know if they'll go for that?"

"My client is buying their debt and, as a result, buying them," Mannes explained. "Given the large amount of money he's depositing, there will still be a significant amount left over to pay for all of the improvements Hard Scrabble requires."

Hubbard sat forward in his chair. His fleshy face entirely flushed. "It's certainly more than enough to do what you say, but it still won't bring people back from Battle Brook. Why, all of the independent mines together are less than half of the Battle Brook concerns."

"But more than enough to give my client a return on his investment," Mannes went on. "We will also be changing the name of the town to Valhalla, and while we can't imagine why you would object to that, we want it in writing that you won't interfere in that regard, either. All investments will be made under an entity called The Valhalla Mining and Investment Company. Its investors shall remain anonymous, at least for the time being."

Hubbard sat back in his seat, breathing heavily. Zimmerman thought he might be having a heart attack and hoped that was not the case. Having to explain his plan to Hubbard's replacement would be time consuming and might not go as well. He needed to put his plan in place now before word reached Battle Brook and someone tried to stop him.

Hubbard's breathing leveled off and he patted his brow with a handkerchief he produced from an inside pocket.

"I don't think it'll work. You're an outlaw. The men with you are outlaws. The money is stolen."

Zimmerman was waiting, just waiting for him to say he could not be part of something like this. He knew Hubbard had done business with worse men than him for much less money.

But the banker surprised him by saying, "If we do this, we must do it very carefully, gentlemen. Helena is distracted by coming statehood now, but once that's over, they'll have time to look at this closely. There will be questions."

Mannes said, "I will be going to Helena on tomorrow's train to make sure all of those concerns are satisfied. When I return, I'll have all of the necessary documentation we require to conduct our business legally."

Hubbard shook his head. "I know you have relatives in Helena, Mark, but this is something different."

Zimmerman waved him off. "Let the lawyers worry about the particulars. You and I are going to make a lot of money together."

Zimmerman got to his feet and stuck out his hand to Hubbard. "Shake on it, and I'll see to it that the money is here in two hours. Mannes will draw up the papers in the meantime and by the time you lock your doors tonight, you'll not only be a rich man, but a powerful one, too."

Hubbard looked at the thick hand, then up at Zimmerman. "And if I refuse?"

"I'll kill you, and your replacement will say yes." He held out the hand anew. "What do you say?"

Hubbard feebly rose to his feet, steadying himself on his desk with his left hand and shaking the outlaw's hand with his right. "Why do I feel like I've made a deal with the devil himself?"

Zimmerman threw back his head and laughed before slapping the banker on the shoulder. "Don't be so dramatic, Hubby. Besides, you'll soon learn old Satan's got nothing on me and my bunch."

Zimmerman looked down at Mannes, whose eyes were still beady and just as frightened as they had been when they had first met. "I want those papers drawn up and ready to sign by the time my men get here with the money. And remember, I know how to read, so if you put anything in there I don't like, I'll know it. And I won't be happy."

He watched his lawyer's Adam's apple bob up and down. "Don't worry, Mr. Zimmerman. I won't."

The outlaw strode out of the office a proud man. "And when you're done, go back to your place and pack a bag. You're taking a trip to Battle Brook tonight. I want you to tend to some business for me before you head to Helena."

The attorney took a fit of coughing before he gasped, "Battle Brook? But I thought I was going straight to Wellspring tomorrow morning to catch the train."

"That's still on," Zimmerman told him as he opened the office door. "I need you to talk to someone in town first before I send you on your way. Don't worry. It's mostly legal."

He almost laughed again as he watched Hubbard and Mannes look at each other as he shut the office door behind him. They looked absolutely terrified.

*If they only knew*, Zimmerman thought.

Not just any bank, he reminded himself. His bank.


Two hours later, Zimmerman remained on his horse while he watched Poe and Monk unload the canvas money bags from the mule and hand them to the chain of bank clerks who passed them along until they reached Hubbard in the vault. Brunet was already inside, making sure the money did not make any detours along the way. He would stay with them while they counted it and gave Mannes the deposit slip.

Blackfoot stood guard out front with his Winchester across his chest while some of Hard Scrabble's rougher residents looked on from the boardwalks at all the bags of money being carried into the bank.

When Poe had handed off the last bag of money from the mule, he ambled over to Zimmerman, pulling at the uncomfortable city clothes the gang leader had given him to wear. "Looks like we're pretty popular with the locals."

Zimmerman did not bother to give them the satisfaction of looking at them. He could already see their reflections in the bank windows. They looked like vultures waiting for an old stag to die. He knew how to handle vultures.

He would handle them once the money was safely in the vault. Nothing else mattered.

Watching Poe pull on his new clothes was beginning to get on his nerves. "Something else on your mind?"

"I don't want to sound like I'm complainin' or nothin', but how come I hafta go to Helena with Mannes? And how come I've gotta dress like this? The shirt itches something awful."

Zimmerman kept himself from laughing at the outlaw's unlikely appearance. He had made him trade in his buffalo skin and filthy clothes at Mr. Jappe's general store for proper work pants and a shirt with buttons on it and a thick woolen coat that came just below his hips. Zimmerman had seen to it that the shapeless thing he had once called a hat had been replaced by a lightly used bowler Jappe had on sale. The store owner had insisted Poe get undressed in the lot behind his store so his clothes could be burned before the lice Poe had living off him infected the rest of his goods.

Zimmerman had allowed Poe to keep his boots as he did not want the outlaw to add blisters to his list of complaints. He had also ordered him to have a bath and a shave, which gave him a more acceptable appearance.

"You're going because I need someone to go with Mannes to make sure he does what we tell him to do," Zimmerman explained for the second time. "You're the least wanted of the rest of us, so you won't draw much attention. Besides, you know how to read and write, which will come in handy should Mannes try to get cute with anyone he meets with in Helena."

Back in Silver Cloud, Zimmerman had learned a bitter lesson about sending men into a hostile situation one at a time. Zimmerman knew Poe could be counted on to make sure Mannes stayed in line.

Zimmerman decided to test Poe. "What are the rules on your journey?"

"Never let Mannes out of my sight, not even on the train. When he's meeting with important people, write down who he's meeting with. When he gets something signed, I take it from him and keep it on me at all times until I hand it to you at the station next week."

It was good, but not good enough. "And?"

"And I'm to send you a wire to Wellspring as soon as I have the signed documents, but not before."

"And what saloon will you be going to tonight before you get the stage to Wellspring?"

"The Hot Pepper Saloon," Poe told him, "and see a man

named Douglas Wycoff. He'll come here to see you if he's interested."

"Excellent!" Zimmerman patted him on the back, causing Poe to cry out.

"Damn it, Ed. I told you this shirt itches like crazy."

But Zimmerman would not let his man's discomfort ruin his good mood. "If this plays out the way it should, we'll all be wearing silk shirts real soon."

"And my right name ain't Poe," the outlaw told him. "It's Kurtzman."

Zimmerman reached down and grabbed him by the collar. "You'll be able to call yourself anything you want if you do your job right." He pushed the new bowler down hard on the man's head. "Now go find Mannes and tell him those papers better be ready for me and Hubbard to sign. I want to move the rest of you boys into Battle Brook before nightfall. We've got some busy days ahead of us."

Poe fixed his hat and pointed down the street. "Looks like they're already here, boss."

Zimmerman ignored the men looking at him and turned his horse around to see the rest of The Spoilers riding into town.

*Good,* he thought. Might as well get this over with sooner rather than later.

He heeled the gray into the middle of the street and signaled for his men to remain where they were. They formed a jagged line that filled the width of the thorough-fare.

Zimmerman looked at the gaggle of disheveled men and women who lined every inch of boardwalk around the bank. They were a forgotten lot who called a forgotten town their home. Some were pulling on whiskey bottles, others looked hungover. All of them looked like they needed a bath. They were young and old and every age in between. He was surprised by the number of black men and Chinese in their ranks. Most were bearded. All of them looked like either the whiskey or the elements would kill them before the thaw. None of them looked like they cared.

Zimmerman was about to change all that. He looked each of them in the eye as he said, "As of today, this town is mine. It belongs to me and my men. I own the buildings you're sleeping in, the places where you buy your whiskey from and where you eat. I own the dirt under your feet, the sky above your heads, and the very air you breathe. We're going to clean up this place and make it fit for living again. I'm paying for all of that, too, and I'll pay a good wage to any man, woman, or child who wants it. If you don't help, you leave. You do what I say and don't give me any sass, we'll all get along just fine. Defy me and there'll be consequences."

He waited until the last echo of his voice died down before he asked, "I think that's plain enough to understand. Anyone have any questions?"

To his right, a group of younger men were in front of the saloon. They had been giggling and elbowing each other throughout Zimmerman's speech. They stifled their laughter as one of them sauntered forward with his hand raised. "Yeah, mister. I've got a question."

Zimmerman drew his .44 from the saddle holster and shot the man in the head. His corpse fell back against his friends, who were no longer laughing. They were covered in their friend's blood.

This time, it was only The Spoilers who laughed.

Zimmerman kept the .44 in his hand as he looked around at the vagabonds who called this town home. "Any other questions?"

Most of them shook their heads and went back to wherever they were living. Zimmerman holstered his pistol and called out to them as they left. "Some of my men will be coming around with work you'll need to do. Your cooperation is expected and appreciated."

He turned his gray around and rode over to Blackfoot.

"Hell of a speech, boss," the outlaw told him.

"I'll be setting myself up in the old jail over there. Tell the boys to come see me once they've gotten off their horses. We've got a lot of work to do."

"I'll bring them with me," Blackfoot promised.

Zimmerman heeled his horse into an easy gait and rode over toward the old jailhouse. The animal did not seem to mind the blood still in the snow from the man he had shot just after noon.

It had not bothered Zimmerman, either.

# Chapter 14

After a breakfast spent in the dining room of The Standard Hotel avoiding Sandborne's questions about the shoot-out in The Wild Cat Saloon the night before, the two deputy marshals walked over to meet McBride in the jail.

But the change in scenery did not quell Sandborne's curiosity.

"Guess Ringham's not as slick as he thinks he is," Sandborne said. "Otherwise, he wouldn't have tipped you off to the two men behind you like he did."

Halstead had never been one for reliving his kills. The dead were dead and posed no harm to the living. He had never shot a man unless it was out of necessity, save for the one time in El Paso and even that was debatable. Even the jury had sided with him that time.

"You would've done the same thing had you been there," Halstead told him. "A man tries to point a gun at you, your instincts go to work. Not much thought goes into it. At least it shouldn't. Thinking can get you killed at a time like that."

"'Thinking can get you killed,'" Sandborne repeated. "I like that."

Halstead closed his eyes. "Thinking in that kind of situation, I mean. If you think too much, you might miss or you might not shoot at all." The entire subject was beginning to annoy him. "It's always best to not find yourself in that kind of situation in the first place. Having to shoot a man, I mean."

"Then why didn't you let me go into the saloon with you to watch your back instead of sending me off with the horses?"

Halstead knew he had him there. "Because I guess I was trying to make a point. To Ringham and to anyone else who was thinking about collecting Zimmerman's bounty on me."

"I guess that's where the thinking part of it comes in," Sandborne pressed. "Before it happens."

"Something like that." Halstead tried to think of something, anything to change the subject. There were plenty of other aspects of being a deputy besides gunning down men. He wanted the younger man to learn that before he got caught up in the violence of the job.

The hammering and sawing of all of the new buildings going up all over town provided a good distraction, and he decided to focus on that. "Looks like this town isn't done growing."

"Kind of exciting if you ask me," Sandborne said. "Guess that's what happens when they move a town from one place to the other. Get to rename it and everything. Start fresh. Kinda like what they tried to do in Dover Station, only this time I hope it ends a whole lot better."

Halstead could not believe the things Sandborne said sometimes. "You know, you've got a knack for ruining a good mood better than anyone I've ever met. Here I am, talking about something nice and you go and bring that up."

"I'm sorry," Sandborne said. "Just crossed my mind is all."

Halstead knew he had not meant it. Besides, Joshua Sandborne made it impossible to stay mad at him for long. "I know you didn't. I'm just crabby is all."

"Can't say as I blame you. The coffee wasn't very good this morning."

"No, it wasn't."

He stopped walking when he saw a group of people standing outside a building on their side of the street that he remembered as being The Battle Brook Town Hall. He did not recognize any of them, not that he had spent much time getting to know the locals since coming to town.

That was when he remembered Jack McBride had told him about the Town Committee meeting the night before. He had completely forgotten about it, probably because he'd wanted to.

He motioned for Sandborne to stand with him in the doorway of a bakery while they waited to see what would happen next.

They did not have a long wait. Jack McBride walked across the thoroughfare with a ring of keys in his hand. The people out front were complaining about the cold, and he spoke over them. "Hold your horses, everyone. They just put the new lock on last week and I've got the only copy. I'll get you in there in a minute."

The tall man waded through the crowd and opened the door, holding it open for the men and women who were all too eager to rush inside to avoid the chilly morning.

When the last citizen entered, McBride spotted Halstead and Sandborne in the bakery doorway and beckoned them to come over. "Might as well join us, as they'll be telling me to fetch you boys sooner or later."

Halstead and Sandborne walked over to him. "Guess that's our firing squad, isn't it?"

McBride shook his head. "Nope. Just the Town Committee I told you about. And judging by their mood after having to wait so long for me to fetch the keys, I'd say they're not in a cheerful mood."

This was the part of the job Halstead hated most. The same part Mackey had always hated. The political part. The glad-handing part. Put him up against a saloon full of drunks and he could clear out the troublemakers in no time flat. Put him up in front of a room full of civilians with questions and complaints and he was helpless. The same temperament that helped him scare a man into a cell was the same that crippled him in situations like these.

A lawman could not tell the town elders to simply go to Hell and expect to keep his badge. Mackey had managed to do it in Dover Station, but that was because he had grown up there. He was a favorite son. A hero at that. Halstead knew he would not be able to do that now that he was responsible for an entire territory.

Halstead could not do it here in Battle Brook because, like it or not, he was a representative of the federal government.

He tried one last tactic with McBride. "Guess you couldn't just tell them you can't find us."

McBride shook his head. "Afraid I can't do that, Jeremiah, but I'm also not responsible for keeping you here. If things get too hot for you in there, my advice is to just leave before you lose that temper of yours. If you jaw at them, they'll cause you plenty of trouble back in Helena."

Halstead suddenly found himself wishing he was back

in Helena. Or back at the pass dodging bullets. But wishing did not make something so, and, with a deep breath, he walked into the town hall. Sandborne and McBride followed him in.

Halstead took a seat down front, and Sandborne sat next to him.

He thought it was a nice building as far as town halls went. It was far from the ornate stone and marble monstrosity James Grant had built for himself in Dover Station, and it was not as elegant as the capital building in Helena. It smelled of new pine and fresh paint and lacquer. The five members of the town council sat on a stage that was elevated about four feet off the ground. Most of the chairs in the hall were filled with groups of citizens engaged in their own separate conversations.

A squat, angry looking man with white hair sat in the middle of the five members of the council. Halstead took him to be the mayor or whatever they called the head of the town here in Battle Brook.

He banged his gavel like a judge in a court of law until all the attendees stopped talking.

A judge's gavel brought back dark memories that Jeremiah Halstead had spent years trying to forget. A cold sweat broke out along his brow, and he felt his legs grow weak. He hoped they did not make him stand up right away as he did not think he could manage it.

"This emergency meeting of the Town Council of the Town of Battle Brook is now in session." The angry little man looked down at Halstead and Sandborne in the front row. "You boys are new to these parts, and we haven't had the pleasure of being formally introduced. My name is

Philip White, and I'm the mayor of this town. I also happen to own the haberdashery up the street from here. If you boys find yourselves in need of outfitting, I'll give you a fair price."

*I just hope you give us a fair hearing,* Halstead thought to himself.

"We've called a special session today on account of some concerns the public have raised about your presence in town. Namely your hunt for the outlaw bandits named Robert Brunet, Edward Zimmerman, and the men they have riding with them. These 'Spoilers' or whatever they're calling themselves. Now, just before you came to town, they robbed six of our most prosperous mines and stole payroll that equates to approximately one hundred thousand dollars."

He waggled a pudgy hand. "That estimate is in some dispute, but we'll go with the one-hundred-thousand-dollar number for now. And last night, you gunned down two men in The Wild Cat Saloon and arrested a newcomer to the area by the name of Thomas Ringham."

He peered down at Halstead over his glasses. "Now I know you don't answer to me, Deputy Halstead, and this board has no authority over you or your partner here. But there seems to be an awful lot of lead flying around these parts since your arrival and some of us want some answers."

Halstead felt his breathing grow shallow. The thin line of sweat had gotten worse and felt like it ran down his back in buckets. He no longer felt like he was in a town hall in Montana, but in that cramped, humid courtroom back in El Paso where the judge had taken three years of his life away from him as if he was just talking about the weather.

He knew this was different. He knew he was different.

But his body and mind acted like he was in the same fix he had been in only five years before. He tried to fight it. He tried to force himself to say something, anything, but he could not even move.

He barely noticed when Sandborne stood up and said, "I guess you all don't know me, but I'm a deputy marshal, too. Joshua Sandborne out of Dover Station and, as of late, Helena. I'm Deputy Halstead's partner so he's asked me to tell you fine people about why we're here."

Halstead spent the next twenty minutes trying to shake off his nerves while Sandborne, in his own unique way, quietly spun the tale of their pursuit of the outlaws Zimmerman and Brunet; that they had promising leads on where they might be hiding and were intent on following up those leads as soon as they were allowed to leave the meeting.

He also told them about the bounty Zimmerman had placed on Halstead and that the deputy was merely defending himself in the saloon the previous night, just as he had been forced to do in Helena for the past several weeks.

And although Halstead could barely manage to move, by the time Sandborne was done, even he could sense he had them all eating out of his hand.

When he was done, Sandborne sat down next to Halstead and kept his eyes forward, as if they were in church.

The mayor looked at Halstead. "I take it you agree with everything Deputy Sandborne has said?"

"Yes, sir." He cleared his throat as his voice sounded weaker than he would have liked. "Every word."

A woman with a feather in her blue hat called out from the audience, "Make him stand up and address us proper. This ain't no barroom."

Halstead found the strength to slowly get to his feet and turn to face the civilians. All of them looked him over the same as everyone else did. Head to toe first, then at the star on his lapel, then at the silver Colt butt jutting out from his coat. He had not bothered to take his hat off when he had entered the building, and the thought did not occur to him now.

"I'm not as good at this as Deputy Sandborne, so I'll tell it to you this way. Marshal Aaron Mackey sent us here to bring a bunch of rabid killers to justice, and we plan on doing exactly that. We didn't come to town looking for trouble, but if someone draws on one of us, we'll put them down. You make sure your men know there's no real bounty on my head and they'd be foolish to try to collect it. It'll help us avoid a lot of unpleasantness in the future. Now, if you people will excuse us, Joshua and I have some fugitives to catch."

He felt a wave of nausea pass through him as he ignored the odd looks he drew from everyone as he marched past them. McBride was standing by the door and Halstead hoped to God he did not try to stop them. He was glad when the tall man opened the door for them and let them pass.

Halstead rushed out onto the street and threw up. He clung as tightly as he could to the porch post out of fear he might fall over into the street. He emptied the contents of his stomach again until he began to heave dry.

He felt a strong hand on his back to help keep him stand upright. When he felt strong enough to stand on his own, he was surprised to find the hand did not belong to McBride, but to Sandborne.

"You feel better now?" the young deputy asked him.

Halstead drew the mountain air deep into his lungs and spat the last remnants of sickness into the thoroughfare. "Yeah, I guess so."

"I knew those eggs tasted a bit off," he said as he helped Halstead stay steady on his feet. "My stomach's a bit off myself."

"It wasn't the damned breakfast," he said through gritted teeth. "It was something else."

"Yeah, I figured," Sandborne said. "Guess it kinda reminded you of what happened to you in El Paso and stuff."

Halstead had not known Mackey had told him about that.

Sandborne said, "Billy told me about it before we left Helena. It's no wonder you were feeling pretty bad. Hell, I doubt I'd have had the guts to walk in there, much less sit for as long as you did."

Halstead felt a shudder run through him. "Glad you were there to keep me from making a complete fool of myself. Five damned years and I'm out here shaking like a leaf."

Sandborne said, "I was just like that when Aaron found me wandering after the JT got burned to the ground. Said there's nothing wrong with being scared as long as you're brave enough to admit it."

Halstead looked at his younger partner. "He said that?"

"He surely did. And you don't have to be brave all the time, Jerry. That's why I'm here. The Good Lord knows you've propped me up plenty of times."

They both turned when the town hall door opened, and Jack McBride stepped outside. He noticed the condition of the thoroughfare and asked, "You all right, Jeremiah? You don't look good."

Sandborne stepped in before Halstead could say a word. "The breakfast down at the hotel didn't agree with us. Come to think of it, I need a privy myself. Damned stuff is running through me like a spring rain. Where's the nearest one I can use?"

McBride pointed to an outhouse at the end of the alley and Sandborne asked them to wait for him until he got back.

Halstead and McBride watched him go.

"That boy's quite the orator," McBride said. "Didn't know he had it in him."

"Yeah." Halstead swallowed the last of the bile that rose in his throat. "He's full of surprises."

With Sandborne keeping an eye on Ringham down at the jail while McBride grabbed some sleep in his hotel room upstairs, Jeremiah Halstead decided to enjoy a rare moment of solitude. He found an old rocking chair on the front porch of The Standard Hotel and allowed himself to drop into it. He managed not to spill a drop of the whiskey the proprietor had given him from his own private stash behind the desk. He rested the glass on the arm of the chair and began to slowly rock back and forth.

It was going on dusk by then and the town was quietly switching over from day to night. Shops were closing up as saloons came alive. Miners were walking into their favorite watering holes, no doubt eager to cash in on some of the credit Emmett Ryan's company had extended to them.

The Hot Pepper Saloon was across from his hotel and he watched different types of men go into it like bees returning to a hive. He wondered what drew men to a particular saloon over another. A place never mattered much to him, so long as it served decent beer or whiskey, though he preferred tequila when he could find it. Good tequila, not the coyote piss they passed off for the genuine article in these parts.

He remembered he still had a couple of Boddington's cigars in wax paper in his coat and set his glass on the floor as he fished them out. He selected one, bit off the end, and spat it into the thoroughfare before thumbing a match alive with his thumbnail and lighting his cigar. The dark smoke hit home harder than the whiskey had, and he felt himself relax for the first time since coming to Battle Brook.

The day that had just ended with the sun sinking below the western mountains had been a wasted one as far as Halstead was concerned. It had started out with a dust-up with the town council and ended with him no closer to finding Zimmerman than he had been the night before.

All he had to show for his efforts was two more dead men and a gambler locked up in a jail with no bars. None of them had anything to do with Zimmerman, Brunet, or the payroll robberies up at the mines. Possibly a hundred thousand dollars gone, and the best Halstead could do was sit on his ass sipping whiskey and smoking a cigar.

He looked up at the fading light that draped the mountains in deep reds and purples and thought again about another way to hunt the men he had been sent to bring home. McBride had said riding into Hard Scrabble would either be a waste of time or suicide. The dying town had become infested with outlaws looking for a place to ride out the winter.

The sensible thing would be to return to Helena and come back in the spring with more men, just like McBride had suggested. But Halstead could not consider that option. He didn't dare. It felt too much like defeat, and he had no intention of allowing Zimmerman or Brunet the satisfaction of running him off. He was here. They were here. It would end here, and it would end now.

He had made up his mind. Tomorrow, they would ride over to Hard Scrabble and see what there was to see.

"That stuff will kill you, you know?"

The woman's voice shook him out of his brooding, and he looked around to see Abby standing next to him. She was wearing a dark blue dress and, of course, a matching hat and bag. She looked like she had stepped out of one of the catalogs from a store back east, except the models in those catalogs did not smile the way she was smiling at him now.

He lifted up the whiskey and the cigar at the same time. "Which one?"

"Both if you're not careful," she said as she began to walk toward him uninvited. "Especially the brooding part. That's worse than everything else."

Halstead blushed in spite of himself. "I didn't know it was that obvious."

"It was, though I'll admit I'm impressed. You didn't strike me as a cigar and whiskey type. Tom yes, but not you."

He hoped that did not diminish him in her eyes. "I'm full of surprises. As a matter of fact, I was smoking a cigar on the train when I had my first run-in with Tom."

"So I heard," she said as she sat on the edge of the rocking chair next to him. "I wanted to apologize for that. He's never showered me with attention but doesn't like it when other men do." A new thought seemed to come to her. "I know I already thanked you for not killing him last night, but I want to thank you again. God knows he probably deserved it."

Halstead could not disagree. "He was smart enough to not be packing a gun. But don't worry. He's in plenty of trouble as it is."

"I know." She looked at the ground, and Halstead felt any hint of happiness disappear within him.

"He set me up to get killed," he told her. "I can't just let him get away with that. Not even for you."

She shook her head slowly. "I know. I wouldn't ask you to, at least not without a good reason."

The void left by his happiness was suddenly filled by dread of what she was about to say next. "I sure hope you're not going to ask me what I think you're going to ask me."

"It's not about Tom," she said. "He picked his battle and lost. He deserves whatever he has coming to him. It's you I'm worried about."

"Me?" He even laughed. "Why would you be worried about me? I hope it's not because of that price Zimmerman put on my head, because if it is, no one's going to try to collect it. Not after what I did last night."

"Not that," she told him. "It has to do with why you're here in the first place. To find Zimmerman, I mean. I don't think you'll be able to do it. Not your way, anyhow."

He stopped rocking and sat on the edge of his chair. "How did you know about that?"

"I ran into Jack before he went up to your room to sleep," she told him. "We got to talking and he told me about what you're up against. You can't go to Hard Scrabble, Jerry, not the way you want. You're a marked man, whether you believe it or not, and that town sounds like it's filled with people who would love to try to get that bounty on your head, especially since they know Zimmerman is around to pay it."

Halstead would have to remind McBride to keep his mouth shut around Abby. "Nothing's been decided yet."

"Of course, it has," she told him. "You've probably

looked at this from every way possible and think the best you can do is go up there and stir things up. It won't work. They won't tell you anything even if they know something. All you'll manage to do is get yourself hurt or somebody else and accomplish nothing." She laid a gloved hand on his arm. "But there's another way, Jerry. A better way."

Halstead liked her hand on his arm, but not what he thought she was about to say. "What way?"

She held her bag tightly on her lap as she began to speak. "Well, I've already accepted the position as school mistress here in Battle Brook, which also covers the children in Hard Scrabble. I was thinking that Jack and I could ride to Hard Scrabble tomorrow and talk to them about how many children are in the area."

He was about to tell her that was absolutely out of the question when she held up a gloved hand. "Let me finish, Jeremiah. It's not only perfectly safe, but it's part of my duty as the teacher in this part of the territory. The people over there are far more likely to let their guard down around me than around you or even Jack McBride. I'll be talking to people about their children's education and finding out what kinds of troubles they face. Zimmerman and Brunet are bound to come up. And, when I'm done, I can come back here and tell you what they told me. And what I see. Then, if you think it's worth you and Sandborne taking a ride up there with Jack, at least you'll have a better idea of what you're up against."

Everything in Halstead wanted to object. The risks were enormous. If she asked the wrong person the wrong question, they might keep her in town or worse.

But he kept his mouth shut and, for once, kept listening.

"They already know I'm coming, and they know I'm not from around here," she continued, "so even if I ask the wrong questions, they'll probably think it harmless. And I'll be mostly talking to women, Jeremiah. Even you have to admit that women speak differently to each other than when a man's around, especially about other men. Especially bad men like Brunet and Zimmerman."

Halstead sat still as her words took root in his mind. It was not just what she had said, but the way she had said it. So confident and without any trace of fear despite the circumstances.

"Hard Scrabble's just not any other town," he reminded her. "You've got a bunch of outlaws riding out the winter up there and that's not counting Zimmerman's bunch."

"And the way I see it," she continued, "one teacher against twelve men stands a much better chance of surviving than three lawmen riding through the hills trying to smoke them out. It might come down to that anyway, but at least you'll know a little bit more about the place than if you just go riding in there, guns blazing."

All of the objections that rose in his mind quickly wilted away under the logic of everything she had just laid out. Not only that, but Jack McBride would be with her.

"Look at me, Jeremiah," she said. "You know I'm right."

But he would not look at her, for he knew if he did, she would have him agreeing to all sorts of things.

"If Jack agrees to this," Halstead said, "and that's a big if, then I want you to have a gun."

"No," she refused. "I don't have a bag big enough to carry one anyway and even if I did, I wouldn't take it. Someone might see it and it would change the way they speak to me."

*God, she's smart,* he thought. Smarter than he could ever hope to be. He remembered back to that moment in Silver Cloud when he had charged back into town without even thinking about it. But right now, as he sat on a rocking chair in front of a hotel in the mountains, sipping whiskey and smoking a cigar, he found himself completely disarmed by this woman's mind.

Knowing he was beaten, he tried to salvage just a bit of pride. "Let me finish my drink and my smoke and we'll go down to the jail to talk to Sandborne about it. If he and Jack agree, then I won't stand in your way."

He finally chanced a look at her and was glad he had not done it earlier. The way she was smiling at him had him melting completely. He only hoped she did not ask him to let her leave right away because he knew he probably would. "But not until I'm through with my drink and smoke. That's final."

She subtly wiggled herself back into the rocking chair. "I wouldn't have it any other way, Jeremiah."

He sat back in his chair and slowly began to rock. It was a small victory, one of the few he was ever likely to have for however long he knew her, but he accepted it gladly.

He took a pull on his cigar as he watched the evening traffic begin to pick up on the streets of Battle Brook. The new town had settled into the same rhythms as a town twenty years old or more. Couples arm in arm going to dinner. Miners heading into saloons. Shopkeepers going home after a long day.

Across the street, he watched a rail-thin, weasely looking man walk into The Hot Pepper Saloon followed by a shorter man who kept pulling at his shirt. They did not fit the kind of men he had seen going into the saloon that evening, but as he had already determined earlier that night, there was no accounting for why men chose the places where they drank.

Once again, Abby interrupted his thoughts by saying, "I have to admit, it's rather nice sitting out here with you."

He glanced at her through his cigar smoke. "I can't argue with you there. I'm pretty good company, ain't I?"

She cut loose with the same sharp laugh that had drawn every eye in the dining car of the train, but on the streets of Battle Brook, no one seemed to mind. Least of all Jeremiah Halstead.

Ed Zimmerman watched Halstead and his lady friend from the shadows of the alley across the thoroughfare from The Standard Hotel.

He regretted not having brought his Winchester with him when he tied off his horse and tracked Poe and Mannes from the shadows. He wanted to make sure they went exactly where they were supposed to go. They would soon be out of his reach when they boarded the train to Helena tomorrow, and he wanted to control as much of their movements as possible.

He had intended to spend the night in the alley and trail their stagecoach down to the station the following day. It would not be the first night he had spent in such accommodations, and he doubted it would be his last.

But he had not expected to find Jeremiah Halstead in town, much less so relaxed and well within range of his rifle if only he had thought to take it with him.

It was still on the saddle scabbard of his horse, and though he could go back for it and pick him off, he decided against it. He could always pick him off when he returned to the hotel later, for he was sure the deputy was staying there. He had heard the jail was not yet finished, so the hotel would be his only option.

But a bullet would be too good for Halstead. And it would only serve to rob Zimmerman of his greatest prize, surpassed only by his desire to control his portion of the Montana Territory.

That prize being the absolute destruction of Jeremiah Halstead.

Any fool could kill. Many fools had. But only a true genius knew how to kill a man and let him live. The best way to do that was by killing what he loved the most.

The lawman was sweet on his female companion. A blind man could see it. And although Zimmerman was too far away to hear what they were talking about, the way they moved when they spoke to each other said it all.

She was not a whore. That much was clear to him. A pretty brunette in an elegant blue dress told Zimmerman that she had either come from money or had some of her own. And once Mannes's work in Helena was done and his future settled, he would make sure he paid the pretty lady a visit.

And when he did, Jeremiah Halstead would never look at her the same way again.

He smiled to himself in the shadows. At least now he had the thought of vengeance to keep him warm on this cold Montana night.

# Chapter 15

The next morning, Halstead drank his coffee in the hotel's dining room, watching the stagecoach driver loading up passengers and luggage in front of The Standard Hotel. It was the coach for Wellspring Station to meet the Helena train.

Halstead recognized the first two travelers who had climbed into the coach as being the same odd men he had watched enter The Hot Pepper Saloon the night before. The skinny, timid looking man and the shorter, dour man pulling on his shirt. They had not fit the crowd going into The Hot Pepper the night before, and they looked just as out of place here among the passengers to Helena. He had watched them board the coach and saw that there was only one small piece of luggage between them.

That struck Halstead as strange. The train trip to Helena was about four days this time of year, given track conditions and layovers and all. He knew men tended to pack lighter than women, but that case was awfully small even if it was only a one-way journey. And the weasely looking man had kept a smaller bag with him. The same bag he had seen him carry into The Hot Pepper Saloon the previous night.

Strange. Very strange indeed.

From across the table, Sandborne was talking to him, but Halstead had something else on his mind. "Bring that coach driver in here. I want to talk to him."

Sandborne set down his mug and did what Halstead had told him to do. When Sandborne delivered the message, Halstead watched the stocky coach driver pull out a watch from his vest and point to it, undoubtedly telling the deputy that the stage had a schedule to keep.

But Halstead was glad to see Sandborne would not be put off and corralled the bearded man into the hotel. The deputy had learned to not allow his youth to get in the way of his authority. "That boy has grit," Halstead said to himself.

Sandborne brought the stage driver to the table in the hotel dining room where Halstead was enjoying his coffee. Now that he could get a better look at him, he could tell the man was much younger than he had looked at a distance. His brown beard had made him look older, but his anger over the delay of his journey showed a man in his mid-to-late twenties.

"What the hell do you want, mister?" the driver demanded. "I've got a coach full of people and gear sitting and animals setting out in the cold, ready to go. I don't have time for conversation."

Halstead gestured to the star on the lapel of Sandborne's coat. "The deputy here tell you we're Deputy U.S. Marshals?"

"I don't care if you're the president of the United States," the coachman said. "I've got a schedule to keep and a boss who'll take a chunk out of my hide if I'm late again. So state your case and state it plain or you boys are gonna have a hell of a time keeping me here."

Halstead normally would have appreciated the man's fire, but today was not a normal day. "What's your name?"

"Pete Henry. What's it to you?"

"Got a list of passengers on your stagecoach, Pete Henry?"

"You mean the people who are freezing to death right now on account of your curiosity?" Henry took a folded piece of paper from his back pants pocket and flicked it on the table. "There it is. You can take a look at it for yourself. Just be quick about it."

Halstead eyed the insolent coach driver as he took the paper and unfolded it. It was a list of names handwritten on Wellspring Stagecoach Line letter head. Six passengers total. Three of them were women. He was not concerned about them and focused on the names of the men.

He handed the list back to the driver. "Who's that skinny passenger and the ugly one with him? The first two who boarded the coach."

Henry pocketed the list as he peered out the window to see who Halstead was talking about. "That would be Mr. Mannes and Mr. Poe. I'm running them down to the train station along with the others. They're catching the next train to Helena and I intend to see they make it with time to spare. So, if you boys will excuse me, I'll be on my way."

Sandborne took hold of the man's arm and held him where he had been standing.

Halstead asked, "Any idea if the telegraph lines are working yet?"

Pete Henry shook his head at the lawman's naivete. "Those lines snap during the first cold stretch, mister, and no one sets about fixing them until the thaw. Life's not as easy out here as it is for you boys back in Helena."

"But the line from the train station is usually working?"

"Sure hope so," Henry said. "I get paid to deliver telegrams from there every run. Keeps me in beer money. Why?"

Halstead took a coin from his vest pocket and handed it to him. "Because I want you to send a telegram from me to Marshal Aaron Mackey in Helena. Do you need to write that down?"

"Hell, Mr. Halstead. Everyone knows who Mackey is. Can't hardly forget that. Just write out what you want me to tell him and I'll do it."

"It's simple. Just say, 'Mr. Mannes and Mr. Poe are due to arrive in Helena on the next train from Wellspring.'"

The coach driver looked at the coin in his hand. "That's it?"

"That's it. The rest of the change is for your trouble. And, if you send it early enough before you swing back here, and the marshal responds, I'll double it when you give me his response."

Halstead was glad the driver was not facing Sandborne, lest the young deputy's face showed him he thought Halstead was crazy for offering so much money for so little.

Pete Henry pocketed the coin gladly. "You can count on me, deputy. I'll send that message off as soon as I reach the station. Don't you worry. Now, if you'll excuse me, I've got a coach waiting for its driver."

Sandborne made Pete Henry walk around him before he retook his seat across from Halstead, who went back to looking out the window at the stagecoach.

"You made of money or something?" Sandborne asked him.

"What makes you think I am?"

"On account of you promising that nitwit money for sending and delivering something we could've made him do for free."

Together, they watched Pete Henry climb up into the wagon box and release the brake as he snapped the reins and got his four-horse team moving.

The stagecoach may have been gone, but Sandborne did not let his point go. "You gave that insolent bastard ten whole dollars just to send and pick up a telegram when I could've ridden with him and done it for free."

"I need you here." Halstead looked for the waitress. He needed more coffee if he was going to verbally spar with Sandborne. "We have things to do."

"I'm glad to hear it," the younger deputy said, "but that still doesn't account for you giving that nasty cretin ten dollars. After how he talked to us in the beginning? He deserved a rifle butt to the kidney, not ten dollars."

Halstead caught the waitress's eye, and she filled his coffee mug. Sandborne's, too, though he was still too worked up about the coach driver to notice. "Why'd you go and do that for, Jeremiah? One minute, you're gunning down men just because they move funny and the next you're giving out money to insolents like it's nothing." He finally stopped talking long enough to realize his mug had been refilled and sipped some coffee. "You sure are a hard man to figure."

Halstead knew the question would gnaw at Sandborne until he got an answer, so Halstead gave him one. "Money's a tool, Joshua. Always has been, always will be. I paid him so he wouldn't forget to send the telegram. He'll have a layover of two days in Wellspring until the train comes back. Might be the train gets delayed, but he'll be anxious to collect on the money once he brings back Mackey's reply in the meantime."

Halstead had not expected his answer would be enough to satisfy Sandborne, and his expectations were met when he argued. "That idiot is going to take all that extra money you gave him and spend it in the first saloon he finds in Wellspring. And you know what he's going to do then?"

"Buy himself some whiskey?" Halstead guessed.

"Damned right he will," Sandborne said like a man who had just been vindicated. "And he'll tell every miner and drover and traveler in earshot how he just sent off a telegram for you and is waiting to hear back from Aaron Mackey himself. Ten minutes after he hits town, everyone in Wellspring will know what you told Aaron."

"Good." Halstead looked down at his coffee. "I'm counting on it."

Halstead looked up from his coffee and at Sandborne until his reason finally began to dawn on his deputy. The look on his face was worth far more than the ten dollars he had just given the coach driver, for it confirmed his suspicions about the young deputy. He was not dumb. He just was not accustomed to thinking a certain way. But with time and experience and age, he would probably make a fine lawman, just like Mackey had predicted he would.

"You want word to get out about Mannes and Poe and you're using that coach driver to help spread the word," Sandborne concluded. "But why?"

"I don't know," Halstead admitted. "They look odd to me and not just their looks but the way they act. Going to Helena with only one bag between them. And one smaller bag that Mannes kept secure on his lap. It just didn't feel right, so I figured I'd use Pete Henry's big mouth for my benefit. At the very least, word will spread that I'm in this part of the territory asking questions. Word's bound to reach Brunet or Zimmerman somehow, if they don't already know I'm here. If Mannes and Poe are innocent, Mackey will find that out once they reach Helena. If they're not, he'll find that out, too. Asking about them might cause some kind of reaction."

"It's a gamble," Sandborne said.

"It's a ten-dollar gamble that I figured was worth the risk. It'll probably fail. With my luck, the coachman doesn't drink and goes to bed at sunset. And if all he does is send off the telegram to Mackey, then it was still worth it."

"You didn't see the veins on his nose," Sandborne said. "Don't worry. He's a drinker and a talker, too, I'll bet."

Halstead saw Abby Newman come down the lobby stairs behind Sandborne's left shoulder. She was wearing a black dress with a white blouse underneath it. Despite its color, it did not look like she was in mourning. And her matching hat did not look like something a widow would wear.

Halstead got to his feet, and Sandborne turned around and stood, as well, following Halstead's lead.

She waved to them as she walked into the dining room toward their table. She smiled up at the younger deputy. "Good morning, Deputy Sandborne. It's a pleasure to see you again so soon."

Sandborne turned as beet red as he had when they had met at the jail the night before. "Pleasure's all mine, Miss Abby."

She looked at Halstead, and he found himself almost as flustered as Sandborne, though he hoped he hid it better.

"Good morning, Jeremiah. May I join you for a cup of coffee? I still have a few minutes before Jack is supposed to come fetch me with the wagon."

She had already taken a seat before Halstead could answer. The two deputy marshals sat down as the waitress brought over a fresh cup of coffee to her.

"Don't look so sour, Jeremiah," she said. "It's all going to work out just fine. Why even Jack thought it was worth a try if you'll remember."

He remembered their conversation in the jail when Jack had returned from his nap at the hotel the previous night just fine. He remembered how Jack had apparently agreed to her plan of going to Hard Scrabble without talking it over with him first.

"Doesn't mean I've got to like it," Halstead said. "Is he getting you a horse?"

"God no," she said. "Sitting sidesaddle is intolerable and sitting astride is scandalous. That's why he's getting a wagon from the livery. One with a cushion I believe. He claims it'll make all of the bumps and divots on the road to Hard Scrabble easier to take."

"Still wish you'd change your mind about going, Miss Abby," Sandborne said. "My partner here won't be fit company until you're back safe and sound."

"I think your partner here enjoys worrying for the sake of worrying," she said. "When his sulking gets to be too much, just remind him that I won't leave Jack's side the entire time I'm there."

Halstead did not need to be reminded, though he still did not like the idea of her going to Hard Scrabble. Yes, she could find out more information than Halstead or Sandborne could, but it still was not worth her risking her life.

"I'll remind him," Sandborne said, "but I understand why he's concerned. I've heard there's a dangerous element that has taken over that town. It would be a dangerous place for me or Jeremiah to ride into, much less a school-teacher."

She frowned at Halstead. "You put him up to saying all of that, didn't you?"

"Didn't have to," he told her. "It's just common sense. But what difference does it make now. You're going, and that's all there is to it."

She sat a little straighter in her chair as if she had just won a great victory. "I'm glad you're finally willing to listen to reason."

"Listening to reason and being smart enough to quit wasting my time when your mind is made up are two different things," Halstead told her. "If I thought it would do any good, I'd spend the next two hours talking until I was blue in the face about all the reasons why you shouldn't go. But I can tell there's no sense in trying because your mind is already made up. Your decision is final, and that's all there is to it."

The three of them looked out the window as Jack McBride pulled up in front of the hotel with a flatbed wagon pulled by a four-horse team.

"The marshal has impeccable timing." Abby finished her coffee and stood. Halstead and Sandborne stood with her.

"Now, you two stay out of trouble while Jack and I see whatever we can see. And as long as you promise me you won't worry too much, I promise to tell you all of the wonderful things I learned there today over a good bottle of Port this evening."

She looked at Halstead and said, "Would you be kind enough to walk me to the wagon? I always have such trouble climbing up on those things and I wouldn't want to fall over in front of the whole town. Would make a bad impression, seeing the schoolteacher fall flat on her backside and all."

Halstead went to her side and she slipped her arm through his as they walked out of the hotel dining room together.

Despite all of his concerns about her going to Hard Scrabble, he knew there was no point in discussing the matter with her. She had made up her mind that she was going and that was all there was to it. Besides, he enjoyed being this close to her and did not want anything to ruin this moment.

"I wanted to thank you, Jerry," she said as they walked through the lobby.

"For what?"

"For not fighting me too hard on going to Hard Scrabble," she told him. "I know you don't approve, and I appreciate your reasons for it. But I appreciate your faith in my judgment more. Tom would never have allowed it."

He hated the idea of Tom Ringham being with her, much less having a say in anything she did. "I figured you'd go on your own no matter what I said. At least with Jack around, you'll be reasonably safe."

"And useful," she said as they walked out onto the boardwalk. "Don't forget that."

She bid Jack McBride a good morning and he tipped his hat to her.

And as Halstead stood beside her to help her up into the wagon, she surprised him by kissing him softly on the cheek as she easily climbed up on her own power.

"Thank you, deputy," she said as she settled in next to McBride.

"We'll be back around three at the latest," McBride told

him. "We'll meet you over at the jail around then." He tossed a ring of iron keys, which Halstead caught easily. "The place is locked up good and tight now, but I don't like the idea of leaving Ringham unguarded, so if you boys could sit with him a while, I'd appreciate it."

"Keep an eye on our lady friend here," Halstead said with a bit more menace than he had intended.

"I intend to," McBride said as he cracked the reins and got the four-horse team moving along the thoroughfare toward the town of Hard Scrabble.

He watched the wagon until it was out of sight and only then realized Sandborne was standing beside him. "Looks like she left her brand on you."

Halstead had not expected such wisdom from his younger partner. "You can say that again."

"I was talking about her lipstick," Sandborne told him. "It's right there on your cheek."

Halstead pawed at his face and his fingers came away with a pale slick of red. He decided to leave it there. It was one of the few marks he wore that he did not mind the world seeing.

The two lawmen began walking toward the jail. Foot traffic on the boardwalk was light but just beginning to pick up as stores began to open for the day.

"I wouldn't brood over it so much, Jeremiah," Sandborne said. "Jack will see to it that no harm comes to her."

Halstead knew it, but it still did not make him feel any better about it. "I was awake half the night trying to figure out a better way than sending her in there and I couldn't. No one knows where Zimmerman and his men are hiding. No one I'd believe anyway. And with the snow being like it is up in the hills, there's not a good trail worth reading. We could be riding around in circles for weeks and—"

Halstead stopped walking.

Sandborne doubled back to him. "What's wrong?"

"Circles," Halstead repeated more for his benefit than Sandborne's. "Maybe we're onto something after all."

He ignored the confused look on Sandborne's face and quickened his pace to the jail. Some of the answers he had been looking for may have been in plain sight all along, but he had just been too dense to notice them.

Halstead unlocked the jailhouse door and was greeted by a fury of insults from Thomas Ringham.

"There he is," the prisoner said. His leg was still chained to the ring bolted into the wall that did not allow him to move past the white paint on the floor. "The great man himself. I've seen your kind before, Halstead. Buried most of them, too. Without that badge and that fancy rig, you're nothing but a lousy breed who's not worth a dead dog's carcass. How about you chuck that iron, unchain me, and fight me like a real man?"

Sandborne charged the prisoner, who fell backward onto his bed. "How about you shut your mouth before I break your jaw and keep you gagged until we reach Helena?"

Halstead was glad Sandborne had quieted him down because his attention was taken by something else. The large area map on the wall across from McBride's desk.

He used his finger to trace the area on the hilltop where Sandborne had marked the mines Zimmerman and his bunch had robbed. He traced them in order and got the spark of an idea.

"Circles," he said to himself.

The prisoner silenced for now, Sandborne stood next to him at the map. "What about them?"

Halstead talked it out, hoping his thoughts might become something real if he gave air to what he was thinking. "This is the hill where the mines were hit, right?"

"I sure hope so. I marked them on the map myself."

And he traced the robberies in the order they happened. "They hit the Mother and Country first, then the others in order, two a day until they finished the circle and ended almost right back where they started."

Sandborne looked up at the map, too. "We already knew that. I don't see what's so new about it."

"The order," Halstead said. "The order they hit them in. They hit them according to when the payroll was coming except in the last two incidents. The payroll arrived at the last mine on the same day as the Mother and Country. They could've started at either mine but didn't. They could've gone clockwise, even if they only hit two a day, but they didn't. They could've hit Mother and Country last, but they didn't. They started there for a reason."

He could tell Sandborne was beginning to understand what Halstead was saying. "Why?"

"I don't know," Halstead admitted, "but the reason's got to be here." He looked at the area of the map that was west of the Mother and Country mine and east of Hard Scrabble.

So did Sandborne. "Looks pretty unsettled until you get to town."

A ridiculous giggle from Ringham made Halstead and Sandborne turn around to face the prisoner.

Halstead asked, "What's so funny?"

"You two are really something special." Ringham laughed. "I guess they'll pin a star on just about any idiot these days."

Halstead slowly began walking toward him. "You know something about that area we don't?"

"I know something about a lot of things you don't." Ringham laughed. "The answer's right there on the map, but you two are too dumb to see it." He looked Halstead up and down in disgust. "And I thought you people were supposed to be able to read the ground."

Sandborne charged the prisoner, but Halstead held him back. "Tell us what you're talking about and say it plain or me and Jerry are going to take turns kicking the hell out of you until you do."

Ringham got off his bed. "Come ahead. I'll take on the both of you at the same time. Shackled leg or not."

Again, Halstead had to restrain Sandborne. "I'll make you a deal, Ringham. The same deal you offered me when we walked in here." He took the iron keys from his pocket and handed them to Sandborne. "My partner here will unlock that chain on your leg, and you'll have a chance at me. Hell, I'll even let you have the first three swings before I even make a fist. You beat me, you're free to go. But if you lose, you stay locked up here. I'll even keep my coat on and my guns, too."

Ringham ran his tongue over his lips. The very idea of winning his freedom was enough to make him salivate. "Then take the chain off, boys, and let's get going."

Halstead shook his head. "Not until you tell me what we're missing on that map. Tell us and Sandborne here will unlock the chains. You can have your shot at me, but not before."

"It's almost too easy," Ringham sneered as he pointed to the map behind them. "The map's blank because there's nothing out there except a bunch of old trapper shacks scattered all over the woods. When the stupid bastards wiped out the animals, the trappers moved on, but the shacks are still there. Drifters use them now and again as hideouts, especially if they're wanted somewhere. Most of them have trees growing through them by now, but there are a few that are still in decent shape."

Halstead knew that would explain the reports about Zimmerman and Brunet being in the area and remaining unseen. A man might be able to stand sleeping out in the cold for a night or two but would need a roof over his head if he hoped to survive for longer than that.

An old trapper's shack would be exactly what Zimmerman would need. Maybe the rest of the men in his gang, too, if they could find enough shacks to hide them all.

"You sure about these shacks, Ringham?" Halstead asked.

"I ought to be," he said. "I've cleaned the pockets of many an outlaw when I played Hard Scrabble back when it was a thriving town. Ask any old-timer you can find. That's why your friend McBride didn't know about them. He's too new at his job yet."

Halstead and Sandborne looked at each other.

"Easy enough for us to ride around up there and see if we find anything," the younger deputy said. "Snow might cover the tracks, but they'll have a fire lit in the stove if they're holed up there. Should be easy enough to see that."

Halstead was about to agree with him until he heard Ringham rattling his chain. "I lived up to my end of the bargain, Halstead. Time for you to live up to yours. Unless you're too scared." He sneered. "Or a liar."

Halstead considered himself neither and decided it was

time to teach Thomas Ringham a lesson he would not soon forget.

To Sandborne he said, "Unlock the man and stand aside."

Sandborne fumbled with the keys. "You sure about this? He's mighty worked up."

Halstead nodded, and Sandborne approached the prisoner.

"If you kick him or go for his gun," Halstead warned, "I'll shoot you dead."

The gambler kept his leg straight and his hands at his sides as Sandborne worked the lock. "The only one I plan on going for is you, breed."

Sandborne undid the lock and stepped aside, a concerned look on his face.

Ringham flexed his newly freed leg, trying to get the blood moving in it again.

"Take all the time you need," Halstead said. "I don't want you claiming any exceptions after this is over."

"What'll you care?" Ringham grinned. "You'll be long dead by then."

As the gambler brought up his fists and inched his way over the white paint on the floor, Halstead reminded him, "You get the first three shots free, then I start swinging."

Ringham laughed. "All I need is one."

He fired a hard right hand at Halstead's head, which the deputy marshal easily ducked.

*One.*

The gambler closed in and fired a left that would have broken a couple of ribs had it connected, but Halstead had already jumped back out of the way.

*Two.*

Realizing he was down to his last free shot, Ringham took his time. He kept his hands up and bluffed with a right hand before firing a left hook that would have broken Halstead's jaw.

If it had hit its target. Which it did not.

*Three.*

Halstead ducked under the hook and buried a hard right cross that connected solidly with Ringham's liver. The shock of the blow sent the air from the gambler's lungs and made his legs buckle as he crumpled to the jailhouse floor in a heap.

Halstead looked at Sandborne. "Drag him back and lock him up again like the dog he is."

Sandborne eagerly complied, dragging the gasping Ringham back behind the white paint and chaining his leg once again to the ring on the wall.

Halstead flexed the fingers on his right hand, as he had hit Ringham a bit harder than he had intended. "Now, the deputy and I are going to ride out to that spot on the map. If we find those shacks you talked about, you'll continue to receive good treatment. If we find you lied to us, I'll see to it you're hogtied until we get to the courthouse in Helena."

Halstead took his Winchester '76 and '86 down from the rifle rack while Sandborne removed his rifle before locking the jailhouse door behind them.

And as they began the long walk to the livery where their horses were kept, Sandborne said, "Never saw a man drop like that before. Not from no punch to the gut, anyway."

"Liver shot," Halstead told him. "You could hit Goliath in that spot at just the right time and even he'd crumple to the ground. Don't ask me why. I just know that it works. And now, so do you. It's a good trick to know, but it doesn't work unless you hit them right on the button, so don't count on it working every single time."

"I'll remember that," Sandborne promised. "Where'd you learn that trick anyway? Your time in that prison in El Paso?"

"Nope. The Sisters of Saint Dominic Academy for Children where I grew up."

Sandborne did not look like he believed that. "You mean a preacher taught you that?"

"Nuns," Halstead said. "Sister Rosella and her yard stick could break up a playground fight in no time flat."

Sandborne seemed to consider that information for a while. "Wish she was here with us now. I've got a feeling we'll be needing her before this is over."

"Yep," Halstead said. "Me, too."

# Chapter 16

Halstead had never seen so much snow.

The snow on the hillside leading toward the mines was deep and treacherous. It had drifted as high as the chests of the horses he and Sandborne rode. But it was mostly powder, so they had little trouble plowing their way through it. The animals quickly recovered from any stumbles from the ice that lay beneath the snow.

As the drifts had obscured any path on the ground, Halstead and Sandborne found themselves following a trail above ground. Sandborne rode point, looking for broken branches and spaces in the overgrowth that still poked up from the snow. Halstead knew they might be riding to nowhere, but even if this turned out to be a waste of time, it was better than sitting back in town wondering what was happening with McBride and Abby.

About an hour into their excursion on the hillside, they began to find some of the old shacks Ringham had told them about back in the jail. Snow had completely covered most of them, and years of exposure to the elements had turned their wooden roofs to little more than splinters. Trees had begun to grow through five of the structures they had found, just as Ringham had said. The prisoner was many things, but he had told the truth about this.

Halstead pulled Col to a stop when the deputy quietly raised his right hand. Halstead knew he may have had more experience with a gun, but Sandborne had grown up in Montana. He knew country like this, and it would be foolish to not heed his warning.

Halstead looked in the direction his friend was looking but could not see anything. It was only when Sandborne waved him to join him that he was able to see why they had stopped.

About fifty yards away from where they were standing was an old wooden shack where the snow had been cleared and fouled by horses. A lot of horses according to the discoloration of the snow. The doorway to the shack had been cleared by footprints, not a shovel or broom. A thin stream of white smoke rose from the chimney, which Halstead figured explained why there was only a thin layer of snow on the roof.

Someone lived there. Someone who had a lot of friends.

Halstead knew there was only one thing to do.

"Stay here," he whispered to Sandborne. "I'll ride over and check it out."

But Halstead was surprised when Sandborne gripped his arm as he began to step out of the saddle. "Not this time, boss. You know what you're doing in town, but you're a tenderfoot out here in the timber. I'll take a look at it first and let you know if it's safe."

Again, Halstead knew the younger man was right and remembered his place. Mackey had sent Sandborne with him for this very reason, so he might as well let him do his part of the job.

Sandborne handed him his horse's reins before he

dropped from the saddle and unsheathed his Winchester before he slowly began to creep through the snow toward the cabin.

Unable to sit there and do nothing, Halstead quietly eased his Winchester '76 from the scabbard and held it on his hip. If Sandborne got into trouble, he would be ready to return fire.

The sun was directly overhead and the sky was as blue and clear as a man could hope for. If anyone moved inside that cabin, Halstead would see it.

He watched Sandborne move silently through the snow. He did not step over it as much as he plowed through it as their horses had done. He moved slowly, too slowly for Halstead's taste, but deliberately. He kept his rifle ready without taking his eyes off the shack.

He approached it at an angle, away from the doors or windows. Smart, Halstead thought. He would have charged up to the building, dismounted, and kicked the door in before anyone inside knew he was there. He was learning quite a bit just by watching the younger man.

Halstead gripped his Winchester tighter as he watched Sandborne reach the side of the cabin, where he stood completely still for a minute or more before continuing onto the porch.

Halstead turned Col and Sandborne's horse toward the cabin. He brought his Winchester up to his shoulder and aimed at the front door. The more he looked at it, the more he could see the door appeared to be open. On a cold day like this, anyone with good sense would have made sure it was closed. He began to doubt if anyone was in there, but kept his rifle trained on the door anyway.

He watched Sandborne reach the door, then use his rifle

butt to slowly force it completely open as he dropped to a knee.

Halstead peered into the open doorway, waiting for any target to present itself. He waited for movement. A rifle flash.

But nothing happened.

Sandborne slowly got to his feet and crept into the cabin. His Winchester led the way.

The younger man was smart enough to stay in the doorway while he looked over the inside of the shack.

Halstead shifted his aim to the surrounding area in case someone might be lying in wait for them in the snow. And even though he did not know what to look for, he could not see anyone there. Everything he saw began to look purple after he blinked his eyes and he wondered if he was going snow blind. He had heard about it but had not experienced it yet.

Sandborne cut loose with a whistle and Halstead saw him back out onto the porch waving him toward the shack. Halstead kept his Winchester against his hip as he led both horses toward it.

Sandborne took his horse's reins and wrapped them around a porch beam as Halstead did the same.

When Sandborne spoke, he spoke in a low tone. "Keep your voice down out here. Sound carries for miles and we don't want to risk marking us."

Halstead nodded, but was more concerned about the shack. "Find anything in there?"

Sandborne beckoned him to follow him inside. "You're definitely going to want to see this. Just step as softly as I do."

Winchester still in hand, Halstead entered the shack.

The smell of the one-room place struck him first. The smell of wet dog and horse dung mixed with the wooden fire that was blazing in an ancient iron stove. Two filthy bedrolls were still laid out against the far walls but the fabric looked frozen, like they had not been slept in for days.

That was when he saw what Sandborne had been talking about. A crooked table had been placed in the middle of the floor away from the stove. On the table was an old bear trap pried open and locked.

A stick of dynamite sat on the pan that triggered the jaws and he noticed the fuse was long and upright.

In front of the trap was a piece of paper with handwriting on it. And although he had only glanced at it, he could see it was addressed to him.

"What the hell is this?" Halstead asked Sandborne.

"I don't know," the deputy admitted, "but whoever left it knew what they were doing. That stick is mighty old, which makes it dangerous. Look at it closely. See how it looks almost wet?"

Halstead had not noticed it at first, but now that Sandborne had called his attention to it, he did. "Glycerin."

"That's right," Sandborne agreed. "You don't have to light it to make it go off. Just dropping it could do the trick. And even if it didn't, the jaws of that trap are liable to make a spark if they close, setting that fuse to burning."

"Just what I'd expect from Zimmerman," Halstead told him. "How should we handle it."

"Real carefully." Sandborne reached out with a gloved hand and gently plucked the stick from the bear trap, then crept outside and laid it in the snow several feet away from the shack.

When he came back inside, he said, "That's about as

stable as we can make it, but the sooner we get out of here, the better I'll feel. That thing can still go off at any time."

Halstead turned his attention to the letter. He did not want to read anything from Zimmerman but found he did not really have a choice.

Knowing Sandborne was still working on how to learn to read, he took the letter from the envelope and read it out loud.

*Dear Jeremiah:*

*If you're reading this, I'm disappointed because it means my plan to kill you failed. I had arranged this setup fully expecting you to come barging in here in your usual way, set off the glycerin or the trap I set and blow yourself to kingdom come. I'll be watching the treetops constantly in the hopes that I'll see a large plume of smoke signaling your demise.*

*But since you* are *reading this, I suppose my plan failed. Pity. You deserve to leave this world in the same manner of fire and fury with which you have stormed through it. I believe a man's death should reflect the way he lived his life, don't you?*

*And although I'm disappointed that you're still alive, I'm heartened by the fact that you'll live to see what I've become. To see what I shall make of this place. In many ways, you're the one responsible for it. For just as you no longer appear to be the angry brute who kicks in doors and blasts away, I am no longer the nomadic outlaw you knew back in Silver Cloud. I'm better and I have a plan.*

*By the time you've read this, the wind has already pushed a small pebble from the mountain top, sending it downhill with exceptional speed. That pebble will continue to pick up dirt and debris as it rolls, growing larger and larger until it causes an avalanche that brings the entire mountainside down with it.*

*There's no one to blame for an avalanche. It's just a force of nature, just as you and I are forces of nature. And the most constant force of nature is change.*

*People do change, Jeremiah. Even people like you and me. I plan on proving that to you and everyone else before my work is done.*

*I know words are cheap to men like you and me. We believe only in what we can see. And you will see, Jeremiah. See so many wonderful things through my eyes. You'll see the empire I plan to build. You will live to see your own irrelevance and, slowly, your own destruction.*

*I'm not going to kill you, Jeremiah. Any fool can die. I'm going to do what my trap apparently has failed to do.*

*I'm going to destroy you from the inside out and my greatest joy will be that you will live long enough to see it.*

> *Until that glorious day,*
> *Zimmerman.*

Halstead crumpled the paper and threw it into the stove. He watched it burn until the last trace of it was gone.

Sandborne cleared his throat. "Sounds to me like Zimmerman's lost his mind."

"No, he hasn't," Halstead said. "That's the problem."

Sandborne took off his hat and ran his gloved hand over his curly hair. "Don't know what you want to do next, boss. We can ride up through the hills and look for him, but I wouldn't suggest it. I see a lot of empty pegs on the walls where these trappers liked to hang their traps, so it stands to reason he might've buried a couple of them out there in the snow."

But Halstead already knew what he had to do. "We're going back to town and wait for Jack and Abby to come back. We'll figure out what we have to do next." He pulled out his knife and took a bullet from his belt. "But I need to do something first."

Sandborne watched him take his Bowie knife and carve something into the brass casing.

It was the letter "Z." And he placed the bullet standing upright on the pan of the bear trap.

"Let's go," Halstead told his partner.

Sandborne walked outside and climbed into the saddle. Halstead did the same thing right after him.

As they traced their steps back through the ruined snow, Halstead found he had to get something off his chest. "He was right, you know. In the note. I was planning on riding up to that place and kick in the door. I didn't is thanks to you." He looked at Sandborne. "That's twice now you've saved my life."

The younger deputy shrugged. "Guess it's becoming a habit."

Halstead supposed it was. "I hope it's one you don't plan on breaking any time soon."

# Chapter 17

One question had bothered Abby Newman during the hour-long ride to Hard Scrabble Township. And now that the place was within sight, she decided to ask it.

"Jack, why do we have a four-horse team to pull a one-horse wagon?"

"Just my way of putting people off is all," he explained. "See, if we come trotting into town with just one horse, people are liable to figure it's just a friendly visit. But showing up with a team of horses will set folks to wondering what that crazy bastard McBride is up to. Might be coming to haul some folks back to Battle Brook with him. Might be for some other reason. Pays to keep them guessing. Besides, four horses got us here much quicker than one, which means we'll get back quicker, too. That ought to put a smile on Deputy Halstead's face, and, in my experience, it always pays to make those federal types as happy as you can when you can."

Abby had not thought about it that way. "What do you think of Deputy Halstead? Just between us, of course."

McBride seemed to consider the question as they rode past a battered old sign welcoming them to Hard Scrabble

Township. "If I didn't like him, I'd keep my opinion to myself and just tell you he's a good man so I could leave it at that. But it just so happens that I really do think he's a good man, Miss Abby, and not just with a gun, either."

That intrigued her. "What do you mean?"

"Gun work of any kind never impressed me much," McBride explained. "Any fool can shoot a man dead for any number of reasons. But it takes a special man to know when to shoot and when to keep your gun holstered. Skill isn't enough in our line of work. Neither is the ability to kill. And if you think too much, you're liable to get yourself shot. If you think too little, you'll probably shoot the wrong person."

She figured he must have seen the look of confusion on her face, because he explained further, "There's a fine line a lawman has to walk, and it's a crooked one at that. It changes with every new challenge we face, and if we don't change with it, we become predictable. And predictability, Miss Abby, will cause you to walk into a bullet every damned time. That's as close as I can come to an explanation of the kind of lawman Jeremiah Halstead is."

She had a clearer picture of what McBride had meant but knew she could never understand it fully. Only someone who did that kind of work could truly appreciate it, just like McBride or Halstead would never know the joy of seeing the look in a student's eyes when they finally grasped a mathematical equation or appreciated the words of Shakespeare for the first time.

She held her shawl a little tighter around her shoulders. "Jeremiah is a good man, isn't he?"

But Jack McBride did not answer. He was too busy looking at all of the activity taking place in Hard Scrabble.

They rode through a bustling place that rivaled Battle

Brook in terms of activity. She saw men and women in the process of sprucing up every building in town. Broken planks on the boardwalks were being pried up and replaced. Windows were being washed and boards that covered them removed. Old signs were taken down only to have new signs replace them.

Wagons hauling goods and tools from the general store crossed their path several times and she knew it was only thanks to McBride's skill with horses that he avoided a collision.

She saw men on ladders at what appeared to be the general store. They were lowering the old sign to drop to the ground as they raised the new sign in the air by rope. It read: "Valhalla General Store" in fancy black lettering.

She was certainly impressed, if not confused by everything that was going on around them. "Hard Scrabble certainly doesn't look like a forgotten town to me," she said to McBride.

"Me neither." She noticed the town marshal looked more concerned than impressed by what he saw. "Something's wrong, and I'm afraid I can't honor part of our deal, Miss Abby. I'm not going to let you out of my sight. Not until I know what the hell is going on around here."

He steered the team through the gangs of workmen who were heading in both directions on the thoroughfare and pulled the wagon to a halt in front of the bank. He pulled the brake lever and began to climb down from the wagon box. "You just stay right where you are until I talk with Cal Hubbard. He's the bank president, so if anyone knows what's going on around here, it'll be him."

But Abigail Newman had no intention of sitting alone in a wagon in the cold mountain air while work crews went back and forth amid the hammering and banging and sawing all around her.

"I'm coming in with you," she said as she began to climb down on her own power before he could object.

McBride was waiting for her when she came around the other side of the wagon. "I don't think that's a good idea. You'd be better off waiting out here."

She was beginning to lose patience with the town marshal's idea of chivalry. "Damn it, Jack. It's a bank, not a whore house or a saloon. I'll be fine."

Startled by her frankness, he followed her into the bank.

The inside of the bank reminded her of similar places she had seen in Denver. Not as ornate as New York or Chicago institutions, of course, but its high ceilings and brass teller cages conveyed a certain timeless stability that investors would find comforting.

She walked past the people lined up waiting for tellers and went straight to a desk where a sour young clerk with dark, curly hair sat writing in a ledger. She judged him to be in his mid-twenties, just as she was, and was too taken with whatever he was writing at the moment to care about what happened beyond the boundaries of his desk.

"Excuse me," she said, interrupting his work. "But Marshal McBride and I would like to meet Mr. Hubbard." She looked back at McBride. "That is his name, isn't it?"

McBride nodded. "You've got a good head for names, Miss Abby."

She turned her attention back to the sullen youth whose mood had brightened considerably. She decided he looked better when he was frowning. "Miss Abigail Newman and Marshal Jack McBride to see Mr. Hubbard. Now if it's convenient."

"And even if it's not," McBride added. "Tell him we're in a hurry and not apt to wait around."

The young man wrote the names down on a piece of paper and ran to the back where she imagined Mr. Hubbard's office was located.

She turned again to McBride. "Strange little man, isn't he?"

"Can't say I blame him. Hard Scrabble's a strange place. Especially because I kept seeing signs out there calling it Valhalla."

The curly haired clerk returned and asked them to follow him. He led them to a door where Abby saw "H. Calvin Hubbard—Bank President" hand-painted on the door.

The clerk held the door open as they went inside.

The bank president, who had a fleshy pale face and impressive white mutton chops and a matching moustache, got to his feet and extended his hand across his desk. "You must be Miss Newman, I take it. The new schoolteacher from Battle Brook."

She took his hand. "I'm afraid my reputation precedes me."

Hubbard laughed in that automatic way that bank presidents tend to do before the matter of money is discussed. "Your reputation is sound, Miss Newman, I assure you, and our need for a teacher in these parts is great. As I'm sure you saw when you rode in here, our town's fortunes have recently changed for the better."

Hubbard looked at the tall lawman looming behind Abby. His smile dimmed a little as they shook hands. "Morning, Jack. Always good to see you."

Hubbard beckoned them both to sit in the chairs opposite his desk. Abby was glad to sit, while McBride preferred to stand. She imagined he planned to use his great height to his advantage as a way of intimidating the bank president.

"What's the story with all the work going on out there?" McBride asked him. "And what's with this Valhalla business?"

Hubbard brightened again. "A miracle, Jack. Nothing short of a miracle. Why, only last week, our tiny town was destined to be forgotten, withering on the vine while all commerce moved to Battle Brook when, lo and behold, an investor came along and infused new capital into our community."

He looked out the window at the ladders and workers passing back and forth. "It does my heart good to see a sense of life begin to course through the veins of the old town again."

McBride strode over to the window and looked for himself. "You're laying it on pretty thick, aren't you, Cal?"

"I don't think it's possible to lay it on thick enough, to borrow your term." Hubbard laughed. "This time last week, we were getting ready to pack up and leave, and now we have a renewed sense of purpose."

Abby watched McBride look out on the town. His long nose and busy moustache gave him a decidedly dour look. "See you changed the jail some. Took down the sign and the bars from the windows, too."

Hubbard laughed it off. "Think nothing of it, Jack. You'll still be the town marshal around here as in Battle Brook. We'll also be hiring a constabulary of our own soon to keep an eye on things here. We don't want disorder creeping in to spoil all of our new success."

"First time I've ever heard you give a damn about that."

McBride nodded out the window. "What's with all these signs I'm seeing with "Valhalla" written on them?" He looked at Hubbard. "You changing the name of the town?"

"Our new investors insist upon it," the bank president said. "They believe a new name will spruce up the place. Make people think about it differently. And, as I'm sure you remember, I was never particularly fond of the name 'Hard Scrabble' anyway."

"You ain't the mayor, Cal," McBride reminded him. "And you can't just up and change the town's name on a whim. That can only be done if the town approves it and if Helena goes along with it."

Abby watched Hubbard's eyes grow hard. "We're doing that, Jack. As we speak."

McBride took a final suspicious look out the window and turned back to Hubbard. "Who's this new investor of yours anyway?"

Hubbard held his chubby hands apart. "I'm afraid that part is confidential for the moment. They wish to remain anonymous until everything is official, you see."

McBride crossed his thin arms. "I'm not going to ask you again, Cal."

Abby watched the bank president frown and look around his desk as if he might find something there that would help him keep the town marshal at bay. Finally, he looked up at McBride and said, "I hate to be rude, but I think this is a conversation best held in private." He smiled at Abby. "No offense meant, Miss Newman."

McBride did not budge. "She might not be offended, but I am. You've got public work going on out there on a public street. What's more, you've changed around the jail, which is a building under my jurisdiction, not yours. Since that work's going on in public, the public has a right to know who's paying for it. Now, you can either tell me here, or you can tell me in the jail back in Battle Brook. We've got a real nasty prisoner back there who'd be awfully glad to make your acquaintance. What's it going to be?"

Abby was glad McBride could be forceful when he chose to be.

Hubbard shut his eyes as he let out a long breath. "Sometimes I forget you're an educated man."

"West Point," McBride said. "Now talk."

Hubbard looked down at his desk again as he said, "The Valhalla Mining and Investment Company."

"And just who the hell are they?"

"I don't know," Hubbard said as he looked up at McBride. "And, quite frankly, I don't care, either."

"That's a dangerous way to look at things, Cal."

Hubbard surprised Abby by slowly getting to his feet. "I came to this town ten years ago when it was little more than a mining camp. I supplied a safe, reliable place where hard-working men could sleep well at night knowing their money was in safe hands. In all that time, we've helped hundreds of families have a better life through loans and investments. We've weathered every financial crisis that has struck this country because of me and me alone. My judgment has kept this institution solvent, sir. My management has allowed this community to thrive when others were wiped off the map and forgotten. You know that as well as anyone. You were here for what, four years?"

"Less than that," McBride allowed, "but just because you've been right before doesn't mean you're right now. I've seen some smart people do some pretty stupid things when they're desperate and Hard Scrabble's just about as desperate a place as I've ever seen."

He pointed a long finger out the window. "Stuff like this is never free. It always comes at a price, and I want to know who's behind it."

Hubbard surprised her by holding his ground. "And I already told you that I don't know. Those men out there bringing this town back to life were hired by the investment company. Some are miners who've volunteered to give their time to bringing Valhalla to life. I should think a man in your position would appreciate that."

"A man in my position is responsible for having answers," McBride argued. "And I don't believe you're going headlong into something like this without knowing who's behind it. So I'll break my own rule and repeat myself, Cal. Either you tell me here or you tell me in the Battle Brook jail."

Hubbard clasped his hands behind him and walked over to the window next to McBride. He looked outside and beamed at what he saw. "Just look at all the progress those men are making in such a short amount of time. Why, by the end of the week, neither of us will be able to recognize the place. You can take me to Battle Brook in shackles if you want, Jack, but it won't change my answer and it won't bode well for you."

Abby watched McBride turn to face him as he balled his hands into fists. "Meaning?"

"Meaning it's not against the law for me to refuse to share investor information with the public," Hubbard explained. "You have no good reason to arrest me, but if you do, my investors won't like it. They'll make noise in Helena and, with statehood only a week away, there'll be an awful lot of people looking for friends all over Montana.

They won't stand for the kind of lawless bullying abided by a territory. And they won't look kindly on a small-town lawman overstepping his boundaries."

Abby gasped as McBride snatched Hubbard by the collar and pulled him away from the window. "You threatening me you little son of a bitch? Fine. I'm arresting you for impeding justice and anything else I can think of between here and the jail."

Hubbard did not try to break McBride's grip on his collar. If anything, he stood perfectly still. "I'd be quick to unhand me if I were you, Jack. In fact, I'd do it right now."

McBride jerked the banker toward him. "Give me one good reason why I should."

"The town's full of good reasons," Hubbard told him, "but I can see five standing across the street right now. Go ahead. Take a closer look for yourself. Don't take my word for it. Tell me what you see."

Abby rose to her feet and joined them at the window. She saw five burly men standing in the thoroughfare. The filthy, matted hides they wore looked like they had never been washed, save for the occasional rain or snowfall. The men wearing them were all different heights, but bore the same dead looks in their eyes. The rifles in their hands left no doubt in her mind about the kind of men they were or what they would do if they saw Jack McBride hauling H. Calvin Hubbard off in a wagon.

McBride had clearly seen them. "They won't do much when I have a gun at your belly."

Hubbard laughed. "Don't let their ragged appearance fool you, Jack. They're dead shots, all of them. You'll be dead before you reach the wagon. And if they miss, I can almost guarantee you their friends won't. You're a tough man, McBride, but no one's tough enough to live against odds like that, particularly when it's not worth the bother."

She watched McBride's left fist redden as he gripped the banker's collar tighter. She wondered if he was actually considering taking Hubbard with them anyway, despite the risk. She wondered what Jeremiah would do under similar circumstances and prayed he would see reason. She prayed that Jack McBride would see reason now.

Hubbard seemed to sense a shift in the lawman as he added, "I can guarantee your safety if you leave without me, but not if you insist on taking me in." He glanced over at Abby. "And if I can't appeal to your own sense of well-being, there's Miss Newman to think about. I won't be held responsible for what happens to her after your death, but I don't think you want to put her through that ordeal."

McBride rammed Hubbard's head against the window hard enough to crack it and draw blood on the left side of the banker's head. He drew his Colt and slid the barrel under Hubbard's chin before cocking the hammer.

Abby saw the men in the thoroughfare begin to walk toward the bank.

"Jack," she called out. "Please don't."

McBride kept the Colt where it was as he leaned in closer to speak directly into Hubbard's ear. "I don't know what you're up to, Cal, but I've got a pretty good idea of where all this new money is coming from. If any of this filth finds its way to Battle Brook, I'll come back when your friends aren't around. And I will hold you accountable then. My way."

McBride released the banker with a shove and withdrew his gun but did not holster it. Without looking at her, he said, "Come on, Miss Abby. I think it's time to go."

She grabbed her purse tightly as she moved behind McBride, who followed her out of the office.

Hubbard called after them. "You'll stay out of Valhalla if you know what's good for you, McBride! You and that half-breed marshal friend of yours. Valhalla is the home of the gods, McBride, not mice!"

Abby suddenly felt very small as she walked through the bank lobby as fast as she could manage, praying her feet did not get caught up in her skirts. She could feel every eye in the bank following them as they left, the way she imagined a pack of wolves watch their prey in the wild. She just wanted to get on that wagon and back to Battle Brook as soon as possible. Back to safety. Back to Jeremiah.

She shrieked when she walked into a man blocking her path and recoiled, backing up into McBride as she did so. She looked up and saw a tall, dark-haired man with broad shoulders and the blackest, deepest-set eyes she had ever seen. His broad chin was clean-shaven, and he was wearing a new gray suit, but looked every bit the brute as the men outside the bank did.

The grin he offered her made her feel filthy, even as he stood aside and touched the brim of his hat.

"My apologies, miss," he said in a voice she knew would haunt her dreams. "Forgive me and my friend here for being thoughtless."

She stole a quick glance at the smaller man beside him. He looked small and insignificant and vaguely familiar, though she did not dare to try to recognize him. Every fiber of her being wanted to be as far away from this place as possible.

McBride gently urged her to start walking again, which she gladly did.

Once out on the street, she continued to keep her head down as she climbed up into the wagon, willing McBride to move faster than he already was.

The cat calls and whistles she now drew from some of the men on the street sent a shiver down her spine as she drew her wrap around her as tightly as she could and buried her face in McBride's slender arm.

The town marshal released the brake and snapped the reins, bringing the four horses to life. Abby shut her eyes as tight as she could and did her best to drown out the vulgar deeds the men shouted at her as McBride turned the wagon past them and headed back toward Battle Brook.

With a straight road ahead of them, McBride cracked the reins again, bringing the team up to a full gallop.

She kept her head tucked against McBride's arm until she felt the team begin to slow and McBride gently nudged her to sit upright again. "We're safe, Miss Abby. We're more than two miles from them now and no one's following us. You can open your eyes now."

She found the strength to sit up on her own and opened her eyes. She saw nothing but the same snow covered ground she had enjoyed on the ride into town. A ride that felt as if it had been ages ago.

McBride spoke to her in a warm, soothing voice. "I'm sorry we're going to have to travel a bit slower back to town, but I was counting on the horses having more of a rest. Don't worry. No one can hurt us now."

But no matter how tightly she held her wrap around her shoulders, the cold only grew worse. It felt like it was in her bones now, and where it would remain for a long time before it was good and ready to let her go.

If ever.

\* \* \*

Zimmerman pushed Doug Wycoff into the bank president's office and shut the door behind him. He cut a low whistle when he saw the sorry state of Cal Hubbard's face.

A thin stream of blood ran down the left side of his face from a cut just above his eye. He pitched his head forward at an awkward angle, allowing the blood that ran down his face to drip onto the carpet instead of on his suit. Hubbard pulled a handkerchief from his back pocket and winced as he held it against his wound.

"That's one bad looking war wound you've got yourself there." Zimmerman laughed. "A might nastier than them papercuts you're used to."

Hubbard was clearly in no mood for jokes. "It was that big bastard McBride who did this to me. Stuck a gun under my chin and threatened me while he was at it."

Zimmerman put his hands in his pockets and nodded toward the window. A thin crack had formed in it just left of center and ran down to the lower corner. "Looks like his temper took its toll on the glass, too. It'll be a while before we can get a new piece cut. A month or so at the soonest."

"Did you hear what I just told you?" Hubbard kept his head tilted and the handkerchief on his wound as he went back to his desk. "McBride not only cut me. He pulled a gun on me. Threatened me, too."

"I heard you," Zimmerman said. "What about?"

Hubbard was about to answer but stopped when he finally noticed there was someone else in the office with them. "Who's this idiot? And what are you doing here?

I thought you were going to ride to Wellspring to make sure the others got on the train."

"Change of plans," Zimmerman explained as he clapped his companion on the shoulder. "As for this fine gentleman, you might want to have a bit more respect. For he is the man who's going to help us double our fortune overnight. Name's Doug Wycoff, the teller I told you about from the Battle Brook Bank."

"Senior teller, actually," Wycoff corrected him. "Believe it or not, there is a difference."

Hubbard softened his tone. "Forgive my lack of manners, Mr. Wycoff. As you can see, I haven't had the best of mornings."

"No apologies necessary, sir," Wycoff said. "And I hope you know you can count on my discretion. Anything you say in front of me will not pass my lips."

Zimmerman knew he had chosen the right man for the job he had in mind. Wycoff was one accommodating fellow.

The outlaw turned his attention to Hubbard. "What did you say that made McBride go off the rails?"

"He brought that new schoolteacher to meet me," Hubbard explained. "Unannounced, of course, and was full of questions about all of the work he saw on the street. He wanted me to tell him who the investors were, and I refused. I had to give him something, so I gave him the name of the company, but not who was behind it."

Zimmerman observed the banker as he went on to explain his ordeal. He did not care as much about what had happened as he did about how much Hubbard might have told McBride before he left.

McBride was a lawman and would hear things a certain way. The presence of the schoolteacher troubled him. Between the both of them, they would give Halstead a pretty accurate picture of what was going on in town. And of what Hubbard had told them.

When Hubbard had finished relating his run-in with McBride, he glared at Zimmerman. "Well? What are you going to do about it?"

Zimmerman sensed the banker had told him everything and held nothing back. He had told McBride just enough to avoid getting arrested, not that The Spoilers would have allowed him to take Hubbard anywhere. The fact that no harm had come to McBride or the woman was the best result that he could have hoped for given the circumstances.

Hubbard pounded his desk with his right hand while continuing to keep pressure on his wound with his left. "Well? Have you suddenly become a mute? Say something!"

Zimmerman took a seat in front of Hubbard's fancy desk and gestured to Wycoff to do the same. "Not much I can do. He roughed you up some. Sorry I wasn't here to stop that, but I was getting cleaned up after my night spent out of doors and bringing our new friend here from Battle Brook. Running into them as they were leaving wasn't ideal, but I can't do much about that, either. I don't think McBride recognized me."

"McBride doesn't know me," Wycoff offered. "He almost never comes into the bank and I rarely see him in town. I keep pretty much to myself."

Zimmerman rapped him lightly on the shoulder. "But that's going to change real soon after tonight, won't it, Doug?"

The senior teller forced a smile, though Zimmerman

thought he still looked more nervous than happy. Good. His nerves would keep him sharp.

Zimmerman saw Hubbard was still fuming about the assault. He could not blame him. It was tough for a man to get beaten up and not have recourse. It was a feeling that Zimmerman knew all too well. But he also knew sometimes you had to let a man hit you a few times so you could learn how he fought. So you could learn how to defeat him.

Zimmerman heard the grandfather clock in Hubbard's office chime twelve times and pointed at it. "Hear that sound, Cal? That's the sound of success. Because right about now, Mannes and Poe should be wrapping up our business in Helena. And if everything turns out like I know it will, we're going to be untouchable by this time tomorrow."

"That was before McBride came here." Hubbard examined the amount of blood in his handkerchief before placing it back on his cut. "We weren't counting on him getting wind of what we were doing before the paperwork was signed and sealed."

"Relax," Zimmerman told him. "Neither McBride nor Halstead nor that pretty young thing he brought with him will be able to stop us. By this time tomorrow, we'll have more money than any of us have ever dreamed and no one will be able to lay a finger on us ever again."

He looked at the cracked window. "Then we can make McBride pay for the damage he did to you in a whole host of terrible ways."

Hubbard's eyes moved back and forth between Wycoff and Zimmerman.

Zimmerman, on the other hand, knew the plan would work because it was impossible to fail.

"How about you take a seat, Cal, and let Doug here tell us how he's going to help us become the two most powerful men in Montana."

Hubbard's eyes narrowed. "Three. You're forgetting Brunet."

Zimmerman knew Brunet had already served his purpose, though he did not know it yet. "Of course. The *three* most powerful men in Montana."

# Chapter 18

Halstead knew something was wrong as soon as he saw the wagon parked in front of the jail.

Sandborne did not. "Looks like Jack and Abby are back already. See? I told you she'd be just fine."

"They're early," Halstead said. "Too early. Let's go."

He dug his heels into Col's sides and the mustang responded immediately. Sandborne followed.

Halstead slid Col to a stop, dropped from the saddle, and wrapped the reins around the hitching rail before Sandborne managed to catch up with him.

Halstead pushed open the jail door and found Abby hunched over in a chair with her shawl wrapped around her. A steaming hot cup of coffee on McBride's desk had gone untouched.

She turned when she heard the door open and ran to Halstead, burying her face in his chest. "Oh, Jeremiah. I'm so glad you're here."

Her grip was tighter than he thought possible from a woman her size and he returned her embrace.

He looked over at McBride, who was tying a sack around Tom Ringham's head. "What's going on? What happened?"

"We've got a lot to talk about," McBride said as he finished pulling the knot tight around the sack, "and I don't want this lousy bastard to hear any of it."

The cold that began to spread through Halstead's stomach was warmed by the closeness of Abby's body.

Sandborne came into the jail and looked at the strange scene before him. "We hanging Ringham?"

"Nope." McBride wiped his hands on his denim jeans as he stood up. "Just making him deaf for a while. I wrapped a wad of cotton around his ears and slipped that sack over his head to keep him from hearing us. Don't know how much good it'll do, but it'll make me feel better."

Halstead ran a thumb gently along Abby's cheek. She was not crying, but she was not letting go of him, either. "What happened?"

McBride poured some coffee for Halstead and Sandborne before he sat behind his desk and told them all that they had seen in the new township. About all the activity. All the new people. And about the two men they had met while they were leaving. McBride sat behind his desk and sipped his coffee. "Yes, sir. Your Zimmerman has been a busy man."

Halstead's mind was still digesting the information McBride had given him while Sandborne asked, "How many guns do they have?"

"Plenty," McBride admitted. "I saw five, but according to Hubbard, there were a lot more. I'd say the whole town is probably packing. Some of those workers matched the same descriptions those miners at the Mother and Country gave us about the bunch who robbed their pay. The rest I've seen on wanted posters for the past year or so."

Halstead was still having trouble putting it all together. "I expected Zimmerman and Brunet to take the money and head for California or up to Canada. I didn't think they'd use the money to buy a town. It doesn't make any sense. Not for men like them."

"I didn't say that." Jack held up a long hand to caution him. "Just that I'm pretty sure they're part of it somehow. It stands to reason that they're using the money to repair the town, but until I know more about where the money came from, I couldn't swear to it in court. Hell, I don't think I could get a warrant to bring Hubbard in, much less make him give us a look at his books."

Abby began to release her grip on Halstead and flattened down the part of his shirt where she had buried her head. "Look at me. This morning I was Joan of Arc and ready to take on the world. Now I'm quivering like a field mouse."

Halstead slowly eased her away from him and looked at her. "You got shook up is all. No shame in that."

"Guess I had something to do with that," McBride admitted. "I lost my temper when I roughed up Hubbard a little. The outlaws saw it and razzed her some. I shouldn't have done that with you there, Miss Abby, and I'm sorry."

"Nonsense," she said as she went back to her seat. "He was practically begging for a beating. I think you showed remarkable restraint."

But Halstead was concerned about something else. "Those two men you ran into as you left. You recognize either of them?"

"The big fella we ran into as we left matched a lot of descriptions," McBride said, "but I'd bet a month's wages that he was Ed Zimmerman. The little guy with him looked familiar, but he had that kind of face."

Sandborne looked up at Halstead. "Stands to reason that Zimmerman would be close to where his men were. And them living in town makes sense after what we found up in the hills today."

It was McBride's turn to hear what they had found in the shack, and Sandborne conveyed it while Halstead sat beside Abby, holding her hand.

When Sandborne was done, McBride slowly shook his head. "Sounds like Zimmerman's got you pegged pretty good, Jeremiah. If that stick was as unstable as you said, you'd have traded in your guns for a pair of wings and a harp."

Sandborne had left out the part about the letter, and with Abby around, he was glad he had. He could always tell McBride about it later if he had to.

"I'd probably wind up somewhere a bit further south," Halstead said.

"Jeremiah!" Abby snapped at him. "Don't you dare say such a thing."

He reluctantly let her hand go and sat back in his chair. "Jack's right. Zimmerman's got me pegged better than I thought. And I wrote him off as just another outlaw looking to rob and steal and get rich. I didn't see this coming. None of it. I never thought he was trying to build something, much less a town." He hated being wrong, but this was more than that. He had been made to look like a fool by a man who was obviously much more than a common outlaw.

He asked McBride, "What do you think we should do next?"

The town marshal sipped his coffee as he crossed his long legs on his desk. "I don't know and that's the part that bothers me. Technically, Hard Scrabble is still part of my jurisdiction, but as we've already realized, I don't have enough men to ride up there and take a proper look around.

Even with the both of you, it wouldn't be enough. I might be able to form a posse of about twenty or so to ride out there with us, but this bunch would probably kill most of them if not all of us. Zimmerman's pulled together one nasty group of men around him. There's no doubt about that. And I'd bet they're fixing that town proper for a fight."

Halstead caught that. "Meaning?"

"Meaning I've worked that town for a few years," McBride explained. "I know it like the back of my hand. I didn't see them changing the layout of it any, but they were repairing what was already there. That place was difficult to hit before. Now that they're making improvements, it'll be even harder."

Halstead almost flinched when Abby took his hand. "Listen to him, Jeremiah. Everything he says is true. I know you've got your orders. I know you were sent here to bring him in, but it's hopeless."

Halstead was not used to anyone caring so much about his well-being. All he could think to do was pat her hand and say, "Don't worry. We'll think of something."

"Don't think of anything but yourself," she said. "You haven't seen his eyes. Not up close like I have. He's a monster. There's not a drop of human feeling in him at all anymore, if there ever was any in the first place."

Halstead knew that was the fear talking. Yes, she had been around some rough characters in her time. Men like Tom Ringham. But the gambler was no match for men like Zimmerman and Brunet, men who killed for a living. Men who killed because it was as much a part of them as breathing.

Halstead asked McBride, "Telegraph wires still down?"

The town marshal nodded. "I check every morning and the answer's always the same. No one will get around to fixing it until the thaw in the spring. But the wire in Wellspring is still working. I know you're touchy about taking the stage down there, with the price on your head and all, but you can make it there in less than half a day of hard riding if you stick to the trail."

He looked out the window at Halstead's and Sandborne's horses. "That mustang of yours should make it there and back without a problem. And if you're looking to Helena for orders, I don't see you as having any other choice but to do it."

McBride pushed his mug onto his desk and did not seem to care that some of it spilled over. "Damn it, I hate this. I hate not being able to grab hold of a man just because he's got me outgunned. Makes me feel useless."

Unfortunately, Halstead understood how he felt. He forced a smile for Abby's benefit, which made her brighten some.

Sandborne cleared his throat as he got to his feet. "Jeremiah, I've got an idea, but I'd like to talk it over with you outside."

"All ideas are welcome," McBride said, "even dumb ones."

But Sandborne left the jail and it was clear he expected Halstead to follow. Unaccustomed to such a definitive act from his friend, he thought it best to join him.

He squeezed Abby's hand. "Let me go hear what he has to say. I'll be right back."

Halstead joined Sandborne out on the boardwalk and closed the door behind him. "What's so important that you can't say it in there. Jack's liable to think we don't trust him just when we need him most."

"It's not about what Jack needs," Sandborne told him.

"It's about what you need. And what you need is to get Abby out of here."

Halstead had been wondering when the younger man might get around to bringing her up. "She's not doing any harm here, Joshua. She's got a job. A position. She can't just up and leave like that."

"That's exactly what she has to do. For her own good and for yours. I see how you're worried about her. How angry you are that she got scared today. I don't blame you. I like Abby, too, and I'd knock any man on his ass for treating her poorly. But she's a distraction that you don't need. That bunch over in Hard Scrabble or Valhalla or whatever they're taking to calling it now is a lot worse than we thought. We're liable to have to go up against them sooner or later and we can't do that if half of you is wondering how Abby is."

Halstead began to feel warmth spread through him. Warmth that usually began when his temper started to build. "Joshua, you're twenty. You don't know how the world works."

"Maybe not," he admitted, "but I know how gunplay works. Maybe not as good as you or Jack or Aaron or Billy, but I know enough to understand that you can't fight a man and your mind at the same time. I remember that letter Zimmerman wrote. He's not looking to just shoot you, Jeremiah. He's looking to burn you down from the inside. And after seeing her in the bank today, how long do you think it'll take for him to find out she means something to you? What'll he do then? Shoot her? Take her? What will you do then? What will happen to Jack and me when Zimmerman or Brunet uses her against you."

The old warmth was spreading now, and he was beginning to hear the roar of his own blood in his ears.

But Sandborne did not let up. "You can haul off and beat the hell out of me if you want, but while I'm picking up my teeth, you'll know I'm right even if you're too stubborn to admit it."

Halstead shut his eyes and turned away from Sandborne before his temper got the better of him. He wrapped his hands around the porch post until his knuckles cracked. Col began to fuss against the rein the way she always did when Halstead got riled. Sandborne's horse, too.

He had not planned for any of this to happen. He had not expected Zimmerman to put a price on his head. He had not expected to meet Abby, much less have feelings for her.

He had planned on finding Brunet or Zimmerman half dead in a saloon some place, not pulling off a robbery to buy a dying town at the end of nowhere.

He had not expected his young friend to save his life twice, much less be the only man who could talk sense to him.

A cold gust of wind blew along Main Street and tamped down his anger. It would be dark soon, and there was much to prepare.

"Bring the horses to the livery," he told Sandborne, "but make sure you drop off our rifles at the hotel first. We'll be riding to that telegraph office in Wellspring come sunup, and I don't want to come back here to get our guns. Tell the liveryman to feed them well. They're going to have a tough day tomorrow."

Sandborne began to unwrap the reins of the horses from the rail. "Should I get a horse for Abby?"

Halstead shook his head. "She'll be taking the stage. Probably safer that way."

"Yes, boss."

Halstead watched the younger man climb into the saddle and sit a little taller than normal. He had managed to make Halstead listen to reason, and that was something to celebrate.

Halstead called after him. "Don't go getting haughty on me, now. You're still just a hayseed."

Sandborne touched the brim of his hat as he rode toward the hotel and the livery beyond. He decided Mackey had been wrong. Sandborne would not make a good lawman someday. He already was.

Halstead glanced back into the jail and saw Abby sipping from her coffee mug, talking to Jack McBride. She looked like she was even smiling.

He did not know how she would take the news about having to leave town. He did not know how he would take it, either.

Halstead kept eyeing the street as he escorted Abby back to the hotel, her arm comfortably through his.

But Halstead was anything but comfortable. The content of Zimmerman's note aside, he still had a price on his head and a town full of desperate men who might want to take their chance at the ten-thousand-dollar bounty. Two men had died trying to collect it, but memories ran short once the liquor and beer started flowing.

He had asked Jack to walk her back to the hotel, but Abby would not hear of it. She had wanted Jeremiah to take her and left no room for discussion on the subject.

They walked slower than the rest of the people on the boardwalk. Mostly because he wanted to see if anyone was following them or waiting for them in a doorway. He also knew this would probably be the last stroll they took together in town, maybe even forever, and he did not want to rush it.

They were only a short distance from the jail when she said, "I'm going to take the stagecoach to Wellspring tomorrow."

A spike of anger went through him. "Did Sandborne tell you that?"

"No," she assured him. "And I couldn't hear what you were talking about outside, but I figured it was about me. I don't know if my leaving was your idea or his and it doesn't matter. It's my decision and that's final."

Halstead had been caught off-guard again for the third time that day. He wondered if he was beginning to lose whatever edge he had. "It's not something I'm happy about, Abby, but it's the right thing to do."

"No, it isn't," she said. "It's a cowardly, womanly thing to do. I should be willing to stay here and stick this out with you until the end, but I can't. Those men back there put a fright into me I've never known before. I thought I could stand up to any man after being with Tom for so long, but those men back there are a different breed."

Halstead was glad she had come to that decision on her own. "Tom's nothing compared to that bunch. A man like Zimmerman would make Tom his valet and he'd be grateful for the privilege. Not many have been able to stand up to Zimmerman and Brunet. There's no shame in being sensible."

"You have," she reminded him. "Stood up to him, I mean. You beat Zimmerman in Silver Cloud. Jack told me all about it. Said you took on twenty gunmen all by yourself and walked out without a scratch. Said you'd chased Zimmerman from town like a scalded dog."

Halstead could not stop himself from smiling. Months after the incident, and the number of gunmen was already up to twenty. It would probably hit thirty by Christmastime.

But he did not like to dwell on the past, and he did not see any reason why he should correct her. "It wasn't that many and I didn't do it alone. I didn't walk out without a scratch, either. Stopped a bullet with my shoulder."

"Interesting," she said. "Did it leave a scar?"

"Not a very big one. The town doctor was better with a needle and thread than most tailors."

"Guess it's still enough to tell all the ladies in your life," she said. "You probably tell them all about how you looked death in the eye and cut it down with your Peacemakers blazing."

He felt himself begin to blush again. "They're Colt Thunderers, not Peacemakers. And there are no women to tell any war stories to, either."

She made an odd sound as they continued walking. He kept hoping she would explain it, but when she did not, his curiosity got the better of him. "What was that sound for?"

"Just thinking is all," she said. "Trying to decide if I believe that part about you having no women to tell war stories to."

"Well, I don't," he said.

She looked at him in a way that made him feel foolish.

"It's true," he persisted. "Don't get me wrong. I'm not a monk, but a man in my line of work doesn't exactly have the time or inclination to be with a woman."

Her smile made him feel like a complete idiot.

"A real woman I mean."

"Oh? You mean there are fake women running around? Oh, you're so much more worldly than me, Jeremiah Halstead."

He felt his face turn scarlet. "Women of substance, I mean."

"Ah, so a woman like your friend's wife, for instance. That woman you mentioned on the train."

"Katherine," he reminded her. "And yes, women like that."

"Women like me?"

He had never liked it when people laughed at him, but for some reason, he didn't mind Abby's teasing one bit. "You could say that."

She hugged his arm tightly and they began to pick up the pace a bit. "Good, because I'd hate to go back to Helena and find myself duking it out with a horde of harlots for your hand."

Halstead stopped walking and so did she.

He found himself unable to speak, especially now that she was smiling up at him. The lamplight of the street made her blue eyes shine. "Yes, Jeremiah. I'm heading back to Helena where I intend to wait for you until you return." She wrapped her other arm around him. "And you will return to me, Jeremiah Halstead. I'll have to insist on it, and I'll be very cross with you if you don't."

Despite all of the people moving around them on the boardwalk, Halstead brought his lips to hers in the tenderest kiss he had ever known. And for those splendid few moments, all of the gasps and looks of disapproval they drew and all of the Brunets and Zimmermans of the world did not matter.

Abby broke off the kiss first and nuzzled her head into his chest just as she had in the jail, only this time, there was no fear in her, only warmth.

Halstead rested his head on top of hers and held her to him. He stroked her cheek with his thumb and although she had not cried back in the jail, she was crying now.

He had never made a woman cry before. At least not in that way.

"I hope that's a tear of joy," he whispered.

"More than joy," she said into his coat. "So much more."

She was still crying and smiling when she looked up at him again. "Let's get back to the hotel, Deputy Halstead. I want to hear some war stories."

She kept her arm wrapped around his middle as they resumed their walk to the hotel.

He had no intention of denying her request.

# Chapter 19

Zimmerman could feel Brunet and his men were anxious to get going as he held them at bay on the outskirts of Battle Brook. Zimmerman wanted to get to work, too, but this only worked if it was bloodless and it would only be bloodless if they did everything exactly right.

They were downwind from the slumbering town and he listened for any sounds that might signal danger. A barking dog or a restless horse. Loud voices of drunks stumbling home after a long night of drinking. Anything that might signal their approach before he was ready.

But all he heard was the wind in his ears and the voice in his heart telling him the time was right to strike. Not just right. Perfect.

It was a cold, moonless night in Battle Brook. The townsfolk were asleep in the warm beds beneath piles of blankets. Even the few saloons that were still open were quiet. The piano players had gone home, and the fallen women were offering comfort to their customers on a cold night.

Ed Zimmerman knew there was nothing standing between him and glory except a half-mile ride through a sleeping frontier town. The dream that had evaded him for so long was finally at hand.

He was too caught up in his moment of glory to realize Brunet had moved his horse next to his. "We're freezing our nuts off up here, Ed. We gonna do this or not?"

Yes, Zimmerman decided. Why not indeed?

Zimmerman responded by kicking his horse's sides and sending the animal moving toward Battle Brook. Brunet and his men followed in a straight line. The horses fussed a bit more than usual for Zimmerman had ordered all bridles and buckles to be made tighter than normal. He did not want the large group of men to make a sound while they moved through town toward their goal.

And as he led The Spoilers down Baxter Street, which ran parallel to Main, Zimmerman's confidence in his plan grew. The men had followed his orders. The only sound he could hear was the scrape of their shod hooves on the frozen ground.

He held up his left hand as they reached the first house on Baxter Street. It was the signal Brunet would see and each man in line behind him would relay to the next that they were to slow their mounts to a walk.

He remembered how they had been against this idea of a night robbery when he had first told them about it a few nights ago. They wanted to ride in hard and fast and get out of there before anyone knew what hit them. It took him a while to convince them that this robbery was safest if it took place in the middle of the night when risk would be lowest and stealth their friend.

Zimmerman kept his horse at a walk until he reached the back door of the bank where he found Doug Wycoff waiting with a lantern in his hand. One of the night watchmen stood by holding the door open for them.

Zimmerman climbed down from his horse, knowing Monk would be in charge of the animals while the rest of The Spoilers robbed the bank. He patted the guard on the shoulder as he beckoned Wycoff to lead them inside. He carried a small kerosene lantern with him to light the way through the darkened bank.

"It's all working out just like I told you it would," Wycoff whispered behind him as he led Zimmerman to the vault.

Zimmerman would not believe it until everything was over and they were back in Valhalla safely. "Did you get the key?"

Zimmerman could see the senior teller in the weak light of the lantern. "The lock on his office door was easy and the desk gave me no trouble at all." He held up the set of keys and jingled them before Zimmerman forced his arm down. "It couldn't have been any easier."

"That's fine, Doug. Just fine." Zimmerman urged him to keep moving through the darkness. "We're going to be wealthy men just as soon as we get that vault open. Let's keep moving."

Zimmerman could hear the footfalls of the men behind them as they crept into the bank in a line like an army of ants. Even though they had spent a small fortune bribing both the night watchmen in addition to promising a piece of the take, Zimmerman knew there was still plenty of room for something to go wrong. Something beyond their control. One drunken passer-by or, worse, Jack McBride on patrol, and they would find themselves trapped inside the bank. He had no doubt they would escape, but it would ruin his plan.

They found the second nightwatchman at the vault holding a lantern as dim as Wycoff's had been. Just bright enough to make it out in the darkness.

"There it is, Mr. Zimmerman." The guard pointed to the large steel safe door. "Just ready and waiting for you to give it a go."

Zimmerman took the lantern from Wycoff and watched the senior teller spin the dial on the door.

"Mr. Kendrick had this baby brought here all the way from Detroit," Wycoff said as he spun the dial to the right series of numbers. "The maker said it would take a wagonload of dynamite to put a dent in it and still it wouldn't crack. Takes the right combination and the keys to open her up. And being the senior teller and all, it's my job to know the combination."

Zimmerman had already known all that. It was why he had targeted the man to help with the robbery in the first place. He silently watched Wycoff work the dial like his life depended on it. Perhaps because it did.

After slowly turning the dial to its final number, Wycoff grabbed hold of the heavy handle and yanked it down.

"That opens the slots for the keys," Wycoff explained as he slid one key into a hole and turned it clockwise. "You can't turn it all the way around like a regular lock. You have to turn it just right."

Zimmerman heard one of the gears in the door snap open.

"Just like that." Wycoff smiled. The lantern cast ugly shadows on his face. He went on with his tale as he found the other thick key on the chain. "Mr. Kendrick is supposed to keep this on him at all times, but he's a bit of a boozer and he's lost it more times than I can count. No one knows he keeps an extra key here but me, seeing as how—"

"You're the senior teller and all," Zimmerman said, finishing the thought for him. His back was drenched in sweaty anticipation. "Keep going, Doug. We're almost there."

Wycoff slid the key into the lock and, this time, turned it counterclockwise. "They built it so that the key doesn't turn normal. If I had turned it the wrong way, ten extra locks would snap into place and we'd never get it open then. You were right to bring me on, Mr. Zimmerman."

Zimmerman fought the urge to scream at the little man to hurry up until he heard the final lock inside the vault release and the heavy door popped open a little under its own weight.

The second guard helped Wycoff pull the vault door all the way open and Zimmerman walked inside. His lamplight leading the way to riches beyond his imagination.

He walked straight into a heavy brass gate.

Wycoff squeezed in front of him, keys at the ready. "We usually keep the vault door open all day so the customers can see how safe it is, but this gate keeps everyone out. It's trickier than it looks, so give me some time with it."

Zimmerman held his breath as he watched Wycoff work the key until the gate swung inward.

The outlaw's excitement got the better of him as he pushed Wycoff out of the way and rushed inside. He turned up the light on the lamp as bright as it would go and beheld his bounty.

Neatly stacked bundles of greenbacks on polished steel. Rolls of coins. Rows of safe deposit boxes.

Everything he had ever dreamed of and more.

He felt Brunet grab hold of his shoulders and give him a good shake. "We did it, Ed. Just like you said."

But Zimmerman knew they had only begun to get to work.

He ignored Wycoff's chatter as he grabbed two bundles of cash and handed them back to Brunet who handed it to the man behind him and so on until it reached the last man in line. That man would stuff the pockets sewn into his hide coat with the money until he was finished, tap the man in front of him on the shoulder and slowly ride out of town to Valhalla. It would go on like that until every Spoiler's pockets were bursting with cash and coin. If there was still any left in the vault by the time Zimmerman was loaded down, they would leave it behind.

How much they would ultimately take was a number Zimmerman dared not to guess. Whatever the final amount turned out to be, it would be enough to shift the balance of power away from Battle Brook and back where it belonged. To Valhalla.

To Ed Zimmerman.


As he passed the last of the cash back to Brunet, the outlaw whispered, "You're the last, Ed. Time to go."

Zimmerman grabbed a fistful of rolled coins and then another until his pockets were weighted down. It was only then that he paid attention to Wycoff.

The senior teller asked, "Do you want me to take—?"

Zimmerman brought his blade across the senior teller's throat before he could finish his sentence. He stepped over the dying man and walked out of the vault and into the bank. Brunet had already cut the throat of the second watchman, whose life blood was now ruining the bank's carpet.

He regretted leaving the lamp behind him in the safe but did not dare go back for it. It was a fairly straight run to the back door where he knew his horse and Brunet were waiting for him.

Zimmerman had just reached the hallway that led to the back door when a shotgun blast echoed through the town.

Something had gone wrong, and he ran for the door with all possible speed.

# Chapter 20

Jack McBride had been a heavy sleeper in his youth, but the army had cured him of that. Too many days and nights spent out on patrol in Arizona and other frontier posts had made him see sleep as an enemy. Five years out of the army and he still went for his gun when he heard a nightbird call.

His size did not help matters. Even on those few nights when he did not have a prisoner to guard and he could grab a room in The Standard Hotel, the mattresses were always too small. He had to curl up like a cat just to get most of the blankets to cover him.

That night was no different than any of the other countless nights he had spent since he had been hired on to become the Town Marshal of Hard Scrabble and now Battle Brook. The towns and the jails might have changed, but his job remained the same.

He spent most of his nights staring up at the ceiling, thinking of what he could be doing if he had not become a lawman and disappointing himself over his lack of prospects. Gunwork and soldiering were all he knew. All he had ever wanted to know. And as much as he tried to convince himself that he should want more out of the life the good Lord had given him, he did not.

He liked being a lawman. He enjoyed the solitude of his own company. He liked sending bad men to jail and he liked not having anyone to answer to except for the mayor on occasion and his own conscience.

But on that particular evening, he was especially troubled by this Zimmerman business. Or, to put a finer point on it, what Halstead would do about the Zimmerman business. He thought about taking Sandborne aside and asking him to talk some sense into his partner. Convince him the odds were against him and to go back to Helena until the spring. But he did not sense that young Sandborne held that much weight with Halstead.

Besides, the two young men were still fairly new to enforcing the law and undoubtedly still had that feeling of invincibility that comes from youth. McBride was not much older than them. He was not yet thirty, but his time in the army had taught him that a man was only as alive as the next bullet or arrow or infection coming his way. It was a cold way to look at life, but life was often a cold enterprise.

All of these thoughts kept bumping into each other inside his head, making sleep even more elusive than it normally was. A quick look at the wall clock told him it was three in the morning. He decided to give up the fight and make use of his inability to sleep.

He rolled out of the cot and glanced over at Ringham. The prisoner was sound asleep. Even chained to an iron ring in a jail on the Montana frontier, the man sawed logs like he did not have a care in the world. He might have envied him if he did not despise the son of a bitch.

McBride slid his feet into the boots he always kept in

the same spot beside his bed, unlocked the jailhouse door, and walked outside. He did not bother with a gun belt or coat. The cold mountain air did not bother him anymore and neither did the desert. He had grown to be able to tolerate the weather as it was, rain or shine, and continue to perform his duty.

He liked to come outside on nights like this, when there was no moon and the wolves and the coyotes were quiet.

He leaned against the porch post and listened to the wind blow west through town. Every town he had ever been in had its own cadence at night and Hard Scrabble had been no different. The way the building strained against the wind or creaked with too much snow on the roof. The wood that popped as it expanded in the summer heat and the noise horses and other animals who could see at night tended to make in the dark.

Battle Brook had been the same, though only after a month or so in the new town, he was still trying to understand the night noises of the place. All of the new construction going on meant the sounds changed every day. The only consistent feature was the lamplight he saw in windows from the other light sleepers in town. The smells, too.

And as he stood on the boardwalk of his jail on that particular night, he could sense that something in town was off.

He could not quite put his finger on it. It was not tension, not like it had been in Indian country when they were expecting a fight. It was something more than that. The town felt fuller than normal. Fuller than it should have felt at three in the morning. Sounds coming from Baxter Street that he had not heard before.

The longer he stood there, the surer he became. Something was off.

He ducked back inside and strapped on his gun belt. He did not need to bother with the lamp as he always kept everything in the same place.

He pulled on his coat and pulled on his hat before he grabbed the old coach gun he kept in the rifle rack and pocketed a handful of shells to go with it. He normally preferred the Winchester, but at night, the shotgun would make up for the lack of accuracy in the darkness.

He pulled the jail door closed but did not take the time to lock it. If someone really was out there, then he did not want the jangle of keys to give him away in the darkness.

He crept across the frozen thoroughfare and, after checking to make sure Main Street was clear, headed toward Baxter. Battle Brook would be a good-sized town when it was finished, but for now, Main and Baxter were it.

McBride rounded the corner on Baxter and stood next to the picket fence of one of the new houses they were building there. He stood alone in the dark, listening as he strained his eyes to try to see through the darkness. He could hear it clearly now. Scuffling of horseshoes on the frozen ground. The sounds a man makes when he's trying to climb into the saddle and take control of his horse.

He crouched behind the picket fence when he heard the unmistakable sound of a couple of horses and riders walking his way. He could tell they were about halfway up the street. By the bank.

And now Jack McBride understood what was happening. The bank was being robbed.

He waited for the sound of the horses to draw nearer. He was able to see them a little despite the moonless night.

When they sounded like they were in range, McBride thumbed back both hammers on the coach gun.

The walking sounds stopped.

From his position behind the picket fence, he brought the shotgun up to his shoulder and aimed in the direction of the sound. "This is town marshal Jack McBride. Step down from your horses and walk toward me with your hands in the air."

He heard gunmetal scrape leather. He cut loose with the left barrel, managing to close his eyes as the gun fired to avoid being blinded by the blast. A horse screamed and a man cursed.

Something heavy hit the ground as gunshots began to ring out all around him. The flashes from the gun barrels lit up the darkness like fireflies.

Most of the bullets went wide, but one clipped the fence just above his head. He aimed in the direction of where he had seen the flashes and let go with the second barrel before running back to the side of the house for cover.

The dark night was pierced by the sounds of men and horses, of gunfire and panic. Bullets slammed into the corner of the house he was using for cover as McBride's practiced hands opened the coach gun, plucked out the spent shells, and quickly refilled the tubes before snapping the gun shut.

He heard a horse speed by him, its rider not even bothering to fire as it raced away behind him and into the night. It was followed by another and then a third before McBride thumbed back the hammers and triggered both barrels at the fleeing men. He had no idea if he had hit his mark or missed entirely, for the sound of more riders coming his way filled his ears.

Realizing there was no time to reload, he dropped the shotgun and drew his Colt from his hip, firing as blindly at them as the escaping men were firing at him.

He was flat on the ground before he realized one of the bullets had hit him with a lucky shot in the pitch blackness.

He tried his best to roll out of the way of yet another approaching rider, but knew it was hopeless. He used all of his strength to raise his pistol and fire into the thunder as it rolled over him.

Jeremiah Halstead was beginning to doze, gently caressing Abby's hair as she laid on his bare chest, lightly snoring when a shotgun blast shattered the quiet night.

Like McBride and Mackey and men like them, he always kept everything he needed in the same place when he went to bed, even following lovemaking.

In one motion, he swept his feet out from under the covers, tucked them into the boots beside his bed, snatched his gun rig where he had left it across the chair, and was out the door. There had been no time to bother with a shirt, much less a coat.

He was already running down the stairs of the hotel when he heard Sandborne rumbling down the stairs just behind him.

The night clerk was crouched by the hotel's front window as Halstead ran out onto the boardwalk and listened. At first, all he could hear was the cold wind in his ears before another shotgun blast came from the end of town. He thought about running in that direction until he heard shouting and horses coming from the bank just up the street from the hotel.

He drew his belly gun as he ran toward the bank with Sandborne right on his heels. The lamps were still burning in that part of town and he pointed for the younger man to take the alley to the right of the bank. He would take the left.

Halstead slowed his run to a jog as he reached the alley. He had no intention of running into a gun, but he could not let whoever was fleeing get away, either.

He burst from the end of the alley but tripped across something he had not seen in the darkness. He landed on his left shoulder and heard a pop. He knew it was not a gunshot, but his shoulder coming out of its socket.

His Colt still in hand, he looked up and saw the vague outline of two riders struggling to keep their horses under control amid the chaos. He aimed at the largest figure and fired.

The man cried out but stayed in the saddle. One of them shot back, and the bullet hit the ground by his feet where he had tripped.

Halstead fired blindly as the men got control of their horses and galloped toward the end of Baxter Street and the road out of town. He heard Sandborne's Winchester fire several times, which gave him a general idea of where he was.

"I'm here," Halstead called out as he got to his feet, tucked away the empty Colt on his belly, and drew the one from his hip, giving chase to the fleeing men on horseback. Sandborne was running close behind when Halstead yelled, "Take a knee and keep firing. They're getting away!"

His left arm flopped at his side, slowing his momentum as he ran after the escaping robbers.

He raised his right arm as he ran and emptied his gun in their direction. He had no idea if he had just wasted bullets or if he had managed to hit one of them. All he knew was that both men crossed into the pale light at the end of Baxter Street before disappearing from view.

Halstead continued to run off balance toward the place where he had heard the first shotgun blast. When he reached the end of Baxter Street, he saw the outline of a man on the ground and skidded to a halt. He slipped on the frozen ground but managed to keep his feet as he moved toward the fallen man.

"Don't shoot," the man said. "It's McBride. I'm hit."

Halstead took a knee beside his fallen friend. He dropped his Colt somewhere in the darkness as he needed his good hand to check the man for wounds.

Ignoring the fire in his own left shoulder, Halstead yelled down Baxter toward Sandborne. "Get a doctor. McBride's been shot."

One of the townspeople rounded the corner with a lantern and Halstead told him to come closer. He ran his hand over McBride to search for wounds. It was not until his hand reached the center of the lawman's chest when he felt the blood. The dim light from the citizen's lamp showed the hole straight through the middle of his breastbone, but Halstead continued to feel for any other wounds. He had not found any, but the one he had found was bad enough.

The townsman gasped as he began to back away from the dying man. Halstead snatched the lamp away from him and set it on the ground next to McBride. "It's just a flesh wound, Jack. You're gonna be just fine. Sandborne's getting a doctor right now. Just hold on."

But McBride's breathing grew shallow, and Halstead covered the wound with his right hand to try to stop the bleeding. To do his best to try to keep this good, brave man alive.

McBride gripped his hand and pulled it away from the wound. "Have them bury me facing west. I . . . was always partial to . . . sunsets."

Halstead saw him fading but willed him to live. "No one's burying you for a long time yet. Just hold on, damn it. Hold on! The doctor is on his way."

But John Joseph McBride, former lieutenant of the United States Cavalry and marshal of the towns of Tucson, Hard Scrabble, and now Battle Brook, had held on for as long as he could before he slowly slipped away.

And not even all of Halstead's pleas could bring him back.

# Chapter 21

Brunet and Zimmerman rode their horses as fast as they dared to go in the dangerous darkness of the wooded trail between the towns. They caught up with most of the men along the way and they all rode together, which had not been part of Zimmerman's plan at all.

He had told the men to take different routes back to Valhalla and to avoid the main road. But he supposed the shotgunner who had opened fire out of nowhere without warning had rattled the men and, by his count, all but one was now on the main road.

He and Brunet did not halt the group until they reached a clearing an hour later, which put them about halfway between the two towns. He asked Brunet to ride back and keep an eye on their trail in case someone had raised a posse to chase them.

The men gathered around him in a loose circle in the dark clearing.

"All right, boys," he asked the group in general. "Who are we missing?"

"Pete," he heard Blackfoot say. "We were riding out of town as quiet as you told us to when Jack McBride cocked his shotgun and told us to stop."

He had run into McBride and Miss Newman in Valhalla, but did not know that much about him. "How do you know it was McBride?"

"Because he announced himself plain as day is how," Blackfoot said. "I knew he couldn't see us too good, even that close, so I was just gonna hightail it around him, but Pete tried to pull on him, and McBride let go with the shotgun. Pete and his horse caught most of it. I got a pellet in the ear, but I think that's all."

Zimmerman ordered the rest of the men to check themselves over for holes or other wounds. A shotgun had a way of spreading a lot of pain to a lot of people. He had never gotten around to giving Pete a nickname as he had Blackfoot and most of the others. The outlaw had been so plain that a nickname had not readily come to mind. He should have called him "Imbecile" for all of the trouble he had caused The Spoilers that night.

Blackfoot seemed to read his mind. "Don't go blaming poor Pete for what happened, boss. That lawman stumbled into us out of blind luck and nothing else. We didn't make a sound or anything."

Zimmerman knew they had ridden into Battle Brook quiet enough and figured Blackfoot and Pete had ridden away from the bank the same way. McBride must have stumbled into them the way he was sure Halstead had tripped into the alley.

And he was sure it was Halstead. No one else would have been that daring in the dark.

All of Halstead's bullets had come close, but none had hit their mark. He would check with Brunet later to see if he had been hit. He certainly had not been riding like a wounded man since they had escaped town.

After he had given the men a chance to check themselves and their mounts for wounds, he asked them to count off in the darkness so he knew exactly how many men had escaped and, more important, how much money had been taken.

Accounting for Brunet who was watching their flank, it sounded like the outlaw named Pete and his horse were the only casualties. That was better news than he had been expecting under the circumstances.

"You boys head on for Valhalla and go straight to the bank. Hubbard will be waiting for you. Me and Brunet will be right behind you."

The group obeyed his command as Zimmerman rode back to find Brunet and call him to join them. He found his partner a good forty yards away, sitting atop his horse like a statue as he listened to what the wind might tell him.

Zimmerman whispered, "Hear anything?"

"No," Brunet said. "Strange. Things going to shit the way they did, I figured they'd have a posse after us by now."

But Zimmerman did not think so. "I saw McBride on the ground as we rode past. Looked like he was mortally wounded. I don't know which of our boys did it, but that'll make a posse think twice about coming after us in the dark."

Brunet leaned over the side of his horse and spat a stream of tobacco in the snow. "Night won't last forever. They'll be coming after us come morning."

But Zimmerman knew better. "Halstead won't let them do that. McBride surely told them what he saw today. He knows he'll be a dead man if he does."

Brunet kept his eye on their back trail. "You think that was him in the alley?"

"Him and a young man who's his partner. Sandborne

was the one with the rifle. Lucky for us, all their shots went wide."

"Not all of them," Brunet said into the wind.

Zimmerman looked him over but could not see much in the dark, only the great hide that covered him. "Where?"

"The back on the right side," Brunet told him. "Came out the left front. Don't think he hit anything important or I'd already be dead. Still want to have a doctor check it out when we get back home. Just make sure you don't tell any of the boys. How many made it?"

"All of them except Pete."

He could see Brunet wince in the dim light of the forest. "That boy had a lot of cash in his pockets. Him and Black-foot were the first to ride out of town."

"The rest made it, though," Zimmerman said. "I'd call that a good night, though McBride's death casts a pall over things."

"You mean Halstead." It was a statement, not a question.

"Yeah." He tried to listen to the wind in case he might hear something. But all he heard was the cold air in his ears. "He might have allowed McBride to handle the robbery on his own, but now that McBride is surely dead, he won't let that go. His boss back in Helena won't want him to let it go, either."

"The new U.S. Marshal," Brunet said. "Aaron Mackey."

Zimmerman let out a heavy breath. "The very same."

"Heard he's tough," Brunet said. "We're tougher."

Zimmerman decided to let that statement hang in the wind before they brought their horses around and joined the others on the ride back to Valhalla.

# Chapter 22

The early morning sky was gray, and a steady rain was falling as Halstead, Sandborne, bank president James Kendrick, and Mayor Philip White stepped out of the back door of the bank and onto a soggy Baxter Street.

Halstead was glad the gore from the bodies that had been left behind had not upset Sandborne. Kendrick and the mayor were understandably sickened by the scene and had gagged more than once. The cold mountain air did the civilians some good despite the rain.

"Doug Wycoff, dead," Kendrick said as he held a handkerchief to his mouth. "Charlie and Enoch, too. My God. Wycoff was new, but Charlie and Enoch had been guarding the bank since the day it opened. They used to guard the bank in Hard Scrabble before we opened up here."

Kendrick looked at the back door that had closed behind them. He laid his hand upon it as if he might be able to learn something from the steel. He paid particular attention to the lock. "Not a scratch on it. How in the hell did they get in?"

Halstead and Sandborne traded glances. They would tell him, but not until after he and White had walked the length of Baxter Street so they could see what had happened for themselves.

"We'll get to all of that later at the jail," Halstead assured him. "But for now, I want to show you what happened out here. Sandborne and I came running when we heard Jack's shotgun from the other end of Baxter Street." He pointed down at the blood still visible on the base of the bank building. "They'd left the body of one of the guards in the alley and I tripped over him as I ran. I hit the ground and saw two men getting on their horses in the dark."

The mayor was inspired by the detail. "Then you know who they are?"

"Nothing I could swear to in court." Halstead was sorry to disappoint him. "It was too dark, and there was a lot of shooting going on. I think I hit one of them, but I'm not sure. One of them returned fire, missed me, and hit your dead guard in the head."

"A further indignity Enoch did not deserve," Kendrick said.

"Let's keep walking," the mayor suggested. "I want to get in from this infernal rain."

Halstead pointed out the tracks and horse droppings on the ground as they walked down Baxter. "As you can see, they had a lot of horses with them. Twelve by my count, though I can't swear to it. They rode into town real quiet, too. Deputy Sandborne asked everyone along Baxter Street if they'd heard anything, but the first sound they heard was McBride's shotgun going off. A few of them rushed to their windows but didn't see much on account of the darkness. A few got hit by stray bullets, but none of them were fatal."

"Thank God for that much." The mayor frowned as they walked along the deadly landscape.

"Murderous horde," Kendrick said. "They knew what they were doing, didn't they?"

"We'll get to that later." Halstead focused on the ground. He needed these men to understand what had happened there and how. He needed them to know what they were dealing with.

"The ground is slippery even for us," Halstead explained. "You can imagine how bad it was for the horses with metal shoes on their hooves. That's why they came in quiet and tried to leave that way until McBride discovered them."

"But if they were as quiet as you say," Mayor White asked, "how did he know they were here?"

"A guess," Halstead offered. "Intuition. A man tends to get the feel of a town he protects, and I figure he must've sensed something was off. It would explain why he didn't come and get me and Sandborne to back him up. My guess is he caught them just as they were beginning to leave town."

"Jack had always been a light sleeper," the mayor added.

By then the group had reached the dead horse still lying at the end of Baxter Street. "McBride took cover behind the picket fence here when he cut loose with his coach gun." He pointed down at the dead horse. "The blast took off the top of the horse's head and blew the rider right out of the saddle."

The ice still bore the blood from the robber and the horse, even though the body of the outlaw had been removed by the doctor hours before. "The dead man was wearing a buffalo hide he had lined with pockets. Each of those pockets was stuffed with bundles of cash. I already gave you what we found on him. I figure the rest of the group was outfitted the same way."

"He had four thousand dollars in those pockets," Kendrick observed. "The rest of it gone. God only knows where it is now."

Halstead was no god and he had a pretty good idea where it was. But now was not the time to discuss such things.

He pointed at the picket fence, which was shattered in several places. "Looks like the robbers returned fire, but most of their shots missed Jack and hit the fence instead. The only bullet we found in him was in his chest." He brought the group around the corner and pointed down at the spot where he had found McBride. The same spot where he had tried and failed to save his life.

The snow where he had fallen only bore a small amount of the blood he had lost. Most of it had already begun to seep into the ground.

That did not seem fair to Halstead. A good man had died there and soon, nature would wipe away every trace of his sacrifice. It was not right, but that was the way it was.

Halstead tried to tell them his idea of what had happened in the best way he could. "The shot went right through Jack and severed his spine. I was with him at the end, and I don't think he suffered much, for whatever it's worth."

The cold rain beat down on the hats of the four men who looked down at the spot where Jack McBride had taken his last breath. Mayor White patted his eyes that were not wet from the rain.

"Can we please talk in the jail, deputy?" the mayor asked. "I don't think I can stay on my feet much longer."

Halstead led him and Kendrick across the thoroughfare

and into the jail. Sandborne brought up the rear with his Winchester. The boardwalk was eerily quiet for that time of the morning, save for a few people clustered together farther up Main Street. They were undoubtedly talking about what had happened earlier that morning. Halstead hoped they left him alone. He had no patience for idle town gossip just then.

The stagecoach to Wellspring was parked in front of The Standard Hotel, but Halstead had already told the driver he could not leave without his permission. The driver had not liked it but knew better than to argue with him.

Once Halstead unlocked the jail door, Mayor White and Kendrick sat in the first chairs they could find. Sandborne put his rifle in the rack and sat down beside it.

Halstead went to the stove and poured them three cups of lukewarm coffee. The last pot Jack McBride had ever made. There were not enough mugs for him to have one, but that was fine. He was in no mood for coffee anyway.

After handing out mugs to the others, Halstead sat down in one of the chairs in front of the desk. Sitting in the dead man's chair did not seem right just yet.

Mayor White pointed at the vacant bed and the chain dangling from the iron ring on the wall. "Where's your prisoner? Thomas Ringham, I think he was."

"We let him go to help Doc Potter with the wounded," Sandborne explained. "Turns out he was a doctor himself before he became a gambler. Figured he'd be of better use helping folks instead of being chained up in here."

"A wise decision," the mayor said. "Four townspeople were wounded by stray bullets during the robbery, though I doubt it was intentional."

One man was dead, Halstead thought. A good man. And that was one man too many.

The bank president cleared his throat and sat up straight. "I know you have a theory about what happened, Deputy Halstead, and I want to hear it. I have a feeling it's pretty bad, but I want to hear it anyway."

Halstead was in no mood to be delicate. "Miss Newman says she saw a man matching Wycoff's description in the Hard Scrabble bank yesterday when she accompanied Jack on a visit there. He was with a big man who Jack believed to be the outlaw Ed Zimmerman."

Kendrick pounded the arm of his chair. "I knew it. Yesterday, Wycoff told me he had to go home on account of a fever. But when I saw him dead in the vault, I knew he had to be part of this. The guards, too, I imagine?"

"We'll probably never know for certain," Halstead admitted, "but since it doesn't look like they put up much of a fight, I'd say they were probably in on it with Wycoff." He took a ring of keys from his pocket and handed them to Kendrick. "We found these on him. Looks like he worked the lock to your office and the one on your desk and used these to open the vault."

Kendrick drew in a ragged breath as he held the keys. "My God. To think my stupidity made all of this possible. I . . . I can't believe it."

Halstead had neither the time nor the inclination to soothe Kendrick's guilty conscience. "Zimmerman is an awfully persuasive man, gentlemen. He probably tempted them with the promise of a big payday if they let him into the bank only to cut their throats as payment."

"But why?" Mayor White asked. "They had done everything he wanted."

"Because he didn't need them any longer," Halstead told them. "They couldn't help him with whatever scheme he's pulling up in Hard Scrabble, so why keep them alive?"

"Bastards," Kendrick spat. "Barbaric bastards all of them. And you think my money is in Hubbard's safe right now, don't you?"

Kendrick might have been careless, but at least he was not a fool. "Probably," Halstead admitted. "Jack said Hubbard seemed awfully cozy with Zimmerman's men."

"What's this scheme you're talking about?" Mayor White asked Halstead. "This is the first I'm hearing of it."

Halstead spent the next few minutes repeating all that Jack and Abby had told them about what they had seen in Hard Scrabble and how it was now known as Valhalla. The information did not make either of them feel any better.

Halstead concluded by saying, "Since there wasn't much we could do about it, Jack and I were going to tell you about it today. And because the telegraph wires are down here in town, I was going to ride to the station in Wellspring to send word to Marshal Mackey about all of this. I plan on writing a report to him that explains everything in greater detail and send it on the next train to Helena."

"The gall," Kendrick spat. The keys in his hand rattled like chains. "Of all the infernal gall. Why, Cal Hubbard is almost as bad as Aaron Burr himself, the swindler. I'd always known he was a crook, but I never thought he was capable of something like this. And throwing in with the likes of Brunet and Zimmerman? Against his own people?"

Kendrick got to his feet and set his mug of coffee on top of McBride's rolltop desk. "I won't stand for it. Hubbard is always boasting that he has friends in Helena. Well, I happen to have a few of my own. And in Washington, too. More than he has. I'm going to put a stop to whatever he's planning, Halstead. You can rest easy on that score. He might think he's clever, but he's not as clever as me." He looked at Halstead. "When were you planning to head to Wellspring?"

"Later today. Got a few things to tend to here first. You'll be in good hands with Deputy Sandborne here until I return."

"Good," Kendrick said as he headed for the door. "Stop by the bank before you go, and I'll have some letters ready for you to include with your report to Mackey. These men will pay for what they have done here. Pay my way. That I can promise you."

He slammed the door behind him when he left, leaving only Mayor White and the two lawmen in the jail.

The mayor was not an old man. Halstead judged him to be about fifty. But as he sat in the chair, he looked ancient and small. He looked off into space as the coffee mug sat untouched on his leg. He looked like he might fall asleep if he had the energy to do so.

"Jim Kendrick is a boastful man," White told them with a blank look in his eye. "Hubbard is not. If he's really behind this, and I agree that he is, then all of Kendrick's railing and letter writing won't make a bit of difference."

"What makes you say that?" Sandborne asked.

"Because long before I came out here and became a haberdasher, I was a lawyer," White explained. "I used to help men like Hubbard and Zimmerman do exactly what they seem to be doing now. Not to this extent, of course, but something similar. Railroads mostly. It was a good living for a long while until I grew weary of it and came out here for a more peaceful life. A peace that Hubbard and Zimmerman and Brunet now seem intent on destroying. And there's nothing to be done about it."

Halstead did not like the way the mayor was thinking. "Brunet and Zimmerman are still wanted men. I've got paper on them."

"Paper," White repeated. "And that's all you have." He looked at Halstead. "Please don't take that as an insult, deputy. I have as much respect for the law as the next man. Maybe even more. And I've certainly seen how you can handle yourself. But a piece of paper with some names on it isn't worth much if you can't bring them to justice. And right now, it sounds like you don't have enough men to do that. It's my fault, I suppose. I'm the one who led the great exodus here from Hard Scrabble. I promised a new and better town with a higher standard of living than they had in Hard Scrabble. And I lived up to my promise. Rare for a politician, I know, much less a lawyer. And I'll go on making this place as new and as modern as possible. But I made the mistake of allowing Hard Scrabble to sit as fallow as a forgotten field on a farm. Now, someone else has come along and worked the land I abandoned. They've made it their own and I'm afraid the time has passed for any of us to do much about it, at least for the moment."

The mayor surprised Halstead by laughing. "He's even got a great name for the enterprise. Valhalla. A man can do a lot for a town with a name like that."

Halstead was beginning to lose his patience. "Kendrick will find a way to get back the money they took from him."

But White slowly shook his head, looking off into space again. "Hubbard is a thief, but he's not a fool. What we know and what we can prove are two different things. He'll just respond to any accusation we make by saying the money came from an investor and the money will be deposited in the bank slowly, not all at once. He'll get the independent miners to come together as a combine now, a feat not even Emmett Ryan and all of his money could accomplish. They'll join Hubbard now after the robberies of the mines here in Battle Brook. They can't risk the losses the Ryan mines could absorb. And Cal Hubbard will be only too glad to offer them the security they seek."

The mayor nodded slowly as he continued to gaze at nothing. "Jack McBride was a popular man among the miners. They would have come to town to pay their respects to him anyway once Doc Potter is finished embalming him. We won't be able to bury him because the ground is frozen, of course, but they'll still come."

Halstead was beginning to worry about White's state of mind. He was rambling. "What's that got to do with anything?"

White slowly looked over at Halstead. "Because while they're in town, they'll be looking to pull their money out of Kendrick's bank and deposit it with Hubbard's bank. After all, who wants their money in a bank that can't protect it? They'll figure their money will be safer with Hubbard."

Halstead was beginning to understand what he was saying.

"It's called a run on a bank," White explained, "and once they all pull their money from The Bank of Battle Brook, it will fail. Ever see a run on a bank, deputy?" White shook his head. "They're not pretty. People get awfully nervous when their savings are at stake. And they're capable of anything."

Halstead had not thought of that, and the notion made

him dizzy. With everything else going on, he and Sandborne now had a possible riot to worry about.

Mayor White pulled out a timepiece from his vest pocket and glanced at it before he slid it back into his pocket. "It's seven in the morning now. I'll bet people are already lined up outside the bank waiting for it to open at nine. We'll probably have a riot on our hands by noon, if not sooner."

Halstead watched the mayor look out the window. Out at the rain beading on the edge of the porch roof before it fell to the ground. "And on such a peaceful day, too. I've always loved the rain. I've always found the sound of it hitting the roof to be soothing to the mind. But after today, I don't think I'll ever be able to see it again without remembering the sight of Jack McBride's body in the muck of it. I guess I have Cal Hubbard to thank for that, too."

He set his mug on the floor as he got to his feet and shuffled to the door. "I'll be at the Town Hall if you need me for anything, boys. I had McBride make me an extra key so I wouldn't have to bother him anymore." He set his hand on the doorknob but did not open it. "I liked Jack. I really did. I'll miss him."

Halstead and Sandborne watched the mayor open the door and gently close it behind him. They watched him pass by the window like a man who had just lost everything. Perhaps he had, Halstead wondered. He had certainly lost whatever innocence he had brought with him from wherever he had lived before.

Sandborne finally took a sip of coffee. "What the hell are we gonna do about this, Jeremiah? We're in a whole lot of trouble here."

"I know." Halstead sat forward and ran his hands over his face. Things had been bad before the bank robbery, but at least they still had Jack to lend a hand. Now that he was dead, he and Sandborne were the only law left in town.

Sandborne wasn't done with his good news. "And the mayor's not lying about that bank run. They had one in Dover Station once when I was a boy. Before Aaron came back to town and became sheriff. Saw it get ugly real fast, too."

Halstead had never seen one himself. No one he knew in El Paso ever had enough money to put anywhere except in a hiding place inside their home. Never in a bank. And anyone foolish enough to rob an El Paso bank had never made it to the town limits.

But he had heard of them and knew how ugly they could get. He had heard they could tear a town apart if they got up enough steam behind them.

Halstead would have to set almost everything else aside and focus on maintaining order for the time being. Chaos in Battle Brook would only benefit Zimmerman and Brunet in Valhalla.

But he would need to send the outlaws a message first. A message they would understand.

"You get any better with your reading?" Halstead asked Sandborne.

"Better than I was," Sandborne said. "Why?"

Halstead got to his feet and got going. "Check McBride's desk for that list of posse men he said he could call on in an emergency. If you can't find it there, go to one of the saloons and make them help you find some men. If that fails, go to Mayor White in Town Hall, though I don't think he's in the right state of mind to help us. Get whoever you can find to stand with you at the bank and do whatever Kendrick tells you. Do it now. The quicker we can show we're in charge, the less likely people will be to step out of line."

Sandborne did not hesitate to begin going through the dead man's desk. "And what if they make a run at us."

"Fire a shot over their heads," Halstead told him as he headed for the door. "If that doesn't work, fire into the crowd. I'll be there as soon as I can."

"What'll you be doing?" Sandborne called after him.

Halstead opened the jailhouse door. "Sending a message of my own."

# Chapter 23

Halstead stormed past all of the people who had gathered on the boardwalk. They cleared a path when they saw him coming and did not bother to ask him questions. He supposed his pace and the look in his eye was to thank for that.

He ignored the stage driver when he reached The Standard Hotel and walked into the lobby. The place was crowded with travelers and their luggage. He was glad to see Abby was already sitting in the lobby with two of her bags packed.

He did not like seeing the tears that streaked her face as she ran to him. "Thank God you're here," she said as she buried her face in his chest. "I thought we were going to leave before we had the chance to say good-bye."

The fat coach driver moved behind Abby in an attempt to get his attention.

Halstead cut him short by saying, "Start loading their bags. You can begin with Miss Abby's first, then the others. She'll be along in a minute."

The driver took Abby's bags with him as he headed out the door.

Now that they were alone again, he spoke to Abby.

"I know you probably didn't have time to get everything, but don't worry. I'll bring the rest of your stuff with me when I come to Helena."

"I don't care about my stuff, Jeremiah. I care about you. I don't like leaving you at a time like this. Not after what happened last night."

He gently lifted her head so he could see those beautiful blue eyes one last time. "A lot of bad things are liable to happen here today, and I want you safe from all of that. By this time tomorrow, you'll be halfway to Helena. You see anyone on the train you don't like, you tell the conductor or one of the porters, and they'll take care of it. You have that present I left for you in your bag?"

She nodded, confirming that she had the small .22 derringer in her purse. "It's Tom's isn't it?"

"Think of it as part of his repayment to you for all of the kindness you've shown him this past year. It's really easy to use. Just point and squeeze the trigger."

That instruction only made her hold on to him tighter. "But I still don't understand why you and Joshua can't come with me. This is town business, Jeremiah. Not federal. Let them handle it while you come back to Helena. Get more men and come back and do it right the way Jack wanted you to do it."

He did not dare tell her that Mackey might order him to do exactly that. He did not want to get her hopes up, only to disappoint her later. "I'll be a whole lot safer if I know you're out of danger. You're not doing this for yourself. You're doing it for me, and I love you for it."

She squeezed him tighter as he noticed the crowd in the lobby was beginning to thin out. Most of the passengers were already on the stagecoach and he began walking her toward the front door. She went, but reluctantly.

"You promise you'll be careful?" she asked. "What happened with your shoulder scares me."

"I dislocate it all the time," he told her. "I snap it back in and I'm as good as new." He did not tell her the pain of snapping it back into place had made him black out for a few minutes.

They got closer to the stage and she added, "And be nice to Sandborne. He looks up to you, you know? He deserves a little kindness now and then."

He smiled. Even at a time like this, she was thinking of someone else. "I promise."

When they reached the stagecoach, the driver was standing by the door, tapping his boot on the floorboard. She kissed Halstead on the cheek and allowed him to help her up into the carriage. She mouthed "I love you" to him as the driver shut the door and went to climb up into the wagon box.

Halstead grabbed the driver by the arm. "Anyone riding shotgun with you?"

The fat man shook his head. "Never been any call for one on this run before. Don't need one now." He patted the Colt on his hip. "I'm armed."

"That's good." Halstead's fingers dug into the man's fleshy arm until he almost cried out. "Because if that lady doesn't make it on that train, I'll kill you."

He held on to the fat man's arm until he was sure he understood, then released him with a shove.

The driver dug a yellow envelope out of his shirt pocket and threw it at him. "And here's your damned telegram you were waiting for. Don't ask me to send another, either."

Halstead picked up the envelope and stood on the boardwalk, looking at Abby as the driver got ready to get underway. She mouthed the words to him again and he found the courage to mouth them back.

The driver cracked the reins, bringing the six-horse team alive, and they sped along Main Street toward the main road that would lead them to Wellspring and the train to Helena.

He watched the stage until it disappeared from view. He wished he had been riding with them. He wished he could deliver his message to Mackey in person instead of the few hastily scribbled sentences he had asked Abby to give Mackey. It was something he had not dared share with Kendrick or Mayor White. The fewer people who knew she was on the train, the better.

He had a deep, sinking feeling in his gut as the stage made the turn and disappeared out of view. Sandborne had been right. With her out of town and safe, he could concentrate on what he had to do.

And it was just about time he got to doing it.

He remembered the telegram he was holding and removed it from the sealed envelope. It was from Mackey and it was typically brief:

MESSAGE RECEIVED. BE CAREFUL AND
HOLD FAST.

He slipped the telegram into his pocket and looked at the bank just up the street. The mayor had been right. A small group of about five men and women had begun to mill around the entrance. All of them were working hard to look calm, but he could practically feel their anxiety from here.

Halstead hoped the four thousand dollars he had recovered from the dead outlaw would cover Kendrick in case everyone tried to pull out their money at once.

And even if it did, it would only make matters worse for the town. With all that cash in the open, thieves were bound to try to steal it from beneath their mattresses or the Bibles where they were likely to hide their savings. A small wave of crime was liable to wash over the town, leaving only Halstead and Sandborne to handle it all. The fact they were not locals would not help matters any. And the idea of one of them being considered a half-breed would be even worse.

He had to act and act now.

He walked over to the livery at a faster pace than he wanted.


With both Winchesters now in the scabbards under his legs, Halstead rode Col over to Doc Potter's office at the edge of town. He climbed down from the saddle and wrapped Col's reins around the hitching rail, then walked into the crowded waiting area.

One of the townswomen was acting like a nurse, examining patients in the waiting room while the doctor and Tom Ringham were handling the more dire cases behind the curtain in the back.

Halstead parted the curtain and saw Tom Ringham working on stitching up a nasty gash on a man's leg.

Halstead said, "Looks like we've finally found a way to put you to good use, Ringham."

The man on the table moaned as Ringham continued

to stitch the wound closed. "This fellow here was foolish enough to stick his head out the window when he heard all the shooting. A bullet hit the window instead of him and he backed into his chamber pot, fell over and gashed his leg. The pot was full, so it'll be a miracle if he doesn't lose this leg."

The man was just as crude now as he had been on the train. "You've got one hell of a bedside manner, Tom. I'll give you that."

"Hope to have the chance to work on you before all of this is over," Ringham said without looking up from his work. "That would make me the happiest man in the world."

Realizing there was nothing to be gained by continuing to spar with him, Halstead moved to the back where Doctor Earl Potter was pulling a bullet out of a woman's lower back. The short, frail-looking man was too focused on the operation to greet Halstead properly.

"Your friends left quite a mess on their way out of town," Potter said as he dropped the bullet into a steel pan. "This poor woman lives on the first floor of one of the new places along Baxter Street. Got shot while she was talking with a friend of hers." The quick glance he gave Halstead said he was putting a finer shine on the truth than it deserved. "She's about the worst of it, though. The others are all minor in comparison, though one man did catch a splinter of glass in the eye. I'm hopeful I can save it for him, but only time will tell."

Potter pinched a thick lump of cotton and swabbed the woman's wound. "I take it you're not here to check up on our patients, deputy."

Halstead was not. "I'm here for the outlaw."

"I figured that was the reason," the doctor said. "You'll

find him in the barn out back next to poor Jack. I'll set to embalming the marshal later, but I don't plan on wasting another moment on the bastard he killed. The vultures can have him for all I care."

"I like the way you think, doc." Halstead pulled his Bowie knife from the sheath on the back of his belt and headed out the back door toward the barn. "I really do."

# Chapter 24

As he sat on the porch of what had once been the Hard Scrabble Jail, Ed Zimmerman finished his mug of coffee. He picked up the pot he had placed on the floor next to him and refilled it. It was a cold morning, but the coffee was fresh. He had never developed a taste for piping hot coffee and preferred it to cool a little before he drank it. He could drink a whole pot in half an hour if the mood struck him, and it struck him to do so now. It never made his hands shake like it did other men. If anything, it had always served to steady him. To heighten his senses and make him think clearly.

He wanted to think clearly now. He wanted to celebrate this moment.

Not even the constant hammering and banging and sawing and cursing that filled the streets of his new Valhalla could dampen his mood. He looked over at The Miner's Bank and Trust building. The bank. His bank.

This morning, he and his men had made a deposit of just over fifty thousand dollars of Battle Brook's money. It would have been more if Pete had not gone and gotten himself killed by McBride. He knew there was a reason why he had not given the odd outlaw a name and now he was glad he had not wasted the effort. He had not deserved a proper nickname like the rest of The Spoilers did, and his death proved it. The rest of his men had gotten away clean, or at least as clean as they could have hoped. The entire scheme had been running beautifully until McBride went and ruined it.

At least he was dead for all the trouble they had caused. Zimmerman counted that as something of a victory.

He looked toward the doctor's office, directly across the street from the old jail and behind the bank, when he heard Brunet cut loose with another blood-curdling scream. Doctor Alfred Nesser had already told Zimmerman that he was having a tougher time getting that bullet out of him than expected. Brunet had thought he had only been shot once, but in fact, he had been hit twice. One of the bullets had gone straight through him as Brunet had said.

But a second bullet—the one Brunet had not felt—was buried deep in his lower back and was dangerously close to the spine. So close, in fact, that the timid little doctor begged Brunet to leave the bullet where it was so that it might move to a location where he could remove it easier at a later time.

But Brunet knew as much about bullet wounds as Zimmerman did. He had seen the agony men went through as a bullet many years old wormed its way through a man's body. Nesser only agreed to do the operation after both Zimmerman and Brunet swore on a Bible that they would not shoot him if the operation left Brunet paralyzed or dead.

The trite rite had amused Zimmerman. He was surprised the Good Book had not burst into flames as he placed his hand upon it. But it had not, and Zimmerman gave his oath, which seemed to placate the doctor some.

The little fool had no idea that he would be doing Zimmerman a favor if he crippled or killed Brunet. The outlaw would only serve as an obstacle now that his plan was fully underway. It was no fault of Brunet. Zimmerman's plan had simply moved beyond Brunet's usefulness.

The Bank of Battle Brook would fall. He had already seen to that. Wycoff had spent days whispering in enough ears about the bank's insolvency before the robbery. About Kendrick's drinking and other irregularities whose seeds had already been sown deep in the fertile ground of town gossip. Now after last night's robbery, those seeds would blossom into a full-blown panic.

The four thousand dollars they had left behind in Pete's pockets might save the bank for one day, but not two. By this time tomorrow, people would be pounding on the bank's doors, looking to withdraw money that was no longer there, but safely secured in Cal Hubbard's vaults.

And when the bank fell, so would the half-built town of Battle Brook.

That would be the moment when Ed Zimmerman's plan would finally come to fruition.

He took another sip of lukewarm coffee and cursed the sun for not moving fast enough across the sky, for the sooner the next day came, the sooner he would come into his glory. He would no longer be Ed Zimmerman the outlaw but Mr. Edward J. Zimmerman, late of California and other parts west. Mr. Edward J. Zimmerman, Financier.

He peered up at the sun that had only begun to rise above the mountains behind the bank. *Move, you lazy bastard. My destiny awaits.*

He looked away when he saw a driver crack the whip at a team of four horses pulling an old coach from the livery and park it in front of the bank. The coach was in sad shape for it had been neglected for years. It was dusty, with cracked brown paint and the glass in all the sidelamps broken long ago. He imagined the damned thing had become a haven for spiders and other vermin as it sat forgotten and untended to in the back of the livery yard. He convinced himself that he could almost smell the rat shit from where he now sat.

But Cal Hubbard had insisted on the formality of using his own coach, as sorry as it looked, as he was about to embark on the greatest journey of his career. One that would allow him to see the vengeance he had craved for so long. For that day, Hubbard was riding to Battle Brook to assure the frightened people that he would honor their savings by offering them credit on their deposits at a very low rate.

Zimmerman had to admire the banker's cunning. He was not only going to loan the poor bastards the money he had stolen from them but charge them interest on top of it.

The idea made Zimmerman laugh out loud. He liked the way Hubbard thought and, unless he got greedy or stupid, Zimmerman was sure they could make each other wealthy men.

No, he decided as he sipped his coffee that cold morning. They were already wealthy men. Soon they would be powerful men.

He watched Cal Hubbard toddle out of his bank and wave across the thoroughfare to Zimmerman. He was wearing a new suit or at least one that was new to him. It was a blue suit with felt along the collar that was several years out of fashion, but Zimmerman had to admit gave

Hubbard a certain look of authority. And the poor people of Battle Brook would need a competent man now.

Zimmerman noticed the nasty cut he had received when Jack McBride had tried to shove his head through the window had healed enough to look like he had nicked himself shaving, though above the left eye was an odd place for such a cut.

Zimmerman watched the banker climb into his dusty, dilapidated coach when the driver called out, "Hey, Mr. Zimmerman, who's that?"

He was pointing to the east, toward the road that led from Battle Brook.

Zimmerman got to his feet as soon as he saw what the driver was pointing at.

It was a lone rider, dressed in all black atop a brown mustang. Even that much was clear to him from this distance. The morning sun glinted off the silver handle of the Colt he wore holstered on his belly.

Even if he had not been able to see such detail, he would have known the rider was Jeremiah Halstead simply by the way the man carried himself on top of a horse.

He could not see the man's face but knew he had stopped just outside the established limits of what had once been Hard Scrabble and was now called Valhalla.

He was holding something in his right hand. Something long, like a flag staff, perhaps, or a spear.

Zimmerman slowly stepped off the porch and into the thoroughfare to get a better look at the man. *Why in hell would a gunman be holding a spear?*

By then, some of the other men of Valhalla, Spoilers and hired workmen alike, had seen the man as well and stopped what they were doing to look at him.

Monk happened to be closest to Zimmerman and asked, "That Halstead, boss?"

Zimmerman squinted at the distant figure, but still could not make out what he was holding, and it troubled him. "Sure looks like him, don't it?"

Then he watched Halstead raise the pole and plunge it into the ground. It was only then that Zimmerman realized it was, indeed, a staff of some kind for there was something hanging from the top of it.

He continued to watch as Halstead slowly backed his horse away from what he had planted. He did not turn and ride away. Instead, he made the horse walk backward until he was just around the bend and out of view.

Monk said, "He sure wasn't hiding. That's for sure. Want us to mount up and run him down?"

"On our nags?" Zimmerman shook his head. "He's riding a mustang. He's probably already a half a mile away by now. Get someone to ride out there and fetch what he left us."

Monk relayed the word to the others, and within a few moments, Scar was on his horse and heading for the staff at full gallop. He doubted Halstead would be waiting to ambush him. If he had come for a fight, he would have ridden into town shooting, just like he had done back in Silver Cloud.

No, this was something else. This was a message, like the bullet he had left for Zimmerman back at the shack. The bullet he now carried with him in his shirt pocket.

The same bullet he would one day use to end Halstead's life.

Hubbard struggled to lower the dusty window of his coach before he yelled out to Zimmerman. "What's the hold up, Ed? I need to get to Battle Brook before the riots start, not after."

But Zimmerman did not take his eyes off Scar. Not when he paused to ride around and examine the staff. Not when he plucked it from the ground and carried it back into town, either.

"Simmer down, Cal. You'll get there. Just gotta see what Halstead left for us first."

He stood alone in the thoroughfare, watching Scar approach him at a good run. He only drew rein on the horse about ten yards away from Zimmerman, when he brought it to a walk and planted the staff in the ground for Zimmerman to see.

It was, indeed, a flag staff, or at least had been at one time. A bloody buffalo hide was draped atop it now. The front of it full of bloody holes from a shotgun blast.

Jack McBride's shotgun.

This was Pete's coat.

He noticed something sticking out of the coat pocket. And although he recognized it for what it was, he pulled it out for the benefit of all those who were watching.

It was a scalp with long, curly brown hair that had once belonged to Pete. A piece of paper fell out of the pocket as Zimmerman removed the scalp and he placed a foot on the paper to keep the wind from taking it.

With Pete's scalp still in hand, he bent over and picked up the note from under his boot.

The wind had died as quickly as it had come, so he was able to read the note easily. He read it out loud for all of the men to hear.

"It says, 'Figured you could add this one to your collection. You're next.'"

Zimmerman laughed as he folded the piece of paper

and stuck it in the same pocket that held Halstead's bullet. "Why, I do believe Jeremiah Halstead has just declared war on us, boys."

The men whooped and hollered, Scar atop his horse loudest of all.

Hubbard stuck his head out the coach window and lost his breakfast.

Zimmerman tossed the scalp up to Scar, who caught it easily. "Burn it and burn Pete's coat, too. I only keep the scalps I take personally."

As Scar removed what he had brought, Zimmerman slowly walked over to Hubbard. The banker was back in his coach, patting his mouth with a handkerchief.

Hubbard said, "Come to think of it, I don't think today's the best day for me to go into Battle Brook, Ed. Not after this."

"Nonsense," Zimmerman told him. "Now's the perfect time. Show them we're not scared of them."

Hubbard blinked at him twice. "The man just rode up here and planted a bloody coat with a man's scalp in the ground and you're telling me I shouldn't be scared?"

"That was for me, not you," Zimmerman assured him. "Besides, none of this works unless we bring down the bank. And we can't do that from here. You'll have to do that from there."

Hubbard looked like he might be sick again.

Zimmerman took a step away from the coach, but when the threat passed, he said, "I've already done the easy part, Cal. This is your part. It's just as important as mine, and you know it."

Hubbard nodded quickly but kept the handkerchief at his mouth when Zimmerman told the driver to get moving.

Zimmerman slowly walked back to the old jail and sat

down. He picked up his mug of coffee from the porch and drained it. He poured himself another.

Delivering Pete's coat and scalp on a spike was a nice touch. "You're next" was good, too. To the point.

He raised his mug to the east and offered a toast. "Deputy Halstead, I do believe I'm beginning to like you."

But trusting him was another matter. The trap he had laid for him in the cabin had failed, but that had been before McBride's death and before he had a possible riot on his hands. Despite his act of bravado just now, the deputy marshal was a man on the brink of disaster. All it would take was one tap to make him go over the edge and make a mistake.

He remembered back to the Siege of Dover Station and how confident Darabont had been that Mackey would either crack or the people would turn him over. Neither had happened and Darabont had paid with his life.

But Jeremiah Halstead was not Aaron Mackey. Just a cheap imitation.

He decided it was time to prove just how cheap.

"Bullet! Blackfoot!" he called out to the outlaws as he waved them to come to him. "I've got a job for you boys, but I'm afraid you're gonna have to make yourselves a bit more presentable first."

# Chapter 25

Halstead did not bring Col into a full gallop on the way back to Battle Brook, but he did not allow her to walk at her own pace either. With the possibility of a riot breaking out at the bank, he knew he needed to get back there as soon as possible.

He knew Mackey would not have approved of him taking valuable time in the middle of a crisis to deliver a message to Zimmerman and Brunet.

But Halstead knew violence was the only thing that men like Zimmerman and Brunet understood. And since the outlaws had surrounded themselves with too many gunmen for him to arrest them, a symbolic message was all he could deliver. A message written in blood.

Halstead and Col had made it back to town just after eleven that morning and, even from the outskirts of town, he could feel the tension that had settled over Battle Brook.

The hammering and sawing that had become part of the music of the town had stopped and, as he rode down Main Street, he could see the thick cluster of people that had gathered in front of the bank. He steered Col in that direction.

To call it a chaotic scene would have been kind.

Joshua Sandborne was doing his best to direct two men with rifles to use their weapons as barriers to keep the front entrance of the bank clear. Men and women were standing in a crowd six or seven people deep in the thoroughfare in the hopes of getting into the bank.

"We need everyone to form a line," Sandborne was trying to shout over their pleas for admittance. "Line up over to my left and we'll make sure everyone has a chance to get inside."

But Halstead knew the deputy might as well be yelling into a gale for all the good it did him. The people did not budge and held their bank books aloft as they crammed toward the entrance, demanding to be allowed inside.

Halstead had never seen the two riflemen at Sandborne's side but recognized the look of fear in their eyes. If things continued to remain nasty, they would run and Sandborne would be swamped.

Halstead steered Col toward the crowd and rode her close to the boardwalk. The mustang easily pushed her way through the knot of people. Those who did not back up were moved aside by the eight hundred pounds of muscle and power that pushed through them.

He kept Col moving until he reached Sandborne at the entrance and turned the horse so that it cleared a circle in front of the bank. The people who had been pushed back had remained at a distance and did not crowd the animal. They all knew how deadly a frightened horse could be.

Halstead looked down at the crowd from his saddle and said, "You will form two lines on either side of the bank entrance. One on the right, one on the left. You'd better form a line quick because the sooner you do, the sooner you'll get your money. Anyone still in the thoroughfare who is not on a line by the time my horse turns around will be arrested for loitering. Good luck getting your money from jail."

The townspeople scrambled to form lines on either side of the guards Sandborne had managed to get.

Only one man stood in his way. He was a miner of indeterminate age whose skin and clothing were as dark as the ore he hacked from the ground with the pickaxe he now held in his hand.

Since the miner kept the axe at his side, Halstead kept his Colts in their holsters.

"Same goes for you," Halstead told him. "Pick a line and stand on it. It'll only get longer if you wait."

But the miner did not move. "Every cent I've got is in that bank, mister. And not you or anyone else is going to keep me from going in there to get it."

"You'll be allowed in," Halstead assured him, "as long as you get on a line."

The miner brought up the axe to waist-level and held it in both hands. "And I told you no one's going to keep me from going in there to get my money."

Halstead drew the Colt from his belly holster and aimed it down at the miner. "Money's no good to a dead man. Get on a line or die where you stand." He thumbed back the hammer, which made some in the crowd flinch. "Right now."

The miner looked him over with squinted eyes. His arms were thick from swinging that axe since the time he had been old enough to hold it. His back was stooped from all the years he had spent in the gloomy, candle-lit terror of the mines, laboring so other men could get rich while he drew a wage and slowly became a cripple.

Halstead did not want to kill this man, but he needed to

maintain order. If order cost this man's life to maintain it, Halstead would pay it.

He was glad when the man lowered his axe and lumbered off to his right to find a place with the rest of the townspeople.

He holstered his Colt and turned his horse around and saw two lines along the boardwalk flanking the entrance to the bank. It was the first hint of good news he'd had all day. He began to think that maybe Ed Zimmerman would not win after all.

"Thank you," he called out to everyone. "I know it's cold and you're scared and hungry. I'll see what we can do about getting some coffee brought out to you while you wait. Just remain calm, and I can promise, as bad as this is, we can keep it from getting any worse."

Some of the people grumbled back at him, that it was easy for him to say since his money had not been stolen. He beckoned Sandborne to come to him as he and Col were out of earshot from the rest of the crowd.

"Besides the obvious," Halstead asked him, "what's the disposition?"

"Better now that you're here," Sandborne told him. "There's about a hundred out here by my count, but I hear it'll be double that number before noon. Word about the robbery has already spread through the mining camps, and I hear they're anxious to come to town for their money."

Halstead had been afraid of that. "And they won't be in a good mood when they get here." There was also nothing he could do about it, so he focused on the part of the problem he could control. "What about those two men you got to stand with you."

"I'm lucky they're standing at all," Sandborne told him.

"One's the old bouncer at The Hot Pepper and the other is a freighter looking for work. I found him in The Blue Belle. They're reasonably sober, but I didn't trust them enough to give them loaded rifles. I couldn't find any list in McBride's desk of posse men, and the mayor just looked at me like I was crazy when I went to ask him about it. I think the old boy's off his nut."

Halstead could not blame him. One day, he had been in charge of a boom town. Now, all he had was a bank about to go bust, a bunch of half-built buildings, and a town on the verge of ripping itself apart.

Everything in Jeremiah Halstead told him to ride hard for Wellspring and dash off a telegram to Mackey. Maybe he could arrange to have regulators come from the capital and put a stop to this. Or maybe Mackey himself could bring a few marshals with him to help him enforce the warrants that would bring Zimmerman and Brunet to justice.

But the more he thought about it, the more he realized that there would be no help coming any time soon. With statehood coming in a few days, the capital was a sea of people from across the country to celebrate the occasion. The problems in a couple of small towns at the far end of the territory would not matter much amid the dream of being admitted into the Union finally being realized.

Mackey would care, of course, but there was not much he could do about it. There were no extra marshals to send to help. More than half of them had retired when Mackey had taken over. Most of them had served much longer than they should have. A few were angry they had been overlooked for the position.

And even if Mackey and Billy came all the way out here themselves, it would be days before they got here, and it would be four against an entire town of outlaws. Maybe fifty or more by Jack McBride's guess.

Halstead had no doubt that Zimmerman had planned for that, and all the work he had been doing throughout the former Hard Scrabble had served to turn Valhalla into something closer to a fort than a town.

Halstead looked down at Sandborne and saw nothing but resolve in the younger man's eyes. "Is the bank open?"

Sandborne nodded. "They're only letting in about twelve at a time. When one comes out, we let one go in. It'll run a lot smoother now that you helped set up the lines for us. I tried my best to keep them in order, but—"

"Enough." Halstead could not afford to allow Sandborne to begin doubting himself. "You kept them from rushing the bank and that's all that matters. I didn't do anything." He patted Col's neck. "She did all the work."

"There's plenty of work still to do," Sandborne pointed out. "This crowd's only going to get bigger and rowdier the closer we get to closing time. And these two I got with me are going to start getting the shakes soon if they don't get some drink into them."

"That's my problem now." He climbed down from the saddle and handed Col's reins to Sandborne. "Tie her up to the post in front of the bank. I'll go inside and ask Kendrick how he's holding up. If he runs out of money and closes his doors, we'll need to know that ahead of time. It would be nice to get ahead of a problem for once, wouldn't it?"

Halstead found the bank president in his office, looking at his cluttered desk as if seeing it for the first time.

"Mr. Kendrick," Halstead said, which caused the man to snap out of it. "How's the bank holding up?"

"Fine for now," he said barely above a whisper. "It's all my fault, you know? The robbery, I mean. I never should have kept a spare key to the vault in my desk. I should've kept it in the small safe over there, but I didn't. Bad habits creep up on us so slowly, don't they, deputy?"

"There'll be plenty of time for guilt later," Halstead told him. "Right now, I need to know if you're going to remain open or shut your doors. I need to keep a riot from breaking out."

"We have a little over ten thousand in cash on hand," he said flatly. "That includes the coinage they left behind."

Halstead thought that was great news. "I didn't know you had so much. That should see you through, shouldn't it?"

"For today," he allowed. "Maybe. My clerks are out there right now bringing people over to the vault, showing them we have plenty of cash on hand. Some have decided to keep their money with us, but a great many more have insisted upon cleaning out their accounts. Once the miners come down from the hills after their shifts, I doubt we'll have more than a thousand left over. Most likely less. You see, most of that cash back there is my own. Every cent I have in the world. And when that's gone, it's all over. For the bank. And for me, too."

Halstead did not have a head for numbers and had no idea how banks worked. But if Kendrick was worried, Halstead figured he should be worried, too. "What can I do?"

Kendrick looked at him wearily. "All that can be done has been done, young man. I've sent a rider to Wellspring to send a telegram to Helena asking the banks there to move some of their deposits here. But they won't arrive until two days from now at the earliest, even if they come by special train. Mr. Ryan has committed to making a deposit, too, but we're too far away for him to make much of a difference. Everyone will get their money back eventually, but we will never get their trust back again. I'm afraid that's gone for good." He ran his hand over the ruined lock on his desk drawer. "That damned key."

Halstead was glad he could give him some good news. "We've got the crowd out front calmed down. They're in two lines on either side of the door."

"Mr. Sandborne did an admirable job under the circumstances," he said. "He's forceful beyond his years."

Halstead already knew that. "You might want to send someone to the dining halls and hotels to give people out there some coffee. It's cold, and the gesture might do you some good."

Kendrick said he would. "It also might make some of them need to use a privy. That should thin out the line a bit."

Halstead watched Kendrick's look of sad concern turn to something else as he looked out the window into the lobby. "My God. What's that bastard doing here?"

Halstead turned to see a dilapidated coach had pulled up outside the bank. He stood next to Kendrick as they watched the burly driver jump down from his box and struggle to open the door.

When he finally managed to pull it open, a round man with impressive white mutton chops stepped down from the coach.

"Who's that?" Halstead asked.

"Calvin Hubbard," Kendrick told him. "From The Miner's Bank and Trust in Hard Scrabble or whatever they're calling it these days. He's probably here to gloat."

But Halstead doubted that was the only reason why he had come to town. He rushed out the door to hear what the man had to say for himself. He doubted it would be anything good.

By the time Halstead reached the front door of the bank, he found Hubbard shaking hands of miners and embracing weeping women. All of them were fearful for the savings they had inside the bank. They asked him questions for which he had no answers. Had their money been stolen? How would they pay their bills? Were they ruined? Hubbard spoke to them the way a father speaks to a crying child and telling them all would be fine soon.

The people on that side of the boardwalk had maintained their spots in line as Hubbard moved among them like a missionary tending to the poor, but those on the other side of the bank entrance had become a mob again. They clamored to get the attention of the banker they had known and trusted for so long. Sandborne and another guard urged them to keep their place in line with mixed results.

Halstead saw the coach team was blocking Col between them and the rail Sandborne had tied her to. The mustang had never been fond of being penned in, so close quarters like this were causing her to buck and pull on her reins. It was only a matter of time before the horse panicked and hurt herself.

Halstead found the burly coach driver next to Hubbard and pulled him away from the banker. "Your rig is blocking in my horse. Get up there and pull it back. Now."

The taller, wider man pointed at Hubbard. "I take my orders from him, breed, not you."

Halstead snatched the bigger man by the throat and threw him against the coach face first. He followed it up with a boot to the backside as the driver steadied himself. "Get up there and move that rig or go to jail. Your choice."

Still smarting from the boot to the pants, the driver climbed up and did what Halstead had ordered him to do while Hubbard continued to work the crowd. Halstead quickly feared he might have started a riot by being rough with the coachman, but the crowd was too focused on Hubbard and the promise of hope he offered to notice.

"Keep calm," Hubbard implored as he moved amongst them as a healer might move among lepers. "Keep calm. Help is here now, I assure you."

Customers from the other side of the doorway ignored Sandborne completely now and rushed to Hubbard. Halstead had to stand in front of them to keep the bank entrance clear. The people remained a few feet away but were growing more anxious to move forward by the second.

Sandborne broke through the crowd and stood at Halstead's side. "Looks like the two guys who were helping me with the crowd took off. What do you want me to do, boss?"

Halstead knew there was not much they could do while Hubbard was there. He had to yell directly into Sandborne's ear to be heard. "Keep these people back while I go see what this idiot is up to."

Halstead saw the coach driver back at Hubbard's side. The banker was about to embrace another crying woman when Halstead took him by the arm and forced him to walk out into the thoroughfare with him. The coach driver yelled something at Halstead, but he could not hear him over the crowd.

When they reached the relative quiet on the other side of the coach, Halstead let go of the banker's arm. "What the hell are you doing here, Hubbard?"

The banker smiled at the lawman. "I see my reputation precedes me, sir. I take it from your complexion that you must be that Jeremiah Halstead everyone is talking about."

Halstead decided to ignore the comment about his looks. "You've just ridden into a dangerous situation, Hubbard, and I want to know why before you make it worse."

The driver tried to intervene, but Halstead pointed at him. "You keep your mouth shut and go help the deputy keep that crowd in line before we're overrun."

Hubbard motioned for his driver to obey Halstead. "I'm here to provide comfort, Deputy Halstead. To offer assurance to a scared and frightened people. I mean no harm, only hope. And if you're as smart as I hear you are, you'll allow me to defuse this situation before you find yourself with a burning town on your hands."

Halstead resented the implied threat. "I've never been overrun yet and it's not going to happen now."

The banker raised his round chins to an area behind Halstead's left shoulder. "Oh, but I'm afraid you are."

Halstead turned around and saw a thick crowd of miners had just turned the corner from the hills and were coming toward the bank. Some of them were riding in buckboards. Most were on foot. He did not bother trying to count them. He just saw a wall of people coming his way in a hurry.

Their clothes and faces were smeared with dirt and sweat. Some of them had brought shovels and pickaxes with them. He was sure some of them were armed in other ways, too. They were already yelling and raising their fists in the air as they moved along Main Street.

They were coming for their money like a human locomotive and nothing on earth was going to stop them from getting it.

Halstead fought the urge to grab Hubbard by his lapels

and demand him to admit he and Zimmerman and Brunet were behind the robbery. Part of him wanted to throw him to the growing mob and let them tear him apart.

But he knew that would only make things worse. He felt like he was being squeezed between the people at the bank, the approaching mob of miners, and Hubbard's smug confidence.

Halstead forced himself to keep his hands at his sides. "I need to know what you're going to say to these people before I let you say it."

The banker was enjoying his triumph. "Sounds like you're a smart boy after all. I'll make a deal with you if you promise to listen to reason."

The miners were getting closer. He looked over at Sandborne, who was now using his rifle as a bar again to keep the crowd back from the bank entrance. The coach driver was having an easier time of it on his side of the door.

Halstead did not have a choice but to hear him out. He had to raise his voice as the shouts of the townspeople grew louder as the miners got closer. "Go ahead."

"You let me go on top of this coach and address the crowd. Mayor White should do it, but I imagine he's too shaken by McBride's death to be much good to anyone at the moment. I give you my word that I will not only calm them down but cause them to disburse in peace."

Halstead thought it over and thought it over fast. He hated the idea of allowing the man who was likely responsible for the robbery to speak to them, but he did not have much of a choice.

Hubbard seemed to sense his deliberation and added, "Let me speak, and I will give you something you've been looking for since the day you rode into Battle Brook."

"What's that?"

The banker smiled. "Ed Zimmerman."

Halstead heard the miners approaching ever closer now, chanting, "Where's our money? Where's our money?"

Halstead made his choice, though it was really no choice at all. "Get up there and start talking. But if you say one word that gets them riled up, I swear to Christ I'll blow you right off that coach."

He stepped aside as the driver stepped forward to assist the fleshy banker up into the wagon box. As Hubbard got his bearings, Halstead shouted to the driver, "You got a rifle?"

The driver reached up and pulled down a Spencer rifle from the coach box.

Halstead knew the driver would guard his boss, so telling him to stand there was pointless. Halstead unwrapped Col's reins from the rail and climbed into the saddle and rode out to meet the approaching miners.

They stopped, if only to glare up at Halstead. There was conviction in their eyes. Murder and fear, too.

A red-headed, bearded miner up front said, "If you think you're stopping us from going in that bank—"

Halstead interrupted him. "Mr. Hubbard has come over from his bank in Hard Scrabble to give you all some news. You can gather 'round and listen to him, but I don't want anyone to cause any trouble. If you still want to get into the bank afterwards, you'll have to get on the line like everyone else. That's all we're asking."

"And what if we don't?" one of the miners in the crowd called out.

He looked in the direction of the man, though he could not point him out. "Then a lot of people are going to get hurt or killed. Some of you men have seen bank runs before. We don't want that happening here."

Not wanting to force a confrontation, Halstead pulled back on the reins and forced Col to step backward. The mare did not like it, but she did it until she was backed up against the boardwalk in front of the bank entrance.

The miners fanned out and filled the thoroughfare as Halstead gave ground. They not only filled the thoroughfare, but all of the boardwalks across the street. He imagined there were about three hundred men or more.

He decided to leave his rifle in its scabbard. The men were close enough for pistol work if it came down to shooting.

Hubbard stood in the wagon box and called out to the people. "Gather around, my friends, and listen to my words. I know all about the robbery that took place here this morning. I know you not only lost your money, but a good man in the process. Jack McBride was our town marshal. He was also my friend. I admired him, and I know you all mourn his loss as much as I do. I ask you to join me in a moment of silence out of respect for his eternal soul."

Halstead eyed the crowd and saw every head bow at Hubbard's command. The banker had them in the palm of his hand. Whether or not that was a good thing would be proven out in a couple of minutes.

After pausing for an appropriate amount of time, Hubbard raised his head and resumed his speech. "I know a lot of you are blaming my good friend James Kendrick for the robbery that took place early this morning. I ask you to not do that. He did everything he could to safeguard your hard-earned money. He was betrayed by a greedy clerk who saw dollar signs in his eyes instead of his duty. Two good night watchmen also lost their lives due to Doug Wycoff's betrayal."

"Hang him!" cried out one miner, who was quickly joined by the rest of the townspeople who took up the cry.

Hubbard held up his hands to silence them. "He was killed by the cutthroats who stole your money, but not before he murdered the guards in cold blood."

The chants died away and were replaced by murmurs from the crowd.

Halstead eyed the crowd as Hubbard spoke. He had to admit the banker was handling them well. And had managed to pin the entire robbery on a dead man.

"Now, as most of you know, my bank and I have been of service to this community for more than a decade. The Miner's Bank and Trust has not only kept your money safe but provided the loans you needed to work your claims and build your houses. And even though Mr. Ryan and his partners decided to build up its holdings here in Battle Brook, we have managed to remain in operation. You held faith in us for years and now, in your time of need, you will find that faith has been well placed. That is why I have come here today to assure each and every one of you that your deposits are secure."

Halstead heard another murmur ripple through the crowd and wondered if they were getting ready to turn.

Hubbard resumed speaking over them. "You have my word that my bank will honor all deposits The Bank of Battle Brook cannot. If you decide to withdraw your money here, you can deposit it in The Miner's Bank and Trust with no extra charge. And if The Bank of Battle Brook fails, my bank will honor all of your accounts in the amounts listed in your bank book. We will grant you a line of credit for those amounts at a very low rate of interest."

The crowd shifted as men and women looked at each other to discuss what the banker had just told them.

One of the women from the line on the boardwalk called out, "At what rate?"

"Five percent," the banker answered. "I hope to bring that to an even lower rate, but at present, five percent is the number."

Halstead did his best to mask his disgust. The son of a bitch had stolen their money and now he was charging them to get it back.

One of the miners standing in front of Halstead called out, "So what you're saying is our money is safe, even after the robbery."

Hubbard replied instantly. "I'm telling you that should The Bank of Battle Brook fail, then The Miner's Bank and Trust will honor your deposits through an extension of credit at a very low rate. So, if you wish to withdraw your money from here, do so. If they run out of money, do not panic for my bank is here to help." He held up his hand as if to warn them. "Provided you have a bank book that verifies your deposit, of course."

Halstead watched many of the crowd hold up their bank books and shout at the banker, but he held out his hands again to ask them for calm. "There is one condition, however. All of you must follow Deputy Marshal Halstead's orders and conduct yourselves in an orderly fashion. We are most fortunate to have him here to keep the peace at this difficult hour, and it is up to all of you to ensure that peace is kept. My bank will not honor the claim of any man or woman arrested for rioting or looting or violence of any kind, especially in the unfortunate event that the bank must close its doors. Deputy Halstead and his partner have asked all of you to form an orderly line on either side of the bank and I ask you to do so now. That is all I have to say at the present time."

The miners rushed toward the banker as he began to climb down from the wagon, but his driver used his long Spencer to keep them back. Others scrambled to get in line as Hubbard had asked.

Halstead drew Col up next to the banker before he climbed all the way down. "You're some piece of work, Hubbard. Charging people for the money you stole from them."

Hubbard did not even bother to deny it. "Do you want Zimmerman or not?"

"Looking to get an even bigger piece of the pie, aren't you?" He almost admired the man's cunning. Almost. "Sure. Tell me."

"He's meeting the train from Helena tomorrow morning," Hubbard said. "He'll likely have some of his thugs with him, but I'm sure you can handle them. Though don't take them too lightly. Jack McBride did and look at what happened to him. I'd hate to see the same thing happen to you."

Halstead reluctantly pulled Col away to allow Hubbard to step down and scramble into his coach. Halstead moved Col between the miners and the rig as the wagon driver climbed up into the box and cracked the reins, sending the team of horses in motion.

Halstead watched the banker wave to the crowd from his dilapidated coach as if he was royalty speeding away from the throngs of people along Main Street.

But Hubbard had proven to be a man of his word. He had promised to give him Zimmerman and he had. For his own purposes, yes, but now he knew exactly where and when the outlaw would be in the open. And arresting Zimmerman had been his entire reason for coming to Battle Brook in the first place.

Now all he had to do was live long enough to grab him. And as he looked over the hundreds of people who had lined up on each side of the bank entrance, there was no guarantee that would happen.

For the town of Battle Brook was no longer just a town in western Montana.

It was a tinderbox. And it would take only the slightest spark to make it go up in flames.

# Chapter 26

Halstead's stomach began to tighten as five o'clock approached. According to the hours painted on the front door, the bank normally closed at that time.

After Hubbard left, the crowd had remained as orderly as Halstead could have wanted. The various food establishments in town had begun to serve coffee to the people waiting in line. Some paid. Some did not. Halstead told the waiters that the bank would cover all losses.

Some of the working girls at the saloons began to bring mugs of beer to the miners and some of the other men, but Halstead stopped the practice. He did not want a drunken mob acting up in case the bank ran out of money.

Sandborne now manned the bank door. The bank had abandoned their practice of allowing twelve in at a time. Now, as one person left, one person was allowed in. One from the right side, then one from the left. The line moved in slower, but movement was constant, which kept their nerves in check.

Halstead patrolled both sides of the line atop Col. He even gave some of the children waiting in line with their parents a ride on the horse, which only improved the mood of the crowd.

The miners, on the other hand, seemed content to leer up at him after he had stopped the beer runs from the saloons. But he had allowed the working girls to stay with them, which made them as happy as the children had been with the horse rides.

Halstead kept an eye on two particularly grizzled men who stood out from the rest.

The man on the right side was stooped and swarthy in an old coat and rumpled hat. The man on the left wore a fur cap and had no neck to speak of.

If they had been standing together or were on the same line, Halstead might not have noticed either man. But seeing as they had both arrived at the same time and were at similar points on their respective lines concerned him.

He could feel both men eyeing him as he approached only to quickly look away when he came by. While most of the crowd watched the line with anxious attention, these two seemed only interested in him.

The swarthy man on the line at the right was constantly scratching his reddened face, as if he was accustomed to a beard that was no longer there.

Halstead had noticed a similar redness of the other man's face, as well.

Even that could have been written off as a coincidence. But the shifty look in the eyes of the men whenever he passed by told Halstead that something was wrong. These men did not look like the type who deposit their money in banks. If anything, they looked more like cleaned up versions of the man Jack McBride had shot and killed during the robbery the night before. He began to wonder if they might belong to Zimmerman's bunch.

He was about to ask one of the men to show him his bank book when the line shuffled forward again. Halstead watched two miners come out of the bank and head in opposite directions while two more customers were allowed inside.

Halstead saw the swarthy man get off the line and approach one of the miners who had just left the bank. He tried to engage the man in conversation, but the young miner clearly did not know him. The miner managed to pull away when the stranger took him by the arm as he yelled, "What do you mean they're closing the bank? Are they out of money already?"

"They've run out of money!" yelled the man Halstead had been watching on the other line. "The bastards have been lying to us!"

Halstead tried to call for calm but the noise from the crowd began to pick up again. He brought Col around to try to get them to maintain order when the man with no neck shoved another man into the group of miners behind him. The victim knocked over one of the sporting ladies working the line, and the miners rushed to her defense.

At the opposite end of the bank, he saw a scuffle break out between the troublemaker and three men who had rushed to silence him.

Halstead sensed a crackle go through the crowd. The thin string that had been holding them in place had snapped and they made a mad dash for the bank door.

The line on both sides of the entrance broke and the customers rushed the front door like a horde.

Halstead dug his heels into Col, and the mustang responded by lurching deep into the crowd, casting aside the men and women in her wake. He brought Col into a tight turn, disbursing even more people from the area, and watched Sandborne use his rifle as a club to push people away from the bank.

Halstead saw that he had managed to keep them at bay until several frightened customers pushed the doors open and fled from the bank, knocking Sandborne forward, where he fell at Col's hooves.

Halstead reached down and grabbed hold of Sandborne's collar as he helped him to his feet.

A panicked bank clerk inside the bank had managed to lock the doors as the angry mob began beating against the glass as they demanded to be allowed inside.

Halstead looked up when he heard the unmistakable sound of glass shattering and saw several of the miners had driven their pickaxes through the bank window. Others joined in using shovels and axes and hammers to clear away the remaining shards from the frame as they climbed inside.

Now on his feet, Sandborne fired his rifle over the heads of the rioters. It served to make some of them run away, but most went back to pounding the door.

"Get back into line!" Sandborne commanded them. "Now!"

The remaining customers joined the miners who had begun to crawl through the window they had smashed. One man screamed out, his arms and legs flailing as he remained half in and half out of the bank window. A couple of anxious men took him by the belt and hauled him backward and into the street. Halstead saw a shard of window glass stuck deep in his belly.

A single pistol shot rang out from somewhere inside the bank and Halstead knew the situation had finally gotten out of hand.

Halstead pulled his Winchester '76 from its scabbard and leapt down from the saddle.

"Scatter them," he yelled to Sandborne over the shouts and screams of angry men and women. "Now!"

Sandborne took the left side, and Halstead took the right, where the window had been shattered. He wanted to break up the crowd on the boardwalk first before he handled whatever was happening inside the bank. There were too many damned things happening at once.

Halstead used his Winchester as a bar and shoved a group of men backward and into the thoroughfare.

Five of the men fell back but one of them was foolish enough to reach for Halstead's belly gun. Halstead slammed the man in the throat with his rifle' stock and batted him aside with his rifle butt. He knew he had not killed the man, but at least he was out of the fight.

The men and women behind them had no choice but to spill out into the muddy thoroughfare; the boardwalk was blocked by the miners who were still clustered together trying to climb through the window.

Halstead brought down the stock of his Winchester at their exposed kidneys, causing them to cry out in pain as he pulled them away from the window and tossed them into the street. He had managed to clear five of them out of the way before two of them saw him coming and came at him.

One of them threw a right hand that he easily dodged while another came in low to tackle him. Halstead brought the rifle butt down hard on the charging man's head as he sidestepped him and slammed the butt into the face of the man who had tried to punch him. The man stumbled back, clutching his shattered nose as he fell. The rest of the men on the boardwalk ran off along Main Street.

Halstead ducked as a chair came sailing through the broken bank window, barely missing him. He ducked beneath the window and crept back to the left side of it before coming up, Winchester at his shoulder.

"Any man in there had better throw up his hands now unless he wants to get shot."

A pair of hands rose up from beneath the window and grabbed hold of the barrel of Halstead's rifle. The deputy tried to pull it away but the man holding on to it was pulled to his feet and would not let go. Halstead squeezed the trigger, blasting the man in the chest at point blank range. He fell backward into the bank.

He could see more men moving around inside but could not tell who was a civilian and who was a clerk.

He stepped on the back of one of the men who had fallen in front of the window and boosted himself up and inside.

He landed on his feet. His Winchester ready. "Everyone stop where they are right now."

The ten men behind the teller cages threw up their hands. Halstead heard the pounding and splintering of wood as one of the tellers pointed to his right and yelled, "They're trying to break down the door!"

Halstead shifted his aim to the left side of the bank where a group of five miners with axes and hammers were hacking away at the door that led back to the cages.

Halstead levered in another round and fired a shot just above their heads.

The men stopped and looked his way as if he had just shaken them awake from a dream.

Halstead levered in another round. "That's it, boys. Just stop what you're doing and lay those tools on the floor. There's been enough people hurt for one day."

The miner with the pickaxe withdrew the tool from the door. He and his four friends looked at Halstead as the man said, "One more hit and that door will give, boys. Just one more hit, and we can have all the money owed us and a bit more for our trouble."

Halstead lowered his aim to that man. "Put them down. Last warning."

He watched the man grip the axe handle tighter. "You boys think you can get him?"

One of the men at the front was already in a crouch. "He might get one or two of us, but not all four of us. Just tell us what you want to do, Sean."

Sean, Halstead thought. The man's name was Sean. He probably had a family. So did the other four. They were not bad men. They were hard-working men scared that all that work now added up to nothing. They had not gone looking for trouble. They had gotten caught up in all of this just like he had. Just like Zimmerman and Brunet had planned.

But now they were breaking the law, and he could not let that go.

He watched their muscles tense. They had made up their minds. He knew they were coming for him.

"Don't do it, boys. You can't spend money if you're dead."

The man with the axe shifted his grip on the handle. "Can't have much of a life without it, either."

He raised the axe and Halstead took him with a single shot to the head.

The four men rushed him as they cut loose with primordial screams. Their weapons raised and ready to strike.

And Halstead cut loose with his Winchester, shooting down every man who charged at him.

The last man fell dead to the bank floor more than twenty feet away.

None of them had had a ghost of a chance of reaching him, but they charged him anyway. Desperate men will do things. They die for no good reason except fear.

Halstead could feel the eyes of the bank clerks on him as he stood alone in the middle of the bank, feeding fresh rounds from his belt into his rifle.

He only looked up at them when he knew his weapon was fully loaded. "Anyone manage to get back there?"

The clerk who had pointed out the miners was the only one who managed to speak.

"No. That was all of them."

Halstead was glad to hear it. "Anyone get hurt? I heard a shot."

"It wasn't any of us," the clerk told him. He pointed toward the back. "It came from Mr. Kendrick's office."

Halstead stepped around the bodies of the men he had just killed and reached the door they had been hacking at. The dead miner had not been lying. Halstead kicked it in easily and moved in behind the cages.

The clerks kept their hands up as Halstead marched past them to Kendrick's office. He paused just before he reached it and, with his left hand, tried the doorknob. It was locked.

He kicked in the door and was not surprised by what he found.

James Kendrick, president and founder of The Bank of Battle Brook, was sitting lopsided in the chair behind his desk, a neat hole in his right temple from which a thin stream of blood had run.

Halstead remembered when he had heard the shot. The

poor bastard had panicked when the miners broke the window.

Halstead walked back to where the clerks were still standing, only they had lowered their hands to their sides.

"Your boss is dead," he told them.

One of them crossed himself. Halstead wished he felt the urge to do the same.

"Tell me something," he asked none of them in particular. "Did you really run out of money?"

"No," said one of the clerks. "We had more than enough to cover all deposits, especially since the mine owners weren't making any withdrawals."

The first clerk who had spoken to him had to grab on to one of the brass rails of the cage to keep himself upright. "Poor Mr. Kendrick died for nothing."

Halstead looked through the brass bars at the miners he had shot. He looked out the shattered bank window and saw bank books lost in the chaos floating in the mud of Main Street. He saw a woman helping a man with a bleeding head wound on the opposite boardwalk, heading toward Doc Potter's place.

So much death. So much destruction.

"They all died for nothing," he said. "Nothing but a single man's greed. Every last one of them."

# Chapter 27

Back at the jail, Mayor Philip White held his head in his hands while his wife, Emily, did all the talking for him. "And you're sure the men who started all of this were outsiders?"

Halstead had cast ceremony aside and was sitting at McBride's old desk. His boots crossed atop it. A cup of coffee going cold in his hand.

He looked at Sandborne, signaling him to answer her. He was in no mood for questions just then.

"That's what we think," Sandborne told her. "I was busy minding the bank door, so I didn't see too much of it myself, but Jeremiah here said they didn't fit in with the rest of the crowd. The man they stopped as he left the bank was in here an hour before you, begging us to believe him that he never told the stranger the bank was closing. We believe him."

Mayor White slowly lifted his face from his hands. "Six dead. Scores injured. There's so many wounded outside Doc Potter's place, people are saying it looks like Gettysburg. Jim Kendrick dead, too. So soon after Jack McBride."

He shook his head before lowering it once more into his hands. "What are we supposed to do?"

Halstead had seen too much blood and destruction to tolerate the whining of a politician. "You can start by getting out there and putting your town back together. You should've been up on that carriage today instead of Hubbard, not hiding in your office hoping all of this would just go away."

The mayor lifted his head from his hands. "I certainly hope you're not saying that I'm responsible for what happened."

"I'm saying you didn't do much to stop it." Halstead decided to drop it, since arguing with the man would get him nowhere. They had more important matters to discuss. "In an hour or so, I'll be riding to Wellspring on business. Don't bother asking me why because I don't trust you enough to tell you. While I'm gone, Deputy Sandborne here will be in charge. You will make an announcement and post it publicly that he and I are the final legal authority in Battle Brook for the time being. You are to state that the use of lethal force is authorized at our discretion. We don't have the manpower to declare martial law or enforce a curfew, but I want you to spread the word amongst the saloons that we're the law now. Anyone steps out of line gets a bullet if we say so. I know that's harsh but that's the way it's going to have to be unless you want your town to burn."

He had not discussed any of this with Sandborne, and hoped the younger man had the sense to keep his mouth shut until the mayor and his wife left.

The mayor surprised him by saying, "I'll draw up the order tonight and have the printer run off copies immediately."

That was not good enough for Halstead. "Not tonight. Now. Do it now. The sooner those notices go up, the sooner everyone will know how things stand. I'll have more news from Helena when I return from Wellspring."

The mayor simply nodded. "How long will you be gone?"

"No longer than necessary," was all he felt comfortable telling him. "Now I'd appreciate it if you two would leave us alone. Deputy Sandborne and I have a lot to talk over."

Mrs. White helped her husband to his feet, and he flattened down his rumpled suit coat. He cleared his throat and said, "I hope you'll accept my thanks for what you did today, Deputy Halstead. You kept a terrible situation from getting much worse."

Halstead was not so sure he had, but the mayor did not need to know that, either. "You can thank me by acting. Mr. Sandborne will have more instructions for you in my absence."

The mayor and his wife left and Sandborne shut the door behind them.

"Were you serious about going to Wellspring?" Sandborne asked as soon as the door closed. "Tonight?"

"The train from Helena is due in tomorrow morning," Halstead told him. "Hubbard told me Zimmerman will be meeting the train. He didn't tell me why he was meeting it, and I don't care. It'll be our best chance to grab him and, by God, I plan on taking it."

Sandborne leaned against the door and folded his arms across his chest. "He won't be alone. You shouldn't be, either. Hubbard could also be setting you up for something."

"I doubt it." Halstead went to the rifle rack and began replacing the spaces on his belt with bullets. "Hubbard's greedy and he knows I've got paper on Zimmerman. With him out of the way, Brunet and Hubbard get bigger pieces of the pie."

Halstead slid a round into the last vacant space on his belt. "I don't like the idea of leaving you here alone, but I'm doing it because I know you can handle it."

Sandborne swallowed. "But?"

Halstead almost smiled. The boy was getting smarter by the day. "But I want you to promise me something before I leave."

"That depends on what it is."

"I want you to promise me that you'll run at the first sign of Zimmerman's men coming to town while I'm gone."

"No, Jeremiah. That's about the only thing I won't do and damn you for asking me to."

"I'm not asking you. I'm ordering you. If they show up, you get on your horse and you hightail it down to Wellspring to meet me. Take the main road. You'll be there a lot quicker than the roundabout route we took."

"I can hold them off from in here," Sandborne protested. "Just like you did back in Dover Station."

"No, you can't," Halstead told him. "This isn't even a proper jail yet. You can't hold out like I did, so let The Spoilers have the town if they come for it. We can always get it back later if we have to." He paused for a moment to allow his words to sink in. "Promise me."

Sandborne clearly did not like it, but he accepted it. "I promise."

"Good man." He got up from the chair and went to the rifle rack. He took down his Winchester and held out his hand to the deputy. "I'll send word back on the stage from Wellspring about how things go with Zimmerman."

Sandborne shook his hand. "Kill him, Jeremiah. Kill him dead. None of us will be safe until you do."

But Halstead already knew that.

# Chapter 28

Jeremiah Halstead puffed on the last of Sheriff Boddington's cigars as he sat on a crate at Wellspring Station, waiting for destiny to find him. The sky had begun to show the first signs of morning, something he had heard called a false dawn.

He allowed smoke to drift from his nose as he welcomed the coming day. Whether or not he lived to see another was out of his hands.

But if this was to be his last day on earth, then he decided he should go out with the taste of a fine cigar on his lips. Something to remind him of the goodness of life as he sank into death.

He had chosen to hide himself among the crates at the eastern end of the station since he figured Zimmerman would come in from the west where the towns were. Whether or not he came alone, Halstead could not say. He had no power over that. He was only certain of one thing. He may not live to see another sunrise, but Zimmerman certainly would not. Alive or dead, today would be the last day the outlaw enjoyed the taste of freedom.

He was more than halfway through his cigar and the sky had begun to brighten when he heard the unmistakable sound of boots scraping the frozen ground of the freight area behind him.

But the uncertainty of the steps put Halstead on his guard. So, as he continued to puff on his cigar, he withdrew the Bowie knife from its sheath on the back of his belt and held it low against his leg.

"Unless my nose fails me," a rough voice came from behind him, "I'd say that's one fine cigar you're smoking, fella."

"A Havana that's as black as the night." Halstead grew still as he heard the man approaching now. "A nice way to greet the morning."

"You'll get no argument from me on that score," the man said as he stepped into view.

It was the same swarthy, red-faced man who had started trouble at the bank yesterday. But he had not looked at Halstead yet. He was stretching his arms as if awaking from a long sleep. "I guess I'm gettin' too old for these cold mornings."

In one motion, Halstead pinned him against the crates and slid the blade under the outlaw's rib cage. The man recognized Halstead then. The deputy placed his hand over his mouth to prevent him from screaming. Halstead's gloved left hand muffled his death rattle as his eyes bulged and he slowly sank to the ground.

Halstead silently held the dying man's gaze, saying nothing as he watched the eyes grow vacant as his head went slack.

It was not until Halstead withdrew his blade that he saw

something on the man's lapel. He took a closer look at it as he wiped his blade clean on the dead man's shirt.

It was a star stamped with the words:

# DEPUTY
# TOWN OF VALHALLA

*Zimmerman had not wasted any time in declaring his own kingdom, had he?*

Halstead pushed the corpse over on its side and slid the knife back into its scabbard. He grabbed the Winchester he had placed on the crate beside him as he waited for daylight.

He chanced a quick glance at the platform, knowing that if one of Zimmerman's men was here, then the great outlaw himself must not be far behind.

Halstead saw a woman in a fur coat, her luggage at her feet, shivering against the cold morning air as she waited for the early train to arrive. A couple of children were on the bench beside her, dozing against each other.

Then he saw the doors to the station building open and watched Edward Zimmerman stride out onto the platform. The man was positively beaming. He wore a buffalo hide coat and round hat. He was smiling at the coming dawn as two men stepped out behind him.

Halstead watched him draw in a great breath and hold it for a moment before exhaling in a great mist.

"Ah, just taste that clean air, boys," he told the two men with him. "That's what glory smells like and don't you soon forget it."

Halstead took the warrant out of his inside pocket as he stepped out onto the platform. He raised his Winchester to his shoulder and drew a clean aim on Zimmerman.

He waited until the outlaw noticed him and watched his joy slowly disappear as Halstead yelled, "Edward Zimmerman, I have a warrant for your arrest. Throw up your hands. The men with you, too."

But Zimmerman did not throw up his hands and neither did the two men with him. The people on the platform, including the woman with her children, scrambled back inside the station building, leaving the four dangerous men alone on the platform.

Somewhere behind him in the distance, Halstead heard a train whistle blow.

Zimmerman glowered at him. "You! Now? Today?"

Halstead tossed the warrant at him, though it only went a few feet before fluttering to the platform. He kept the Winchester aimed at the middle of him.

Halstead tried to keep his voice even as he said, "I've got you now, you son of a bitch."

He watched Zimmerman's wide face turn into a sneer and his gloved hands ball into fists at his sides. Halstead had him dead to rights and all four men knew it.

The men on either side of him also wore buffalo hides that covered the pistols Halstead figured were holstered on their hips.

Zimmerman crouched just a little toward him, the way the four miners in the bank had crouched before they charged. He hoped Zimmerman would do the same. He had not prayed in years, but he found himself praying for that now.

The only reason why he did not shoot him where he stood was the piece of paper fluttering on the platform at his feet. The warrant.

The Law.

Instead of charging, the outlaw remained where he was. "If he shoots me, cut him down, boys."

"They'll be in Hell right behind you if I shoot," Halstead told him. The Winchester steady. "Last warning. Open your coats real slow or I set to shooting. And we're not in Silver Cloud now, Zimmerman. This time, I won't miss."

Zimmerman stood up to his full height, trying to save some of his dignity as he slowly opened his coat. He was not packing a gun. "You shoot me, you'll be shooting an unarmed man." He inclined his head toward the station building. "In front of a whole lot of witnesses, too."

"Now tell your men to do the same thing."

"Do what he wants, boys," Zimmerman commanded. "I want to see how this plays out."

Both men at either side of him slowly opened their coats, revealing gun belts and holsters tied down on their right legs. Just as he had expected.

The desire to shoot all three of them almost overpowered him, but he kept his finger off the trigger. "With your left hands, untie those guns and unbuckle your gun belts."

Once again, Zimmerman told his men to follow Halstead's orders. He grinned as he looked over Halstead's shoulder.

"You want the man I've got behind you to do the same thing, deputy?"

"You mean the crooked fella with my knife in his belly?"

Zimmerman's grin disappeared.

"He won't be troubling anyone except the undertaker. And unless your men want to join him, they'd better do as I say."

The man on Zimmerman's left untied his gun first and

slowly reached for his buckle. "Blackfoot was a friend of mine, you miserable bastard."

He drew a pistol from his belly.

Halstead shot the outlaw in the chest before he could raise it. The impact sent him sprawling off the platform and onto the tracks.

Halstead levered in a fresh round and aimed the Winchester at the man on Zimmerman's right. "You want to die, too?"

The man untied his pistol and, with his left hand, undid the buckle of his gun belt and allowed it to drop to the platform with a thud before raising both hands.

"If either of you has a hideout gun on you," Halstead told them, "now's the time to come clean. Next time I shoot, you get it in the belly."

"Now we're both unarmed," Zimmerman said. "And you've got a lot to answer for, Halstead. You just gunned down a sworn deputy of the Town of Valhalla."

A second blast of its whistle told him the train was only a few minutes out. Halstead knew he had to get Zimmerman off the platform and into a cell before the train pulled into the station. He would lose whatever advantage he had over Zimmerman once the platform began to fill up with innocent civilians.

"Both of you have been here before," he said. "You know where the jail is. Turn around and start walking to it. Either of you duck or try to run, you die."

Zimmerman laughed as he turned around first, followed by the man beside him, and they started walking at a slow pace.

Halstead closed the distance between them, but not too close so as they could make a play for his rifle.

"Speed up," he ordered them as they reached the muddy

street that served as Wellspring's main boulevard. "Jail's right in front of you."

Zimmerman walked faster and so did his deputy. "Whatever you say, Halstead. I'm gonna have a whole lot of fun watching you work your way out of this one."

The few bystanders on the street at that hour quickly got out of the way as they saw one man walking two men to the jail at the end of a Winchester.

They stopped when they reached the boardwalk of the jail. The sign nailed next to the door read: John Howard, Sheriff. Town of Wellspring.

Halstead was glad to see the lantern light inside was still on. He hoped it meant Howard was still on duty and had not snuck off for home.

"This is your show," Zimmerman said. "What do you want us to do next?"

Halstead refused to allow Zimmerman to frustrate him. "Your friend can go up and open the door and wait. If it's locked, knock, then step on back here. And if you make a play for the sheriff's gun, I'll kill you."

Zimmerman's deputy did as he was ordered. He opened the door and let it swing inward. He stood in the doorway and waited, just as Halstead had ordered him to do.

"What in the hell?" came a sleepy voice from inside the jail.

Sheriff John "Red" Howard, who looked well north of sixty, was in the process of pulling up his pants when he came to the door. A Colt was tucked into his belt. "What's going on here?"

Zimmerman's deputy snatched the pistol from Howard's belt and moved behind him before the old man knew what was going on. He wrapped his arm around the sheriff's neck and held the Colt Peacemaker to his head.

Zimmerman turned around slowly, flashing a smile a mile wide. "How about that, Halstead? I'll bet you didn't see that coming. Now, do I have to tell you to let us go or isn't it obvious?"

Halstead did not answer him. He did not even breathe. He fixed his aim on the man holding Sheriff Howard hostage.

Zimmerman's deputy laughed as he drew his arm tighter around old Howard's neck. "Looks like you're the one who has to drop 'em now, half-breed."

"Don't move," Halstead said.

Zimmerman hung his head. "Damn it, Halstead. I thought we'd be past all that now."

Halstead fired. The bullet sliced through Zimmerman's left ear and kept going through the deputy's hand and into his left eye.

Halstead levered in a fresh round and set his aim back on Zimmerman. "I wasn't talking to you. Now, get inside or the next one will catch you in the belly."

Zimmerman cursed a blue streak as he cradled his bleeding left ear and trudged up the stairs into the jail.

"Sheriff Howard," Halstead called out. "I need you to get that cell door open. Right now."

He heard the old man fumbling with keys before he heard the familiar squeal of iron grating on iron. He had managed to get the cell door open.

Now in the jail, Halstead saw only one cell was inside and it yawned open before them.

Taking no chances he shoved Zimmerman hard into the cell before slamming the door shut. Howard's hands were still shaking something fierce as he locked the door and withdrew the key.

Halstead lowered his rifle and leaned against the wall

before he fell over. The warm, thick air of the tiny jail felt good.

He had finally done what he had been sent here to do. Ed Zimmerman was under arrest.

That's when he noticed Sheriff Howard was shaking all over while repeating, "What the hell? What the hell?" He had been unable to take his eyes from the gory sight of the corpse on his floor.

Halstead got up and grabbed hold of the old man and eased him over to a worn cloth chair behind a desk. He took a knee, blocking the sheriff's view of the dead man. "My name is Jeremiah Halstead. I'm a Deputy United States Marshal out of Helena, and this man is my prisoner. I'm sorry I couldn't tell you about this earlier, but there was no time."

Halstead knew that last part was a lie. He did not trust anyone in town who might give word to Zimmerman that he was walking into an ambush. Given the old man's sorry state, he knew he had been right.

Sheriff Howard's eyes grew clearer, though he was still shaking all over. "Halstead out of Helena you said? You work for Mackey?"

He was glad to see the old boy was snapping out of it. "Yes, I do, sir. And this man is my prisoner. Edward Zimmerman. You've probably got paper on him around here somewhere."

Howard's eyes grew larger. Not from fright, but from acknowledgment. He pointed a crooked finger at the wall where posters for other wanted men were hung. "You mean that Edward Zimmerman? In my jail? Now?"

Realizing Howard was steadier now, Halstead got up. "Yes, sir. And you helped me bring him in. They're going to hear about you in Helena. Might even get some kind of commendation."

Howard looked down at his desk. "Ed Zimmerman. In my jail. I can't believe it. I was asleep, then—"

As his voice trailed off, Halstead remembered Zimmerman's deputy still had Howard's gun. He reached down, plucked it out of the dead outlaw's hand, and put it in the top drawer of the sheriff's desk. He was in no condition to be using it now.

Zimmerman still had his hand to his left ear. "You shot me, you bastard. And you killed a good man, too."

Halstead looked down at the corpse on the floor. It was a gory sight, even by his standards. He found a sheet on a shelf near the cells and threw it over half of him. "Anyone who rides with you is no damned good, Zimmerman."

The prisoner kicked at the cell door. "You think you ended anything here today? Boy, you don't know what you've started."

Halstead allowed himself to enjoy Zimmerman's rage. "Whatever I started ends with you dancing at the end of Judge Forrester's rope."

Zimmerman smirked. "Wouldn't it be nice to think so?"

Halstead stepped over the dead outlaw's body and carried his Winchester with him as he went out onto the crooked boardwalk of the jail.

The train from Helena had pulled in while he had been locking up Zimmerman, and the road from the station was already a hive of activity. Some of the people he figured to be locals were pointing at the jail and gesturing with their hands, probably retelling all they had seen.

In a little while, he would go around and ask any of them if the sheriff had some deputies who might be able to lend a hand guarding Zimmerman. But for now, he allowed himself to catch his breath.

He reminded himself that he had finally done what he had come to Battle Brook to do. He had arrested Ed Zimmerman. If that did not call for a pause of celebration, he did not know what would.

He was enjoying the chill breeze of the morning when he saw two men making haste toward the jail. He could not see them clearly at first in the dull light of dawn, but they were definitely heading his way and with purpose.

Halstead stepped back into the jail and raised his Winchester. He had not gone through all of this trouble to get killed now.

He aimed the rifle at the two approaching men. "You two in the street. Throw up your hands and walk toward me real slow."

The two men complied and as they got closer to the jail, he realized he had seen them before. They were the two strange men he had first seen when he had been sitting in front of the hotel with Abby and again when they had taken the coach to Helena. One was tall and skinny with dishwater blue eyes and a weak chin.

The other was much shorter and broader. He had been pulling at his clothes as if they scratched him in Battle Brook, but he was not pulling at them now.

And as the pair stepped closer, he could see the shorter one had a gun on his right hip.

Halstead aimed the Winchester at him. "You with the gun. Use two fingers to pull it out real slow and let it drop on the ground. I've already killed three men today. A fourth won't make much of a difference."

The shorter man did as he was told. They also opened

their coats to show they were unarmed when Halstead ordered them to.

Halstead lowered his rifle, but kept it ready. "What business do you two have here?"

The skinny one said, "My name is Mark Mannes, and I am Mr. Zimmerman's attorney."

"Congratulations," Halstead said. "He's going to be keeping you pretty busy until his hanging."

"There isn't going to be any hanging, deputy." He gestured toward his coat. "I have proof of that if you'll allow me to show it to you."

Halstead did not like the sound of that. "Go ahead. But if anything more than paper comes out of that pocket, you catch one in the belly."

Mannes's hand shook as he pulled out a piece of paper that looked an awful lot like the warrant he had just lost at the station. "Is this a copy of the warrant you have for Mr. Zimmerman's arrest?"

Halstead read it over. It was the same warrant he had carried with him from Helena. "What of it?"

Mannes reached into the same pocket and produced another paper that was much cleaner than the warrant. It was in an envelope sealed with wax. The territorial seal was embossed in it.

"What's this?" Halstead asked.

"You acknowledge it is an official document?"

Halstead really did not like where this was headed now. "As far as it goes. Why?"

"It's addressed to you," Mannes said. "Open it. I can read it for you if you don't know how."

Halstead cracked the seal open and pulled out the letter inside.

As he opened it, the surprising weight of it almost made

him drop it. It was heavy because it also bore a seal atop a ribbon and a signature.

From Charles M. Owen, Governor of the Territory of Montana.

Halstead forced himself to open the rest of the letter and his breath caught when he finally managed to read it. The words and letters swirled before his eyes at first, but eventually, they stopped moving long enough for him to make sense of what it said.

Halstead looked into the attorney's dead eyes. "This is a pardon?"

Mannes smirked. "So, you can read after all. That'll make all of this go much smoother."

Halstead looked at the document again to make sure he had not made a mistake. "A goddamned pardon from the governor? How is that possible?"

Mannes smiled primly. "The governor's full name is Charles Mannes Owen. We're first cousins and members of my family are spread as far and wide as Montana herself. I was sent here to learn the law concerning mining and banking interests, and I think you'll agree I've done quite well. But you shouldn't trouble yourself about the whys of the situation, deputy. Just concentrate on what is."

He handed him a second sealed envelope. "I also have a pardon for one Mister Robert Brunet. The governor of the Montana territory has seen fit to grant both of these men full pardons for any crimes they may have committed, which means you must release Mr. Zimmerman immediately or find yourself in violation of the law."

Halstead stepped back until he found himself against the wall.

The struggles of the past week all swam before his eyes at once. The long ride up to Battle Brook. The men he had killed. The men who had died. The hurt and wounded and scared in the riot. The lives destroyed by this man. All of it mixed before him now, only to be wiped away by a piece of paper that said Zimmerman was free?

"No," was all Halstead could think to say. "No way he gets out after what he's done. He stays locked up until I get a telegram or something official that tells me otherwise."

Mannes nodded to his shorter companion who handed him two envelopes. One was a telegram and the other a letter. At least neither of them bore an official seal.

"The telegram was waiting for you at the telegraph office at the station back there. We took the liberty of bringing it up here with us after we learned what happened. The second is a letter from Marshal Aaron Mackey himself."

Halstead opened the telegram first. It was from Mackey. It read:

ZIMMERMAN AND BRUNET GOT PARDONS
FROM GOVERNOR. IF YOU HAVE THEM
IN CUSTODY, RELEASE THEM.
LTR TO FOLLOW.

Mannes and his partner were about to walk into the jail when Halstead blocked their way. "Not yet, damn you. Not yet."

They could give him all the pardons and proclamations from the governor they wanted, but he would not let Zimmerman go until he heard it from Mackey himself.

The envelope was from the marshal's office in Helena and the handwriting on the envelope was Aaron's. He tore it open and quickly removed the letter inside.

He would have recognized Mackey's scrawl anywhere. It read simply:

*Jerry,*

*I hate to have to tell you like this, but the wires are down between here and Battle Brook. There was no other way to get word to you. The pardons are real. Don't ask me how Zimmerman pulled it off, but he did. They also got the governor to agree to allow them to form The Town of Valhalla in the old town of Hard Scrabble.*

*If you have Zimmerman or Brunet, you have to let them go. I know it's hard, but not as hard as it was to write this letter to you.*

*The bastards will hang. Just not yet. Send me a telegram when you get this.*

*Aaron*

Halstead felt everything drain from him as the reality of it all settled in. Despite all the damage he had done, all the chaos he had caused, Ed Zimmerman was a free man. And there was nothing he could do to stop him.

This time, he did not have the energy to prevent Mannes or the man with him to enter the jail. They took the keys from Howard's desk and unlocked the cell door to set Zimmerman free.

That was when more than Mackey's training returned to him. He was standing just like Aaron always did when facing a target. With his left shoulder forward. His belly gun an easy draw. Himself a narrow target.

He dropped the telegrams and the papers and the official

documents and drew his Colt from his belly holster. He held the gun at his waist, aimed at Zimmerman's middle. Mannes shrieked and dashed to the side. The shorter man at least held his ground.

Zimmerman looked him up and down the way people always did. First at his face, then at the star on his lapel, then at the Colt now in his hand.

The outlaw placed his hands on the bars and peered at him through the open cell door. "I could. You can't. If you could, you'd be in here right next to me."

Halstead thumbed back the hammer. Every part of him wanted to shoot. Just one squeeze and all of the death and destruction this man had caused would be over. His victims would all be avenged.

All except one. The life Jeremiah Halstead would be sacrificing if he killed this man this way.

His own.

Halstead kept the gun cocked and trained on Zimmerman as he moved away from the door and stood next to Howard, who had remained seated in his chair in his own world the entire time.

Zimmerman took his hands down from the bars and buttoned up his coat. He looked at Mannes, who was still cowering against the cell. "Go ahead, ladies. And mind you don't step on poor Plato there. He met an unfortunate end."

Mannes scurried from the jail, practically skipping over the corpse as he tried to avoid it. The shorter man eyed Halstead as he stepped around Plato's body and went outside.

But Halstead kept his Colt on Zimmerman as the man proudly walked out of the cell and headed for the door. He did not look at Halstead once.

He did stop by the door and flip up the thick collar on his buffalo coat. He closed his eyes as a rush of cold, free air reached him. "Don't come after me, Halstead. You'll die if you do."

Halstead willed himself to keep his finger off the trigger. All he could think to say was, "Wouldn't it be nice to think so?"

Halstead kept his Colt aimed at the door until he heard the men climb on their horses and ride away.

It was only then when he could manage to thumb the hammer down and tuck the Colt back in his holster.

He had done what he had been sent there to do. He had put Zimmerman in jail.

He just did not have the power to keep him there.

Sheriff Howard shook his head and repeated, "Ed Zimmerman. In my jail. No one would believe it."

Halstead picked up his Winchester from the wall and walked down to the train station. He had a telegram to send.

He ignored all of the frightened looks he drew from the people who were still in and around the station building. The porters had not been able to pull the dead deputy from the tracks before the train rolled into the station. Several women and a few men were still recovering from the sight.

The clerk in the telegraph only looked at him when he asked for a pad. Halstead had to reach behind the desk and take it himself before the clerk realized he had done it. The man sat in his chair and pushed it away from the desk. "Whatever you want, Deputy Halstead. I'll send whatever you want."

He grabbed a pencil and wrote out a reply to Mackey. He kept it brief.

MESSAGE RECEIVED. ZIMMERMAN AND
BRUNET FREED. BATTLE BROOK IN BAD
WAY. BANK GONE. MCBRIDE DEAD.
ME AND SANDBORNE STAYING ON UNTIL
NEW TOWN MARSHAL HIRED.

He shoved the pad back at the clerk who read it over quickly. "That's good, deputy. Real good. Real fine handwriting."

Halstead picked up the Winchester and walked out of the station building. He walked past the porters and conductors who were still trying to figure out how to pull what was left of the dead man out from under the train. He kept walking past where Blackfoot's gutted corpse was lying, still undiscovered among the crates.

He walked up the same slight incline he had come down that night as he laid in wait to kill or capture Edward Zimmerman. He found Col right where he had left her, tethered to a thin dead tree where some dead grass poked through the snow.

He slipped his Winchester into the saddle scabbard before he freed her from the tree and climbed into the saddle.

He cast a final glance toward the east where the sun had already risen to begin a new day.

As fate would have it, this would not be his last day after all. He was not dead yet, and neither was Zimmerman.

He gently bounced his heels into Col's flanks to get her moving back to Battle Brook. To Sandborne.

And toward the battle that was sure to lie ahead.

Keep reading for a special excerpt
of the first Jeremiah Halstead Western.

## BLOOD ON THE TRAIL
A Jeremiah Halstead Western

by
TERRENCE McCAULEY

Silver Cloud, Montana. A mining town
welcome to all seeking to make their fortune.
And a place where a lawman has to watch his back
before some hardcase empties his pistol into it.

Deputy U.S. Marshal Jeremiah Halstead is escorting
notorious outlaw John Hudson across the territory for
trial when he's ambushed by Hudson's gang. Although
outnumbered and outgunned, Halstead puts the blast on a
couple of the bushwhackers without giving up. Halstead
holes up in Silver Cloud with prisoner Hudson.

The folks in Silver Cloud, though, are none too happy
playing host to the lawman or his kill-crazy prisoner.
Unable to trust the sheriff to back his play,
Halstead finds himself standing alone against Hudson's
gang as they slip into town, recruiting gunmen
to help free their leader.

Except for Ed Zimmerman. He's spent his whole
criminal life in John Hudson's shadow.
He wants Hudson dead and buried so he can become
the leader of the gang. And if he has to, he'll put
everyone in Silver Cloud six feet under—including
Deputy U.S. Marshal Halstead . . .

**_Look for_ BLOOD ON THE TRAIL**
**_where books are sold!_**

# Chapter 1

"Come on, Col!" Jeremiah Halstead yelled as he spurred the mustang on. "Faster, girl. Faster!"

The Deputy United States Marshal crouched low beside the mustang's neck as bullets from the Hudson Gang cut through the air all around him. High and low and right past him. None of them had found their mark yet. None of them would, if he had anything to say about it.

He knew it was almost impossible to hit a man from the back of a running horse. Returning fire would only be a waste of ammunition. Urging the mustangs to run faster was a much better idea.

The horse Halstead was pulling on a lead rope was also a mustang and Col's sister. She had no trouble keeping up the pace despite the prisoner tied over her saddle like a dead deer. He imagined John Hudson must be complaining something awful. His ribs were probably mighty sore given the pounding they were taking, but the wind in Halstead's ears drowned out the cries of the outlaw.

Halstead could feel Col begin to reach her top speed as the air and blood began to flow through her body. The young mare had been Texas born and usually needed a little bit of time to limber up in the cold Montana weather, but once she did, she was the fastest horse Halstead had ever ridden. He knew he would need every bit of that speed now if he had any hope of out-running the Hudson Gang.

Halstead kept the horses running straight across the flatland in hopes of putting as much distance as he could between himself and the gang.

He stole a quick glance back at his pursuers and saw the group of ten outlaws was quickly falling behind. Halstead knew this was not only because of the speed of his mounts. They were only a few miles out of Rock Creek, and the Hudson Gang's horses were already showing signs of being winded. The animals had spent too much time in the town livery being overfed by the hostler.

The Hudson Gang were overfed, too, but in a much different way. They had managed to cow the sheriff and take over the town of Rock Creek for the past several months. The outlaws had grown soft on whiskey and women. They robbed drunks in alleys and took a share of the winnings at the gambling tables whenever it had pleased them. Easy living in the town they terrorized had made man and beast soft, much to the benefit of Jeremiah Halstead.

But experience had taught Halstead to know better than to take the gang lightly. The Hudsons, as they were known, had a reputation throughout the territory as being a brutal, determined band of stone-cold killers. He knew that even if he managed to get away from them now, these men would continue to stalk him every step of the two-day journey to the federal court in Helena. U.S. Marshal Aaron Mackey wanted to see John Hudson hang in the territorial capital and Halstead had no intention of letting his boss down, especially since this was his first official assignment as a deputy.

After a quick overnight stop in the town of Silver Cloud, he would head on to Helena and see to it that John Hudson received the justice he deserved.

Halstead saw a stand of pine trees in the near distance and steered the mustangs to head in that direction. He was glad the second horse with John Hudson across her back had been able to keep pace with them despite the large prisoner she carried.

Halstead had to crouch even lower in the saddle as he rode among the low-hanging branches of the pines.

He drew his mustang to a gradual halt and brought the horses around to see where his pursuers were now. They had spread themselves out in a line about three hundred yards away and were moving at a much easier pace.

*Smart,* Halstead thought. *They know where I am. Best to rest the horses while they plot their next move.*

Halstead pulled out the field glasses from his saddle-bags and took a closer look at the men. He could see the thick vapor coming from the muzzles of the horses. They were blowing hard and fast in the cold autumn air. They were not used to riding this hard anymore. The speed and distance had taken a toll. They were fat and out of shape and would need a long rest before they were ready to take up the chase again. The liveryman back in Rock Creek had been too generous with the oats, and the lack of exercise had made them sluggish. If the men of the Hudson Gang continued to chase him now, he doubted all of the mounts would make it even halfway to Helena.

Judging by the way they were breathing, he figured at least three of them would come down with pneumonia if they did not already have it. An outlaw was not much of a threat without a horse in open country like this. And since Halstead had their leader tied over the saddle of his mustang, he hoped the remaining members of the Hudson Gang knew enough about horses to know chasing him would get them killed.

But relying on another man's common sense to save his own life did not sound like much of a plan to Jerry Halstead. He had never been much of a gambler as he preferred to make his own luck.

Halstead had bristled at Mackey's orders that all of his men wear all black when picking up a prisoner. He felt like he looked like a preacher or a mortician but did not dare question his friend's orders. Now that he was among the pines, he understood Mackey's reason. Black made for good cover in many situations. At night, for instance, and now among the shadows of the pines. The Hudsons knew where he was, but they could not see him. They were on tired mounts in open ground. All of that was in his favor.

It was time to tilt the odds even further in his favor.

Keeping hold of the rope of the second mustang, Halstead climbed down from the saddle and led both horses to a pair of pines. He slung Col's reins around one of the branches and tied the second mare carrying John Hudson to a tree close by. Col had a tendency to nip at her sister when her blood was up, which it certainly was now.

John Hudson began squirming, but Halstead had bound his hands and feet tightly under the barrel of the mustang too well for him to get free. His prisoner wasn't going anywhere.

Halstead took a knee and took a good handful of Hudson's hair as he raised his head to look at him. The prisoner screamed through his gag in protest.

"Quit fussing," Halstead told him. "You're not hurt, just uncomfortable. And you'd be sitting upright now if you and your boys hadn't given me so much trouble back in Rock Creek."

Hudson struggled in vain to pull his hair free from the deputy's grip. His fleshy face was red from anger and from riding across the saddle for so long.

"Now, I'm going to have a conversation with your men in my own way. If this turns out like it should, I'll see to it you're riding proper. If it doesn't, then you'll stay as you are until we reach Silver Cloud."

Halstead gripped the hair tighter as he pulled Hudson's head up even higher. "But if you cause me any trouble or try to get away, I'll catch you and I'll drag you all the way back to Helena. Not fast, but real slow so you make the journey." He shook the prisoner's head. "Look at me so I know you understand."

John Hudson did look at him, causing Halstead to smile. If looks could kill, Jeremiah imagined he would be dead. He figured that must have been the same icy glare that had cowed the good people of Rock Creek for so long while he and his gang controlled the town. The same glare that had held them in check until John Hudson had pushed them just a bit too far.

"Don't be angry with me, Hudson. If you hadn't gone and killed the mayor, I wouldn't be here, and you wouldn't be tied over a horse."

Halstead released his grip with a hard shove and left the outlaw to dangle helplessly over the saddle. The deputy had no sympathy for him. John Hudson was a bully and Halstead hated bullies.

He went back to Col and rubbed her neck. The horse had barely broken a sweat despite all the running and seemed content to eat the shoots of grass that had grown up around the roots of the pine trees.

"There's my girl," he said as he dug a carrot out of his saddlebag and fed it to her. He did not dare give her another because he might need her to run again at a moment's notice and did not want her belly too full of food. But he liked to reward a horse as soon as he could following a good effort, and Col had given him her all.

He dug out another carrot and fed it to Col's sister, who he had not gotten around to naming. Both animals had come north with him from Texas and had proved themselves many times on the trail. They might have been smaller than most horses in Montana, but he would put them up against any other mount for durability and speed.

While the animals enjoyed their treat, Halstead slung the field glasses around his neck and pulled his Winchester '86 from the scabbard on the left side of the saddle. He had an old Winchester '73 in his right scabbard but selected the '86 for its range and stopping power. He figured he would need to take these boys at a distance, and the '86 was the right tool for the job.

He walked toward the edge of the trees but remained in the shade. He raised the field glasses and took a closer look at the men following him.

He saw they had stopped completely now and kept their mounts in a straight line as they looked at the stand of pine trees where he was hiding.

"Ten men in the gang and not a brain between them," Halstead said to himself as he looked them over. Then he remembered none of the men who rode with John Hudson had ever been called upon to do much thinking. Hudson had always been the brains of the outfit. All the outlaws had to do was rob what he told them to rob and kill whomever he told them to kill and everything worked out fine. That's the way they had done it for years, or so Halstead had been told when Mackey sent him to bring John Hudson to justice.

The marauders had left a trail of blood behind them that spanned from California all the way to Wyoming and back again. The West was littered with the bodies of stagecoach passengers they had robbed, mining camps they had hit, banks they had held up, and Indians they had massacred and scalped.

As he looked through his field glasses, Halstead saw three of them still had those scalps tied to their saddle horns, dangling from ropes like morbid trophies. A few people had stood up to them of course, but none of them had lived long enough to tell the tale.

That was until John Hudson had been foolish enough to go and kill the mayor of Rock Creek, and the towns-people rallied against him and threw him in jail. The rest of the gang had managed to get out of town before they were lynched and made camp somewhere in the rocks that overlooked Rock Creek, waiting to make their move.

And as he looked them over now, Halstead could tell they were a motley, grimy bunch despite having spent the better part of the past three months in the relatively refined comfort of Rock Creek. The outlaws were of all shapes and sizes and colors. He even remembered some of their names Mackey had given him back in Helena, though he could not tell which outlaw corresponded to which name as he looked them over now.

He figured one of the younger men was probably Hudson's little brother Harry. The others were known simply by whatever title John Hudson had seen fit to call them when they joined his murderous gang. Men with names like Bug and Cree. Pole and Mick. Weasel, Bandit, and Ace. Cliff was the easiest to spot in the group, even from this distance, as he was the only black man in the bunch. The broadest of them, too, with a black patch over his left eye.

Besides Harry, only one of them was said to go by his given name. Ed Zimmerman, who Mackey said was every bit as bad as John Hudson himself. Maybe even worse. He sported two guns, just like Halstead and had acquired a reputation as something of a gunman even before he had joined up with the Hudsons.

Halstead wondered which of the men he was looking at now might be Zimmerman, but there was no way he could tell something like that from this distance. Jeremiah thought of himself as being pretty handy with a pistol, too. He figured he would probably have to go up against Zimmerman at some point between here and Helena. He would be interested in the outcome, especially because his life would be on the line.

He kept watching the men as they maintained a ragged line and although none of them looked at each other, he could see their mouths moving. The small puffs of vapor that rose from them as they spoke confirmed as much.

Halstead did not have to read lips to know they were talking about what they should do next. The lawman had taken their leader into the pines, where there were plenty of shadows and cover to be found. A man could hold off a group their size for quite a while, especially if he knew how to shoot. And they had enough experience to know a deputy marshal knew how to shoot. He might not have his uncle Billy Sunday's eye or his Sharps rifle, but Halstead could still kill a man at a fair distance with his '86.

And the longer they talked, the more he began to wonder if they might not be a bit smarter than they looked.

He hoped not. For his sake.

# Chapter 2

Harry Hudson had somehow found himself in the middle of the line, though he had not planned it that way. It was just where he had happened to end up when that damnable lawman rode into the pines with his brother.

Although he was John's brother, there had only ever been one leader of the gang and that had been John. That had always been fine with Harry. He had never been one to make decisions on his own, especially when he could avoid it. He supposed that was why he had followed his brother off the family farm in Kansas and into the life of an outlaw in the first place.

"He's your brother," Cree said to him. The man's dark, swarthy complexion had reminded John of a Cree Indian who had managed to stick a knife in him once. As Harry remembered, Cree was simply a French-Canadian with dark features. "It ought to be your call about what we do next."

Harry was about to stroke his bushy beard as he often did when faced with a difficult decision but stopped himself before he did it. He remembered John's admonishment that the motion made him look like a weak fool. "He might be my brother, but it's all of our hides at stake here, fellas.

I think we ought to come to some kind of agreement, don't you?"

"If it was my brother," the red-haired man named Mick offered, "I wouldn't take any chances. We've run that fancy lawman to ground. No shame in that. I say we wait until dark and ride in after him when we're on more even footing."

"What the hell do you know about anything?" Bug said. His wide, wild blue eyes had earned him his name. "I'd bet they don't even have horses in Ireland."

"I was born in California," Mick countered, "same as you, you bug-eyed bastard."

"Simmer down," Bandit told them. He was the best-looking man of the group; clean-shaven except for the moustache he waxed into a tantalizing curl. John had named him Bandit on account of the ease with which he stole the hearts of the ladies he wooed, preferably wealthy widows if one happened to be in the vicinity. "We won't get anywhere with you two barking at each other like a couple of dogs."

"I ain't never been one for waitin'," Weasel offered. He was a pinch-faced man with a long neck that John had thought made him resemble his namesake. "I say one of us distracts him with a manner of peace offerin' while I ride around the side and come at them that way. Sneak up on him and put a bullet in his back, then free John. Best to do it now afore he gets too settled."

"Just like a weasel," Ace concluded. John had called him Ace because he was something of a card sharp. The gang had relied on his winnings in gambling halls to keep them afloat when times were lean. He was good enough that he did not have to cheat all that often. "I say we ride right at him together before our horses get sluggish. Damn it, boys. It's only one man in there."

"One man with a fancy rig," Pole noted. He was the tallest of the group, more than six feet tall by plenty and as skinny as a bean pole. "You see them irons he was sporting in town? A Thunderer on his right hip and another holstered above his belt on the left. Never saw a man with a rig like that. Probably knows how to use them, too."

All of the chatter was giving Harry a headache. He had agreed with every man who spoke as each of them had a point to make. They had been bad men long before they had joined up with John and him. He felt like a fool telling any of them they were wrong and did not want to risk the consequences if he was.

Fortunately for him, not all of the members of the gang had spoken yet. He looked at the large black man at the far right of the group. "Cliff, you haven't said anything yet. What do you think?"

The black man with the patch over his left eye did not speak often, but Harry knew that when he did, the rest of the gang listened. He had gotten his name because John said he resembled a cliff. Anyone who tried to go over him always wound up busted up or dead. He stroked the neck of his horse where the scalps of three dead Indians hung. "Our horses ain't used to this kind of work anymore, boys. They're just about played out. I know mine is and all of yours are, too. I can hear a rattle in Cree's mare, which tells me she's down with pneumonia or will be soon. They might have one good charge left in them, but not much after that. If this Halstead fella takes off with those mustangs of his, we'll be left with a bunch of tired horses and nowhere to ride them." He looked down the line of men looking back at him. "I love a fight just as much as the rest of you boys, so don't go thinking I'm trying to shirk anything. I want John back, too, but we're not outfitted well enough to do it right now. Them's just the facts as I see them is all."

Harry had hoped Cliff would have come up with something better than that, but he was right. The horses were just about done in. His own mount was shivering from the effort of the chase and he imagined none of the other animals were faring much better.

That left him to ask the final member of the gang for his opinion. He also happened to be the quietest and the deadliest among them now that John was out of the way. He looked to the far left of the group at Ed Zimmerman. "Well, we've heard from everyone else besides you, Ed. What do you think?"

Zimmerman had not taken his eyes off the stand of pine trees since they had slowed down. He was looking into them now as he said, "I never thought I'd say this, but every one of you idiots is right in his own way. We're stuck here with tired horses and a target in thick cover." He nodded toward the trees. "This boy isn't just fancy, he's smart. He's packing two Winchesters. One's a '73 and the other's an '86. Saw them when he tied off his horses in front of the jail back in town. That means we're already in his range, depending on what he's got it loaded with."

Harry was glad he could finally contribute something to the discussion. "It only holds if we stand still, Ed, and there's ten of us. If we rush him, he's bound to miss most of us."

"But not all of us," Zimmerman told him. "And I won't count on him being the type to panic. I watched how he handled himself in town. He's about as cool as they come, and I'd wager my share of the money that he's every bit as good as he thinks he is. He's a fighter and we can't buffalo him like some homesteaders on a wagon train."

He pulled up one of the four scalps dangling from his saddle horn and began to feel the hair between his fingers, as if it might tell him something. For all Harry knew, it just might. Ed had always been the strangest man in their outfit.

Harry hung his head. He had asked the question, hoping someone would have an idea they could all agree upon. But everyone had a different opinion on what they should do next.

"That didn't help much."

Zimmerman cleared his throat and spat over his horse's head. "I say we play it Weasel's way for once. That'll mean one of us rides out there and tries to talk to him. Can't hurt. We can't scare him off, but maybe we can buy him off. We've got enough to spare. A man in his position might be willing to take the money and let John go. You can tell him we'll ride on and away from Rock Creek if he wants. Tell him we'll ride clear out of the territory. Promise him the moon. We can always kill him later after we get John back."

Ace cursed. "No way in hell I'm giving up Rock Creek. The only reason why we left was because they had John. I'd rather see that place burn than have them say they rode us off."

"Then we'll burn it," Zimmerman said, "because even if we get John back, we're going to have to kill that deputy who has him. Halstead doesn't strike me as the kind of loose end you leave unticd."

"So what?" Bandit said. "Won't be the first lawman we killed."

"Won't be the last," Pole added.

"He'll be the last we kill in Montana," Zimmerman told them, "because once word gets out that this Halstead fella is dead, Aaron Mackey will come looking for us. And believe me, boys, you don't want to still be in Montana when that happens."

Weasel was far from impressed. "Hell, I heard all them same stories you have, Ed, and I don't believe the half of them. What's one man against the ten of us? Eleven if we can get John out of this."

Zimmerman continued to stroke the scalp in his hand. "I'm not going on any rumors or fairytales. I'm going on what I've seen, and I can tell you Aaron Mackey's worse than anything you've heard. If we kill Halstead, he'll kill all of us. That's a fact."

"I don't care about Mackey right now," Cree said. "I care about that half-breed whose got us pinned down in there."

"He's not a breed," Zimmerman said. "His father's white and his mother's Mexican. Heard them talk about it in The Railhead last night."

"I don't care what he is," Cliff said. "He's in our way, and someone's got to do something about it."

Zimmerman finally took his eyes off the stand of pine trees and looked at Harry. A shiver went through Hudson when he did.

"I say one of us needs to ride out to talk to Halstead," Zimmerman said, "while Weasel flanks him from the right over there. I'd prefer to send more, but if too many of us disappear, Halstead's likely to notice. It's not perfect, but it's the best plan we've got, given the circumstances."

Harry swallowed hard as he felt the eyes of every man in the gang on him. They did not have to say what they were thinking. Harry was smart enough to know they doubted him. They thought he was weak and stupid. They thought he had lived his life in his brother's shadow. What's more is that he knew they were right.

He also knew it was up to him to decide what needed to be done.

He tried to keep the quaver out of his voice as he said, "Sounds like a good idea to me, Ed. I'll ride ahead a bit to get into shouting distance of him while Weasel here works his way around the right side." Giving orders like this made him feel a little better about what he was about to do. Put a little iron in his backbone. He only hoped he didn't catch any iron in his belly for his trouble. He picked up his reins and urged his horse forward. "No time like the present. Just be ready to back me up, whatever happens next."

The men grumbled their encouragement to him as he walked his horse at a steady pace. But the closer he got to the pines, to the chance of death he knew was waiting for him in its shadows, the more his courage began to wane. He even thought about turning back and having one of the other men do it. But kept on moving.

He feared his own men might shoot him dead if he did anything else.

Visit us online at
**KensingtonBooks.com**
to read more from your favorite authors,
see books by series, view reading group guides, and more.

**BOOK** **CLUB**

## BETWEEN THE CHAPTERS

Visit us online for sneak peeks, exclusive giveaways,
special discounts, author content, and engaging
discussions with your fellow readers.

Betweenthechapters.net

Sign up for our newsletters and be the first to get exciting news
and announcements about your favorite authors!
**Kensingtonbooks.com/newsletter**